"A bit of heaven . . . love, laughter,
adventure, and passion."

#1 *NEW YORK TIMES*

JOHANNA
LINDSEY

THAT
PERFECT
SOMEONE

*A Malory
Novel*

*They were destined for
each other . . .*

FALL IN LOVE WITH LINDSEY!

Discover the passion and excitement of
#1 bestselling author

JOHANNA LINDSEY

*A ROGUE
OF MY OWN*

*NO CHOICE
BUT SEDUCTION*

*THE DEVIL
WHO TAMED HER*

*CAPTIVE OF
MY DESIRES*

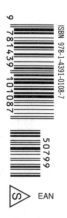

ISBN 978-1-4391-0108-7

9 781439 101087

50799

S EAN

. . . but their hearts
were the last to know!

Enjoy Johanna Lindsey's "mastery of historical romance" (*Entertainment Weekly*) in all of her wickedly witty, lusciously sensual" (*Booklist*) bestselling novels!

THAT PERFECT SOMEONE

A Malory Novel

"The Malorys are the family everyone wishes they had, so returning to their world is like entering a bit of heaven. The way Lindsey writes a seductive battle of wills love story is magic; love, laughter, adventure, and passion collide as childhood foes become lovers."

—*Romantic Times,* Top Pick (4½ stars)

A ROGUE OF MY OWN

"Entertaining . . . with emotions leaping from the pages . . . filled with sexual tension . . . Engagingly satisfying from start to finish."

—SingleTitles.com

NO CHOICE BUT SEDUCTION

A Malory Novel

"In typical Lindsey fashion, untold secrets, hidden relationships, fascinating family interaction, steamy passion, and an intricate plot add to the mix."

—*Library Journal*

"Witting . . . charmingly unique . . . a sexy love story . . . irresistible."

—*Booklist*

That Perfect Someone is also available as an eBook.

"Filled to the brim with . . . richness and believability. . . . A superb read."

—Romance Reviews Today

MARRIAGE MOST SCANDALOUS

"Delightful. . . . The perfect read for a long summer day."
—Wichita Falls Times Record News

"Spectacular. . . . [*Marriage Most Scandalous*] will charm and captivate you."

—Romance Reviews Today

A LOVING SCOUNDREL

A Malory Novel

"A wickedly seductive hero and a wonderfully unconventional heroine . . . [Lindsey] infuses this fairly-tale-like love story with a dash of danger."

—*Booklist*

"Awesome . . . Lindsey's Malory novels are automatic romance classics."

—Knight Ridder/Tribune News Service

A MAN TO CALL MY OWN

"Filled with emotional intensity and sexual tension. . . . Romantic, funny, and poignant."

—*Romantic Times*

"Twists and turns galore . . . a delightful romp."

—*Booklist*

MORE THAN 60 MILLION COPIES OF JOHANNA LINDSEY'S BOOKS IN PRINT!

JOHANNA LINDSEY

THAT PERFECT SOMEONE

A Malory Novel

Pocket Books

New York   London   Toronto   Sydney

Pocket Books
A Division of Simon & Schuster, Inc.
1230 Avenue of the Americas
New York, NY 10020

This book is a work of fiction. Names, characters, places, and incidents either are products of the author's imagination or are used fictitiously. Any resemblance to actual events or locales or persons, living or dead, is entirely coincidental.

First Pocket Books mass market edition May 2011

POCKET BOOKS and colophon are registered trademarks of Simon & Schuster, Inc.

For information about special discounts for bulk purchases, please contact Simon & Schuster Special Sales at 1-866-506-1949 or business@simonandschuster.com.

The Simon & Schuster Speakers Bureau can bring authors to your live event. For more information or to book an event contact the Simon & Schuster Speakers Bureau at 1-866-248-3049 or visit our website at www.simonspeakers.com.

Cover design by Lisa Litwack; illustration by Craig White.

Manufactured in the United States of America

10   9   8   7   6   5   4   3   2   1

ISBN 978-1-4391-0108-7
ISBN 978-1-4391-7690-0 (ebook)

THAT
PERFECT
SOMEONE

Chapter One

⟨ornament⟩

It might seem odd to consider Hyde Park your own backyard, but Julia Miller did. Growing up in London, she'd ridden there almost daily for as long as she could remember, from her very first pony when she was a child to the thoroughbred mares that followed. People waved at her whether they knew her or not, simply because they were so used to seeing her there. The *ton*, shop clerks cutting across the park on their way to work, gardeners, they all noticed Julia and treated her like one of their own.

Tall, blond-haired, and fashionably dressed, she always returned the smiles and waves. She was generally a friendly sort and people tended to respond to that in kind.

Even more odd than Julia's considering such a mammoth park her personal riding grounds were her circumstances. She'd grown up in the upper-crust end of town but her family wasn't upper-crust at all. She lived in one of the larger town houses in Berkeley Square, because it wasn't only the nobility who could afford those town houses. In fact, her family, who acquired their surname in the Middle Ages when a craftsman took on the name of his trade, had been among the first to buy and build in Berkeley Square back in the mid-1700s when the square was first laid out, so Millers had been living there for many generations now.

Julia was well known and well liked in the neighborhood. Her closest friend, Carol Roberts, was a daughter of the nobility, and other young women of the *ton* who knew her through Carol, or from the private finishing school she'd attended, liked her as well and invited her to their parties. They weren't the least bit threatened by her pretty looks or deep pockets because she was already engaged to be married. She'd been engaged nearly since birth.

"Fancy meeting you here," a female voice said behind her. Carol Roberts rode up, and her mare fell into an easy trot beside Julia's.

Julia chuckled at her petite, black-haired friend. "That should have been my remark. You rarely ride anymore."

Carol sighed. "I know. Harry frowns on it, especially since we're trying to have our first child. He doesn't want me to take any chance of losing it before we even know it's been conceived."

Julia knew that horseback riding could indeed cause miscarriages. "Then why are you taking that risk?"

"Because a baby didn't get conceived this month," Carol said with a disappointed pursing of her lips.

Julia nodded sympathetically.

"Besides," Carol added, "I have so missed our rides together, I'm willing to defy Harry for these few days when I'm having my monthlies and we won't be trying to conceive."

"He wasn't home to find out, was he?" Julia guessed.

Carol laughed, her blue eyes sparkling mischievously. "No indeed and I'll be home before he is."

Julia didn't worry that her friend would get into trouble with her husband. Harold Roberts adored his wife. They'd known and liked each other before Carol's first season three years ago, so no one had been surprised when they got engaged within weeks of Carol's debut and married a few months later.

Carol and Julia had been neighbors their whole lives, both living in Berkeley Square, their respective town houses side by side with no more than a narrow alley separating them. Even their bedroom windows had been directly across from each other—they'd arranged that!—so even when they weren't in the same house together visiting, they could talk from their windows without raising their voices. It was no wonder they'd become the best of friends.

Julia sorely missed Carol. While they still visited

often when Carol was in London, she no longer lived next door. When she married, she'd moved into her husband's house, many blocks away, and every few months she and Harold spent weeks at his family's ancestral estate in the country. He was hoping they'd stay there permanently. Carol was still resisting that idea. Fortunately, Harold wasn't the sort of overbearing husband who made all the decisions without considering his wife's wishes.

They continued to ride side by side for a few minutes, but Julia had already been in the park for a hour, so she suggested, "Want to stop by the teahouse for ices on the way home?"

"It's too early in the morning and not warm enough yet for ices. I am famished though and have truly missed Mrs. Cables's morning pastries. Do you still have a breakfast buffet laid out in the mornings?"

"Of course. Why would that change just because *you* got married?"

"Harold refuses to steal your cook, you know. I've nagged and nagged him to at least try."

Julia burst out laughing. "He knows he can't afford her. Every time someone tries to hire her away, she comes to me and I raise her wages. She knows where her bread is buttered."

Julia had been making decisions of that sort because her father, Gerald, could no longer make them. Her mother had never made them when she was alive.

Helene Miller had never taken control of anything in her life, not even the household. She had been a timid woman afraid of offending anyone, even the servants. Five years ago she'd died in the carriage accident that had rendered Gerald Miller an invalid.

"How is your father?" Carol asked.

"The same."

Carol always asked and Julia's reply was rarely any different. He's lucky to be alive, the doctors had told her after they had shocked her with their prognosis that Gerald would never again be himself. His head had suffered too much trauma in the accident. While his bones, seven of which had been broken that day, had mended, his mind would not recover. The doctors had been blunt. They'd given her no hope. Her father would sleep and wake up normally, he could even eat if hand-fed, but he would never speak anything other than gibberish again. Lucky to be alive? Julia had often cried herself to sleep recalling that phrase.

And yet Gerald had defied his doctors' predictions. One time that first year after the accident, and then every few months after that, he would know, however briefly, who he was, where he was, and what had happened to him. So much rage and anguish had filled him the first few times this had occurred that his lucidity couldn't really be called a blessing. And he remembered! Each time he regained lucidity he was able to remember his prior periods of mental clarity. For a few minutes, a few hours, he was himself again—but it never lasted for long. And he never remembered anything of the dead time in between.

His doctors couldn't explain it. They'd never expected him to have coherent thoughts again. They still wouldn't give Julia any hope that he might someday fully recover. They called his moments of clarity a fluke. Such an occurrence was undocumented, never known to happen before, and they warned Julia not to expect it to happen again. But it did.

It broke her heart the third time her father was himself, when he asked her, "Where's your mother?"

She'd been warned to keep him calm if he ever "woke" again, and that meant not telling him his wife had died in the accident. "She's gone shopping today. You—you know how she loves to shop."

He'd laughed. It was one of the few things her mother had been decisive about, buying things she didn't really need. But Julia had still been in mourning herself, and it had been one of the hardest things she'd ever done, to smile that day and keep her tears at bay until her father slipped away again into that gray realm of nothingness.

Of course she'd consulted different doctors. And every time one of them told her that her father was never going to recover, she'd dismiss him and find a new doctor. She stopped doing that after a while. She'd kept the last one, Dr. Andrew, because he'd been honest enough to admit that her father's case was unique.

A little while later in the Millers' breakfast room, Carol was carrying her filled plate *and* the large basket of pastries to the table when she stopped in her tracks, having finally noticed the new addition to the room.

"Oh, good Lord, when did you do that?" Carol exclaimed, turning around to stare wide-eyed at Julia.

Julia glanced at the ornate box on top of the china cabinet that had caught Carol's attention. It was lined in blue satin and edged in jewels, and behind its glass cover sat a lovely doll. Julia took her seat at the table and managed not to blush.

"A few weeks ago," she replied, and motioned Carol to take a seat at the table. "I came upon this fellow who'd just opened a shop near one of ours. He makes these beautiful boxes for items people want to preserve, and that doll is one thing I don't ever want to fall apart due to old age, so I commissioned that box for her. I just haven't decided yet where to place her, since my room is so cluttered. But I'm getting used to her being in here."

"I didn't know you still had that old doll I gave you," Carol said in wonder.

"Of course I do. She's still my prized possession."

It was true, not because Julia valued the doll so much, but because she valued the friendship it represented. Carol might not have given up the doll when they first met, but when she got a new one, instead of putting the old doll away in the attic, never to be seen again, she'd remembered that Julia had wanted it and had shyly offered it to her.

Carol blushed as they both remembered that day, but she finally chuckled. "You were such a little monster back then."

"I was never that bad," Julia snorted.

"You were! Screaming tantrums, bullying, demanding. You took offense at everything! You nearly punched me in the nose when we first met and would have, if I hadn't knocked you on your arse first."

"I was so impressed with that." Julia grinned. "You were the first person to tell me no."

"Well, I wasn't letting you have my favorite doll, not at our first meeting! You shouldn't even have asked for it. But really?" Carol said, surprised. "Never told no?"

"Yes, really. My mother was too weak and indecisive, well, you remember how she was. She always gave in to me. And my father was too kindhearted. He never said no to anyone, much less me. I even had a pony years before I was old enough to ride one, just because I asked for one."

"Aha! That's probably why you were such a little monster when we met. Spoiled beyond redemption."

"It wasn't that—well, maybe I was a little bit spoiled because my parents couldn't bring themselves to be firm with me, and my governess and the servants certainly weren't going to discipline me. But I didn't become a screaming, crying termagant until the day I met my fiancé. It was mutual hate at first sight. I didn't want to ever see him again. It was the first time my parents didn't let me have my way, so you could say I threw a tantrum about it that lasted for years! Until I met you, I didn't have any friends to point out to me how silly I was being. You helped me to forget about *him,* at least between the visits our parents forced on us."

"You changed quickly enough after we met. How old were we?"

"Six, but I didn't change that quickly, I just made sure you didn't witness any more of my tantrums— well, unless my fiancé came for a visit. Couldn't very well hide that animosity even if you were present, now could I?"

Carol laughed, but only because Julia was grinning over the remark. Julia knew her friend was aware that it hadn't been the least bit funny back then. Some of those fights with her fiancé had been quite violent. She'd almost bitten off his ear once! But it had been his fault. From their very first meeting when she was only five and had been so sure they would become the best of friends, he'd dashed those hopes with his rudeness and his resentment that she'd been handpicked for him. Every time they visited each other he would enrage her so that she'd want to fly at him and rip his eyes out. She didn't doubt that he'd instigated all those fights deliberately. The stupid boy somehow thought that *she* could end the engagement that neither of them wanted.

She didn't doubt that he'd left England when he finally figured out that she had no more say in ending their betrothal than he did—and saved them both from a marriage made in hell. How odd to feel grateful to *him* for anything. But with him gone for good, she could see a little humor in what a terrible termagant she'd been—around him.

Julia nodded at their food, which was getting cold, but Carol shifted their conversation to a new subject. "I'm having a small dinner party this coming Saturday, Julie. You will come, won't you?"

The nickname had stuck since they were children, and even Julia's father had picked it up. She'd always thought it was silly to have a nickname that was just as long as her real name, but since it *was* one syllable shorter, she'd never minded.

She glanced at her friend over the scone she'd been about to bite into. "Have you forgotten that's the day of the Eden ball?"

"No, I just thought you might have come to your senses and begged off from that invitation," Carol said grouchily.

"And I was hoping you would have changed your mind and accepted the invitation."

"Not a chance."

"Oh, come on, Carol," Julia cajoled. "I hate dragging my wastrel cousin to these affairs, and he hates it, too. We no sooner step in the front door than he's already looking for the back door. He never sticks around. But you—"

"He doesn't need to stick around," Carol interrupted. "You'll know everyone there. You're never left alone for more'n a minute at parties. Besides, that marriage contract that the Earl of Manford keeps locked away means you don't even need a chaperone. A contract like that means you're as good as married already. Oh, good Lord, I didn't mean to bring that up again. I'm sorry!"

Julia managed a smile. "Don't be. You know you don't have to tiptoe around that distasteful subject with me. We were just laughing about it. Being that we hate each other, that fool I'm engaged to couldn't have done a nicer service for me than to fly the coop as he did."

"You felt that way before you reached the age to marry, but that was three years ago. You can't deny that being called an old maid doesn't infuriate you."

Julia burst out laughing. "Is that what you think? You forget I'm not an aristocrat like you, Carol. Labels like that are meaningless to me. What I find meaningful is having no one to answer to but myself. You can't imagine how wonderful that is. And it's official. The family wealth and holdings are all mine now—unless that bounder comes home."

Chapter Two

JULIA GASPED WHEN she saw Carol's horrified reaction to her thoughtless remark. "I didn't mean *that*! I told you my father's condition is the same."

"Then how can all his wealth and businesses be yours, without him—passing on?" Carol asked delicately.

"Because on one of his rare lucid days a few months ago, he summoned his solicitors and bankers to the house and turned over control of everything to me. Not that I hadn't already been in control since the accident, but the solicitors won't be peering over my shoulders anymore. They can still try to guide me, but I no longer have to listen to them. What Father did that day was give me my full inheritance sooner than I wanted it."

The solicitors couldn't break her marriage contract, though, but then she'd already known that. Her father had tried unsuccessfully to break it years ago when it had become apparent that her fiancé had disappeared. The contract could only be terminated by mutual agreement between the two parents who had originally signed it, and the Earl of Manford, that awful man, wouldn't agree to end it. He still had hopes of getting his hands on the Miller wealth—through her. That had been his plan all along and was why he'd come to her parents not long after she was born with his marriage proposal for their children. Helene had been so thrilled that they would have a lord in the family and wanted to seize the opportunity to wed her daughter to a member of the nobility. Gerald, who was less enthralled with the aristocracy, had agreed to the betrothal to please his wife. It could have led to a happy ending for all—if the engaged pair hadn't hated each other.

"I can see how you might be enjoying that sort of freedom, but does it also mean you've resigned yourself to never marrying or having children?" Carol asked carefully.

Trust her friend to think of children when she was trying so hard to have one of her own. "No, not at all. I want children," Julia said. "I realized that when you first mentioned you and Harry were going to try to have one. And eventually I *will* marry."

"How?" Carol asked in surprise. "I thought they could hold you to that contract *forever*."

"They can, as long as the earl's son is alive. But it's been over nine years since he left or anyone has heard from him. For all we know, he could be dead and buried in a ditch somewhere, the victim of a robbery or some other crime."

"Oh, good Lord!" Carol exclaimed, her blue eyes wide. "That's it, isn't it? You *can* petition to have him declared dead after all this time has passed! I can't believe I never thought of that before!"

"Neither did I, but that's what one of my solicitors advised me to do three months ago when I came into my inheritance," Julia said with a nod. "The earl will put up a fight, but the situation speaks for itself and is thus in my favor.

"I have to admit I'll miss the carte blanche that engagement gives me," Julia added. "Think about it. You said it yourself, I don't even need a chaperone because I'm engaged. Everyone looks at me and sees a woman who's as good as married. How many parties do you think I'll be invited to when people know I'm an heiress looking for a husband?"

"Don't be absurd," Carol scoffed. "You're very well liked and you know it."

"And you're too loyal to see the broader picture. I'm not a threat to anyone right now; that's why the *ton* finds me an acceptable addition to their guest lists. They don't look at me and worry I might lure their sons down the social ladder. They don't look at me and worry I might steal their daughter's prime catch out from under her."

"Nonsense, nonsense, and more nonsense," Carol said quite adamantly. "You, m'girl, don't give yourself enough credit. People like you for yourself, not for your wealth or your 'unavailability,' as you put it."

Carol was still speaking from her loyal heart, but Julia knew that the aristocracy could and often did look down on tradesmen as beneath their notice. But ironically, that stigma had never really touched her. Possibly because she'd been engaged to an aristocrat all her life and everyone knew it. Or maybe because her family was so bloody rich it was quite often an embarrassment, particularly with so many nobles coming to her father over the years for loans, you'd think he was a bank. But Carol's father had also pulled strings, at his daughter's behest, to get Julia into the exclusive private finishing school that Carol attended, and Julia had made other friends from the nobility there.

All of that had opened doors for her. But those same doors would close quite quickly once it became known she was looking for a husband.

"I can't believe we didn't come up with this solution sooner," Carol remarked. "So now that you're about to be rid of that albatross around your neck, have you started looking for a *real* husband?"

Julia grinned. "I've been looking. I just haven't found a man I want to marry yet."

"Oh, don't be so bloody particular," Carol said, and probably didn't realize she sounded like her husband,

Harry. "I can think of any number of suitable—" When Julia laughed, Carol paused and demanded, "What's so funny?"

"You're thinking of your social circles, but I'm not locked into finding another lord for a husband just because I'm currently engaged to one. Far from it. I have many more choices than that. Not that I'm discounting an aristocrat. I'm even looking forward to that ball this weekend that heralds the new social Season."

Carol frowned. "So in the last few months no one has piqued your interest?"

Julia blushed. "Very well, so I *am* a little particular, but let's face it, you were very, very lucky to find your Harry. But how many Harrys are out there, eh? Yet I want a man who will stand in my corner *with* me, just like you have, not one who will put me behind him in his corner. I also need to protect my inheritance from a man who might squander it. I need to make sure it's still there for the children I hope to have one day."

Carol's eyes suddenly widened in alarm. "Look how much time has been wasted! You're twenty-one and not married yet!"

"Carol!" Julia exclaimed with a chuckle. "I've been twenty-one for how many months now? Nothing has changed about my age."

"But you were an *engaged* twenty-one. That's quite different from being twenty-one without a fiancé, and it's going to be in the papers when you have the earl's son declared dead. Everyone will know——oh, stop looking daggers at me. *I'm* not calling you an old maid——"

"You already did, not fifteen minutes ago, right here at this table."

"I didn't mean it. I was just making a point, and, well, deuce it all, this is so different! This is you without a fiancé!"

Julia shook her head. "You're seeing things with your eyes again instead of trying to look through mine. You and the other girls we went to school with all believed you *had* to marry your first Season out the door or the sky would fall. That is so silly and I told you that back then. This year, five years from now, ten years from now, it makes no difference to me when I marry as long as I'm not marrying my current fiancé and as long as I'm still young enough to have children."

"It's a luxury to think that way, you know," Carol huffed again.

"So there are some benefits to not being an aristocrat."

The pointed way Julia said that caused Carol to burst out laughing. "Touché. But you know what this means, don't you? I'm going to have to arrange quite a few parties for you now."

"No, you're not."

"Yes, I am. So do break off from going to that Mallory ball this weekend. You're not going to find very many young men there, and I will widen my guest list now to include——"

"Carol, you're being so silly! You know very well this ball is going to be *the* ball of the Season. The invitations are highly prized right now. Why, I was even offered three hundred pounds for mine."

Carol's eyes flared. "You must be joking."

"Yes, I am, it was only two hundred pounds."

Julia didn't get the laugh she'd hoped for. Carol gave her a stern look instead and said, "I know who that ball is for even if it's supposed to be a secret. You've become chummy with Georgina Malory and have even been to her house a number of times—"

"They're our neighbors, for goodness' sake, and have been our neighbors for what, seven—eight years now? They live just down the street!"

"—but you won't catch me stepping foot in there," Carol continued as if she hadn't been interrupted.

"The ball isn't at Georgina's house. Her niece Lady Eden is giving it."

"Doesn't matter. Her husband will be there and I've managed to avoid meeting James Malory all these years. I've heard all the stories about him. I'm going to continue to avoid him, thank you very much."

Julia rolled her eyes. "He's not the ogre you make him out to be, Carol. I've told you that a number of times. There's nothing sinister or dangerous about him."

"Of course he'd hide that side of himself from his wife and her friends!"

"You'll never know until you meet him, Carol. Besides, he hates social events so much, he might not even attend this one."

"Really?"

Julia held her tongue. Of course he'd attend; the ball was in his wife's honor. But she let Carol assimilate the slim chance that he might not attend and got the response she'd hoped for.

"Very well, I'll go with you." But Carol wasn't that gullible, because she added, "And if he *is* there, just don't mention it. I'd rather not know."

Chapter Three

GABRIELLE ANDERSON STOOD at the helm, steering *The Triton*. The sea was calm today. She was barely having to put any effort into keeping the wheel steady. Her husband, Drew, didn't worry that she'd sink his beloved ship. He knew that during the three years she'd sailed the Caribbean with her father, Nathan Brooks, and his treasure-hunting crew, Nathan had taught her everything there was to learn about running a ship. She really enjoyed steering. She just couldn't do it for an extended period without her arms beginning to shake from the strain.

Drew took over without a word, just a kiss to her cheek. He didn't give her a chance to get out of the way, though, so she was now trapped between his arms, which she didn't mind at all. She leaned back against his wide chest with a sigh of contentment. Her mother had often warned her never to fall in love with a man who loves the sea. With her father away at sea when she was growing up, Gabrielle had taken that advice seriously, until she realized how much she loved the sea as well. So her husband wouldn't be leaving her at home while he sailed around the world; she'd be right there with him.

This was their first long trip since they'd married last year. They'd taken many short ones between the islands and a few to Drew's hometown, Bridgeport, Connecticut, to buy furniture, but this trip was finally taking them back to England, where they'd first met, and where half of Drew's family lived now.

A letter from his brother Boyd had caught up to them at the beginning of the year, giving them the amazing news that he'd married, too, and not long after Drew had tied the knot. Boyd's marriage was unexpected, but it wasn't a complete surprise, since he hadn't been a confirmed bachelor like Drew. The surprising part was that Boyd brought the count up to *three* Anderson siblings who had now married into the huge Malory family in England. But the really amazing part was that Boyd had fallen in love with a Malory no one had known about, including his wife and her father!

And drat Boyd, he'd given them only bits and pieces of how all that had come about. Drew was eager to hear the whole story and would have sailed for England right after receiving his brother's letter if he and Gabrielle hadn't been in the middle of building their home on the beautiful little island Gabrielle had been given as a wedding gift.

But their house was finally finished and now they were on their way to England. Boyd had also suggested in his letter that the whole family gather in England this year for their sister's, Georgina's, birthday, which was a perfect excuse for a family reunion. Gabrielle and Drew would arrive in good time for both events.

An only child, Gabrielle was delighted to have married into a large family. There were five Anderson brothers and one sister. Gabrielle had met only the three youngest siblings so far, but she wasn't worried about meeting the three older brothers. She was looking forward to it.

She'd been feeling chilled until Drew cocooned her with his body. It might almost be summer and they would reach England tomorrow if the wind held steady, but there was simply no comparison between the cold Atlantic and the warm Caribbean waters she had grown used to.

"It looks like you two should repair to your cabin," Richard Allen said with a roguish grin as he came up beside them. "Want me to take the wheel?"

"Nonsense, we're not newlyweds anymore," Drew began, but Gabby had turned around to hug him close and he groaned, "Actually . . ."

She laughed and tickled Drew out of that thought. She could tease, too, but she didn't usually get away with that kind of teasing because she tended to get carried away whenever she was this close to her husband.

"Just yell if you change your mind," Richard offered, adding with a chuckle before he headed down to the lower deck, "I know I would!"

Gabrielle stared after him. Her dear friend had lived nearly half his life in the Caribbean, at least the half that she knew about, and obviously he was feeling the same chill in the air that she was. He was wearing a greatcoat! Where the devil had he got such an English-looking garment as that?

Tall, excessively handsome, a daring young man— maybe a little too daring—but so charming in his humor . . . it was a wonder that Gabrielle had never been attracted to Richard and that they'd become close friends instead. He wore his black hair so long he had to queue it back. A thin mustache gave him quite a rakish look, and his green eyes usually sparkled with laughter.

Richard had been much slimmer when she first met him four years ago. But now at twenty-six his body had filled out and become more muscular. He kept himself meticulously clean. From his hair to his clothes, right down to his polished high boots, he'd always stood out among the other pirates.

He'd joined her father's pirate crew not long after he'd arrived in the Caribbean from—no one knew from where. Most pirates never said where they hailed from, just as most of them used fake names, which they changed frequently. Jean Paul was the fake name Richard used most often, and for the longest time he'd been practicing a French accent to go with the name and always sounded so funny using it! It had taken him a long time to master the accent, but as soon as he did, he stopped using it and the French name as well. He just hadn't been willing to give up until he'd got it right, then he'd happily set it aside as something he'd accomplished.

Her father hadn't been a typical pirate though. He'd turned more or less into a middleman who took hostages from other pirates and ransomed them back to their families. The hostages whose families couldn't afford the ransom, he simply let go. In the interim, he'd hunted for treasure!

But after spending months in the dungeon of a real pirate last year, Nathan no longer associated with his old comrades. Gabrielle's marrying into a legitimate shipping family who considered pirates their enemies might have influenced that decision, too. He still hunted for treasure though, and occasionally took a commission of cargo from Skylark, the shipping line that Drew's family owned—if the cargo was to be delivered in the direction of whichever treasure clue he was currently chasing down.

Deep in thought, she hadn't noticed Richard walk over to the rail on the lower deck. But she saw him there now, staring in the direction of England. Once he'd stopped using that silly French accent, it had been obvious that he was an Englishman. But then she'd long ago guessed as much because of all the times he'd slipped with "bloody hell" or other notable English expressions.

But even though he now sounded like a true Englishman, he'd never admitted he was English, and she'd never pointedly asked—for one good reason. Men who became pirates were usually hiding from something in their past, sometimes from the law, and Richard had been uneasy about going to England with her last year. He'd put a good face on it, had been his usual carefree, teasing self, but when he hadn't known she was watching him, she'd sensed his . . . what? Worry? Dread? Fear of being hauled off to the nearest prison over past deeds? She had no clue. Then he'd met Georgina Malory, and *Gabrielle's* worry had taken precedence.

But looking at him now, she couldn't miss the sudden change in his demeanor, the profound melancholy that surrounded him. She suspected he was thinking of Georgina again, and all the doubts that Gabrielle had been having since they set sail returned tenfold.

"*How* did we let him talk us into bringing him along to England?"

She said it to herself, but Drew followed her gaze and snorted. "Because he's your best friend."

She turned around to assure Drew, "You're my best friend now."

"I'm your husband; he's still your best friend. And you let your other best friend, Ohr, convince you that Richard isn't really in love with my sister. You know, Gabby," Drew abruptly added with a narrowing of his dark eyes, "you have too many male friends."

She laughed at her husband's flare of jealousy, which took her mind off Richard and the dilemma he presented. While Drew was looking down at her, even with that scowl, feigned or not, she couldn't resist leaning up to kiss him. She loved him so much, it really was hard to keep her hands off him for long, and he felt the same way about her.

"Stop that," he warned huskily, "or I'm going to have to take Richard up on his offer to man the wheel."

She grinned. That wasn't such a bad idea. Cuddling up with Drew in their cabin was certainly preferable to thinking about Richard walking into a death trap in England.

But that death trap continued to loom in her mind because Drew said, "A better question would be, how did you talk *me* into letting those two come along on this trip?"

She turned back around so he wouldn't see her wince over that. As much as she loved Ohr and Richard like family, she regretted letting them come along.

But she reminded Drew, "It was a spur-of-the-moment decision and you know it. I'd told Richard no all those months ago when we started talking about this trip and he asked to come along. But then my father broke his leg right before we sailed, which is going to keep him and his crew at home for a month or two, and you know how a crew can get in trouble if they're landlocked too long with nothing to do."

"Yes, but those two could have found something to do—admit it, your father wanted them to come along as your watchdogs again. He doesn't trust me to take care of you yet."

"You don't really think that when he's so delighted with you as his son-in-law? Besides, *he* didn't ask me to bring them along, though he probably would have if he'd thought of it. He does worry about them, you know. They view my father as family and he feels the same way about them."

"I know, one big happy family." Drew chuckled. "I married into it, didn't I?"

"You're the one with a big family who married into an even bigger family. And your brother-in-law might have ignored Richard when they last met, but James had other things on his mind at the time, like rescuing my father from that horrible dungeon. Which doesn't mean that James has forgotten the promise he made that day when he saw his wife slap Richard in their garden for making an inappropriate overture toward her. James told me without mincing words that if Richard ever came near his wife again, he was going to have to hurt him. I didn't doubt for a minute that he meant it.

You know him better than I and you confirmed he was most likely dead serious."

"Of course he was, same as I would be if I saw another man trespassing with my wife. I think you're worrying over nothing, sweetheart," Drew added as she snuggled back against his chest. "Richard isn't stupid. And anyone in their right mind would have to be damn stupid to trifle with that particular Malory."

"Umm, didn't you and your brothers do exactly that when you forced him to marry your sister? After you beat him unconscious?"

"Sweetheart, it took *all five of us* to administer that beating. We tried it one-on-one and it just wasn't working! And I told you, James forced our hand deliberately. It was his bizarre way of getting Georgie married to him without his having to ask her or us, because of some silly vow he made never to marry."

"I think it was rather romantic."

Drew chuckled. "You would. But only a stubborn Englishman would go to *those* lengths to keep his sworn word—about marriage. Had it been about honor, or country, or—well, you know what I mean, it would have been reasonable. But marriage? Remember, that's privileged information I shared with you, since you're my wife. Don't ever let James know that my brothers and I have figured that out. *He* still thinks he put one over on us. And believe me, he's much more tolerable when he's silently gloating than when he's annoyed and going for blood."

"I'm sworn to secrecy," she assured Drew with a grin. "But you're quite right about Richard. He's not stupid. But you know how he is. He's a charming man, humorous, teasing, always smiling—"

"Stop singing his praises!"

"You didn't let me finish. I was going to say, until he remembers Georgina. Then he gets so melancholy it could break your heart."

"It's not breaking *my* heart."

"Oh, come on, you like him, you know you do. How can you not?"

"Possibly because he's in love with my sister. He's lucky I don't swab the deck with his face."

She ignored her husband's growl. "Ohr says Richard doesn't really love Georgina. I believe that, or I wouldn't have let him come along."

She'd been skeptical about Ohr's contention until she found out that Richard had had at least three affairs in the last year. That had pretty much been the deciding factor in allowing her friends to enjoy this trip with them.

"That might well be true," Drew said, "but what difference does that make if Richard *thinks* he's in love with my sister?"

"Yes, but Ohr said Richard is a man who wants to be

in love, that he wants it so much that he easily mistakes lust for love. And he doesn't even *know* that's what he's been looking for. But maybe because he's never experienced real love, he can't recognize the difference between the two."

Drew had experienced the same dilemma and indicated as much when he said, "Exactly, but now you're suddenly doubting it?"

"No, but I can't help remembering the things Richard said about Georgina. When I reminded him that she's a happily married woman, that he ought to forget her, he told me he's tried, but he just can't forget about his 'one true love.' How often does a man call a woman that?!"

"I can count on two, three, a dozen hands how many times I've said or thought it—about you."

She barely heard his reply, though she did swing around again to hug him. But she was remembering a conversation she'd had with Richard back when she'd first realized she loved Drew—and was so sure he didn't return that love. Richard had put an arm around her shoulder and told her, "It will work out, *chérie*. He adores you."

"He adores all women," she'd replied.

Richard had chuckled. "So do I, but I would give them all up for—"

"Shush!" she had told him in earnest. "Richard, please, stop pining for another man's wife. Malory won't tolerate another trespass. You make me fear for your life by not being reasonable about this."

"Who said love was reasonable?" had been the reply, which had stuck in her mind. She repeated that phrase now for her husband.

"And look how true that is," she added. "In your own case, you were an absolutely confirmed bachelor with a sweetheart in every port."

He didn't reply and she glanced up to see the steady "waiting" look he was giving her and realized it had nothing to do with her last comment. She grinned and wrapped her arms around his neck.

"Yes, I heard you," she said. "You can really count on a dozen hands the number of times you've called me your 'one true love'?"

Mollified, he hugged her back as he replied, "No, I was being conservative in that number. But as to your last comment, there was a good reason I was a confirmed bachelor. I was determined never to put a woman through the agony my mother experienced, always staring sadly out to sea waiting for a ship that rarely came home. Not once in all those years did I think I'd find a woman happy to sail by my side. I know my brother Warren's wife sails with him, but I didn't expect to get that lucky. But you've made your case about how unreasonable love can be. It broke down those very firm convictions I had. In fact, it can be so unreasonable that I have no doubt I would have given up the sea for you.

God, I can't believe I just said that, but you know it's true."

He crushed her with his next hug, he was suddenly feeling so much emotion, which made her quickly assure him, "You'll never have to! I love the sea as much as you do."

"I know, and I know exactly how lucky I am that you do. Now you've worried about your friend enough for one day, don't you think?"

She sighed. "I wish I could stop. I'm just so afraid that when he sees your sister again, he's going to throw caution to the winds and—"

"He wouldn't just have James to contend with," Drew warned. "You do realize that?"

"Yes." She sighed again.

"I could always throw him and Ohr overboard— with a dinghy, of course. By the time they row to England, we'll be ready to leave again. Problem solved."

She knew he wasn't the least bit serious and was just trying to ease her out of her concern, but she couldn't shrug off the sense of foreboding she felt. Whether from deeds in Richard's past or threats he'd provoked over a woman he thought he loved, she was afraid something bad was going to happen, and it would be *her* fault for bringing Richard back to England.

Chapter Four

Richard pulled his hat down low. It wasn't that he was worried that he might be recognized. On the London docks? Not a chance. But it would be foolish to flaunt his presence just to tempt fate. Why take the chance that this might be the one day out of a thousand that an old acquaintance might be returning from a trip abroad and be on these very same docks?

He'd put away the greatcoat now that it was too warm for it and was wearing his usual shipboard garb, clothes that were easy to work in. His long-sleeved white shirt was loose for ease of movement, deeply V-necked, and belted on the outside. His black pants were tucked into his boots. He blended in rather well with the common dockworkers, except for his highly polished Hessian boots.

It was highly unlikely that he would be recognized after all these years. He'd left England a skinny seventeen-year-old who hadn't yet reached his full height. He'd sprouted up a few more inches rather late, which had kept him slim longer than he would have liked, but then he'd finally filled out so he could no longer be called skinny. His long black hair even added to his disguise, since it was about as far from fashionable as he could get—in England, that is.

It was a popular style in the Caribbean, so he'd adopted it to blend in. He didn't braid his hair the way Ohr did, but it was so long now that he definitely had to keep it queued at the back of his neck or it became a nuisance aboard ship.

He ought to cut it while he was in England. He'd thought the same thing when he was here last year. But why? He wouldn't be staying and he liked his hair long. Besides, it was a symbol of the rebellion he'd started before he'd left home for good. He would never have been allowed to wear his hair this way while living under his father's iron thumb.

"Lord Allen?"

Richard hadn't seen the man approaching, but now as he quickly scrutinized the man's face, he recognized him. Good God, one of the rakehells he'd been chummy with before he left home? That one-in-a-thousand chance of being recognized? Bloody hell.

"You are mistaken, monsieur. I am Jean Paul from Le Havre." He bent respectfully, but was actually letting his long hair fall over his shoulder to better confirm his lie. "My ship, she only just arrived from France."

Every muscle in his body was primed for flight if his bluff and his thick French accent didn't work, but the rake simply looked disgusted at what he apparently thought was a mistake on his part. "Too bad. That would have been a juicy morsel for the gossip mills."

Indeed it would have—and it would have let Richard's father know he was still alive. But the man rudely walked off. It took a few moments for Richard to breathe easily again. That had been too close. And unplanned for. But at least the man wasn't someone Richard had been well acquainted with, and the fellow hadn't been sure that he was Lord Allen, either. And he had changed enough, Richard assured himself, that no one would really be sure except his family.

"I told you I'd do better at getting us a ride than you would," Margery gloated as she returned to where their baggage was piled and directed the hack driver to wait right there. "Now where's Gabby? Still on the ship?"

Gabrielle's maid glanced out to where *The Triton* was anchored in the middle of the Thames. The ship wouldn't be given dockage space anytime soon, and with summer upon them, the docks were more crowded than usual, so it was quite possible that the ship might not even get a space before they were ready to depart again!

Richard took a deep breath, shook off any remaining tension, and gave the maid a jaunty smile. "She's waiting for Drew. You know how captains are, always a dozen last-minute details to attend to before they can disembark."

Ohr was rowing toward the docks in a dinghy piled high with the rest of their baggage. You'd think they would be visiting for a month, rather than the two weeks they were planning on, they'd brought so much along with them.

"Can you smell it?" Margery said quite ecstatically. "Doesn't it smell wonderful?"

Richard eyed the old girl as if she were daft. "What the deuce are you smelling? All I smell is—"

"England!"

He rolled his green eyes. "It stinks here and you know it. The docks at home, with the trade winds always blowing, smell like a garden compared to this."

She snorted at him. "Gabby must be wrong in guessing this is where you were born and raised. You'd have more appreciation for the homeland if it was. Admit it, the English accent you're using now is as fake as the French one you were using before. You're just much better at this one."

With a wrinkle of his nose that was meant to tease her, Richard merely replied, "One of these days this town is going to pass a law about dumping garbage in the river."

But Margery hadn't expected him to open up to her just because she'd speculated aloud about his past and merely addressed his remark. "Maybe they have. It's not exactly the most law-abiding area of London and never has been. Not that *I'm* complaining. It's wonderful to be home again even if only for a visit."

Margery had elected to follow Gabrielle to the New World, and while she might have adjusted to that very different way of life, she still pined for home. Richard didn't pine for home, but damn, he did miss his brother, Charles. And being this close to him once again, he couldn't help but wonder if he should make the effort this time to try to steal a visit with Charles—without their father finding out about it.

"Here now, none of that daydreaming," Margery said, snapping his attention back to her. "You did enough of that on the ship. Use some of that brawn you've developed and start loading these trunks on top the coach. I was warned the driver only drives, he doesn't load. Uppity man. He knows his hack is at a premium down here. He's going to charge more the longer he sits here waiting, too." Then she added with a brilliant smile, "Nothing changes in this old town. Isn't that wonderful?"

Margery was a chronic complainer, so this bubbly attitude and her gleeful expression were so out of character that Ohr remarked as he came up beside Richard, "Is she going through her 'everything is wonderful because it's in England' routine again?"

"Right on the mark as usual." Richard chuckled at his friend.

"No different than the last time we were here. When you miss something very much and then finally have it in your grasp, you can become a bit euphoric—though the euphoria will wear off as reality returns."

Richard winced. Ohr was too perceptive by half, and Richard knew his friend wasn't just talking about Margery now. Though Richard wouldn't be getting what he wanted, and they both knew it. But that was what Ohr was subtly alluding to, that it would be a fleeting euphoria—and not worth dying for.

"You aren't going to start in on me, too, are you?" Richard asked.

Ohr's intentions were good. So were Gabrielle's for that matter. If Richard didn't know that, he'd have got quite annoyed at how much they'd hounded him about Georgina Malory on this trip. Though Ohr was definitely less obvious about it than Gabby.

Richard was tall at six feet, but just like Drew, Ohr had a few more inches on him and probably about ten years, too, though that was impossible to tell from looking at him. An Oriental half-breed born of an Asian mother and an American father who'd sailed in the Far East, Ohr's face was ageless, and he looked no different today from how he'd looked eight years ago when they'd first met, the day Ohr broke several members of Nathan's crew out of the jail in St. Lucia and Richard just happened to be sitting in the same cell with them. Richard had been able to talk Ohr into letting him come along. When Richard found out their occupation, he hadn't had to think long about joining them.

The Caribbean hadn't been Richard's choice of a destination. It was simply where the first ship out of England was heading the day he'd decided to leave. With thousands of islands, it had been a good place to hide, though he hadn't known that at the time. But it hadn't been a good place for a snobbish young Englishman to work. Seventeen and too fastidious to realize he'd need to adjust if he was going to survive there, he'd been floundering for a year, broke, going from island to island and job to job. He kept getting fired since he'd been too bloody arrogant for menial labor. Nor was it the first time he'd been tossed in jail for being unable to keep up with the rent for even the most wretched of hovels.

He and Ohr had ironically ended up in the West Indies for opposite reasons. Ohr had landed there hoping to find the father he'd never met, while Richard had landed there to escape from a father he couldn't stand. Meeting Ohr that day in the St. Lucia jail had probably saved Richard's life. He'd found a new family in Nathan Brooks and his crew, new friends closer than any he'd ever had, and an occupation he actually enjoyed!

" 'Too'?" Ohr said now. "Has Gabby been beating you over the head again with her concern?"

"When does the darling girl ever mind her own business?" Richard rejoined.

"There's only one thing she beats your brow over, and I hate to say it, but—"

"Yes, yes, you're in complete agreement," Richard cut in with some exasperation.

"Touchy, you. But answer me this: do you love Georgina Malory because you actually know her, or are you merely enamored of her beauty? Actually, you don't need to answer, just *think* about it."

Did his friends really think his love was that insubstantial? Richard didn't mind answering. "I spoke with her at length, Ohr. I've never come across another woman so easy to talk to—well, other than Gabby. But I know Georgina has a wonderful sense of humor, too. I saw firsthand how devoted she is to her children. She's brave—look who she's married to—and adventurous— last year she came along to help rescue a friend. She's perfect for me in every way!"

"Except that she loves someone else."

One tiny wrinkle in the life he wanted for himself? The women he usually came into contact with were tavern wenches, delightful romps, but none of whom he could picture as the mother of his children. All these years he hadn't met a single woman, other than Gabrielle, whom he could imagine giving him the large, loving family he craved—a family completely different from the one he'd been born into. If Gabby and he hadn't become such good friends, *and* she hadn't been his captain's only daughter, he would have pursued her. He'd met no one else as suitable for him—until he'd met Georgina Malory. She symbolized everything he wanted in a wife. He couldn't give up on this woman.

But, ironically, the man she was married to didn't scare him off. On the contrary, he gave him hope. *How* could she love a brutish fellow such as James Malory? Richard simply didn't believe that she really could. Because of that he was determined to wait until she came to her senses and left the man. He wanted her to know he'd be waiting for her with open arms.

Ohr shook his head. "Very well, I will say no more—actually, I will say one last thing. I don't like funerals. Do *not* make me have to attend yours."

Richard flinched. "Contrary to what you and Gabby think, I really would prefer to live out my life to its natural conclusion, not have it end at that behemoth's hands. I'm *not* going to try to lure her away from her husband again, Ohr; I swear I'm not."

"Fair enough. You stay away from her and all will be well."

Richard didn't reply, he just glanced away.

Ohr snorted. "As I thought. But remember, Malory's warning wasn't about you making advances to his wife, it was about you getting anywhere near her."

"An exaggeration. Most threats are made for effect. How often are they carried through?"

"That depends on who makes them. James Malory? If he says he's going to hurt you, you can stake your life on it."

"I thought you weren't going to say anything more about it," Richard mumbled.

Ohr chuckled. "You're the one who is dragging out the subject, my friend. Perhaps because you keep losing sight of reason and need help keeping it in view?"

Did he? Richard had assured himself that he wouldn't try to tempt his love away from her husband again, but what if he couldn't help himself? No, he *wasn't* an idiot.

"Why are you two just standing there?" Gabrielle asked as she came up behind them with Drew. "You should have had our trunks loaded and ready to go. You're not being very helpful."

"We were waiting for your husband," Ohr said. "He has more muscle."

Gabrielle cast an admiring glance at Drew, who was close enough to have heard Ohr. "He does, doesn't he?" she agreed with a grin.

Drew might have scoffed at the muscle remark, but his wife's look had him blushing instead, which caused the rest of them to laugh. Humor restored, Richard put aside his worries about this trip. Now if his friends would just do the same . . .

Chapter Five

JULIA MILLER KNEW that the Eden ball was definitely going to be *the* event of the Season. Not only had every invitation been accepted, but from the crush in the ballroom on Park Lane, a lot of party crashers were apparently there, too. Which would account for their hostess, Regina Eden, looking so frazzled. As it was a masked ball and hard to recognize most of the guests who were wearing the more elaborate masks, she couldn't very well point her finger and say, "You weren't invited, get out."

Actually, Regina Eden, a niece to the four eldest Malory brothers, was too sweet to do something that rude. Julia would have had no difficulty doing so if the food and drink she'd arranged for a social event weren't going to be enough to go around because of party crashers.

Julia was wearing her two favorite colors tonight. Her new ball gown was aqua silk, trimmed with turquoise double cording that was bound together with silver threads. The aqua and turquoise did wonderful things to her blue-green eyes, lightening them and darkening them respectively, giving her the shade somewhere between the two colors that she preferred. It was too bad she had to wear a domino that partially shaded her eyes, but as masks went, the domino was the narrowest of the three styles, covering just her eyes, and hers was rather fancy with the opening for her eyes rimmed in sparkling gems.

The domino was too narrow to conceal a person's identity. She had no trouble recognizing a domino-clad Lord Percival Alden, who pushed through the crowd to get to her side. She'd met him through the Malorys, since he'd long been a friend of the younger men in that family. He was a bit infatuated with her despite her being engaged. He was tall, in his early thirties, and quite easy on the eyes.

Percy, as his friends called him, fumbled for her hand when he reached her, so he could gallantly kiss it. Then he sighed.

"You take m'breath away, Miss Miller, 'deed you do. I'm in no hurry to marry, but I s'pose I will have to eventually. Gad, all m'friends have already put the chain on. But if *you* were available, I'm quite sure I would be thinking of marriage much sooner."

She blushed. It wasn't the first time he'd voiced that thought to her. Percy had a bungling tongue, thoughtlessly saying things he shouldn't, and she'd seen how he could frustrate his friends because of it. But Percy was harmless for the most part. She just didn't tell him her circumstances might soon change. While he was quite acceptable as a husband, he didn't steal her breath away. But it was definitely high time she started looking for a man who could . . .

She gave the expected response to such bold words: "Fie on you, Percy, everyone knows you're a confirmed bachelor."

With one of his friends calling Percy to join him, she wasn't sure he even heard her. He didn't appear to want to leave her side, though, but finally sighed again.

"Please keep me in mind if your circumstances ever change." As he hurried off, he yelled back at her, "And save me a dance, do!"

Dancing in this crush? Julia chuckled to herself. There was to be an unmasking at midnight, and she didn't doubt that at least a third of the guests would disappear before then. But by that time they would have got what they came for, a look at the one Malory who *never* socialized and thus was a prime target for rumors and speculation. Tonight was an exception and James Malory was attending the ball because it was being given in his wife's honor.

The Malorys weren't just a large family, they were

rich and titled as well, and it appeared they were all in attendance tonight at Georgina's birthday ball. Julia had met most of them, and she even knew some quite well.

Her neighbor Georgina had actually befriended her long ago, and Julia had been invited to her house for small social events, even for quiet "just family" dinners. Georgina was an American whose brothers were considered "in trade" just like Julia's family. One of Georgina's brothers had made a deal with Julia's father before his accident, a contract for regular cargoes of wool for their shipping business. Textiles was just one of the Millers' many enterprises.

Late last year Julia had helped out Georgina's youngest brother, Boyd Anderson, who had just married a Malory himself and was looking for a house for himself and his bride in the city. Julia's father had acquired quite a few fine properties in London over the years, some of which, in the highly sought-after upper-crust neighborhoods, he had accepted as payment for debts. Once her father acquired a property, he never sold it. She wholeheartedly agreed with that investment strategy. So while she wouldn't sell Boyd the town house he wanted, she'd given him a long lease on it, which he was happy with.

Yes, she knew the Malorys well, and she knew that some of them, like other members of the *ton*, felt sorry for her. Not because she was becoming an old maid, but because they knew she couldn't marry until her long-gone fiancé returned to England, which seemed unlikely to happen.

Julia didn't really mind that sort of pity. Good heavens, she'd be feeling the same thing for someone else who found herself in her pathetic situation. Although most people were polite enough not to bring up her engagement in conversation—Percy being the exception!—that wouldn't be the case for much longer. She hoped. After that talk she'd had with Carol, she'd visited her solicitor the next day. He'd already started working on it, though he'd warned her that the Earl of Manford would likely do everything possible to delay the legal action. So it might take longer than she'd thought to be rid of that horrid contract.

"I knew it!" Carol exclaimed as she came up to Julia. "You just have to look at him to know it's all true, every brutal, ghastly thing ever said about him."

Julia managed not to laugh. Carol sounded so serious! But when Julia looked closely at her friend's face, which was partially covered by a pale pink, jewel-studded domino similar to her own, she realized Carol *was* serious. She'd be walking out the door in a moment if Julia couldn't get her to see how silly she was being in basing her opinion of James Malory on nothing but rumor.

The two younger Malory brothers, James and Anthony, might have been such rakehells in their day, never losing a duel whether with fists or pistols, that they were well known for being quite deadly. No one could dispute that, but all of that had occurred years ago! Unfortunately, that could easily lead to much worse allegations, and now some speculation about James Malory's long absence from England after such a jaded career was simply ridiculous. Sent to the penal colony in Australia, where he'd killed all his jailors to escape, a pirate on the high seas who sank ships just for sport, the leader of the Cornwall smugglers finally imprisoned for murder—those were just a few of the more outlandish things whispered about the man by people who didn't personally know him or his family.

Not that it was anyone's business why James had disappeared for so many years, or what he was doing during that absence. But the *ton* was notorious when it came to gossip, and while most of them were quite satisfied with real scandals, others who wanted answers that weren't forthcoming simply made up their own!

Julia didn't doubt that most of the rumors about James Malory had no basis in fact. His menacing aura was what made it so easy for people to speculate in the wrong direction, and his elusiveness, which kept people from getting to know him. Yes, she didn't doubt he could be deadly if provoked, but who in his right mind would provoke him?

Big, blond, handsome, James would draw eyes even if people hadn't guessed who it was hovering over the beautiful, petite guest of honor in her ruby-colored gown. They made such a striking couple. But James wasn't wearing a mask tonight like everyone else. His mask was hooked over his wife's arm, and Julia had even noticed Georgina prompt him more than once to put it on. He'd just stared at her without expression, refusing to comply. Julia had found that amusing. It was so like James to abhor anything of a frivolous nature.

The more elaborate masks covered the whole face or just half the face, and unlike the domino, those did actually conceal people's identities. But Julia was certain she would have recognized James even if he were wearing a full mask. His body was quite distinctive, brutish one might say, it was so muscular. And no one else wore his hair so unfashionably long that it floated about his shoulders as did James's. Perhaps if he had worn a mask, Carol might have got through the evening without fearing him.

Julia needed to bring her friend up-to-date. "You know, Carol, James Malory hates social gatherings, really can't tolerate them. Yet he's here tonight because he loves his wife and wouldn't dream of disappointing her by not attending her birthday ball."

"Really hates them?"

"Yes."

"That would explain why he's never at any of them, wouldn't it?"

"Indeed."

"I thought it was because he was such a pariah," Carol then added in an even lower voice, "in the extreme, so that no hostess would include him on her guest list."

Julia managed to hold back the laughter that was threatening to burst out, but she did say drily, "You do know who we're talking about, right? One of the more powerful families in the realm? They get invited to everything."

"I'm sure the rest of them do, but I doubt he does," Carol huffed in disagreement.

"Him especially, Carol, or haven't you noticed how bloody crowded it is here tonight? You don't really think Lady Eden invited this many people, do you? If his reputation weren't so notorious, the *ton* wouldn't be so eager to finally be able to meet him in this social setting, which was what made the invitations so prime, and why so many extra people have shown up without one. You don't think he knows that, too? Yet just for his wife he still came here knowing quite well that he'd be on display."

"That does seem rather decent of him, doesn't it?"

"Let me introduce you," Julia suggested. "He can be quite gracious to the ladies. Once you meet him, you'll never believe those silly rumors again."

But Carol dug in her heels and with an adamant shake of her head said, "That's quite all right. We'll let him stay on that side of the room, and we'll stay on this side, thank you. There might not be a jot of truth to any of those rumors, and he's much more handsome than I expected, but he's still not the least bit approachable. Why, he hasn't smiled once at his wife, probably doesn't even know how to smile! And I don't see anyone else daring to make his acquaintance. No matter what you say, Julie, there's still that certain something about him that makes me want to shudder. It's as if he's primed to jump at anyone who gets near him to bite their head off."

"What a dreadful image that is," Julia said, still managing not to laugh at her friend's graphic imagination. "Shame on you."

"Yet it's true! He might be the nicest chap imaginable. Prob'ly is. There, you see, I *have* listened to your logic. But he still *looks* like the ogre you called him."

"I called him nothing of the sort," Julia protested. "I think my words were more to the point that you should stop thinking of him as one."

"He's not an ogre?" Carol said with sudden triumph. "Look at him now and say that. If that isn't a man with murder on his mind, I don't know what is."

Julia frowned and followed Carol's gaze, and, darn, she had to agree. In all the times she'd been in the same room with James Malory, she'd never once seen him like that. If looks could kill, someone in the room had already expired.

Chapter Six

I CAN'T BELIEVE YOU'VE shown up here," Gabrielle said, poking Richard in the back to get his attention.

He swung around with a groan of frustration. He'd done a good job of staying out of Gabby's view, James's view, and the view of two old acquaintances he thought he recognized, even though he knew his face was well hidden under the sad-clown mask, a full face mask that was damned hot. But he wasn't going to let her castigate him again when he had his own bone to pick with her.

"And I can't believe you didn't tell me Georgina's birthday celebration was going to be a masked ball. Didn't you realize how perfect this is? It negates all of your concerns—and how the deuce did you recognize me?"

"Your hair, of course."

"Maybe I should have worn a dress," he quipped. "Why didn't I think of that?"

"Because you are no longer anywhere close to slim enough to pull that off, even if there were women as tall as you, which there aren't. And do duck down before he sees you," she hissed as she dragged Richard back to the edge of the crowd.

This was already beginning to sound like their last discussion. Richard didn't think he could bear being told no yet again. But Gabrielle had been hard-nosed from the moment they'd docked. With only the one coach for the five of them to share, the plan had been for Ohr and him to drop her, Margery, and Drew off at the Malory town house before they looked for accommodations for themselves, but Gabrielle had vetoed that idea before they'd even left the docks. She had pulled Richard aside and explained that she didn't want him going anywhere near that particular house, even as close as the curb in front of it.

"You aren't being reasonable about this. He isn't likely to even remember me. He's nigh twice my age and probably quite forgetful because of it."

Gabrielle had choked on an incredulous laugh. "You're calling James Malory old when the man is in his prime? Don't kid yourself. You might have put on a little weight to fill out very nicely since he last saw you, but your face is the same, and, Richard, you have a *very* memorable face as handsome as you are. I'd recognize you anywhere—so will he. Hell, your old nanny would probably still recognize you."

"I never had a nanny," he'd replied stiffly.

"Don't try to ignore the point I'm making. You won't escape his notice, and he *will* remember the man he saw his wife slap after you made overtures to her in her own garden with her two toddlers right there! He would have tracked you down that very day if I hadn't promised him you'd never go near her again, and still, he made it clear what would happen if you *broke* my promise."

As if he didn't know all that? As if it made a difference when he craved the sight of Georgina with his whole being?

"Have a heart, Gabby," he'd said, appealing to her softer side. "I won't go near her, but you have to let me at least see her this one last time. You could arrange it for me. That brute she's married to won't have to even know I'm there. Pick a day when he's not home."

"Why can't you—?" Gabrielle had begun, but then she'd actually digested what he'd said and abruptly amended, "One last time? And you'll put her from your mind after that?"

He didn't want to lie to her, but he could relieve her worry without doing that. "She's a lost cause for me. D'you really think I don't know that?"

He'd thought she was coming around to his side when she said with a worried frown, "This is just asking for trouble, Richard." But then her little chin got that mulish angle and she'd added, "In fact, no. I'm sorry, but you're my dearest friend and I'm not going to help you down this path to destruction you seem intent on. *Forget about her!*"

Stymied and utterly frustrated because of it, he'd thrown up his hands. "Fine! You win! I'll just drown my sorrows for the duration. I'm sure Ohr, who agrees with you, will assist me with that at least," he'd said, and marched back to the coach.

He'd decided not to argue with her anymore. He'd just have to find his own way to see Georgina again. And he'd got lucky in that endeavor.

"And how did you get evening clothes this quickly?" Gabrielle was demanding now with an angry once-over at his black formal wear. "We only got here two days ago. I thought your old clothes didn't fit you anymore."

"They don't. But I have a good tailor in St. Kitts I've been using for several years, and I came prepared for anything on this trip."

"You came prepared to die! My God, I can't believe you're in the same room with him!"

"You have blown this so far out of proportion, Gabby. He's not going to kill me for just looking at her."

"His dire warning was that you couldn't get *anywhere* near her, and while you might easily ignore a promise like that from any other man, you can't from *him*. And how did you even find out about this ball?"

"*You* should have told me about it."

Her scowl darkened over that accusation. "No, I shouldn't have, which is why I didn't. *How?*"

He sighed over her obstinacy. "That hotel you dropped us off at—by the by, thank you for that, it's one of the best in town—keeps several coaches on hand for guests. I made use of one yesterday, even gave the driver the day off after he parked the vehicle across from Georgina's residence. I sat there merely hoping for the briefest glimpse of her if she happened to leave the house, but she never did."

"She has guests, so of course she wouldn't leave, but that still doesn't explain how you found out about this ball and where it was being held."

"I'd been hiding there most of the day when two ladies from the area strolled past me, and I suppose because the Malory house was right there across the street, the subject of this ball came up. I nearly fell out of the coach trying to catch the end of what they were saying."

Gabrielle sighed now. "You usually have perfectly good sense—until it comes to her, then you don't have any at all. And how did you get in here without an invitation?"

He grinned suddenly. That had actually brought back memories of the hellion he'd been when he'd been trying anything and everything to get his father to disown him, none of which had worked.

He told Gabrielle, "The same way the two young lords I found out front discussing access did. I followed them around to the back of the house and watched them climb over the garden wall. Deuced small garden compared to Malory's, and crowded, too, but mostly with others who'd got in the same way. Those who noticed our irregular entrance merely laughed."

She tsked. "Ohr agreed to this madness? He was supposed to keep an eye on you. Aren't you sharing a room with him so he can do that?"

"We were, but I made him angry enough to find somewhere else to cool off before we came to blows."

"You didn't!" she gasped.

"It wasn't easy. You know how imperturbable he is."

"You deliberately riled him up?" His guilty wince had her scold, "You owe him an apology."

"I know."

"Now would be a good time to apologize. Get out of here, Richard, while you still can."

He weighed his options and decided that arguing with her any further would get him nowhere, so he nodded at Gabrielle and headed to the garden. At least he'd seen Georgina. Gad, she was as beautiful as he remembered, and he still wanted her so much! Time wasn't making that go away. He hoped Gabrielle would believe he'd got what he'd come for and trust that he was leaving. But it wasn't enough, this one sight of his love, not as long as he was in England and so close to her.

Apparently, Gabby didn't trust him completely

when she considered so much was at stake. She actually followed him to the terrace doors that opened to the garden, which forced him to leap over the wall and out of her sight. He went no farther, but he did wait at least ten minutes before he peered over the wall to make sure she'd gone back to join Drew in the main room.

It was a simple matter to make sure she didn't discover him again. A wonderful thing, full face masks—at least tonight they were. They covered the entire face, except for the eyes, which of course was why they weren't comfortable to wear. He'd already noticed another fellow in a full mask quite different from his standing alone below the terrace in the garden.

Richard vaulted back over the wall and quickly approached the man. He kept one eye on the terrace to make sure Gabby didn't reappear. It took him a moment to realize the chap in the full mask was also eyeing the terrace.

"Care to swap masks, old chap?" Richard asked.

"No."

The man didn't even look at him! His glance went from both exits to the terrace, then to the pocket watch he held in his hand. He was obviously waiting impatiently for someone to join him. But it was like fate that this man's mask was different from Richard's, since a few he'd seen inside had been identical to his, so he tried again.

"Ten pounds?"

The fellow glanced at him now, even laughed. "Aren't you the desperate one. I'd actually take you up on that if my mistress didn't buy this mask for me specifically so she'd have an easy time finding me in the crowd. But I left word for her to meet me in the garden instead. Had a feeling this place would be a bloody crush."

"Then there should be no problem. You'll recognize her, won't you?"

"Can't say for sure, and I'm not about to miss her tonight for any reason."

Since the man's mistress was already late and would probably arrive at any moment, Richard suggested, "After she shows up?"

The fellow still shook his head. "Can't do it. She bought it. You do realize what happens if you give away something your ladylove buys you?"

With no one else outside the ballroom wearing such a perfect disguise, Richard's sigh was poignant. He should just leave. This was probably fate prompting him.

But the young lord must have heard his sigh. "You can't have mine, but I came with a friend. Perhaps he'll accommodate you."

Being a good sport after all, the young lord even went to fetch his friend and the swap was soon made. Unfortunately, the new mask wasn't at all to Richard's taste; a devil's face replete with ceramic horns, it was not even a full mask. The half mask left his mouth exposed, but what the hell, mouths weren't all that distinctive. And he had no other options. At least Gabrielle wouldn't recognize him so easily, though she might accost the fellow wearing his old clown mask. But she'd just end up a little embarrassed and give up looking for him, assured that he'd left.

Armored once more to his satisfaction—he even stuffed his long hair beneath his coat this time— Richard was prepared to risk all again for a few more hours of just gazing at Georgina from afar. In the back of his mind was the distinct worry that he might be tempted to do more than that, but he ignored it. He had to ignore it. He didn't *really* want to die for love of another's man wife.

Chapter Seven

THE BALEFUL EXPRESSION in James Malory's eyes wasn't fleeting. It persisted, and because it did, Julia's curiosity got the better of her. But she couldn't see who or what had drawn his furious attention. Whoever it was, was on the same side of the room as she, but dozens of people in the way blocked her view. So when Carol tried to steer her back to her husband, Harry, to introduce her to the friend Harry was conversing with, Julia excused herself for a few minutes and wove her way quickly through the crowd. She had to peek over people's shoulders and rise up on her toes every now and then to catch glimpses of James to see if she was lining up with his sight.

After a few minutes she got a clear view of him, but she was quite disappointed to find that she was too late. James had turned his attention back to his wife as he leaned down to tell her something. He even kissed her cheek, which caused an immediate oh-ah-isn't-that-sweet collective sigh in the room, then quite a few embarrassed chuckles over it.

Georgina laughed, hearing the crowd's reaction. James looked up at the ceiling in exasperation, no doubt, because he couldn't help but hear that sigh, too. But then Georgina was distracted by one of her many relatives who had come up to talk to her, and James's gaze went right back to where it had been before.

Like Carol, Julia couldn't help the shudder that passed over her when he seemed to pin that feral gaze right on her! She realized that he must be staring at one of the four people who were standing in front of her on the edge of the crowd facing the dance floor. The music stopped briefly, so the few couples who had been dancing left the floor, which gave her a clearer view of James. While his stone-faced expression still gave away nothing, his green eyes had turned lethal. Amazing how he *could* have murder on his mind and you simply wouldn't know it unless you caught that gaze.

Then it occurred to her that the man really did usually keep his feelings to himself, so he must be exhibiting them deliberately now. Was he sending someone a message? She tried to figure out who had James's undivided attention.

Of the four people standing with their backs to her, a woman and three men, the woman and one of the men were obviously together. The second man was a short, stocky fellow easy to see over. The third man was tall enough to easily stand out in the crowd.

The couple were so engrossed in conversation that they hadn't noticed anything amiss, and as soon as the music started again, they moved onto the dance floor. James's gaze didn't follow them, which left the two men. The short one suddenly turned and hurried off behind Julia, and she couldn't mistake *his* shudder as he passed her. He disappeared beyond the open doors to the terrace, and James's gaze didn't follow his departure, either. That pretty much left the tall fellow.

She didn't know many men outside of Malory's family who were this tall, and James wasn't likely to be this furious with a relative—actually, that had to be it! Georgina's brothers, of course! How could she have forgotten James made no bones about his animosity toward them? He could barely tolerate them.

This tall, broad-shouldered man could be any one of Georgina's five brothers. Julia hadn't met all of them, though those she knew didn't have black hair like this man. And come to think of it, James might not like the Anderson brothers, but he wouldn't give any of them killing looks either.

She began to realize how silly her quest was. Unless she recognized this man, which was doubtful with everyone wearing masks tonight, what did she think she would discover? She couldn't point out to him that he was about to die and ask him why. No, she wasn't going to find out a single thing.

As she turned around to look for Carol, a rather loud sigh stopped her and made her glance at that wide, masculine back again. Had the man finally noticed James's dire attention? If so, she expected to see the man run past her and out of the room, but he didn't. Actually, that sigh had sounded rather pitiful—almost heartbreaking. That certainly wouldn't have anything to do with James Malory, so this fellow probably still didn't know he was in danger.

Should she warn him? While the titled ladies present might be constrained by the rule of not speaking to a man they hadn't been introduced to, that rule didn't apply to her. In the world of business, she had to speak to strangers all the time. But this really wasn't any of her concern, and besides, her curiosity was prompting her to make assumptions that might not be accurate.

She turned to leave again, but then, appalled, found herself tapping the man's shoulder instead. It was that pathetic sigh! How could she ignore something that forlorn?

"Are you all right?" Julia asked.

He swung around, and she was startled for a moment by the devil's mask he was wearing. It was only a half mask though, with beneath it the shadow of a mustache, a pair of sensual lips, and a firm chin. But he barely spared her a glance before looking back over his shoulder where he'd been gazing.

With another sigh he said, "Look at her, she's magnificent, isn't she?"

He had a slight accent, though Julia couldn't quite place it, but she wondered if he'd even heard her question. "You sound smitten," she said, noting the obvious.

"More than smitten. I've been in love with her since I first clapped eyes on her last year."

"Who?"

"Lady Malory."

Julia managed to choke back a laugh because that had to be the last thing she'd expected to hear. But that certainly explained James's animosity. Her curiosity had been satisfied after all.

The Malorys were extremely family-oriented. No matter which of their women this man was talking about, those present tonight were all married, so James would take exception. "Trespass against one and you've trespassed against them all" might as well be their family motto. Unless . . . no, this fellow wasn't one of the Malory husbands merely admiring his wife from a distance. They were all present and accounted for elsewhere in the room, easy to recognize in their dominos.

"Which Lady Malory would that be?" she asked. "There are at least five of them here tonight and they're all—"

"Georgina."

"—married women!" she finished with a gasp. If he

had to be hopelessly in love with one of them, he couldn't have picked a worse one than James Malory's wife.

"I am excruciatingly aware of that appalling fact," he replied.

"But are you aware that her husband has been looking daggers at you for at least fifteen minutes?"

That got his eyes off of Georgina immediately and back to Julia. "But he can't know it's me! I wasn't invited. He'd have no clue!"

She shrugged. "Whether he knows who you are or not, it's rather apparent that he objects to how long you've been staring at his wife."

He groaned. "I'm dead."

Her thought exactly, but she was compelled to scold, "You didn't even notice he's been watching you?"

"When I couldn't take my eyes off of her?"

Blinded by love? She was still feeling a smidgen of pity for him, though it was definitely tempered now because she knew the couple involved and how happily married they were. And they were her friends. This fellow wasn't.

So she said, "You should leave."

"It won't help. He'll hunt me down—unless he thinks he's made a mistake. You could help to make him think that. Would you be willing to save my life?"

"You want him to think you're with me?"

"Exactly."

"We could dance, I suppose."

"Thank you, but that won't be enough. He must

think you are the only woman in my life, perhaps even married to me. And married couples kiss—"

"Now just a minute," she objected sternly. "I'm not willing to go *that* far when I don't even—"

"Please, *chérie,*" he cut in again in such an appealing tone.

The sudden French startled her. He'd been speaking such clear English, she would never have guessed he was a Frenchman. His accent became more pronounced as he continued, "If I just leave without this demonstration that my affections are with another, he will hunt me down. He has promised to do that very thing if I ever went near his wife again."

"Then you shouldn't have come here!"

"I know." He sighed that abject sigh again. "But I couldn't resist when I've longed so much for just the sight of her. Have you never been in love to know what it's like?"

He was making her feel sorry for him again. Of course she had no idea what it was like when she'd been stuck with her god-awful fiancé all her life, which had kept all the men of her acquaintance at arm's length. In fact, she'd never even been kissed before. Who would have dared when she was already spoken for? Yet with his introducing the subject of kissing, she was having a hard time getting her eyes off his lips . . .

"Oh, very well, just be quick about it," she said, and hoped she wouldn't regret it. "I don't want anyone other than James noticing."

Chapter Eight

I F IT WEREN'T going to be her first kiss, Julia would never have agreed. But having gone twenty-one years without ever experiencing any kiss of a romantic nature was a compelling incentive. This wasn't fleeting curiosity, it was a powerful desire to know, which had been with her since she was fourteen. Which was about the time her friends were getting kissed and telling her how exciting it was.

More fury to add to the fire of discontent that her engagement had caused her. So many things she'd missed out on while growing up because of it. The excitement of a first Season; good God, for an entire year her friends had talked and giggled over nothing else. The titillation of harmless flirtation, they were all experiencing it even prior to that first Season, but Julia couldn't. And each time she'd realized just how much she was missing because of *him*, it added one more reason why she'd shoot him if he ever came back.

But not to be kissed, at least once, just to know what it was like, was probably the thing she'd regretted the most, that she'd had no way to experience it. It could have been the easiest thing to find out, too, since she *did* have a fiancé, after all. But the last time they'd seen each other, when she was ten and he was fifteen, they had agreed to kill each other if they ever got close enough again to do so. They hadn't just made empty threats either. They despised each other so much that every one of their meetings had ended in violent discord of one sort or another. So they had avoided any more visits after that, and then he'd thankfully disappeared two years later so she hadn't had to clap eyes on him again.

But it would have been nice if she'd had at least one other kiss to compare this one to. Then she might not have been so completely swept away by it.

The kiss began the moment she agreed to it. He didn't remove his half mask because nothing was preventing his sensual mouth from reaching hers. She felt a moment's disappointment that she wasn't going to see the rest of his face. Green eyes were all she saw before she closed her own eyes to more fully enjoy the novelty of having her lips pressed to another's.

It was more exciting than she could possibly have imagined. That he was a stranger might have added to that. That she didn't even know what he looked like probably did, too. She could imagine him to be anyone she wanted, the most handsome man she could think of—well, he would have to be a duplicate of Jeremy Malory then, since he was probably the most handsome man she'd ever seen, but he was already taken . . . or his uncle Anthony . . . or wait, there was his cousin Derek, too, oh, darn, never mind, they were all married. Besides, it didn't really matter what he looked like, not in that sublime moment of discovery of something she'd waited this long for.

But he sure didn't kiss like a man who was in love with someone else. He seemed as involved in this intimate act as she was. He'd slipped one arm about her shoulders and the other about her waist and had drawn her steadily closer to him until no space was left between them for anything resembling a chaste embrace, far from it. But he was simulating a married-couple kiss, so she ought to keep in mind that he probably wasn't really getting carried away by the moment, that it meant nothing more to him other than a ruse to fool James Malory.

Yet she did nothing of the sort because it was very real to her, and so exciting. Who would have thought a kiss was so much more than just the touching of lips? It was the embrace, too, the exciting sensations of having his arms around her, of being pressed to such a hard male chest. The tickle of hair on his upper lip caused an interesting shudder. The rasp of his tongue that had tried and failed to get her lips to open because she didn't know that might be part of the kiss. Delicious flutters in her belly, her legs getting steadily weaker, making her hold on even tighter to him.

"You're being a very good sport about this. Another moment or two should do it."

He said that against her lips before continuing the kiss, but being reminded that this first kiss of hers wasn't actually a real one, just a demonstration for someone else, was quite a splash of cold reality. Enough of one that the pleasant haze she'd been floating in was already waning before he stepped back, ending their brief moment of intimacy.

"A bit tardy, I know," he was saying in a jaunty tone, his lips quirked upward in a half grin, "but allow me to introduce myself. I am Jean Paul, and forever in your debt."

The grin bemused her so much it actually stole her breath. She'd only just tasted those lips! She found his mouth entirely too fascinating now, couldn't take her eyes off it.

"Is Malory still looking this way?"

She had to take a few deep breaths to concentrate on what Jean Paul was saying. "I shouldn't look," she said. "He isn't dumb. He'll know we're talking about him."

"True."

"My name is Julia, by the way."

She heard the shyness in her tone and was astounded by it. Shy? When was she *ever* shy? This man was having such an unusual effect on her. Just because they'd shared her first kiss?

"A very pretty name on both sides of the ocean," he replied.

"Which places on the other side have you been to?"

"I'm just visiting England with friends."

She realized he wasn't actually answering her question, though that might not be intentional. "So you don't live here?"

"No."

"But you sound so English."

He chuckled. "I try to, *chérie*."

"Oh." She was embarrassed for having forgotten so quickly the accent that kept weaving in and out of his words. But just for clarification, in case he was actually an Englishman who'd been raised in France, she added, "So you are French?"

"Nice of you to notice."

Now that was an odd thing to say. It occurred to her that despite his seeming to have a perfectly good grasp of the English language, at times he might still not find the right words to use—thus, a little confusion could arise.

Now that she'd helped him, for whatever it was worth, she knew she should leave him and return to Carol, but found herself reluctant to say good-bye. She realized, belatedly, that she probably hadn't helped him as he'd hoped. She'd only been thinking of herself, not his circumstances, when she'd allowed him to kiss her. She needed to warn him. It was the decent thing to do.

"That kiss may not have fooled James at all, since he knows me."

"Gad, I should have asked if you're married."

That was the only thing he gathered from her warning? She raised a brow at him and pointed out, "Marriage doesn't appear to deter you."

"I wish it wasn't so, *chérie*. It is painful, loving someone you know you can't have."

His sigh confirmed it and had her feeling sorry for him again. She guessed he was even blushing under that half mask, though the lower half of his face, even his neck, was too sun-bronzed for her to be sure.

In case she was right, she admitted, "As it happens, I'm not married."

"But you must have suitors."

"No, actually—"

"You do now."

She laughed, couldn't help it. The man was actually flirting with her? She'd gained a little experience in flirting after her eighteenth year, though not flirting of this harmless sort, where she knew the man wasn't serious. She'd actually encountered a few men of less than strong moral fiber who, knowing of her frustrating betrothal circumstances, had tried to lure her into clandestine affairs. Although she was ashamed to admit it, she'd actually been tempted! But that was before she'd discovered an end to her horrid situation. Besides, she hadn't been *that* tempted.

But Jean Paul was actually rather charming, when he wasn't sighing over his broken heart, so she played along, enough to say coyly, "Need I remind you that you're in love with someone else?"

He ran the back of his finger over her cheek. "You might be able to get my mind off her. Would you like to try?"

Luring him away from another woman sounded a bit unsavory, but that other woman wasn't his, she was already married. In that case, could it actually be considered a charitable thing to do? To help to mend his broken heart?

Julia pulled in the reins abruptly. What the deuce was she thinking? Just because he suddenly sounded serious she was considering it? It *was* tempting. She couldn't deny it. But she didn't really want to encourage an acquaintance with someone who, from the sound of it, wouldn't be staying in England for long. That could put her in the same situation he was in, wanting someone she couldn't have.

Before she could change her mind, she said, "I must return to my friends, and you should leave the ball or our effort to get you out from under James's murderous gaze will have been for naught."

"Sound advice, *chérie*. Adieu, until we—"

She didn't stay to hear the rest of his good-bye and started weaving her way quickly through the crowd. Before she reached Carol, she did steal one more glance at James Malory and saw that his full attention was back on his wife. So perhaps the ruse had worked after all.

Chapter Nine

How disappointing, though not a total dead end, eh? Julia couldn't get Carol's words out of her mind.

When she had reached her friend, Carol had asked, "Well, who is he?"

"Who?"

"Who else had your undivided attention for so long?" At Julia's blush, Carol giggled. "This is so exciting! It almost feels as if I'm having my come-out all over again, now that you're finally having one."

"I'm not yet—"

"Of course you are. Just because no one else knows it yet doesn't mean it hasn't started for you. It's all about finding that perfect someone who you'll want to spend the rest of your life with. And you did say you are looking already—you *are,* aren't you?"

"Yes."

"I went to find you, but when I saw you so deep in

conversation with that tall chap, I wasn't about to interrupt. So, who is he? With that mask he was wearing, I couldn't begin to guess."

"He's only visiting England."

"A foreigner? Well, darn, that's not ideal—I would be devastated if you moved away from England—but other foreigners have settled in our fair country."

That was true. Julia had put up roadblocks in her mind without really thinking about it. But that she and Jean Paul lived in two different countries meant nothing when those two countries were neighbors. She'd been to France herself on business. She knew how little time it took to cross the Channel. Why, it took longer to make the trip to northern England to confer with her managers there than it did to visit France. So that, at least, wasn't a good reason not to see the man again.

But she teased her friend, "You're getting a little ahead of yourself, aren't you?"

"Nonsense, we have to think of everything, you know, when it comes to picking a husband for you, including where he'll want you to live. But you won't find very many men with pockets as deep as yours, so I'm sure you could convince your chap to live wherever *you* want to. You could even put it in your marriage contract!"

Julia laughed. She wasn't in the habit of thinking that far ahead, not where men were concerned, and certainly not on a first meeting.

But she admitted with a half grin, "France isn't so far away."

"Oh, my, a Frenchman? No indeed, a hop, skip, and a jump, as Harry would say. And I've even met a few Frenchmen recently, so perhaps I know him?"

"Jean Paul is his name."

Carol's brow knitted thoughtfully before she shook her head. "No, that doesn't sound at all familiar. But the important question is, are *you* interested? Do you hope to see him again?"

The excitement Carol had encouraged waned suddenly when Julia had to admit, "He's charming, intriguing, and I even found myself quite stimulated by our interaction, but I'm afraid he's spoken for, or at least, he's already in love with someone else, although she's married."

"How disappointing, though not a total dead end, eh?"

No indeed, and with that in mind, Julia went looking for him a while later. But he'd taken her advice. He was gone. Realizing that she'd probably never see him again, she felt a distinct sense of loss. Which was silly. She didn't even know what he really looked like, though the half of his face that had been visible hinted that he was handsome. Yes, she'd been drawn to him. He could be amusing when he wasn't overcome by dejection. He'd made her laugh. He'd made her thrill to the touch of his lips. And he'd stolen her breath—how long she'd waited for something like *that* to happen!

But he wasn't available in the normal sense, and she didn't have the least idea how to win over a man who'd already been won over!

She tried to put him from her mind. Some of the crowd unexpectedly thinned out even before the unmasking, though many more left just prior to it. But enough were gone that the dancing picked up and she stopped declining when asked. She even had the opportunity to share a mild flirtation with another young man who didn't know her circumstances yet, but she wasn't really interested by then, so she actually confessed that she was engaged, which ended his efforts abruptly. She didn't even know *why* she did that. She just knew that all the gaiety she'd felt earlier had gone out of her.

As the night wore on, her mood didn't improve. It became almost as melancholy as Jean Paul's. So she was glad when it was time to go home. Crawling into her bed that night, she was struck by the irony of her situation. Here she was on the brink of finally becoming available, of finally having her own come-out, of finally putting herself on the marriage mart, as the *ton* fondly called it. It should have been the most exciting time of her life and it had been. Until tonight. Until she got run over by emotions she'd never before experienced. And maybe that was it. What Jean Paul had made her feel was what she'd always imagined it would be like when she found her perfect someone. Why else would her mind be filled with nothing but him after only one meeting? Her dejection came from knowing there wouldn't be any other meetings.

She'd walked off before letting him know how to find her—if he cared to try. And he was French. No one there knew him, at least Carol didn't, and so she doubted anyone else did either. He wasn't even supposed to be there tonight. So she had no way to find him even if she wanted to. Did she want to? But two people there did know him. One he loved, the other wanted to kill him for it. But asking them would be really bad form. Wouldn't it?

Chapter Ten

"WHAT THE HELL?"

Ohr said it as he leapt forward to help the hotel employee drag Richard into their room. The door bursting open hadn't startled him. The sight of Richard did. The young man, probably no more than a boy, was definitely having trouble with Richard's mostly dead weight.

"Found him lying on the curb out front," the young man said as Ohr took over and easily got Richard to his bed.

"The hack driver wouldn't help any further," Richard mumbled. "He was angry that I got blood all over his seats."

With a frown, Ohr tossed the boy a coin for his assistance and closed the door behind him. He lit another lamp before he approached the bed again.

The dead silence prompted Richard to ask, "That bad?"

"What ran you over?" was all Ohr said.

Richard was curled on his side, holding his ribs. He couldn't imagine how many were broken, but it had to be a lot. Each breath was excruciatingly painful. But he supposed he was lucky to still be alive. And he'd been so close to escaping! He'd been about to jump for the same wall he'd climbed over earlier to enter the ball when a hand swung him around and a fist landed in his gut.

Bent over, gasping for breath, he'd demanded, "Why'd you do that?"

"You really have to ask?"

He hadn't seen who landed the punch, not that he didn't know. But that dry voice confirmed it. Ever since he'd vaulted over another wall, the one in Georgina's garden, after she'd slapped him and he'd turned to see that her husband had witnessed it, he'd known this day was coming. But he'd had to take that risk that day, he'd wanted her so much. And now he had to pay for it. It was his own fault for letting his last encounter with Malory deceive him into thinking James wouldn't *really* kill him, when the man had come to the Caribbean to help Gabby rescue her father and had completely ignored Richard's presence while he'd concentrated on the task at hand. So Richard hadn't given sufficient credence to James's warning that he'd harm him if he ever came near his wife again.

Tonight, he'd tried to tell James, "I was leaving—!"

"Not soon enough."

The second blow, an uppercut, connected with his cheek and knocked him on his arse. He was vaguely aware that at least half of the men who'd been on the terrace and scattered around the small garden were now scurrying over the garden wall, no doubt thinking that Lady Regina's uncle had been elected to get rid of the party crashers.

"Enough," Richard had said as he managed to get to his feet. "You've made your point."

The thin porcelain of his mask had shattered completely with that last blow, small pieces of it littering the ground around his feet. With the mask smashed against his cheek, he'd felt the sharper sting mixed with the wider area of pain where the hammer of James's fist had landed, but his cheek was already turning numb.

On his feet again, he got a good look at James Malory and took heart. The man didn't look angry. He could have been utterly bored, he was so lacking in expression.

So Richard felt his stomach turn in dread when James said, "We've barely begun."

If the man weren't such a brute specimen, Richard might have stood a chance. Ohr had taught him some unusual Asian maneuvers that had kept him from getting even a scratch in the many brawls he and the rest of Nathan's crew tended to get into in all the rowdy taverns they frequented. He'd done everything right tonight in the way of defense, he'd just known it wouldn't do any good. This particular Malory couldn't be stopped. Gabrielle had made sure he knew that when she'd delivered James's warning that he was going to kill him if he ever saw him again. The man was extraordinary in the ring. He'd never, *ever,* been beaten, she'd told him. But then you only had to look at Malory to guess that, he had so much power in his upper body, and fists like sledgehammers.

It was a grueling punishment for Richard's trespass, absolutely the worst beating of his life. James didn't stop until Richard was unconscious. He wished he'd been knocked out sooner. Most of those men who had vaulted out of the garden when the violence began had actually stayed to watch the show, hanging from the wall on the other side of it, feeling safe with the wall between them and Malory. A few of them had felt enough pity for Richard to help him out of there and into a passing hack after James went back into the ballroom.

"So?" Ohr prompted now.

"Malory," was all Richard said.

"Then you're going to need a doctor."

Ohr moved quickly to the door to try to catch the young hotel employee before he disappeared down the hall, but the chap had had the same thought. Ohr found him about to knock on the door when he opened it.

"It occurred to me your friend might need—"

"A doctor, yes, thank you." Ohr gave the lad another coin.

"Right away, sir."

Ohr closed the door with a chuckle. Richard knew it amused his friend no end to be called "sir," a form of address that simply didn't fit a pirate and never would.

A room over a tavern was usually one of their better accommodations unless they were in St. Kitts, where Richard and Ohr had rooms at Nathan's home. But this hotel was in the better end of town, in Mayfair no less, an area of London that had been developed for fashionable residences mostly by the powerful Grosvenor family back in the seventeenth century. The area included several large squares in the north, including Berkeley Square, where Georgina lived. Their hotel had once been one of those fancy residences, and it was the first place where Ohr had ever been called "sir."

When Ohr came back to the side of the bed to look down at Richard, he said, "Let me guess, you went to her party, didn't you?"

"It was a ball, and a masked one at that. He never should have noticed me."

"Then how did he? No, let me guess again, you got stupid, didn't you? Couldn't just have a look and leave, eh?"

Richard might have flinched. He couldn't tell, his face was too numb. "I don't think he knew it was me to begin with, he just caught me staring at her too long."

"Don't kid yourself. Gabby was there, so he'd immediately think of you. And what's that stuck on your cheek?"

"Porcelain shards probably. He broke the mask I was wearing when he punched my face."

"He didn't notice the mask?"

"I'm sure he didn't care."

"Your face is bloody. You better hope it doesn't scar. But you've got more blood on you than a few punches would account for. Did he take a knife to you? I find that hard to—"

"No, his fists were quite enough. The mess is probably from my nose when it broke. It bled a lot before it stopped. That, at least, I've experienced before and is the least of my concerns. I'm more worried about my ribs. It bloody well feels like one or more has broken through my skin."

Ohr tsked. "Let me have a look."

"No! Don't move me. I'm actually able to breathe in this position."

"I'm only going to open your shirt. Don't be a girl about it," Ohr scolded, but after doing so, he added, "I suppose you're allowed to be a bit girlish about this. Damn, Rich, you're already a solid mass of bruise, right down to your belly."

"Any ribs poking through?" Richard asked with dread.

"Not that I can see on the front side, but I'm not going to try to get you out of that jacket and shirt to examine the rest. I'll leave that to the doctor."

"Do we have a bottle of rotgut?"

"I never travel without a few. And good idea. If those ribs are broken, the doc will probably have to push them back into place before he binds you up. It would help if you can't feel it by then."

Richard groaned. He didn't think he could stand any more pain than what he was already enduring.

But Ohr was saying, "It's probably going to take a while for a doctor to be found at this time of night. Don't worry, you've got time to drink yourself into a stupor."

It took Ohr a few minutes to stuff enough pillows under Richard's head so he didn't have to change his position, which was at least tolerable, and could tilt the bottle without spilling the whiskey.

"You were lucky, you know," Ohr said after Richard had downed a third of the bottle. "Malory could have messed up your face so bad you wouldn't recognize yourself even after mending. And why didn't he?"

"Not enough pain to suit him, I'm sure. And his strategy was sound. He kept me in a constant state of gasping for every breath—or flat on my back."

On an angry note, Ohr demanded, "What the hell, did you forget everything I taught you?"

Richard downed another third of the bottle before he replied, "Not at all. I was a good student. You even said so. I didn't even try to hit the man, I was so busy defending myself. It bloody well didn't work. Have you forgotten what he looks like?"

"Even mountains can be cut down to size, but I get the point. Malory is the type you have to hurt early, or it's all over—for you. And you should have stayed down when he knocked you down."

Richard started to laugh, but that hurt too much. "Think I didn't try that? He yanked me back to my feet every bloody time." Richard's words were starting to slur. "By the by, sorry for making you angry earlier tonight. Didn't mean a bit of it."

"I realized that—too late. By the time I got back to the room, you were gone. But I wasn't away *that* long," Ohr added with a frown. "What'd you do, grab your fancy duds and race out of the room to dress somewhere else?"

"Had to. Knew you wouldn't be angry for long. You never are."

Ohr sighed. "I really didn't think you'd be this foolish over a woman you can't have. You have no trouble putting her from your mind when you're bedding someone else. Have you never wondered why that is?"

Richard didn't answer. He'd already passed out.

Chapter Eleven

It took two days for Julia to get up the nerve to visit the Malory house down the street because she wasn't going there simply to visit her friend Georgina. She was hoping to find out something, anything, about Jean Paul that might lead to her seeing him again. It was rather bold of her to try, but how could she not, when she couldn't get the man out of her mind? Or the notion that he might really be her perfect match. How could she let him just slip away without finding out for sure? That had, in the end, convinced her. She would always regret it if she made no effort at all.

She wasn't going to mention him to James, of course. But she reasoned that Georgina might not mind talking about him and might even be flattered that such a strapping young man was in love with her.

The Malory house wasn't in its usual quiet state, however. She'd forgotten that all five of Georgina's brothers had come to London for her birthday this year, and none of them had yet gone back to sea. Only Boyd lived permanently in London. While Warren and his wife, Amy, also had a house in town, they were usually at sea for half of each year.

When she was introduced to the two brothers that she hadn't met before, Clinton and Thomas Anderson, just as they were leaving, she assumed they were staying with their sister until they sailed back to America.

It was the first thing she remarked on after she joined Georgina in her parlor and more introductions were made. Two of Georgina's sisters-in-law were present, along with Boyd, her youngest brother. Julia was already acquainted with Boyd's wife, Katey. And while she'd met Drew Anderson once before several years ago, and she'd seen his new wife at the ball, she hadn't actually met Gabrielle until now.

"Actually," Georgina said with a wry grin, "this is the first time ever that none of my brothers are staying with me. But then it's a perfect opportunity for Clinton and Thomas to get to know the new wives in the family, so Boyd's putting them up, thanks to that house you found for him."

"And thank God for that," James said drily as he sauntered into the parlor. "Can't thank you enough, Julia, for leasing him that place that's big enough for the lot of them. Now if they'd just stop spending all their waking hours here . . ."

The derogatory remark was typical of James when it came to his five Anderson brothers-in-law. Even Julia knew that. And no one there took it seriously.

Katey Anderson, who had only discovered last year that she was also a Malory, chuckled. "You aren't getting rid of me that easily, Uncle James."

"You and Gabby are the exception, puss," James said as he bent to kiss the top of Katey's head on his way to Georgina's chair, where he half-sat on the arm of it. "And if either of you would like to come to your senses, I know which arms to twist to arrange for a quiet divorce."

Boyd used to have quite a temper according to his sister. Although he'd apparently mellowed with age, it didn't sound like it when he said, "That's going a little too far, Malory." Then, turning to Georgina, he inquired, "Isn't he supposed to at least pretend to be nice when you have company?"

"Well said, Yank!"

Boyd nodded to acknowledge the compliment from James, but Georgina said, "If you mean Julia, she's our friend and neighbor, and he doesn't rein it in among friends, so do try not to encourage him."

"Don't *dis*courage him, George," James said. "He's finally getting the hang of it."

Georgina rolled her eyes toward the ceiling.

Julia grinned. She was used to this sort of banter in this particular household. She had been present when

James had brutally disparaged his brother-in-law Warren and no one in their family had raised a brow over it, Warren included. But James didn't only put his hooks in the Anderson men. If none of them were present, he could be just as abusive to his own brother Anthony. Their niece Regina had summed it up nicely once when she'd confided they were happiest when they were fighting, either each other or joining forces against a common enemy.

Definitely not a good time to come asking about secret admirers, Julia thought, when Georgina was surrounded by her family. Julia couldn't deny that she was disappointed. After she'd finally worked up the nerve to broach the subject, she was going to have to leave empty-handed. Yet uppermost in her mind was the knowledge that Jean Paul wasn't going to be in London for long, so she didn't have time to dally if she hoped to see him again. All of which made her realize she probably wasn't going to see him again.

She tried to enjoy the visit anyway. The Malorys were always entertaining. But her disappointment put a definite damper on her mood. She was about to give her excuses to depart when James beat her to it.

"I was supposed to meet Tony at Knighton's Hall for a round or two in the ring this morning. I suppose I should at least make an appearance."

"We have company," Georgina said pointedly as he stood up to leave.

"Yes, but now you ladies can discuss ladylike things, and frankly, m'dear, I'd rather have Tony pound on me than suffer through yet another discussion of fashion. What about you, Yank?" he added with a glance at his brother-in-law. "Care to tag along?"

Boyd shot to his feet instantly. "Are you joking? I'd love to!"

Katey laughed as soon as the men left the room and said to Georgina, "That was quite a boon for Boyd. He was sure he'd never get invited to that private pugilist hall those two are members of and have a chance to watch them have at each other. Is Uncle James feeling all right? He's not usually so—dare I say—kind to your brothers."

"If his invitation extends to inviting Boyd into the ring, it wouldn't be so kind, now would it?" Gabrielle remarked.

"Actually, Boyd would consider that a privilege! He so admires their pugilist skills."

"I doubt that's James's intention," Georgina said. "As it happens, he's been quite benevolent now that the ball is over and done with. You can't imagine how much he hated having to attend, knowing he'd be on display. He was at his most sardonic the prior week, and I couldn't even let him know that I sympathized with him, since I wasn't *supposed* to know about the party."

"It was a smashing success, though, wasn't it?" Gabrielle said. "Regina must be pleased."

"*Smashing* is a good word for it," Katey replied. "It was such a crush, I could barely move about."

"And Regina wasn't pleased a'tall," Georgina informed them. "She expected a few party crashers, but not in those absurd numbers."

Gabrielle had been looking at Julia during this discussion and finally said, "I was hoping to meet you again before my husband and I leave town. Georgina mentioned you're in trade just like her family, but that you also run your family businesses and have been for quite some time now. I find that fascinating, as young as you are."

Julia grinned. "It's not all that hard to do when you've been involved in it all your life. My father wasn't lax in making sure I could take over for him one day."

"You don't run into trouble because you're a woman?"

"Certainly. When it comes to negotiating new contracts or buying new businesses, I make my decisions, then simply let my solicitors speak for me. This keeps ruffled feathers to a minimum, my own included!" Julia chuckled. "Everything else is fairly simple because my father already employed very competent managers."

"So you don't do the hiring and firing yourself?"

"Just the managers, and I've only had to replace one

so far. He was a good man, he just got it into his head that he could take advantage of a 'female' employer. But what about yourself? I was told you and Drew have settled in the Caribbean instead of America."

"I've loved the islands since I first went to live with my father there. And I was given a lovely little island as a wedding gift."

"A whole island?" Julia asked, amazed.

"Really, it's tiny!" Gabrielle laughed. "But Drew agreed to build our home there since he's been trading in the islands for years anyway."

It was too bad, Julia thought, that Gabrielle and Drew would be returning there soon. The young woman was so easy to talk to, Julia was sure they could have become good friends. But with the subject of the ball having been introduced, Julia grabbed the opportunity now to mention what had been preoccupying her.

"By the by, Georgina, I met an admirer of yours that night at the ball," Julia said. "A young Frenchman by the name of Jean Paul."

"A Frenchman?" Georgina shook her head. "I'm pretty sure I don't know any."

"No? So he's kept his love a secret, even from you?"

"He professed to love me?" Georgina said with a frown now, and then a tsk. "Is this some new romantic notion young men are favoring these days, that they must risk all for love?"

"This isn't your first secret admirer?" Julia guessed.

"No, unfortunately."

Katey laughed. "That *would* be risking all, wouldn't it, to fall in love with you?"

"That's why I find this so absurd," Georgina said. "They must know I'm happily married. They're more'n likely terrified of my husband for whatever reason. Perhaps it's like a rite of passage, their picking the most unavailable woman to moon over, the one they're most likely to get killed for pursuing. It quite annoys James, you know."

Katey was laughing harder. Gabrielle was looking up at the ceiling. Julia sighed inwardly. She wasn't sure what she'd expected to learn here today, but it wasn't that Georgina didn't even know who Jean Paul was.

"You weren't interested in that French fellow, were you, Julia?" Gabrielle asked, casting a worried look her way.

"No, of course not," Julia replied, but her blush probably gave away the lie.

Chapter Twelve

Julia's nerve was beginning to desert her. She stood outside Jean Paul's hotel. Did she really want to do this, make her interest so obvious to a man she hadn't fully seen yet? That she was even there was so unexpected, she was still amazed.

When Gabrielle Anderson had followed her outside the Malory house, Julia had thought she'd left something behind. But, no, Gabrielle had said, "I know who you were talking about. Jean Paul is a dear friend of mine."

"But Georgina doesn't know him?"

"She does; he just probably neglected to tell her his name. He's not only careless when he's around her, but thoughtless as well."

"I suppose love does that to a man."

"Among other things," Gabrielle had cryptically

said. "But you appear to be aware of the situation yet you are still interested in him?"

"Was it that obvious?" Julia said with a blush.

"No need to be embarrassed. I'm not even surprised. Jean Paul is not only handsome, he can be delightfully charming, too. But this obsession he has with my sister-in-law isn't good for anyone involved, most of all him. He's been lovesick too long over a lost cause. He needs rescuing. And while I wouldn't ordinarily interfere, it occurred to me that a pretty girl like you could be his salvation."

"That's—a tall order," Julia said uneasily.

"I merely meant, you could help him to forget about Georgina."

Hadn't Jean Paul said nearly the same thing? And hadn't *she* been thinking it as well? She'd been intrigued by a masked charmer, and now he was even more acceptable in her mind. He was a friend of the Andersons' and Gabrielle had confirmed that he was handsome and charming. Julia couldn't find any reason not to pursue an acquaintance.

Gabrielle had put that thought in Julia's head when she'd added, "He's staying at Coulson's Hotel if you'd like to leave him a message. Perhaps you can arrange a meeting somewhere to further your acquaintance. Wait, you didn't bring your maid to chaperone, did you?"

"No, I live down the street here, close enough to walk, so it wasn't necessary."

"Well, no need to delay! My carriage is right here. I'll go with you," Gabrielle had offered. "It won't take long just to leave a note."

This innocent suggestion still put Julia in the role of pursuer, and Jean Paul would know it. She would have preferred a meeting by chance. Even if she arranged it, at least he wouldn't know she did. But with her new friend going to the trouble of escorting her, she couldn't back down now. She couldn't get the time constraint out of her mind, either. Jean Paul was only visiting England. He'd said as much. He could leave at any time.

Actually, Gabrielle might know, might even be the friend he was here visiting. She'd called him a dear friend. She must know a lot about him.

As they entered the hotel together, Julia asked, "What kind of work does Jean Paul do?"

"He didn't tell you?" Gabrielle replied in what seemed a careful tone.

"No, we didn't say much about ourselves at the ball."

"Well, it will give you something to talk about with him."

Was Gabrielle deliberately avoiding that subject? Julia tried another, asking, "Do you know how long he is going to be in England?"

"Not long. Too long," Gabrielle said, somewhat distracted, then with a glance at Julia, she sighed. "I'm sorry, he just causes me such worry over his infatuation with my sister-in-law. Which is why I thought—" Gabrielle paused. She even frowned. Then she added unexpectedly, "Have you ever thought of visiting the Caribbean?"

Julia chuckled at such an abrupt change of subject. "Oh, my, no. I can and do make quick jaunts to France on business, but I can't be away from my responsibilities here for more'n a few days at a time."

"I understand, and maybe this wasn't such—" Gabrielle paused again. "Oh, what the heck, fate has impulsively gotten us this far. I'll leave the note. Actually, why don't I see if he's available to join us for lunch here?"

Julia grinned. A much preferable arrangement that made her pursuit of him less obvious.

At the desk, though, they were informed that Jean Paul was already having lunch in the garden. The clerk called one of the hotel employees to take them to him.

The clerk explained, "You'll need direction, since it's still a bit of a maze out there once you get beyond the small dining area. Some of our guests prefer their privacy, so we have a few tables set up behind the hedges. The young gentleman is using one of them."

With quite a few tables set under the shade of two large oak trees in the center of the garden, Julia and Gabrielle walked past a lovely area where guests could partake of breakfast, lunch, or tea, weather permitting, to a maze of tall hedges at the back of the garden.

Julia was desperately trying for some composure so it wouldn't be so obvious that she was giddy with excitement. She couldn't manage it. She was going to see him! Today. Within moments.

But she got unexpected help when she was nearly run over! The employee waved an arm indicating the final hedge, and Julia no sooner stepped around it when a tall man did the same. He was quick enough to put out his hands to keep her from colliding with him. He looked slightly oriental, due to the long black braid that hung over his shoulder. He blocked her view of the table behind him.

He looked her up and down. "Well, definitely not the lunch we ordered," he said, sounding English, then added to the employee, "You forgot this table is already in use?"

"We were told Jean Paul—" Julia began.

"Right place," the man cut in but then, noticing Gabrielle behind Julia, muttered, "Uh-oh."

Gabrielle was raising her brow at him over that "Uh-oh," but all Julia heard was Jean Paul's voice from behind the man. "My angel of mercy from the ball? What an unexpected *pleasure, chérie*. Do come join me. And, Ohr, be a good sport and go find out what happened to that food, eh?"

Ohr started laughing. "I would, but your 'angel' isn't alone."

Julia couldn't help grinning over the emphasis Jean

Paul had placed on the word *pleasure*. But as Ohr stepped aside so she could actually see Jean Paul, her grin faded at the sight of him.

"My God, what happened to you?" Julia gasped.

"James Malory happened to me."

"When? Surely not that night?"

"Indeed, he caught up with me as I was leaving the ball. Another few moments and I would have been gone." Then he winced when he saw Gabrielle step next to Julia.

"My God, didn't we give you enough warnings?" Gabrielle said in an appalled tone as she looked him over. "Maybe I should have taken a club to you myself and saved James the trouble?"

He gave his friend a half grin. "Your sympathy warms my heart, *chérie*."

"Oh, shut up," Gabrielle huffed, then stabbed a finger at Ohr. "You come with me, I want a full accounting." To Julia she said, "I'll be back in a moment."

Julia barely heard her. She was drawn forward almost in morbid curiosity as Jean Paul stood to pull out the chair next to him for her. He was dressed too casually for a hotel of this caliber, no jacket, no cravat or tie, and perhaps that's why he was tucked away at this private table. Or was it because of his bandages? When he bent slightly, she saw the upper edge of the bandages that were apparently wrapped around his chest, and the bruises above them. She saw him wince, too, and how stiffly he moved as he sat again. But his poor face! Whatever damage had been done there required a thick bandage that crossed the bridge of his nose and covered a good portion of the left side of his face.

"How badly are you hurt?" she asked as she took only a few steps closer to him. She resisted the chair he'd pulled out. She shouldn't sit next to him, at least not until his friends returned.

The right side of his mouth rose in a cheeky grin. "Truly, not as bad as it looks."

"But your chest is wrapped, isn't it?"

"Merely bruised. I thought it was much worse, but the doctor assured me I'd be in a lot more pain if my ribs were broken. Malory was rather accurate in not hitting me in the same place twice."

"Bruises that require bandaging?"

"Just as a precaution. The doctor couldn't be absolutely certain there isn't a small fracture hidden in there. Besides, while it might not look like it, I can breathe much easier this way."

She winced. What a trouncing that must have been! But considering who had administered it, Jean Paul was lucky to have walked away from it.

"I take it your nose is broken though?" she said, staring at the bandages on his face.

"A minor nuisance," he replied with a shrug. "Having been broken before, it breaks rather easily now. I'm usually much better at avoiding blows to my face."

He said that with a wide grin that showed off some white teeth. He certainly didn't *sound* seriously injured, but it definitely sounded as if he was no stranger to fisticuffs, which made her wonder again what sort of occupation he held, or leisure pursuits he indulged in. A young rakehell who frequented too many unsavory taverns? A pugilist like the younger Malory brothers, who took their exercise in a sporting ring? She wished Gabrielle had said more about him.

"All of those bandages can't be for your nose," she pointed out.

"Let me guess, you're a nurse?"

She chuckled. "No, certainly not."

His green eyes sparkled with laughter. "Well, if you were, you'd be leery of London doctors! They have such newfangled notions. This one first wanted to wrap my face up like a mummy's. I refused. Then he suggested fish glue to stick the bandages to my skin. No thank you!" She smiled with him over his anecdote. "But truly, *chérie,* the doctor was just overly concerned with scratches on my cheek, so he did more than was warranted. And my nose will mend as it did before."

"So no scars?"

"From scratches? But your concern is warming my heart. Perhaps if you visit me each day during my recovery, I will mend perfectly. You are my angel of mercy, after all."

She blushed. She knew it wasn't just compassion

making her ask so many questions about his injuries, but her nervousness over being there. And some very real disappointment. She had assumed she would find out what Jean Paul looked like today. She'd been quite excited about that. But thanks to James Malory's ire and an overzealous doctor, his face was just as distorted as when he'd been wearing the mask.

Despite all of the bandages, it wasn't hard to tell that he was as young as she'd guessed him to be, somewhere in his mid-twenties. Nothing concealed his forehead today, so she could see that it was wide and smooth, with thick black eyebrows. And at least one cheek was undamaged, broad and masculine. His mouth was still just as fascinating as she'd found it that night, supple, quick to grin and quirk that thin mustache to a jaunty angle. Quite a dark tan he had, too, so he must enjoy the outdoors as she did.

"You're not wondering how I found you when I didn't know Gabrielle was a friend of yours?" she asked.

"I do not question gifts, *chérie*. Come, sit here and let me bask in your beauty." He patted the seat next to him again. Had he moved it a little closer to him?

She knew she shouldn't, but she found herself sitting down demurely anyway. Some unexpected heat washed over her, being this close to him. She must be blushing again.

His lack of curiosity struck her as unusual. Or perhaps hers was overabundant, since she had to know everything about every little thing—and had yet to really learn anything about him. But she'd always been that way, in her studies, in life, while learning the intricacies of conducting business from her father.

And a good deal of that curiosity was aroused by this man. "Georgina doesn't know you're French."

"No, I didn't want her to misunderstand my intentions, so I spoke my best English with her."

She dropped her eyes to her lap before adding, "She doesn't even know your name."

He laughed. "I'd be devastated if I thought I'd told her and she so easily forgot, but I can't recall mentioning it to her. My thoughts get quite scattered in her presence—as scattered as they are right now."

Her blush got hotter, or maybe *she* was getting hotter. She feared she would let out a nervous giggle. She wasn't used to this sort of excitement. It was a bit overwhelming. Her simply being there alone with him was so naughty! This must be what a lovers' tryst felt like.

She shouldn't have taken her eyes off his face. The distortion the bandages caused was quelling her excitement and kept her mind focused on his condition, which raised her sympathy, not her attraction. So she lifted her eyes slowly, but didn't get any farther than his shoulder. He'd turned in his chair to face her more directly, and his hair had fallen over his shoulder. It was that long!

She waved a finger toward it with a laugh. "Is that a French fashion?"

"The reason I wear my hair this way is actually a long story which I'd rather not recount. Suffice it to say, it delights me to wear it this way."

"It's nearly as long as my own hair!" she exclaimed.

"Is it? Let your hair down and show me."

Now his tone was too husky by far. She felt a fluttering in her belly and her pulse was quickening. This was getting out of hand! It occurred to her that he might be thinking she'd come here to tryst with him. Why wouldn't he? She shouldn't be there!

"I should leave," she said abruptly, and started to stand.

"No, no, don't do that! My pain went away the moment you appeared."

What a whopper, though she smiled anyway over the blandishment. Then he put his hand on her arm to stay her, and all she could think about was his touching her.

She finally got out, "Your friend Gabrielle thought you could use some cheering, but she obviously didn't know about your injuries."

"She worries too much about me."

"With reason?"

He grinned. "Be my shield, *chérie*. She won't yell at me while you're here."

She chuckled. "I have a feeling she—"

She stopped with a gasp when he suddenly leaned

out of his chair and nearly across hers. But then she heard the buzzing sound of the bee close to her ear and instinctively moved away from it, which brought the side of her cheek up against his chest. He was batting at the insect to get it away from her. She heard his grunts. That was too much stretching for his bruised ribs. But she didn't hear the bee anymore either—he'd swatted it away. What a chivalrous thing to do, despite the discomfort it had caused him.

"Thank you."

She leaned back at the same time he did and saw immediately that the bandage on his face had fallen to the ground during his exertions.

"It was a nuisance and due to come off this afternoon anyway," he said, then grinned as he leaned closer so she could see for herself. "Just a few scratches, correct? I don't look too scary, do I?"

No, just too handsome, she thought before she met his eyes, realized she was far too close to him now—and felt his lips brush across hers. Her gasp was lost in the pressure that began immediately, her surprise so sudden, she didn't even think to close her lips this time. His tongue slipped inside her mouth, carefully exploring, amazing her with his taste, with her instant, passionate response. He was holding her there against him with just one arm, but she wasn't trying to get away. Oh, no. She was right where she wanted to be.

Carried away by that kiss, she put up a hand to

caress him. Thoughtlessly, so thoughtlessly, her fingers got too close to his nose. She felt him wince and shoot backward as if burned.

"I'm sorry!"

He was giving her a wry grin. "Not as much as I am, *chérie*."

She could see his whole face now. Despite the bruising on both sides of his nose and the abrasions on his cheek, she saw just how handsome he was, even more than she'd imagined that night at the ball. But his features seemed familiar to her. Had she met him before?

Maybe he'd ridden in Hyde Park—no, she would have noticed someone this handsome on her riding grounds, wouldn't she? But she must have met him somewhere for him to look so familiar. She just couldn't pinpoint where.

And then she did.

The anger didn't creep up on her slowly; it burst instantly from inside her where it had been hidden away, just waiting for the sight of *him* again to spark it to life. Even after all these years he could still provoke her. This couldn't be happening. He couldn't show up when she'd just petitioned to have him declared dead and out of her life for good!

"*Dieu*, what's wrong, *chérie*?"

Her relief was tremendous when she heard his French accent. He was French, not English. This wasn't her fiancé. But, good God, it had been frightening to think he was, however briefly. And of course, it wasn't. Jean Paul bore only a minimal resemblance to the fifteen-year-old Manford whelp she'd last seen eleven years ago, and it wouldn't be the first time someone had shared a trait or look with him that had brought that skinny, arrogant boy so clearly to mind again.

She was still shaken, though. She'd had no idea that such rage had been lying dormant inside her all these years.

She had to take a few deep breaths before she could trust her voice to sound normal. "Sorry, it was an old, horrid memory that snuck up on me." Then she grinned to make light of it. "Your cuts are mostly superficial, but there's an obvious dent in your nose. Will it go away once your nose mends?"

"My nose is fine. The bump is from an old break when I was young that wasn't treated."

"Broken when you were twelve?"

What was she doing? Did she still have doubts? *She'd* broken her fiancé's nose when he was twelve and she'd been so glad that she'd done so.

But he was frowning over her question, then his green eyes flared wide with the same memory she was having. "If you tell me you're Julia *Miller,* I'm going to wring your bloody neck," he said in a snarl.

She shot out of her chair so fast, she almost tripped.

"You son of a bitch! *You son of a bitch!* How dare you come back when I'm almost rid of you for good?!"

"How dare *you* not be married so I *can* come home? My God, I can't believe I've been trying to seduce *you!*"

The way he shuddered, or pretended to so as to insult her, made her see red. She almost flew at him. It was so close! But just enough of a sense of self-preservation remained that she quickly walked away before they picked up where they'd left off and tried to kill each other.

Chapter Thirteen

"WHAT HAPPENED DOWNSTAIRS?" Ohr asked Richard from the doorway when Ohr returned to the room. "Gabby and I got back to the table and found you and the young lady gone. Gabby was still in high dudgeon after chewing my ear off and thought you two might have gone off somewhere more private. I'm thankful she just huffed off without another word."

"Sorry about the ear-chewing."

Ohr shrugged. "Since I was pretty much tasked with keeping you out of trouble, I deserved it. I finished lunch, though, to give you a little time in case you did manage to get the lady to come up here."

"If you thought that was a possibility, you were dead wrong."

Ohr finally noticed that Richard was stuffing clothes in his travel bag. "Did Gabby send up a message that we're leaving early because of this?"

"No, but I am." Richard didn't look up to say it. The panic he was feeling was similar to what he'd felt nine years ago while waiting for his ship to sail away from England, afraid his father's henchmen would find him and drag him back to Willow Woods, his home outside Manchester, Lancashire—his personal hell.

His fear had been very real that night because he'd known the search for him had already begun. He had a little more leeway now. Unless his father was currently in London, which was unlikely since he rarely traveled so far from home, it would take a day or two for a message to reach him, depending on the messenger's mode of travel. Richard didn't trust Julia not to send that message. But as long as he vacated this hotel, he could still control the situation.

"Let me guess," Ohr said next. "The young miss wanted a ring on her finger instead of a nice tumble."

"Exactly."

"Er, I was joking. You haven't been here long enough for a woman to insist on marriage."

"Time is irrelevant if the woman has been engaged to you nearly since she was born."

"That would actually make time more than relevant," Ohr pointed out. "This sounds more like an arranged marriage from my culture, not yours."

"My people are half yours, or rather the Americans are, but it's still archaic no matter how you look at it, and I didn't escape from this horrid situation all those years ago to end up getting trapped by it again. Bloody hell, I really thought she'd be married by now to someone else whom she could torment for eternity."

"Why didn't you marry her if you were obligated to?" Ohr asked carefully.

"Obligated because my father signed a contract, thereby signing away my life? Not bloody likely."

"Still—"

"No, by God, don't try to make me feel guilty for not honoring the word of my tyrant father, who thinks he can live my life for me. Besides, there's no polite way of saying this, Ohr. The girl and I hate each other. If I had asked her to marry me, then I might feel obligated, but I didn't. I never wanted any part of her or her bloody fortune that my father covets."

"I begin—to understand."

Richard snapped his bag together before he glanced at Ohr and, with a nod, said, "Thought you might. Not every culture instills in children the importance of honoring their parents above all else. Which isn't to say I wouldn't honor mine out of love, if I had a parent left who was worth loving. I don't. But I'm not catching a ship out of here until I break all my old ties to this place for good, and I can't do that until I've seen my brother one last time."

"The brother you mentioned a few years back when you were so drunk you couldn't stand up?"

"I actually told you about him? Why didn't you ever mention it?"

Ohr shrugged. "Figured it was something you didn't want to talk about since you never did—unless you were drunk beyond remembering."

"You have an amazing lack of curiosity, my friend."

"It's called patience. If I'm meant to know, then eventually I will know."

Richard chuckled. "You miss out on knowing a lot of things with that attitude."

"Would you like some help in locating your brother?"

Richard's instinct was to say no. He didn't really want his friend to know how pathetic his life here had been. But he couldn't go anywhere near Willow Woods himself. Time hadn't changed his appearance as much as he'd thought it would. His body might have changed, but apparently his face hadn't altered drastically in nine years, or in eleven years in Julia's case. She had recognized him, or thought he looked familiar enough to pry with her question, which made him realize who she was.

Good God, he hadn't seen that coming. She bore absolutely no resemblance to the scrawny little savage who had tormented him when they were children. He couldn't even say what color eyes she'd had back then, they were always so narrowed on him with rage. Her hair had been much lighter, nearly white, when she was a child, not the ash blond it was now. She'd actually turned out pretty! Who would have thought? But he knew the vicious little termagant was still inside her.

Look how quickly her rage had sprung forth the moment she'd guessed who he was.

"I know where to find Charles, at least I assume he and his wife, Candice, are still living at Willow Woods with my father," Richard said. "I just can't go near the place myself, or I'll risk being dragged back into the fold."

"So you do feel you have obligations?"

"No, not a single one. But actually I could use your help."

Ohr nodded and started packing as well. He didn't ask what Richard feared would happen if his father found him. His restraint really was amazing.

Richard decided to volunteer a little bit about his life anyway. "It's a complicated story, Ohr. I might be my own man now, but my father won't take that into account. He uses—harsh means—to see his will done and employs brutes to enforce that will. He's Milton Allen, Earl of Manford."

"That makes you as aristocratic as the Malorys?"

"Yes, but I'm the second son. I won't be inheriting the title. My father, while not poor, is by no means rich either. Comfortable in the pocket barely describes his lot. So uncaring tyrant that he is, he decided to barter his sons to improve his circumstances."

"That's not an uncommon practice, to plump up the coffers through marriage."

"Agreed, but in this day and age, parents take their

children's preferences into account. My brother and I should have been allowed to choose our own wives, keeping our father's criteria in mind. But we weren't even consulted; we were simply told who we were going to marry, and before we even came of age.

"Charles, with the title coming to him, was logically used to marry up the social ladder, and you can't ascend much higher than marrying a duke's daughter. That's so lofty, it wouldn't be conceivable for an earl's son under normal circumstances. But Candice, the girl to whom Charles became engaged, was so unappealing in appearance and disposition that her father, the Duke of Chelter, couldn't get rid of her after three Seasons of trying. She's what you might call a screecher. She's also a habitual complainer. All of which made her suitors, and there were plenty of them who sought the connection to the duke by marrying his daughter, go running in the opposite direction long before they got to the altar. It was becoming something of a joke, the number of engagements broken off with her. So the duke jumped at my father's offer of his eldest son, despite that the girl was four years his senior. They were married two years before I left home, and his marriage became the nightmare Charles and I guessed it would be."

"You apparently left to avoid the marriage your father arranged for you. Why didn't he?"

"As the eldest son, he had much more to lose. And he's not the rebel that I turned into. He might have raged and bemoaned his fate, but in the end he always did whatever Father told him to do. He wants to become an earl someday. God, I used to get so furious at him, for always buckling under. And look where he is now because of it, married to a woman who makes his life a living hell. She drove him to drink, you know. I don't think I ever saw him sober after the day he married her."

"You thought the same thing would happen to you, didn't you?" Ohr guessed.

"Are you joking? I knew it would be exactly like that. Actually, I was afraid I'd end up killing my intended, if she didn't kill me first. We hated each other on sight."

"Why?"

Chapter Fourteen

RICHARD HAD TO think about Ohr's question for a moment. From the day they were born, he and his brother had never been allowed to make their own choices about anything. Their toys, their pets, their friends, their clothes, even the way they wore their hair, everything had been decided by the earl, not them. He wasn't just a hard taskmaster, he was a tyrant in his domain, and an overzealous disciplinarian. Richard couldn't remember ever loving his father. So it would be easy to say that Richard's arranged marriage had been the clincher, the worst instance of his father's controlling every single aspect of his life. That was why he'd resented Julia Miller before he even met her.

He tried to remember that first meeting, which wasn't easy. All the angry, rambunctious ones after that stood out in his mind.

He hadn't even known about her for the first four

years of their engagement. When his father finally told him a month prior to their meeting that he was going to be marrying down for money, he'd told his father he wouldn't do it. A rather bold statement for a ten-year-old, and he'd been severely punished for that insolence. The stick his father used to discipline him and his brother had actually broken on Richard that day, and the welts hadn't completely healed by the time he met his intended. Perhaps he'd transferred some of the hate he felt for his father to Julia without even realizing it.

But the true rebellion against his situation had begun when he was fifteen and he and his bratty fiancée had promised to kill each other. He'd told his father about that and had asked him to break the engagement contract. Milton had laughed and told him, "If you can't get along with the chit, ignore her after you get an heir or two. How simple is that, eh? It's bloody well what I did with your mother, may she rest in peace, the witch."

Richard had no memory of his mother. She'd died the year after he was born. But Charles had told him how bitterly their parents used to fight. Apparently, they'd had no choice in their marriage either.

So knowing there was no way out of that horrid match unless his father disowned him, Richard had actually started a campaign to accomplish that very thing by running up high gambling losses that could break the earl financially. But that campaign never bore fruit. It hadn't been the least bit easy to find men who would gamble with him at that young age, and when he'd succeeded in finding a few dissolute bucks he could lose to, none of them had been willing to go to his father for payment of those debts because his father was a peer of the realm. Instead, they'd politely hounded Richard and had been too bloody congenial about it, willing to wait for however long it took him to pay up. Two years later he knew he'd have to leave England. That was his only way out.

But his memory of that long-ago day at Willow Woods, when Julia's parents had brought her to meet him for the first time, was so vague all he could remember was the pain she'd caused him. Hard to forget that. And she'd been only five years old!

She'd approached him on the wide lawn behind the large manor house where he'd been throwing sticks for his dog to chase. She wouldn't raise her head to actually look at him so he could see her face. Pretending to be shy, no doubt. Her white pigtails tied with pink ribbons lay over her bony shoulders. Her little bonnet was a mass of white and yellow flowers. Her rose-and-white gown was made of the finest linen money could buy, he was sure. Such a darling little girl, anyone might think—until they got a peek at the little monster's eyes.

He knew their parents were watching them from the terrace. His father had called out to him, notifying him of the Millers' arrival, and was probably seething because Richard hadn't immediately run back to the house. But the girl had been sent down to join him instead. Surely he'd been on his best behavior despite his resentment at having to meet the fat purse he was being forced to marry.

Had he actually said something about it? He couldn't recall, but she'd amazed him when she'd unexpectedly burst into tears. He did recall wondering what the deuce had brought that on, so it must not have been anything he'd said. But the girl's tears hadn't lasted more than a minute before she suddenly flew at him with her fists flying, and one of those fists had struck his groin, probably unintentionally, but it had brought him to his knees. That put him more or less on her level, unfortunately, so she kicked him in exactly the same spot, that time quite intentionally he was sure, and thus began the war.

Her father had been appalled and had rushed down to tear her off him, but not before she'd bloodied Richard's lip as well while he'd been groaning on the ground. She'd screamed at Gerald Miller that she didn't want to marry a damned Allen. Her mother had been red-faced with embarrassment and speechless. Gerald had actually turned to Milton and said, "Perhaps this wasn't such a good idea after all."

Milton had scoffed at the concerned father and made light of it, assuring him, "Children will be children. Mark my words, they won't even remember this incident when they're older. And it's too late to reconsider.

The engagement has already been announced. Your daughter will reap the benefits even before the marriage. The moment the contract was signed, she gained entrée to the *ton*. So do try and teach her some manners before they meet again."

It was so typical of Richard's father to react that way. Gerald Miller wasn't pleased. It wasn't the last time Julia's father tried to persuade Milton to tear up that contract. At one point he'd even offered to pay the entire promised dowry to end it. But Milton had grown even greedier by then. The Miller name appeared often in the papers because of some new business deal, acquired property, or other success, and Milton crowed every time he read something about the Miller family's good fortune because it would soon be his. Richard had hoped for a while that Gerald Miller would break the contract anyway, but, apparently, the harm it might do to his business reputation as well as the social scandal his wife, Helene, feared had stayed his hand.

If Julia had ever learned any manners, she certainly never displayed them around Richard. He had a scar on his ear from when she'd tried to bite it off. His nose had been disfigured for life when she'd broken it and he'd been too ashamed to admit it, so no doctor had been summoned to fix it. Not once did they ever get along on those visits, which, thankfully, were infrequent. But always in the forefront of his mind was the knowledge that he was going to have to marry that little monster.

Just because his father wanted the enormous dowry and the access to the Miller fortune that would come with her. Why in the bloody hell didn't he try to marry her if he wanted her in the family that much?!

He'd actually asked his father that question one of the many times he'd tried to get out of that contract himself. "Don't be ridiculous, boy," Milton had chided him. "You see, her father loves her. He's not going to saddle her with a man even older than he is."

"But they're marrying up, so why should that matter?" Richard had demanded.

"Because Miller is a rare commoner. He isn't a social climber. He's so rich he doesn't care about titles or the opportunities that would open to him with an aristocrat in the family."

"Then why did he even agree to this mismatch?"

"The females in his family apparently feel differently about it. If I hadn't found out when I researched their family that one of the Miller women had bought herself a lord to marry a few centuries ago, and another did the same thing just two generations ago, I probably wouldn't have had a leg to stand on. But I used that information as the cornerstone of the deal. The Miller line will go forward as aristocrats now, once you produce some offspring, exactly what they tried but failed to do before. Miller's wife was certainly thrilled with the betrothal. Still, Gerald might not have committed his daughter to a marriage partner at so young an age if you didn't take after your mother and weren't such a fine-looking lad that his daughter couldn't help but be pleased with you."

"She's not pleased with me a'tall; she despises me as much as I do her!"

"Which makes not a jot of difference, boy. Her mother agreed with me that it would be a fine match, which clinched the deal."

That was the bottom line, a deal that was going to make the Allens as rich as the Millers, and Milton wasn't giving that up for any reason, least of all because the young couple couldn't stand each other.

But Milton had added that day, "So grow out of this ridiculous animosity you two have developed. She's still a child. She's not old enough yet to be attracted to you. When she is, you won't see the spitfire anymore."

In that prediction, his father had obviously been wrong, so it was just as well that Richard hadn't held out for that false eventuality. Julia had been attracted to him today, right up until she realized who he was and then turned into the she-devil that he remembered so well. But even if his father had been right, and as an adult now he had to allow he might be able to woo her out of her animosity, it was pointless to try because he still wouldn't have her. He wasn't about to give that bastard who'd sired him and put him through hell what he wanted most—the means to bring the Millers and all their wealth into the Allen family fold.

Having told Ohr most of that, Richard ended with, "No one was happy with that engagement except my father, and he wasn't the one getting married. But I didn't just leave England because of her. It wasn't even mostly because of her. I left because I wanted to live my own life, not have my father live it for me. And I hated him too much to make him happy with that marriage."

"I'll get us a coach," was all Ohr said to that.

Richard almost laughed. That was so typical of Ohr. He was a firm believer in fate. He never interfered with it. He might make suggestions, he might point out things he thought were being overlooked, and he'd offer help. But he wouldn't try to change someone's mind once it had been made up. That would be tampering with fate.

"I think horses will get us there more quickly," Richard said.

"Me on a horse?" Ohr asked. "You're joking, right?"

Richard grinned. "I guess I am."

Chapter Fifteen

JULIA HAD GONE directly home and locked herself in her room. She'd thought about finding Carol. She really needed someone to talk to. But she was in such a state that she feared she might unintentionally lash out at anyone. She didn't really want her friend or anyone else, including the servants, to see her like this.

She was beyond upset. Agitated, enraged, and feeling some potent fear, she couldn't even sit down she was trembling with so much emotion. Her worst nightmare was back, now when she was so close to unlocking that chain his horrid father had wrapped around her neck when she was just a baby.

But she hadn't dreamed it. She'd seen him with her own eyes, heard his nasty remarks, felt the rage overcome her the way it always did in his presence. Eleven years had passed since she'd last seen him, and except for his appearance, he hadn't changed, not even a little. The proof was in the first thing he'd said to her when he'd recognized her. Wring her neck? And he hadn't been joking! Once, when she was a child, he'd held her over a balcony railing two stories up just to terrify her.

But she had changed. She no longer took offense so easily. She no longer let anger rule her actions. She no longer let anyone upset her so much that she wanted to hurt them the way she'd always wanted to hurt him. She'd outgrown that kind of impulsive behavior. Look at her today. She hadn't tried to scratch Richard's eyes out. She'd run away from him instead. The sensible thing to do!

But her anger wouldn't go away. Was he back to fulfill that horrid contract? Or had he never even left England? That remark he'd made about falling in love with Georgina Malory last year implied he'd been here then, and London was certainly a big enough town to disappear in. Had he been in town all these years, laughing at her for being stuck with their engagement without his having to actually marry her?

That would be so like him, despicable rogue that he was! But she could live with that. As long as his father didn't find out about his presence and drag them both to the altar. She certainly wouldn't tell the earl that his son was back in England. She would proceed with having Richard declared dead. Gabrielle Anderson knew he was alive, but Julia wasn't sure if Gabrielle knew who he really was or simply knew him as Jean Paul, as she'd called him. But Gabrielle was only visiting and would soon be gone anyway. And the Malorys, who might know him by sight, didn't know him by either name! So she could proceed with her petition. She'd just have to make sure that horrible contract was destroyed in the process.

Could it still work? As long as no one else knew of his existence, why not? And with the contract gone, Richard wouldn't have to hide anymore. Actually, she ought to make a deal with him to make sure it happened exactly like that—no, good Lord, what was she thinking? Knowing him, he'd reveal his presence in England just long enough to thwart her plan, then disappear again. She'd have to wait another ten years before she could try again!

But whether he'd been in England all along or was just visiting as he'd mentioned, he obviously had no intention of marrying her. He hadn't gone home. The earl would immediately have sent her notice if he had. Instead Richard had gone to a London ball to moon over his love! And even though he was in love with someone else, he'd admitted that he'd tried to seduce her! It was so like an aristocratic rake to be ruled by rampant carnal instincts. Why should she be the least bit surprised that that was what Richard had turned into?

How could she have been attracted to him? She was disgusted with herself for thinking him charming even for a moment! What a pathetic, desperate old maid that made her! His charm was probably just as fake as he was, with his pretense of being a Frenchman. How could she have even found him handsome today when his appeal was so superficial? Nothing about him on the inside was handsome. He was mean, spiteful. He was the worst sort of snob, the kind who couldn't keep his mouth shut about his supposed superiority. He'd always looked down on her, thought she wasn't good enough for him, and let her know it. Good grief, the memories were flying at her. She'd thought she'd put all that behind her, never thought about those days.

But then Richard Allen hadn't been around to remind her.

Chapter Sixteen

Y**OU MUST BE** so excited," Helene Miller said to her daughter. "He's such a fine, handsome lad. And a lord! You'll be a lady just like your aunt Addie was!"

Julia's mother was certainly excited about it. She so rarely made up her mind about anything, but, apparently, this engagement was the one exception because she'd been in favor of it from the beginning. Julia was excited about it, too, mostly because her mother's excitement was contagious. As long as all she and her mother did was talk about it, Julia was content. The earl's son did sound like a wonderful boy. But marriage was so far off. Honestly, she'd rather have a new doll than a husband.

She'd never not known about this splendid boy she was promised to. His father actually sent progress reports to her father, and Gerald related them to her. Lord Richard was doing well in school. Lord Richard got a new dog. She wanted one, too. Lord Richard caught a huge fish in his lake. Why had no one ever taken her fishing? Her parents wanted her to feel as if she knew Lord Richard before she met him. It seemed to work.

But meeting him was so far off that she never really thought about it. Then the day arrived soon after her fifth birthday, and her reaction wasn't the least bit expected. On that long ride to Willow Woods, the Earl of Manford's estate near Manchester, she got so nervous that she broke out in a rash that splotched her cheeks bright red. Her mother cried when she noticed. Gerald had chuckled at them both for being silly. Julia couldn't even say why she was so nervous. Because she wanted Richard to like her and was afraid he wouldn't? Because he'd never truly seemed real to her until then?

Julia almost had to be dragged into that big mansion in the country. Then she was awed by the size of Willow Woods as they were led through some of the rooms on the way to the earl and she caught glimpses of other rooms. Her home was big, but not like this. Here every single room was large, and the entire house was spread out wide as well as tall. Everything blended in so well, antique paintings that had to be centuries old, huge crystal chandeliers, muted wall coverings that you barely noticed. Nothing was gaudy and glittering like the fancy French decor her mother preferred.

She'd met the earl before, but she had only the vaguest memory of his visiting once just prior to her fourth birthday to see how she was turning out, since he hadn't seen her since she was a baby. He hadn't brought his son with him on that visit. The boy wasn't there at Willow Woods when they arrived, either. He was outside with his dog. She was so relieved! She almost cried.

"Go introduce yourself, Julie," Helene urged her. "You two will get along famously. I know it!"

Her father moved to accompany her, but Helene put a hand on his arm. "They'll be more relaxed if they don't feel constrained by our presence," Helene said, as if Julia couldn't hear her. Her mother often talked about her in her presence as if she didn't have ears. "Let this first meeting be natural for them."

Julia walked down the lawn with leaden feet. What was she supposed to say to the boy? She could talk about his dog and mention that she had three. One hadn't been enough for her. She could tell him about the pony she'd just got and that her riding lessons were to begin that summer. Or she could ask him to teach her how to fish! Her father had said that he would teach her soon, though her mother had complained that it wasn't something appropriate for her to learn. But a lake was right there on the property beyond the boy, a big one, and she knew he knew all about fishing.

He hadn't noticed her yet, but as she got closer to him, she realized how big he was, twice her height! She hadn't expected that. She didn't know any other ten-year-olds. With his short black hair and finely cut jacket, he looked like a miniature adult, while she was still dressed in a little girl's shapeless frock. He was as handsome as they'd told her, perfect in every way, though perhaps a little thin. But that didn't count. She was thin, too.

Her steps slowed as she became dazzled by this first sight of her fiancé. When he finally noticed her, she instantly looked down at the ground. She could have walked off into the lake for all the attention she was paying to where she was going. She felt so nervous again she could almost feel more rashes breaking out on her cheeks. But she continued walking, her head down, until she reached him and could see his legs from beneath the rim of her bonnet.

"So you're the fat purse I'm supposed to marry?" he said to her.

She glanced up at him, not understanding what he meant by that. She wasn't fat.

"What a pity," he added in a nasty tone as he stared down at her cheeks. "At least you could have been pretty. That might have made this match a little more tolerable."

She didn't quite understand condescension or snobbery yet, but she did understand that he didn't like her. She'd been so apprehensive about meeting him, terrified, really, and now her feelings were so hurt she burst into tears. Then mortified that she was crying, she was overcome by anger, the likes of which she'd never before experienced, and she flew at him, pummeling him with her fists.

Her parents had had to drag her off him. They were upset, too. She recalled her father's saying that he might not have done such a wonderful thing for her after all, in arranging a marriage to an earl's son. But Richard's father just laughed about the incident, assuring her parents that children were just being children. Julia had been unable to calm down until she was in the coach on the way home.

Helene simply didn't know how to deal with her daughter's temper tantrums, and there were plenty of them after that day—whenever she or Gerald suggested another visit to Willow Woods. Helene was frantic that Julia was going to ruin the family socially by insulting nobles. Gerald had snapped at his wife to stop it, that the match was a mistake and he would never have agreed to it if she didn't think so damned highly of those very same nobles. Helene had always been somewhat indecisive, but she became incapable of making any decisions after that.

Julia did have to meet Richard Allen again, but a whole year passed before that happened. It took that long for her not to burst into tears and start screaming when the suggestion of another visit was made. She still wasn't old enough to understand how their first meeting had gone awry, but she did guess that it had to do with their both being so apprehensive about it. She also understood snobbery by then and realized that's exactly what he was, a snob, though she hoped she might be able to forgive him for it so they could start anew. She must have imagined a thousand such meetings where he apologized and was as wonderful as he ought to be.

None of which happened when the first words out of his mouth were "You hit me again and I'll hit you back."

But he didn't say that to her until after they'd been in the same room with their parents and his brother, Charles, for nearly an hour. The adults were afraid to leave them alone again. Almost by silent agreement, Julia and Richard had been on their best behavior. It had been easy as long as they didn't speak to each other. Julia took it a step further by pretending Richard wasn't there and talking to Charles instead.

With no violence erupting this time, their parents began to relax. The men even went off to play a game of billiards. Left alone with the two boys and her uncontrollable daughter, Helene was soon having a nervous reaction and had to excuse herself.

The moment she left the room, Charles, who was three years older than Richard, sighed in boredom and said he had better things to do. Suddenly the engaged children were alone, staring at each other warily, and Richard gave her that warning about hitting her.

"You'd hit a girl?" she asked.

"You're not a girl, you're a little monster. I got a beating because *you* attacked me. Father didn't believe that I didn't provoke it."

"You did start it, and I'm glad he beat you," she replied, her lip already beginning to tremble.

"You little witch, do you even know what it's like to be beaten?" he snarled. "You don't, do you? Well, it bloody well hurts!"

With him shouting at her, she couldn't stop the tears from rolling down her cheeks. Oh, God, she was behaving like a crybaby in his presence again! They were never going to like each other, yet they were stuck with each other!

She latched onto the finger he was angrily shaking in her face and bit it as hard as she could. He was furious, but he didn't bite her back or hit her. Instead he dragged her by her pigtails out of the house straight down to the lake behind Willow Woods! Then he tossed her off the little fishing-boat dock into the water. She couldn't swim, so she flailed around, panicking as she tried to scream. He'd been even more furious that he'd had to wade through the cold water to drag her back out. With both of them soaking wet there was no way to hide what had happened from their parents. Her parents took her straight home. She hoped Richard got another beating.

Time passed. The friendship she developed with her neighbor Carol progressed until they became best friends. She never thought about Richard when she was with Carol, and they became inseparable. She did know that her father had tried again to get her out of that horrible engagement. She'd heard her parents talking about it and how bitter Gerald was that the earl wasn't going to release them. Her mother was still in favor of the match, though, and would always remind her father that the children were bound to grow out of their animosity. She begged him to give it time and not to do anything rash, and he finally agreed that it wasn't necessary to pick a big fight with the earl over a matter that might work out later.

By the time Julia was seven, she'd grown a bit but was still quite thin. She was also so sure that she was mature enough now to deal with her offensive fiancé without letting her emotions get out of hand that she even suggested another visit. Her mother was delighted. She was still expecting great things to come of the match.

They were going to spend the entire weekend at Willow Woods this trip. The children weren't going to be left alone for even a moment.

The visit started off pleasantly enough. Charles played a game of checkers with her. She liked him. He was as handsome as his brother, just much older, though not quite an adult yet. She was sure he let her win, but it put her in a good mood anyway. Then Richard took his place, sitting across the table from her. They'd never been so close to each other without violence erupting.

"My friends call me Julie," she shyly told her fiancé as their first game of checkers progressed. "Not so many syl'bles as Julia."

"No, that's still too much work for the tongue," he replied without glancing up. "I like Jewels better.

Rich and Jewels, we make a wealthy couple! Get it?"

Unfortunately she did. "I don't like it."

"Wasn't asking your permission. And it's too bloody on the mark, Rich and Jewels. That's all we're good for, isn't it? To fill my father's coffers with wealth."

"I said I don't like it," she hissed at him.

"Too bad, Jewels."

He would call her that from then on, and every single time it made her see red, just as it did that day. She abruptly left the table and went out on the terrace to count to one hundred. Her nanny had taught her that trick and it was working! Exactly what a mature young lady would do! She hadn't kicked him under the table. She hadn't flipped the table over into his lap. She hadn't even thrown the checkers at him, which would have hurt because they were made of painted heavy metal. She'd left the room instead. When she returned, she didn't expect him to still be sitting at the little game table waiting for her.

Stiffly, she rejoined him. He promptly won that game. She demanded another. She thought he'd refuse but he didn't. She wished he had. He beat her every single game and smirked about it. She refused to give up trying and kept insisting on another round, and another, right up until dinner.

They'd managed to get through the day without fighting. She'd restrained herself and had ignored his insults. She was mature enough to deal with him now and was so proud of herself!

She went straight to bed after dinner and, glowing with success, even went straight to sleep. Which was unfortunate because she arose too early the next morning, before the adults did. Richard walked into the breakfast room while she was sitting there alone.

He started to do an about-face when he saw her. She should have kept her mouth shut and let him leave. But she actually thought she could survive another day controlling her temper, even though he went out of his way to provoke it.

"Shall we play checkers again today?" she asked. "I still haven't won yet."

"Nor will you, when you have no clue how to play. You're still a baby, aren't you, Jewels? Can't even master a simple game like checkers yet."

He wasn't going to even try to get along with her, she realized. Yesterday, under the watchful eyes of their parents, didn't count.

"I hate you!" she yelled at him.

He laughed bitterly. "You're too young to even know what that means, you silly chit. But I know it well."

She threw her plate at his head. It didn't hit him, of course. The plate, which was too big and heavy to even get close to him with her meager strength propelling it, clattered on the floor. But his eyes narrowed on her.

Her intent had been clear. He actually started coming around the table to get his hands on her. She screeched and ran around the other side of the table and out the door. She didn't stop running until she was back upstairs, safe in her room.

But he followed her! He burst inside before she could even think of locking the door, and within seconds he dragged her out to the little balcony off her room and shoved her over it. She thought he was throwing her to her death! She was too terrified to scream. But he'd latched onto her ankles and dangled her upside down over the railing.

She'd never known rage before she'd met Richard Allen. But she'd never experienced this before either. Pure fear. She was paralyzed with it as he held her over that railing. He didn't have the strength to do this! She was sure she was going to die!

When he finally dragged her back up, he laughed before her feet were back on the balcony floor. "You're as skinny as I thought!"

Her loose frock had settled back over her body, but it had turned inside out when he'd dangled her over the railing, covering her face and exposing her bare legs and underclothes. But the very second her feet were solidly back on the floor, all the terror he'd just subjected her to turned instantly into the worst fury she'd experienced yet. She didn't even know how she broke his nose. Her fist? Her palm catching him just right? But suddenly he was backing away from her into her room, a hand holding his nose. He ran out of there, but not before she saw the blood escaping below his hand.

She stood on the balcony panting, and crying great sobs now that she was safely alone. She could see Richard running across the lawn, then disappearing into the woods at the other side of the house.

She didn't mean to break his nose, it had just happened, but she was fiercely glad of it, after what he'd done to her. At least it got rid of him. He'd run off with his bleeding nose into the woods like a wounded cub, or maybe just to pout. But she didn't even wait to see if he'd come back. As soon as her parents arose, she convinced them to take her home. She didn't tell them what had happened. She didn't think Richard would ever mention it either.

She flatly refused to ever go to Willow Woods again, and she was sticking to it this time. Six months later Richard came to London to visit her instead. It was too soon. The horror of that last visit hadn't faded yet. There would be no more talking to him or trying to become friends again. She utterly despised him now.

He kept coming to London though. His father forced him to. He even brought his dog with him and used the animal as an excuse to spend most of his time in the park instead of visiting her. Which was a good thing, because with each of his visits, the animosity between them grew worse.

She would attack him anytime they found themselves alone, immediately, viciously. She had a fear of heights now, thanks to him. But he always held the advantage because of his superior strength, so attacking him normally rarely got her anywhere; he'd just laugh at her and hold her off, which only infuriated her more. So whenever she did get close enough, she'd been rather quick and vicious. Yes, vicious, and she wasn't even ashamed about it. He deserved it!

She bit his leg until she tasted blood and was glad of that, too. He locked her in her own attic for an entire day for that! No one had heard her screaming to be let out. He'd waited until the maids who might have heard her were done cleaning upstairs. When he finally let her out, he had the gall to tell her he'd gone to the park, got distracted by his dog, and simply forgot about her.

She couldn't even recall what he'd done to provoke her on what turned out to be his last visit, but instead of holding her off at arm's length, he'd been angry enough to toss her over his shoulder and march off with her. She didn't know where he was taking her, but still remembering being locked in the attic all day, she reared up and bit his ear. Because of his strength, biting seemed the only way she could hurt him, and she wanted to hurt him! He dropped her to the ground.

"You make me bleed again and I swear I'm going to kill you!" he shouted at her.

Her ankle twisted in the fall. She didn't even feel the

pain, she was so furious. "Not if I kill you first! I will if I ever see you again. See if I don't!"

She'd been ten that day, he'd been fifteen. Two years later her mother told her that he'd left England. How she'd rejoiced! Until she found out that the earl still wouldn't tear up the marriage contract. He was confident that Richard would come home. She was only twelve then, still a long way off from a marriageable age. But even when she turned eighteen, the earl wouldn't give up the contract. Probably because he was still angry about failing to get guardianship of her after her father's accident. Thankfully, her solicitors had thwarted the earl's attempt since he couldn't produce the groom.

Julia's memories of Richard were horrible. She'd kept them locked away in the back of her mind for so long it was no wonder she hadn't recognized him immediately. But those memories were all fresh now, and she realized that every single time they'd met, they'd ended up fighting.

Their parents should never have introduced them when they were so young. If their parents had waited another few years, Richard might have been more mature and not so nasty and snobbish. Another few years and she might have been able to restrain herself, instead of reacting so angrily to his rudeness. It was the worst sort of luck that the animosity between them ran so deep that it was still there after all these years! If they'd met under different circumstances, they might have made the perfect couple, like Carol and Harry, instead of the worst mismatch imaginable.

Chapter Seventeen

REASON RETURNED! AND in good time, too, Julia thought, since a few hours of daylight were still left. Not that nightfall would have stopped her now that she had a course of action in mind.

She'd simply needed to remind herself that she was a woman of business. She knew how to make deals. She'd been buying new businesses and directing her solicitors in negotiating contracts for five years now. Of course those contracts merely involved people's livelihoods, not the intimate aspects of their lives, but a contract was a contract, and she was going to make a new one with Richard Allen.

After she'd calmed down, she'd realized that dealing directly with Richard instead of leaving their circumstances to chance was a brilliant idea. He would agree— she knew he would. The plan she had in mind would sever all ties between them, and that's what they both wanted. She just had to suffer his presence briefly once more, long enough to propose that he stay hidden a few more weeks until he was officially declared dead, then he could reveal himself or not, but he'd never have to worry about hiding again to avoid marrying her.

So she returned to Coulson's Hotel and once again found herself approaching the desk. She did so decisively this time, now that the end of his dominating her existence was within sight once again. But when she requested that he be asked to join her in the lobby, the clerk told her, "They've left, ma'am. Both gentlemen are no longer guests here."

Julia didn't panic, she was actually relieved, surmising that Richard was wasting no time in leaving England, probably because of his run-in with her. She much preferred his disappearing over her having to deal with him. But just to be sure he'd left the country, she had her driver take her to Boyd Anderson's house, where she hoped to find Gabrielle. No luck there. The butler informed her most of the Andersons were at Georgina's house again. So on the way home she stopped there, too. Well acquainted with the crusty, old sea dog Artie, who opened the door, one of James Malory's two unusual butlers, she asked him if he would just fetch Gabrielle for a brief word, rather than ushering her inside.

Which he did, and then the panic set in again. No, Gabrielle said, Jean Paul wouldn't leave the country without telling her. No, she hadn't seen him since yesterday when they both went to his hotel, nor did she even get a chance to talk to him there, so she had no idea why he and Ohr would change hotels when the one they were at had already been paid for. Julia thanked Gabrielle and hurried off, probably leaving the young woman quite confused. But Julia was sure by then that Richard hadn't merely changed hotels to be out of her reach again. She got the maggoty thought that he was on his way home to visit his brother before he left England again and was terrified that his father would find out.

But she might still be able to stop him before he reached Willow Woods and ruined both of their lives even worse than they'd already been ruined. If she could find him.

She almost left town immediately, but she still had enough presence of mind to know she couldn't race down country roads in the dead of night. With his injuries, surely Richard wouldn't be traveling as fast as she could. So she sent her cousin Raymond a message that she needed him as an escort for a quick trip to the country.

They left at dawn the next morning, traveling the swiftest way possible, on horseback, which was why she didn't take a footman along instead. Raymond, at least, was as adept on horseback as she was. The day-and-a-half trip was reduced to half that time with her stopping five times to quickly rent rested mounts so they could continue on at her grueling pace. She'd never galloped such long distances before. Raymond complained all the way. Her backside did, too, and was quite numb by the time she neared her destination.

Her panic hadn't lessened much. She'd hoped to find Richard on the road, though that had been unrealistic as she'd galloped by so many vehicles. But they'd passed through numerous towns and villages, too, and he could have been in an inn in any one of them. She couldn't afford to waste time searching on the way. But with their swift pace, she was at least reasonably certain that she was ahead of him now and only had to stop by Willow Woods briefly when they arrived late that afternoon to be sure. Hopefully, she wouldn't even have to speak to the Earl of Manford. She could then simply wait down the lane to his house and stop Richard before he went any farther, even if it took the rest of the day.

She was going to have to get rooms for herself and Raymond though. She was sure it would be dark before she was done dealing with Richard, and she refused to stay at Willow Woods even for one night. A hamlet was closer to Willow Woods than the town of Manchester, just down the road, really. She even knew it had a hostelry.

Her family had passed through there on each of their visits to that area of the country, and her mother had once mentioned stopping there just to freshen up before they arrived at Willow Woods, which her father had laughed about. But that wasn't a bad idea in her present situation, since she was covered in dust from that mad dash across country. It was almost comical, the dust cloud she created as she tried to get rid of some of it before she entered the hostelry. Raymond had told her not to hurry and went directly into the tavern next door.

She didn't get more than a step inside the door before she froze, her eyes latched onto the tall oriental man coming down the stairs into the main room. Richard's companion. What had Gabrielle called him? An oar, or ore, or whatever, something odd like that. His presence meant she was either too late or just in time. She was almost afraid to find out which.

He had stopped, too, upon seeing her and stood there like an unmovable barricade to those stairs. She had to wonder what Richard had told him about her. He certainly didn't seem very approachable at the moment with his arms crossed over his chest.

She marched over to him anyway and stated the obvious. "This is too close to Willow Woods for Richard not to have gone straight home."

"He's not going there."

"Then he's here?"

He wasn't going to tell her. He just stared at her without expression. How annoying. She didn't miss that he hadn't asked who Richard was, so he knew Richard's real name. Did Gabrielle know it, too, but just hadn't mentioned it to Julia when she'd referred to him as Jean Paul? How embarrassing if they both knew why Richard had gone into hiding.

Impatiently she told the man, "Never mind, I'll just knock on every door. There can't be more than a few."

"First one at the top of the stairs, but if you have a weapon on you, you're not getting past me without handing it over."

She flushed bright red. So the man did know about her. She was sure Richard had put all the blame on her. She did have a weapon, but she certainly hadn't intended to use it on Richard to get her point across.

She might dress like the veriest lady and was often mistaken for one because of it, but she only traveled with chaperones if she was going to an upper-crust party, since the *ton* expected it, or on long trips like this one. Otherwise she often moved about London by herself or with her secretary when she was merely attending to business. But in either case, she'd got into the habit of keeping a pistol close to hand in case it might be needed. She kept it in the small valise she was toting, which also contained a change of clothes.

Too impatient to rummage through the valise for the weapon, she shoved the bag at him, then slipped past him to go upstairs. She was relieved that he didn't follow her. Only two rooms were up here, both on the same side of the short corridor. On the other side, three windows were open, letting in a warm breeze.

She knocked briskly on that first door. It opened within seconds, but she only caught the briefest glimpse of surprise on the face of the man standing there before the door was slammed shut again with Richard's snarl "No way in hell."

Julia gritted her teeth and pounded on the door more loudly. All fear gone that she wouldn't find him in time, she was her usual indomitable self. The racket she made resulted in the door's opening again and her being yanked inside the room.

"We are not causing a scene here," he said angrily. "If you draw notice to me, I'll—"

"Shut up, Richard." She turned to face him. "I'm just here to stop you from making a mistake we'll both regret."

His cheek was still scratched, and bruising was still on both sides of his nose, but he was behaving as if nothing was wrong with his ribs.

"Mistake? You thought I was going home?" He laughed harshly. "Not a chance. But I bet that's where you're going. Get out."

He was still holding the door open. She shook her head at him. "I'm not leaving until we discuss our options and come to an understanding. That's the adult thing to do. We can even put it in writing."

"Another contract?" he said incredulously. "Are you out of your mind?"

"One we can both agree on."

"You and I will never agree on anything, Jewels, so do us both a favor and get out!"

"No."

"You see? We can't even agree on something so simple as your not being welcome here!"

"Relax, my teeth are sheathed."

She was trying to put him at ease, but apparently her comment only reminded him of their violent encounters in the past. His face turned livid with anger and he reached for her. She squeaked out a protest, but didn't get out of the way in time. But after he grabbed her, he only threw her out of the room. Before she could even turn around and express her indignation over the way he'd just treated her, the door was slammed shut again.

Chapter Eighteen

JULIA'S INSTINCT WAS to pound on Richard's door again, but she'd heard the key turn in the lock. He wouldn't open it again. And he was right, she didn't want to draw attention to him by making a racket up here. He was too close to home. He'd probably even snuck in here the back way after his friend got them the room.

Besides, she needed to calm down. His attitude infuriated her just as it always did. They'd never been able to have a civil conversation, except recently when they hadn't recognized each other. But it was too late to go back to that point. Or was it?

She ought to make an effort to show him that she wasn't the child who had so little restraint she tried to bite off ears! She was a grown woman in control of her emotions and, hopefully, her destiny.

So she marched back downstairs and snatched her valise back from Richard's friend without a word. He was still there with the bag at his feet as if he'd guessed she wouldn't be long in returning. She checked to see if the other room upstairs was available. It was. A few minutes later she was behind a closed door of her own, staring with narrowed eyes at the wall that separated her from Richard.

If he had been reasonable, they could have come to a quick agreement and she would be on her way back home. She might still be able to start the journey back to London today if she could be on her way within the hour. She just needed to quickly tidy up, then try again to speak to Richard.

As she took off her jaunty riding hat, she saw it was so caked with dust that even the pink feathers drooped with it, then she realized her face must look just as clownish. Thankfully there wasn't a mirror in the room to confirm it, but she had no doubt and was surprised Richard hadn't made some nasty remark about it. But then his own appearance hadn't been without its shortcomings and certainly hadn't been appropriate for the son of an earl.

He'd been wearing a billowing white shirt that wasn't tucked in, but was girded low on his hips with a wide, gaudy belt. Loose black pants had been cut off at the knee. Which had looked a bit outlandish with knee-high boots that gleamed. His excessively long hair was queued and quite visible. All of which made her wonder if he was wearing a disguise.

But she didn't give it another thought once a pitcher of fresh water arrived with several towels. The maid, or the owner's wife, directed her to a tub in a closet next to the pantry downstairs, if she wanted a bath. She politely declined and made good use of the water, then donned her extra riding habit, though she left the matching lavender jacket off. She wouldn't need it until she was ready to depart the hostelry.

She knocked softly on Richard's door this time. It fooled him into opening it and she rushed inside past him before he could stop her. Successful, she had to tamp down the urge to smirk as she turned around to see him closing the door with an angry look.

"Hear me out before you turn brutish again," she said quickly. "If you're not here to go home, what are you doing here so close to Willow Woods?"

"I'm here to see my brother."

"Just that?" At his nod, she said with some disparagement, "Then you're a fool to take this risk, showing your face so close to home. You should have sent someone to bring Charles to you in London instead."

He seemed to grow angrier at her calling him a fool, probably because he knew she was right. It was obvious with his lips tightening, his green eyes glaring at her. She ought to keep her own eyes off his damned face. It was disturbing her train of thought and making her say things she shouldn't. She'd always known he'd turn out handsome. That had been apparent when he was a boy. She just hadn't expected him to be this handsome, even with a messed-up face. That it was having even a small effect on her, as much as she hated him, was insane!

No doubt those kisses she'd shared with him had made a greater impression on her than she'd realized. Now, seeing him again, she was reminded of how exciting they'd been. But she'd kissed Jean Paul, someone else entirely, or so she'd thought, not her detestable fiancé. She had to keep that in mind.

She focused on his clothes instead. All clean, but hardly the garb of a gentleman, which had her point out, "You call that a disguise?"

"I call this comfortable, and it's no bloody business of yours what I wear. I'm only going to say this once this time, Jewels. Get out."

He said it so calmly it was easy to ignore. She warned him, "That contract still binds us, you know. Your father still has it. He was even offered the entire dowry to hand it over, but he wouldn't."

"I know that. He's not just a tyrant, he's a greedy tyrant. He wants it all."

"So we can agree on something?" He just narrowed his eyes on her so she quickly added, "Your absence hasn't changed that. Nine years have passed and he still won't relinquish the power that contract gives him to marry us if you show up."

"That isn't going to happen. I'm not bound by a piece of paper I didn't sign, nor am I a boy any longer under a tyrant's control. That contract is meaningless to me."

Brave words, but she could see in his eyes that he didn't quite believe that, he just didn't know for certain. She did.

"It's not an ordinary contract that might have been negated when we came of age, it was a contract made by families, yours and mine, an agreement to join through marriage. The courts see it as binding as if you and I signed it. A priest will see it as binding and won't even need to hear an aye from you to pronounce us man and wife. Don't pretend you didn't know that and disappeared before it could happen."

"Don't give yourself so much credit, Jewels. You're not the only reason I left."

Denigrating her already? Actually, when did he ever not? She had to grit her teeth to go on, "But I'm in the process of getting it from him, as long as no one in this country knows you're still alive."

He laughed. "You're having me declared dead?"

She actually blushed a little. "Yes, but it will make no difference to you. As soon as I have that contract destroyed, you can return from the dead, as it were. You can even go home and see your brother as often as you like."

"No, I can't," Richard replied bitterly. "It won't erase

what I did to get Father to disown me before I left."

She frowned. "What did you do?"

"It doesn't matter, but that vindictive bastard will make me pay for it, if he ever gets his hands on me. He probably even has legal recourse to have me imprisoned."

"He wouldn't do that to his own son."

"Are you kidding me? He would, and faster than you can blink. You really don't know him, do you?"

"No, thank God, I've had very little exposure to him and am only well acquainted with his unreasonable stubbornness."

"Well, rest assured I will avoid, at all costs, clapping eyes on him again."

"Then you will leave the country again, for good?"

"Of—course."

That pause was brief, but noticeable. She didn't doubt for a moment that he was thinking of Georgina Malory. His love was here. He probably would return, just to see her. Not that Julia could trust his word anyway. She wished she could, she really did. But he was Richard Allen and he'd never done anything she'd hoped he'd do. He couldn't even stay gone long enough to be dead! On paper, that is.

"At least put that in writing, dammit, so I can have some peace of mind." That was as close as she'd come to begging him.

But he merely replied, "You think I care about your

peace of mind? Pay attention. If I won't honor my father's contract, why would I honor one with you? I like you even less than I like him, and I bloody well despise him."

That could have hurt, but it didn't, since it mirrored her own sentiments for him. But she was quite annoyed that he was giving her no choice but to accept his word on this matter that was so important to her. So she stalled for a moment to try to think of some other way to get more assurance from him.

Letting her gaze roam over his tall frame, she mentioned what was so obvious: "You healed rather fast."

"I'd merely been pampering myself at the doctor's suggestion. It certainly wasn't necessary." He slapped his chest without a wince.

"I see. And I should have remembered. You're quite used to beatings, aren't you?"

What was wrong with her? She'd been unable to stop herself from goading him. Just because he was frustrating her? They still couldn't get along, even for a few minutes!

"And you never did find out what it's like, did you?"

He said that in such a deceptively quiet voice, but his expression warned he was about to give her a demonstration.

"You lay one hand on me, and I'll have you tossed in jail," she promised.

"Dead women tell no tales."

She blanched, reminded of his superior strength, which he'd always lorded over her. As a full-grown man now with those brawny arms, he could probably snap her neck without even half trying. And if he'd snuck into this hostelry without anyone's noticing, who would know?

Chapter Nineteen

T‍HE FEAR HIT Julia with a vengeance. He'd come close to killing her before when he'd dangled her over a balcony and one slip of his hold would have had her falling to her death. It was a terrifying experience she'd never forget. He'd promised to kill her if he ever saw her again. It was a wonder he'd restrained that urge this long. Her death would put an end to his problems. Not for a minute did she believe that his father was keeping him from going home for any other reason. The earl would probably welcome him back with open arms if she wasn't an issue between them anymore.

She was already edging around him toward the door, ready to bolt for it if he moved an inch. Then she saw his smirk. He'd frightened her deliberately!

The fury that consumed her was more powerful than anything she'd felt as a child. Unable to control herself, she charged at him, stupidly putting herself within his reach. She ended up on the bed, facedown, with his heavy weight holding her there.

"Let me up!"

"No, I don't think so," Richard said matter-of-factly. "I rather like you in this position. It definitely brings to my attention that there are—other ways to scare you away . . . and it keeps your teeth off of me."

She struggled underneath him so earnestly, she soon wore herself out. He only laughed at her efforts because she couldn't budge him, couldn't even reach back to claw him because he was holding her wrists to the bed as well.

Then he leaned close to her ear and whispered provocatively, "What do you think, Jewels? Want to take this fight to a new level?"

"You're contemptible."

But her statement lacked heat, possibly because his suggestion had ignited powerful emotions in her, which she understood well enough. One, she wanted children, and that's how they were created. And she was still afraid that her petition wouldn't go through now, even if he did leave England again, because someone would step forward to say he'd seen him on this visit, hence he wasn't dead. His brother could do this, if Richard followed through on trying to see Charles while he was here. And she couldn't deny that her curiosity was demanding that she find out what came after kissing in courtship. Hearing about it from her married friends for the last several years had only sparked her curiosity all the more. Could she put aside her aversion to him long enough to find out?

She was out of her mind! He couldn't have reinforced that conviction more when he added, "If I don't have to look at you, I can pretend it's not you I'm making love to."

She bucked again and this time caught him off guard. He slid halfway off her and released one of her arms. She pushed to her side so she could slam her elbow backward into his chest. That dislodged him even more and got her halfway off the bed. But it wasn't far enough for her to have gained purchase to free her other hand. He used the hold he still had on her to draw her back.

She fell on top of him, backward, glaring furiously up at the ceiling. Immediately, he wrapped his arms tightly around her, crossing her own arm over her belly, since he still had that wrist in his grip. But her other arm wasn't much use to her trapped under his and with her covering most of his body with her own.

"This works, too." He laughed.

Oh my God, she realized, he was enjoying this, having her so at his mercy. But then he'd always taken some sort of perverse pleasure every time he'd dominated her with his male strength. But she wasn't as helpless as she'd thought in this new position. Her bucking again with impotent rage actually knocked the breath out of him, to go by his grunt. The heel of her riding boot struck his shin hard, too. And the back of her head knocked against his jaw. That one hurt. Her. But it got rid of his amusement.

With a growl he moved her so that she lay half underneath him again, but he couldn't catch her hand in time to prevent her grabbing a fistful of his hair. She was going to yank out every single strand and tried, but she'd caught too much, so all it did was pull his head down toward hers. Their eyes only inches apart, each of them glaring furiously at the other . . . then his eyes dropped to her mouth.

It all happened too fast. The anger had no chance to subside for her to maintain any sort of reason. It transferred instead to a much different passion, just as explosive, just as mindless, the instant his lips pressed against hers. This wasn't just kissing, this was far beyond that, raw desire that ravaged the senses, something so primitive it was out of control.

Her grip tightened on his hair, but this time to keep him there. His hand found her breast, and as his fingers encircled it, the delicate button on her blouse popped off. She didn't know, didn't care, only felt the hard pressure that was stirring her right to her core. He raised his leg so that his knee moved up her body, dragging her skirt up to the apex of her thighs, and pressed there, too. She wrapped an arm around his neck. Her skirt bunched about her thighs now, his hand slipped under her drawers and she nearly screamed at the raw pleasure as his finger thrust inside her.

Then, as fast as it began, it ended. He suddenly shot off the bed. "What the hell? What the hell!? Did you do that on purpose?"

She leaned up on her elbows in a daze. He looked absolutely furious, but absolutely magnificent, too, with his long black hair that she'd ripped out of its queue wild about his shoulders, his breath coming hard, his muscles bunched tight, his fists clenched.

She knew anger could be all-consuming. She'd found that out so many times with him. But she'd had no clue that passion could be, too. A dangerous thing to find out, that he could bring her to the point of wanting him. Really, she could have done without knowing that.

For the moment, she was deflated, all of her own anger having been drained away by that passion, so her voice was perfectly calm when she said, "Do what?"

"Start that?"

"Don't be an ass. I was leaving."

"You attacked me!"

"Did I? Then I'm sure you must have provoked it . . . as usual."

She scooted off the bed—wisely on the opposite side from him. She was leaving a button behind somewhere on the bed, but she didn't yet notice the wide exposure between her breasts. Her coiffure had come undone as well in her struggles, and that she couldn't miss, with a long lock half over her face. Her hair must look as wild as his.

She pushed her hair back before she turned to face him. Thank God he'd come to his senses. She wanted children, but not his. She still wouldn't have him even if he were worth a fortune, which he wasn't. She needed the ties severed with him and his damned father, and that wouldn't happen if she bore him a child.

She caught him staring at her body when she turned. That drew her attention to her heavy velvet riding skirt that hadn't fallen naturally back into place when she stood up. With a tsk she shoved it down over her knees.

He was still obviously bristling, blaming her because his domineering tactics had backfired on him. Too bad for him. She was still calm. That really was remarkable. She'd never been this calm in his presence before.

"Let's hope this is our last meeting," she said.

"It better be," he warned.

"There we go agreeing with each other again."

She actually smiled at him! What the deuce was wrong with her?

She took a deep breath before continuing, "I'm going to take you at your word, since you leave me no other option, and proceed with my petition to be rid of you so I can get on with my life just as you have. If you insist on visiting your brother, warn Charles to keep his mouth shut when I have you declared dead." She said that on the way to the door and paused only long enough to add, "I promise you, Richard, if you or your family foil my effort to break that despicable contract, I will pay someone my entire dowry—to kill you."

Chapter Twenty

"SHE HAD A pistol on her," Ohr said when he returned to the room later that day. "She didn't try to kill you, did she?"

"Just my sanity, she's good at threatening that."

Richard discounted the possibility of Julia's killing him in the heat of the moment when she was screaming at him, but he knew she could inflict a lot of pain. She was good at delivering pain. But he was certain one of them would kill the other eventually if they were forced to marry. They both got too crazy around each other.

That threat she'd made today, though, had definitely given him pause. She'd said it so bloody dispassionately, as if it were something she was used to doing, paying others to see her will done—just like his father.

He shuddered at the comparison and tried to put Julia Miller out of his mind. She was gone. He'd watched from his window as she galloped down the road, back toward London. He'd be out of the country again soon himself. There was no reason for them ever to cross paths again.

"A pretty girl," Ohr remarked. "Too bad you two can't get along."

Richard snorted. "Beauty means nothing when there's a little monster hiding under the surface."

Ohr grinned. "Not so little anymore."

No, dammit, she definitely wasn't little anymore. Julia had filled out with some luscious curves. Nothing about the scrawny, enraged child had indicated she would turn into a beauty one day. Not that it would have mattered. They could have become the best of friends and he still wouldn't have married her, because it was what his father wanted, and he refused to give that bastard any satisfaction at all.

But for a few moments today, too many moments, he'd utterly ignored that conviction, which he'd lived with for most of his life. He'd wanted her. How the hell did *that* happen?

She'd come at him with her claws bared, and with little effort he'd propelled her past him, where she'd fallen onto his bed. He wished to hell it hadn't occurred to him that it would be easy to keep her nails and her teeth off him by holding her there.

So his body had responded normally. How could it not with her squirming and moving so provocatively beneath him? But he should have realized what was happening and got off her immediately. Instead he'd kissed **her and** had been inflamed by that even more.

In **retrospect** it was rather obvious. He could kick himself **for not** realizing that something like that *could* happen if they started fighting physically the way they used to do when they were children. They were adults now. Sex was bound to get in the way of that sort of angry passion. And it hadn't just happened to him. She'd kissed him back just as furiously.

But he thrust her from his mind now to ask Ohr, "Did you have any luck?"

"As good as it gets." Ohr grinned. "I delayed getting back, so he should be arriving any—"

He didn't finish, just chuckled at the sound of some-one knocking at the door and waved a hand toward it. With a laugh of delight, Richard leapt for the door and yanked it open. He was engulfed in a bear hug that he returned wholeheartedly. So many years had passed since he'd seen his family, at least the only member of his family he loved, that such a wealth of emotion filled him, it almost brought tears to his eyes.

"I really didn't believe your friend," Charles said with a laugh. "Secret meeting? You actually here? I even got angry that he was getting my hopes up with lies."

"He did, too," Ohr put in.

"But I couldn't *not* come to see for myself. And you're really home!"

"Not quite," Richard said, pulling Charles into the

room. "But I couldn't leave England again without visiting you this time. God, it's good to see you, Charles!"

"And you! But what's wrong with your face?"

"That's nothing," Richard hedged. "I had a little too much to drink and fell facefirst into a brick wall."

"I know how that is," Charles admitted with a wince, but then he took a step back to have a full look at Richard and finished with an amazed chuckle. "Forget what century you're living in? Or is that a wig to disguise you while you're in the neighborhood?"

Richard grinned and got a tie from his pocket and fastened his hair back. "It's real and not all that unusual where I've been living. But look at you. Not so skinny anymore, eh? Someone feeding you well?"

"Look who's talking." Charles chuckled. "I barely recognize you." Then he added on a sober note, "But it's easy to eat normally when you're no longer feeling twisted with turmoil and anxiety that has you puking all the time."

Richard nodded in understanding. He could recall doing that a few times himself when he'd felt so churned up with impotent fury that had no outlet. But for Charles, the excessive drinking must have added to the difficulty of keeping food down as well. Richard couldn't recall Charles doing anything other than picking at meals after his marriage. But he definitely remembered him always being drunk.

It wasn't easy to tell they were brothers, the resemblance was so minimal. Neither of them actually looked like their father, either, though Charles did take after him more, having Milton's dark brown hair and blue eyes. He even had their father's stocky frame now that he'd put on weight. He was a few inches shorter than Richard, too. Richard also didn't take after his mother either, though he'd been told his black hair and green eyes did come from her side of the family.

But since his brother appeared to be standing there sober and had obviously found his appetite again, Richard guessed, "So you gave up the bottle?"

"Yes, but that's not what gave me peace."

"Don't tell me you actually get along with Father now?" Richard was joking. No one could get along with that man.

But Charles replied, "He and I have an—understanding, but Candice actually did me a good turn. She died. I've been at peace ever since."

Richard wasn't expecting that, and just stared for a moment before he replied, "I'll skip the condolences, if you don't mind."

"Please do. Truth be told, I was hard-pressed not to smile at her funeral. But I can't say that I don't bless her every day now."

"For dying?"

"No. For finally gaining me a son. It took three

years, which was mostly my fault—I could barely stand to touch her. Her complaining didn't stop once we repaired to the bedroom, you know. But we found out she was pregnant right after you left."

"I have a nephew?" Richard said with a beaming smile.

"Yes, Mathew just turned eight, and he's utterly changed my life. You can't imagine how fiercely protective I am of him, or how much I love him. I found out just how much when my father-in-law showed up after his daughter's funeral demanding that I turn Mathew over to him so he could raise him himself."

"Are you kidding?"

"No, Mathew is actually his only male heir, so the duke was quite serious and determined, even brought his solicitor along to make it legal. Some of the threats he issued, including ruination, were rather nasty. And Father took his side, of course. He's afraid that offending that old man for any reason will cost us his benevolence. Which is what my marriage to Candice was all about. Father is also in debt to him apparently, so he was furious when I balked and ordered me to comply."

"Damn, Charles, they took your son from you?"

Charles chuckled. "I can't blame you for drawing that conclusion. I never did tell Father no before, did I? Like you constantly did?"

When every one of those "refusals" earned Richard

a beating, Charles just hadn't found a good enough reason to suffer that pain. But Richard replied, "You weren't as stubborn as I was, nor as rebellious."

"True, at least not until that day." Charles grinned. "I warned Father to stay out of it. The boy is mine. He gives me the courage I always lacked. As for the duke, he raised his daughter to have the worst disposition I've ever encountered in my life, and I told him so. He was *not* going to raise my son to be like her."

"What happened?"

"I told him I'd take the boy and leave the country so he would never see him again. By the by, you gave me *that* idea."

"He believed you?"

"Why wouldn't he? I meant it."

Richard laughed. "Good for you!"

"And besides, I wasn't denying him access to Mathew, far from it. I take Mathew to visit him every few weeks. In fact, we were packed to leave for one of those visits today, but then your friend found me, so I postponed the visit until tomorrow. But, suffice it to say, we've all decided to forget about that original altercation."

"Even Father?"

"Father's attitude changed that day, at least; he no longer tries to force his will on me. You could say he treats me with kid gloves now. I have a feeling you're responsible for that, too. With one son gone, he's realized that I could disappear, too. Mathew and I are the link that keeps the duke happy with the Allen family. Father doesn't want to lose that. So as I said, we have an understanding, unspoken, but there nonetheless, to simply leave each other alone."

"I'm—incredulous."

"I'm not," Ohr put in. "Everyone changes, and nine years is long enough for someone to change."

Both brothers stared at Ohr, but then Charles chuckled. "I wouldn't go so far as to say that. My father is still the tyrant he always has been. He just manages to control his overbearing nature when he's around my son. Not that I would allow it, but not once has he ever tried to enforce his strict rules on the boy, or interfere with the way I'm raising him. And unlike the way Father treated you and I, Richard, I let Mathew make his own choices, and he makes them logically. He's such a bright, caring child. He even loves both of his grandfathers, but then oddly enough, they're both on their best behavior around him."

Richard found it hard to believe that his father had changed for any reason, even for what sounded purely like self-interest. But the changes in his brother were definitely remarkable. Charles seemed to glow with happiness when he spoke of the boy.

"But enough about me," Charles said. "Where on earth did you go? Another country? What have you been doing all these years?"

Richard, his eyes sparkling with laughter, glanced at

Ohr before he gave his brother the toned-down version: "I became a sailor."

Charles stared for a moment, then chuckled. "That's probably the one thing I would never have imagined. You? But you had such a rebellious nature, I was sure you'd gone off to find other battles to fight. At the very least, doing something adventurous."

Richard laughed. "What makes you think sailing can't be adventurous? And I'm well pleased with my life. I've made such good friends, they're like family to me now. I always have a place to sleep, food to eat, good companionship, and more women than I can count. What more could I want?"

"Children."

That was a sobering thought, and of course now that Charles was a proud father, he *would* think of that. But Richard didn't have to dwell on the matter to come up with an answer.

"I'd rather have children with a woman I love than with one who's forced on me."

Charles flinched. "I can't argue with that. And you're young. No special lady, though?"

"Yes—but she's otherwise attached," Richard mumbled so low that only Ohr heard him and rolled his eyes.

Charles said, "What?"

"I'm glad to know you aren't still living in hell," Richard said, changing the subject. "I was actually going to try to talk you into coming away with me, but it sounds like you're quite content here now."

"I am. But I'd be even more content if you told me you're home for good."

"That isn't going to happen, and not just because I despise our father. I just found out I can still be roped in by that damned marriage contract he saddled me with. I really thought Julia Miller would have married someone else by now."

"Father still won't release her from the contract," Charles said with a sigh.

"So I heard."

"You've seen her?"

"Not intentionally. We had a run-in."

"I saw her a few years ago m'self. She turned out to be quite a looker. Are you sure—?"

"You remember how it was with us?" Richard cut in. "It still is. She and I can't be in the same room without becoming furious at each other. Besides, I refuse to make Father happy by giving him what *he* wants from that match."

"It's a shame you and she never got along."

Richard shrugged. "It just wasn't meant to be. But she's taking steps to free us both, so I should warn you, don't try to stop her."

"From what?"

"Having me declared dead."

Charles stared at him, a frown forming on his face. "You're not joking, are you?"

"No."

"But that's—damn, Rich, that's morbid. Don't think I like that idea a'tall."

"You don't have to like it, just ignore it. Once it's accomplished, Julia will be free to get on with her life, and I'll be free to visit you more often."

That didn't remove his brother's frown, but he did nod grudgingly.

Chapter Twenty-one

RICHARD DEAD? CHARLES couldn't get the ghastly thought out of his mind on the short ride back to Willow Woods. He'd been reluctant to cut short his visit with Richard. He'd really hated having to say good-bye. But he had to return home before dark or his father might send the servants out looking for him. Richard refused to stay in the area any longer so they could visit again tomorrow.

Charles detested the obstacles that were preventing his brother from really coming home, but the drastic measure that the Miller girl was utilizing to banish one of those obstacles was even more despicable. He was too superstitious to see it as anything other than a prediction, not the simple means to an end, as Richard and the girl did.

At home, he stopped by the earl's study so Milton would know he was home, and to inform him of his change in plans.

Like the rest of the house, the study had grown shabby over the years because Milton lacked the funds to maintain their home or even keep a full staff of servants anymore. The old brown-and-gold wallpaper in the study was cracked in many places; the large oval rug that covered most of the floor was frayed at the edges. Only one extra chair was in the room. The other two had broken and were never replaced.

It wasn't as if money didn't regularly come in. They had good tenants. But Milton had too many old debts to settle and he used a good portion of his income to retire his debt to the duke since he couldn't stand being indebted to him. He obviously expected Richard's marriage to settle everything else. It wasn't going to happen.

Standing in the doorway, Charles said, "I'll be leaving in the morning for Mathew's visit with the duke."

Milton glanced up with an annoyed look from the letter he was writing at his desk. "You were to leave today. Why didn't you?"

"I lost track of the time" was all Charles said.

It wasn't a lie. As long as it wasn't a lie, Charles had no trouble saying it. He wasn't good at lying, never had been.

Charles started to turn away at the door, but with Julia Miller's plan still weighing on his mind, he wanted to try a less drastic means to help his brother's situation.

Before he lost the courage to do so, he said, "I saw the Miller girl recently." Again, it was not a lie. Two years could be considered recent. "When are you going to release that poor girl from that marriage contract? She's past the age to marry now, isn't she?"

Milton set his quill down and gave Charles a hard look. "What does that matter? When Richard comes to his senses, they'll be married."

Charles's expression turned sad. "Do you realize how many years have passed since he left?"

"Of course I know, to the bloody day," Milton said, getting angry.

It was definitely a sore subject in this house. Since Richard had departed, Charles had never been able to mention Richard to their father without angering him. But for once he had to ignore how uncomfortable that anger could make him feel.

"He's no longer a boy, Father. If he hasn't returned by now, he's not going to. Give it up already, and let that poor girl get on with her life. That contract is useless as it stands."

"It's not useless, that's the beauty of it. The Millers have already offered her dowry and more to get out of it. In five or ten more years I may have to accept that, but not yet."

"She could just get fed up with all this endless waiting and marry someone else despite the contract, you know."

Milton actually chuckled. "She won't. If that were an option, her father would have publicly announced an end to it long ago—before he became incapacitated. A contract means everything in the world of trade, and that's *the Millers'* world. It's a matter of their given word. You could even go so far as to say their reputation is on the line. For them to go back on a deal that is so well known could ruin them."

"Do you really think that will matter when you're already ruining her life?"

"I'm doing nothing of the sort. *She's* already reaped the benefits of being tied to our name, while I've reaped nothing yet. The *ton* accept her as one of their own, you know—because she's bound to us through that contract. Besides, *some* children are actually dutiful and honor the obligations their parents arrange for them."

Charles had done that. He'd married a foul-tempered woman he couldn't stand, but not because he honored his father. Nothing about Milton Allen inspired honor, love, or even duty. Charles had done what he'd been told because at that tender age he'd feared this man sitting before him more than anything else.

"Neither of them wanted that match, or have you forgotten that they despised each other?"

Milton snorted. "That was when they were children. When Richard sees her now, he'll change his tune. She turned out much prettier than expected, didn't she?" Milton suddenly laughed. "This extra time is actually an advantage, because when he does come home, she'll be so eager to finally have a husband, she'll be running to the altar. Old maids are like that, you know."

Charles felt disgusted by Milton's heartlessness and his amusement at Julia Miller's plight. Milton didn't really care whom he hurt, as long as the money he expected to reap eventually filled his coffers. Richard *had* seen Julia—and still wouldn't have her. Though, unfortunately, that had much more to do with the earl than it did with the girl.

Charles said stiffly, "He'd have to return for any of that to happen. I gave up hope that he would come home years ago. Why can't you?"

"Nonsense," Milton scoffed. "This is actually when Richard is more likely to come home, because enough time has passed that he'll think the girl is married and no longer an issue."

"Don't count on it, Father. *You* were the issue. He won't come home because of you!"

Milton suddenly frowned, Charles assumed because of his raised tone, until Milton demanded, "Do you know something that I don't know? Have you seen him, Charles?"

"No—of course not. I—I've just been thinking about him more than usual—ever since I saw the Miller girl."

Charles's cheeks were flaming now. He turned away before Milton noticed and rushed upstairs.

* * *

Milton moved to the doorway and stared after his son's rapidly departing figure. He was still frowning. He knew Charles. He knew his son was lying. He just found it hard to credit what his gut instinct was telling him. If Richard *was* back in England, wouldn't he come here to gloat that he was his own man now, beyond Milton's control? Of course he would.

Milton shook off the feeling. He just wasn't used to seeing his docile son become so emotional unless it involved Mathew. If anything, Charles had probably been lying about the Miller girl. She must have come to appeal to Charles to convince Milton to hand over that contract, knowing full well she'd have no luck doing so herself. Stupid girl. She should be grateful that he was still holding tight to their connection. She had to know by now how many doors would close in her face without it.

As he turned back into his study, not quite satisfied with the conclusion he'd settled on, he caught sight of Olaf, coming down the hall stuffing a pastry in his mouth, and paused again.

He should probably have got rid of this servant long ago. He really had no use for such brute strength anymore, and a man that size made a rather ridiculous footman, which was all he was good for now. Olaf was the only one left of the three bruisers he'd hired so long ago when Richard had got too old for the switch. But having the men administer punishments might have been a mistake because it had only turned Richard more recalcitrant.

But that brute strength might just be necessary again.

After giving Olaf his orders, he sent a message off to Abel Cantel, the local magistrate, inviting him to dinner. It had been nearly half a year since he'd done so. He didn't particularly like the fellow. But he'd planned ahead and cultivated a friendship with Abel soon after Richard had disappeared. He'd even gone so far, in the guise of a drunken stupor, of apprising Abel of Richard's crimes. Abel had told Milton more than once that he'd toss Richard's arse in jail when he came back. As soon as the earl gave him the word, it would be done. But Milton had found out that Abel had a brother who might be even more useful. But whatever course of action Milton took, Abel gave him options for the day Richard came home, and Milton liked having options.

Chapter Twenty-two

DINNER WAS LONG over. Charles and Mathew had retired directly afterward, since they were leaving early in the morning. Milton had taken Abel to his study for some brandy, but he was hard-pressed for an excuse to detain the man much longer.

Milton had ordered Olaf to start searching for Richard at the three inns closest to Willow Woods, then work his way toward London. Manchester was too far in the other direction, so at least they didn't need to search there. If Richard had come north to see his brother, he might even be planning to journey east with Charles to Rotherham tomorrow, to extend that visit a little, so he could still be close by. But if not, the direct route back to London had to be canvassed. He'd given Olaf and the search party he'd been told to gather access to the best horses in his stable, including his own stallion. He wanted the search done quickly and without error, so they couldn't split up, since only Olaf would recognize Richard if they encountered him.

Suddenly the door burst open and Olaf and the old gardener's strapping son dragged a man into the room. Abel shot to his feet, startled at the intrusion. So did Milton. Could it be, finally? He moved quickly around his desk to make sure. The man was unconscious to go by the look of his hanging head and the long hair covering his face. Milton lifted the hair aside and drew in his breath. Richard.

Such triumph filled Milton he could barely contain it. Anger helped in that regard. Olaf was such an idiot! Charles could have been in the study, and that would definitely hamper how Milton could deal with Richard. But at last the rebellious whelp was back under his control!

He gave a moment's thought to sending for Julia Miller to force the marriage immediately, but decided against it. That was too big a risk. The pastor who lived on Milton's estate would of course comply, but the girl might cry foul if Richard was shouting that he wouldn't have her. And with that damn competent legal team in her employ that had thwarted him before when he tried to get guardianship of her, he didn't dare take that chance.

The two men dropped Richard on the floor at their feet. Richard's hands were tied behind his back. He'd grown. A lot. A tall, strapping man was lying there, not a boy. His feet should have been tied, too. Milton didn't want to take any chances on losing him again.

"What's the meaning of this?" Abel demanded of the two servants.

"It would appear my recalcitrant son has wandered close enough to home to be found," Milton replied, staring down in disgust at the appalling length of Richard's hair.

"Richard?" Abel asked in surprise.

"Indeed, Richard. And look at this." Milton bent down to yank the signet ring off Richard's finger and put it back where it belonged, on his. "I'm amazed he still has this ring he stole from me. Not that I wasn't forced to have it replaced, but this one was special, handed down through the centuries from the first Earl of Manford, and he knew that. Obviously he didn't take it to sell, but as another means of flouting my authority and insulting me because he knew how much I valued it."

"I can lock him up for that alone. You've just shown me the proof of it."

Milton was gratified to hear Cantel reacting just as he'd hoped, but he was sure a spell in a local jail wasn't going to convince Richard of anything. But before he discussed what would, he dismissed the gardener's son.

Olaf started to leave with him, forcing Milton to snap, "Not you. *You* make sure the boy doesn't bolt out of here the moment he wakes." Milton then turned to the magistrate to remind the man, "My own son nearly paupered me with his gambling debts. Did I ever mention that? Twelve thousand bloody pounds! And enough witnesses to prove it!"

Abel nodded with some slight embarrassment. "One night when we'd had a bit too much to drink, I believe you did."

"If the Duke of Chelter hadn't bailed me out, I would be in debtors' prison m'self right now. And I'm not even close to paying the man back." Then, as if the thought had only just occurred to him, Milton asked, "Isn't your brother a guard on one of the ships that transport convicts to the new penal colonies in Australia?"

Abel frowned. "He's the captain, actually, but that's a bit harsh, don't you think?"

"It's a moot point if Richard has come home to do his duty. If he has, then all can and will be forgiven. But if he hasn't, well, I wasn't suggesting he be transported to such a place indefinitely. A few months and he'll be ready to meet his obligations, don't you think?"

"It takes more'n a few months just to get there, and some of the convicts don't even survive the trip. If they do, the harsh conditions there usually break a man in the first few weeks. Are you sure you want to send your son there?"

Milton wasn't going to let Richard slip through his fingers again. If the boy couldn't be made to see reason, by God, he *was* going to take steps to make sure he would. Nine years of penury the boy had to make up for. Nine years of impotent frustration because Milton could no longer afford the few things in life that gave him pleasure.

So he reminded Abel, "Men get sent there for lesser crimes, don't they?"

Abel shrugged. "Our prisons are overflowing, and convict labor is free labor, after all. Australia needs a lot of workers if we're going to turn it into a promising new colony for the crown. There's still nothing there except penal colonies, and no way to escape from them. The only ships that arrive are more convict ships. A man really has no hope if he's sent there."

Milton smiled to himself. "Yes, rather harsh, but probably the only thing that will reform this rebel—as long as Richard's release can be arranged as soon as he's ready to meet his obligations. *Can* that be arranged?"

"Anything can be arranged," Abel said a bit uncomfortably.

Milton frowned at the man's apparent unease. Was he being a bit too cold and uncaring even for a commoner like Cantel? Was it not obvious that Richard deserved it? Cantel only had to look around him at the appalling condition of Willow Woods to see the damage Richard had done to his own family.

"Let's see what he has to say for himself first. If he's ready to conform and help this family instead of hurting it, then he can be forgiven. Wake him up," Milton told Olaf.

Olaf's interpretation of that was a hard kick to Richard's side. Abel turned away. Milton glared at the big oaf.

"Some water or smelling salts, you fool."

"Don't see any," Olaf said.

"Not—necessary," Richard groaned, then added, "What the hell?" when he realized he had to struggle to get up, that his arms were bound behind him.

He'd known this could be the outcome when Olaf had kicked his door in—the dumb giant hadn't even checked to see that it wasn't locked. Richard had been alone in the room eating the dinner that Ohr had sent up along with a message that he was going to be detained—by the barmaid in the tavern next door.

Richard had recognized Olaf instantly, one of the three strong-arms Milton had hired when Richard had got too big for the switch. The last memory he had of Willow Woods had been of his father demanding he cut his hair, which had barely reached his shoulders. He'd refused, of course, even knowing he'd be punished for it. But he and his father were at a complete war of wills by then. So Milton had ordered his brutes to cut Richard's hair for him, and they'd dragged him out of his bed from a sound sleep, tied him to a chair, and practically scalped him. God, the impotent rage he'd felt.

He'd left for London that very night and never looked back.

Richard was actually fiercely glad to see Olaf standing there over the broken door, didn't even wonder yet what the brute was doing there. Revenge was all Richard could think of.

Olaf was still much bigger, a damned giant, but he was stupid, and Richard wasn't a boy anymore. But he didn't even have a few moments to savor the thought of beating the hell out of Olaf before five other men crowded in around him, and all six of them charged Richard and wrestled him to the floor. He was overpowered by sheer numbers. They didn't need to knock him out as well, but one of them did.

Now, in his father's study, Richard finally managed to get to his feet. Straining to free his hands proved futile, and so was the glare he gave his father. How did this happen? He'd been so sure no one in the area had recognized him, but obviously someone had and had run straightaway to the earl with news of the sighting.

He and Ohr shouldn't even have been there for this to happen! The cautious plan would have been to leave and find an inn closer to London for the night, a long distance from Willow Woods. But he'd been toying with the idea of trying to catch Charles on the road in the morning, so he could meet his nephew before he left England once and for all.

Milton hadn't changed much at all. His hair was maybe a little lighter shade of brown, his blue eyes were just as cold, and only a little sagging to his jowls marked the passing of the years. But Milton hadn't even looked him in the eye yet. He was staring in disgust at the long hair that fell over Richard's shoulders.

"My God, it's even longer than I thought. You look like a bloody beggar who can't afford a haircut," Milton said, then ordered his brute, "Get rid of that."

Richard turned to the bigger man and calmly told him, "Try it and I'll kill you this time."

Olaf merely laughed, but Milton shook his head and said, "Never mind. It's obvious he's going to be just as defiant as he ever was."

"What did you expect?" Richard turned to snarl at his father. "You, old man, have no say anymore over the way I look or what I do. I've outgrown your control."

"You think so? You haven't outgrown the law, though, and you broke a few of those before you ran away."

"What laws? Yours?"

Milton fingered the signet ring that was now on his finger again. "You stole this before you left. Did you forget about that crime?"

Richard scoffed, "That ring goes to my brother when you die, and he wouldn't have minded my borrowing it—and why the hell don't you die and put us out of our misery?"

Milton sighed and told the other men in the room, "You see what I've had to deal with? He's the most unnatural son a man could have."

Richard frowned over the show of parental disappointment, obviously contrived for the other men. If Milton had ever once shown any real disappointment in him, or even just a little concern or a speck of caring, their relationship might have developed into a more natural one. A child's instinct was to please his parent, after all—until the child figured out that nothing ever would.

"Who are you?" Richard asked the third man.

"Abel Cantel is an old friend of mine," Milton answered for him.

But Abel felt obliged to add, "I'm also the local magistrate, Lord Richard."

Was that a deliberate warning? Richard stiffened. Only untitled gentry or a commoner would use Richard's minor title, and a man of either rank would defer to an earl's wishes. But then he'd always known that his father might try to use those old misdeeds of his against him if they ever came face-to-face again. He'd wanted to be disowned. He'd been too young to realize he might be giving his father another tool to use in twisting his arm to comply with the marriage contract.

But he wasn't really worried yet. It could just be a coincidence that the "law" was represented in that room. And he wasn't planning on sticking around, nor was he alone this time. Charles was in the house somewhere, had said he wasn't leaving until morning for a visit to Mathew's maternal grandfather. His brother had never had the courage to intervene before, but he was his own man now. And Ohr would look at Willow Woods first when he returned from his dalliance with the barmaid to find Richard gone—and the damage left behind in their room was evidence that he hadn't willingly left.

What was the most Milton would—could—do? Have him beaten again? Nothing new in that. Contain him in a room with threats of real imprisonment? For borrowing a ring from his own family, a case that would be laughed out of the courts? Besides, he'd have help escaping long before any threat became more than a threat. That very night, he was sure.

He was more worried about Julia's prophecy, that he could stand there and shout no and yet still be pronounced her husband. Milton did support at least one pastor on his estate who was beholden to him for his livelihood. But Julia was on her way back to London. It would take a day or two to get her back here, and he was sure she'd delay her return even longer if she was told why her presence was required. He didn't expect to be there that long.

"You know, Father, you could have asked for this meeting, instead of forcing it down my throat as usual."

"We both know what your answer would have been," Milton said stiffly.

"Well, I know, but do you, really? What if I was coming home to ask for your forgiveness?"

That gave Milton pause. "Were you?"

Richard couldn't bring himself to say yes, even if it might get him released. "No, but you should have made an effort to find that out before sending your loutish lackeys after me, because if I *was* returning to the fold, this welcome would definitely have changed my mind. But when all you've ever done, Father, is administer beatings or pay someone—"

"Enough!" Milton cut in, red-faced.

Richard raised a brow. "Don't want the magistrate here to know how brutal you made life under your roof? But you are absolutely correct, Father. We both know there will never be a reconciliation between us. So what was the point of bringing me here?"

"A matter of settling accounts. Do you have the money to pay off the huge gambling debts you stuck me with, that I still owe to the Duke of Chelter, who bailed me out—and lords it over me that he did?"

Richard was given pause now. Those damned rakehells had finally gone to his father for payment? Then why hadn't Milton severed all ties with him?

"You were a fool if you paid those losses, when you could have disowned me instead," Richard said.

"So it *was* deliberate? An attempt to force my hand to be done with you?"

"What choice did your cruel tyranny leave me?"

Richard demanded. "And it's not too late to finally disown me. You have a witness. Make it legal."

Milton shook his head. "Even if that were an option, it would have solved nothing back then. You were underage, leaving me accountable for your actions. So I'm to take it that your answer is no? You don't have the wherewithal to make immediate restitution?"

"Of course I don't."

"Then you're ready to marry your fiancée to redeem those debts?"

"Hell no."

"You see?" Milton said, glancing at the magistrate. "Not even apologetic that he deliberately tried to pauper his own family. Nor willing to make restitution the only way he can." Then Milton sighed. "Give me a few moments of privacy with my son. I would be remiss in my parental duty if I don't try one last time to make him see reason before resorting to drastic measures."

Richard didn't like the sound of that. But he still didn't think he'd be there long enough for those "drastic measures" to bear fruit. Milton was a fool if he thought Richard would honor a marriage that was forced on him. Or would his father get what he wanted either way? *That* worried Richard. He didn't exile himself from England so his father could win in the end.

The earl had leaned back against his desk, his arms crossed, waiting for the door to close. He didn't look angry; he actually looked perplexed.

"I've never understood you," Milton began.

"You never tried to."

"I did a good thing for you all those years ago when I arranged that contract binding us to the Millers, assuring you of wealth and good fortune."

"Without asking me," Richard reminded him.

"You were too young to form an opinion back then, much less know what was good for you. And now, you are so stubborn, so determined to thwart me, that you don't even realize what you're turning down."

"My breath is bated," Richard said sarcastically.

"You dare to make light of it? When circumstances have changed so drastically while you were gone? Gerald Miller had an accident five years ago that has left him mindless to this day, with no hope of recovery. This put his only child, *your* fiancée, in control of the entire Miller fortune, and you've come home in time to take full advantage of that. All you have to do is say 'I do' in a marriage ceremony and you'll be married to one of the wealthiest women in England and have control of her huge fortune, which would enhance the standing as well as the social and financial power of all of us, not just me and you, but your brother and nephew, too."

"They are directly related to the Duke of Chelter. They don't need elevating."

"Chelter's fortune is waning."

"He's still rich."

"Not nearly as rich as the Millers!" Milton exclaimed,

then sighed and tried to compose himself again before adding, "Besides, the duke has always made us feel like poor relations."

Richard raised a brow. "*Us?* You mean *you,* don't you?"

Milton gritted his teeth. "Are you even listening as I explain what's at stake here? The Miller enterprises have grown astronomically over the years. Do you know wealth like that can even influence the king? There could easily be new titles for our family along with more land grants."

"There's no *our* in this, Father. *You* don't have to marry a hellion you can't stand."

"I did," Milton growled. "Your mother."

Richard was incredulous. "Is this why you've never shown me any love or affection, or even kindness, when I was growing up? Because you hated your wife? And this is what you're trying to force on me? A marriage as detestable as yours was? Why did you never mention any of this before?"

"You were a child," Milton said stiffly. "Children don't require explanations."

"This child did. From the day I was born, you insisted on living my life for me. But it's *my* life, Father. I'll live it and make my own decisions for good or bad. And my decision is *not* to marry Julia Miller."

Milton was red-faced now with anger, a visage

Richard was actually better acquainted with. "I should have known better than to try to reason with you. You're as outrageously obstinate and foolish as you ever were." Then he shouted, "Abel!" And before the door had fully opened, Milton told the magistrate, "Take him away."

Chapter Twenty-three

JULIA COULDN'T GET that last image of Richard out of her head. She barely noticed when Raymond led them to an inn in the very next town. They could have gone farther. It wasn't dark yet. But she was as exhausted as her cousin was, which was why they both overslept the next morning.

She'd had to pound on Raymond's door repeatedly before she heard him shout, "I ain't budging! We'll go home tomorrow!"

"Today!" she shouted back.

She loved her cousin, but at times like this she didn't exactly like him. He was a true wastrel. All he was ever good for was an escort when she needed one, and only if she informed him well in advance. He was always broke. He was given a nice allowance, but he threw it all away on gambling and women. She'd talked to him countless times about taking on some responsibilities to earn some of that allowance, but he had an endless stream of excuses to avoid any sort of work. At least he was an adept rider and had kept pace with her on this trip, though he'd complained all the way.

Her annoyance over not getting an early start stayed with her that day, as did that haunting image of Richard. It was as if she were running from it. The long hair, centuries out of fashion, didn't detract at all from his masculinity. It merely gave him a wild, primitive look, especially when he was panting with fury. He'd been so angry! Because he'd kissed her—no, wait, he'd blamed that on her, accusing her of starting it, when she'd done nothing of the sort. That kiss had been amazing, though, definitely an introduction to passion. She couldn't help wondering what would have happened if he hadn't brought it to an end.

She set the same mad pace that day, trying to get home before dark. It didn't work. When they stopped to retrieve their original mounts in the first town they'd stopped at yesterday morning, it was dusk, and Raymond balked at going any farther, as he was not used to such long days without a nap or two. Julia was tired enough not to insist, feeling both numb and weighted down with dust again. So she got them rooms for the second night. She just wished she'd been able to sleep this time. Despite her exhaustion, she tossed and turned most of the night, reliving that meeting with Richard and all the things she should have said but didn't, and all the things that could have happened—but didn't.

On the road again just after dawn, they entered London a few hours later. Raymond, annoyed to have to rise so bloody early, as he put it, three mornings in a row, didn't even say good-bye as they reached her house, just continued on to his own home several blocks away.

She was planning to go back to bed herself, still exhausted after so little sleep last night. But as soon as she entered her house, one of the footmen rushed over to her, and she was instantly revitalized by the excitement on his face and in his voice as he said, "Your father—"

She didn't need to hear more. She knew. It happened every time her father woke up, *really* woke up: the whole household got excited. She was already racing up the stairs.

"I'm not too late?" she asked as she burst into her father's room and rushed over to Gerald's bed, where he was sitting, propped up with pillows, and smiling at her. "How long have you been awake? Please tell me it hasn't been long?"

"Calm down, Julie." He patted the bed beside him, indicating she should sit down. "I don't think time is going to matter—"

"Of course it is, you know it is—you *do* know that, correct? You can remember this time?"

"Yes, everything."

She took a deep breath and grinned at him, embarrassed by her anxiety as she sat down. She would have been furious with herself if she had missed this visit with her father—because of Richard. But she finally noticed the cloth or, rather, small sack that was resting on the pillow next to his head, and that Arthur wasn't in the room with him.

She'd hired the servant soon after the accident to be a full-time attendant for Gerald, someone who could feed him, bathe him, even carry him out to the small balcony she'd had built off the room so her father could enjoy the sun when the weather permitted. Arthur even slept in a bed tucked into the corner of the room so he could be on hand round-the-clock.

"What is that for?" She pointed at the little sack. "And where is Arthur?"

"He went to get my lunch," Gerald said with a delighted smile. "I was told they've been slaving all morning in the kitchen making all of my favorite dishes. I'm to get a sampling of each."

"All morning?" Julia shot to her feet again. "*When* did you wake up?"

He sighed over her anxiety that she wouldn't have much time with him. "Julie, there is good news, if you will settle down long enough for me to tell you."

He patted the bed again. That her father could make that gesture was a tribute to Arthur's diligence. The man had begun manipulating Gerald's limbs several times a day to simulate exercise after they discovered his muscles were atrophying due to his inactivity. Now when her father woke up, he could at least move his arms and even his legs a little, though he wouldn't be strong enough to actually walk on them and was never awake long enough to work toward that effort. But Arthur had made sure that if that day did ever come, Gerald's limbs wouldn't be beyond hope due to his being bedridden for so many years.

She sat again, but the dip in the bed this time dislodged the sack from his pillow and it rolled down to land by her hip. She stared down in horror at the spots of blood on it.

"My God, what happened to you?" She poked the bag. It was cold and soaking wet.

"Ice," he explained. "It hasn't been warm enough yet to melt the winter supply in the cellar. The doctor was here yesterday and recommended cold for the swelling— and don't fly off the handle again. I mentioned good news, didn't I?"

He was beaming at her. She couldn't get past the point that he was bleeding. But then it sank in. Yesterday? He'd been awake for an entire day?

Anxiously, but with hope sneaking in, she asked, "Tell me how you got hurt."

"I woke up yesterday before Arthur did. I was sufficiently disoriented to think I had dreamed that horrible accident and that it was a normal morning like any other and time to get up. So I tried to."

She winced. "You fell out of bed?"

"No, I got out of bed. I actually stood up, or at least I put all my weight on my left foot first, and I was half standing before that leg buckled. I fell to the left and hit my head on the corner of the night table. You'll notice it's not there? I hit the table hard enough to break it. Scared the hell out of Arthur with that fall, or so he said. I was out cold again."

"But not for long?"

"Long enough for Arthur to send for Dr. Andrew. I woke up when he started poking around my head. He was fascinated that I'd hit my head in nearly the same place as my original injury."

She gasped.

"It's only a small cut, though it's swollen now, which was why he recommended cold compresses. Arthur suggested we try ice, since we have some on hand. Thought it might work quicker."

Gerald paused and slowly raised his left hand to feel the wounded area. The worst of the original injuries to his head had been high up on the left side. There had been others, but none as bad as that one.

"That's quite a lump," she said, appalled that she could see it through his hair.

"No, it's smaller than it was, so the ice must be helping," he reassured her.

"How bad does it hurt?"

"I barely feel it, so don't fret. I'm not lying here in pain, dearest, I promise you I'm not."

"Why was Dr. Andrew so fascinated?"

Gerald snorted. "He mentioned an amnesia patient who had regained his memory when he received another injury to his head, which is hardly comparable, and I told him so. But they know so little about the brain, he was hesitant to treat this new injury at all. In fact, he said the cut wasn't wide enough to warrant more than a stitch or two, and he was going to wait until I lost consciousness again to close it. He might have been fascinated, but he wasn't very optimistic. But when he came back later that afternoon, I was still awake. He tried again last night before he retired, but I was still awake."

Gerald was grinning again widely. Julia started crying, couldn't help it. Her father had never stayed cognizant for this long since the accident, mere hours was all she'd ever had with him, and once, only minutes, before he'd slipped back into that dead fog of no awareness.

Though tears were rolling down her cheeks as she gripped his hand, she was also grinning just as widely as he was. "My God, you've finally come home—for good."

Chapter Twenty-four

JULIA BARELY LEFT her father's side that week. She wanted someone awake by his side at all times, and while she had a houseful of servants she could have assigned that task, she performed it herself, merely switching off with Arthur, so one of them was always with Gerald even while he was asleep. She ignored all visitors that week, even Georgina and Gabrielle, even Carol. She simply had the footman tell them the good news about her father and that she would see them soon.

She didn't know how soon that would be though. She couldn't help but fear that her father would suffer a relapse, that her days with him were still borrowed. Because of that fear, the old constraint of time, of wanting to squeeze in every minute with him while he was awake, was still present. Despite his rising every morning with that wonderful smile that so warmed her heart, her anxiety wouldn't go away. Every morning she awoke feeling sick to her stomach until she ran back to his room to see with her own eyes that he was still with them, *really* with them.

Dr. Andrew was writing a paper to send off to his colleagues, documenting Gerald's recovery, just as he'd done with the unusual effects of the first injury.

Gerald wanted to know about everything he'd missed, of course, and there'd been so many subjects they'd skipped before, when there'd been so little time to discuss them. Bringing him up-to-date on his business empire had taken nearly a full day! Julia had acquired seven more businesses, had only had to fire one of his managers, who wasn't keeping up with the others.

They didn't get around to talking about her until her father asked, "How old are you now, Julia? I've always been hesitant to ask. I was afraid, really, to know how much time was passing me by."

"Oh, God, Papa, five years have passed since the accident. I'm twenty-one now."

She was already crying, loud racking sobs this time. That so summed up the horror of his injury, that it had taken five years of his life away from him—and from her. But even worse, she had to tell him about her mother. She'd already mourned for her mother, but her father had never had a chance to. He'd never really been there with Julia for more than minutes or hours at a time, certainly not long enough for her to break the news to him that only he had survived the accident. He'd loved Helene, loved her enough to put up with all her idiosyncrasies and her social-climbing desire to elevate the Millers into the aristocracy.

She'd been dreading it, but she knew she couldn't put it off any longer. "And Mama—"

"Hush, dearest," he said in a choking voice. "I've already guessed."

He held her close as she cried all the harder, but for him this time. And he cried, too. She tried to tell him why she'd kept it from him, but he told her she didn't need to explain, he understood.

All those tears brought her such relief. When she finally got her emotions under control, she realized the terrible weight of uncertainty had been washed away as well.

She told him everything, held nothing back. There was so much else to talk about, it was like a dam bursting for her. Because Richard had been on her mind so much recently, she even mentioned him later that evening, though briefly. At least she tried to keep it brief.

"I honestly didn't think he'd ever come back," Gerald admitted.

"He hasn't really. No one else knows he's back, except his brother, who he came to visit. Which is why I'm going to go forward with having him declared dead."

Gerald shook his head. "You can't do that, dearest. It isn't right. It was a solution when you actually thought he was dead, with so much time having passed. But now that you've seen him, you know that isn't the case. And you two still don't want the marriage? You're certain?"

"Absolutely. Nothing has changed. We still can't stand each other." She didn't mention that Richard was in love with someone else, which was beginning to annoy her when she thought about it.

Gerald snorted. "That pompous arse Milton. He was so sure that you children would outgrow that animosity, he even managed to convince me of it."

"Is that why you didn't offer him more to sever the ties between our families?"

"But I did, triple your dowry. It was obvious by then that he expected a hell of a lot more from the marriage. So I stopped trying to reason with him. You were still a child. There was also still the possibility that you might look favorably on Richard one day. So I postponed making decisions of any sort until you were of a marriageable age. And now that you are, get on with your life, dearest. Find that perfect someone who's out there waiting for you—which I failed miserably to do for you."

She couldn't believe he was suggesting that. Eyes wide, she said, "But we can't go back on your word."

"It's my decision. You aren't to worry about it."

She realized he was still viewing her as a child. That was understandable, but she wasn't any longer a child who could accept Father's assurances and let it go at that. They had to discuss this.

"What is the worst that can happen?" she asked, then answered her own question. "The earl could take it to legal jurisdiction and could be awarded recompense."

"Possibly, but it would be a pittance. It's not as if the groom is standing at the altar willing to fulfill the Allens' part of that contract."

"But the backlash for breaking your word—"

"You let me worry about that. You've been held fast long enough to this deplorable situation because of *my* actions. If there's any backlash because of it, I'll consider it justified for my own foolishness. And it will all be forgotten soon enough."

Julia was afraid it wouldn't be as easy as her father made it sound. They would be thwarting a lord, after all, and they didn't have that same social distinction themselves. The earl was bound to make trouble, creating a scandal at the very least, even impugning their integrity for not honoring the contract, the very things that had stayed her own hand in the matter. Gerald wasn't sufficiently recovered yet to deal with that sort of whiplash.

But Julia didn't mention that to her father. She nodded, allowing him to think she agreed with him. But she couldn't agree, not yet, not without at least seeing the earl and trying one last time to make him see reason so they could end this betrothal amicably.

Chapter Twenty-five

HE KEPT HER waiting! Half a bloody day!

Julia hadn't seen Milton Allen, the Earl of Manford, in five years, not since her parents' accident, which had devastated her life. The earl had come to her mother's funeral and offered his trite condolences, but his real reason for coming to town had been to start proceedings to gain guardianship of her. Her family's solicitors had told her how angry he'd been when he'd failed to do so. It would have given him what he'd wanted all along, complete control over everything the Millers owned.

It had been even longer since she'd been inside Willow Woods. The house she'd been so impressed with as a child looked quite different through an adult's eyes. Had it been in this shabby state back then? Surely not. But the house's poor condition actually added to her confidence that she could finally break the tie to the

Allens. The earl had refused money in the past to end it, but if his finances were in such dire straits he couldn't even maintain his home properly, he might accept that solution now.

Julia had left her maid at the hostelry nearby. She'd been lucky to get a room there after the innkeeper accused her of being responsible for damaging his property the previous week. She didn't know what he was talking about, but paying him triple the price for the room had shut him up. She hadn't intended to sleep there anyway when she already had a room at the much nicer inn where she'd stayed last night. But like her mother, she'd wanted a little privacy where she could freshen up before her audience with the earl.

She'd traveled by coach this time, so she'd been able to bring her maid instead of having to ask Raymond to escort her again. But traveling by coach was much slower than simply riding, and now she would be lucky to leave Willow Woods before nightfall, since the earl hadn't deigned to see her yet, which could turn this trip into four days instead of the three she had figured on.

She hadn't told her father where she was going, knowing he would have tried to talk her out of it and would probably have succeeded. She'd told him instead that she needed to make a brief business trip to the North Country. She didn't like lying to him, but she didn't want him to worry over her absence, and she would explain when she got back, hopefully with good news. If the earl ever made an appearance.

Charles wasn't even at home to keep her company. The butler had told her he hadn't returned yet from taking his son to visit the boy's other grandfather. So the time dragged that afternoon. And her annoyance mounted.

It *was* actually turning to dusk when the footman arrived to lead her to Milton's study. She didn't doubt for a moment that he'd deliberately left her to stew all afternoon. So while she had intended to be polite and deferential, now she was just angry and eager to get out of there.

She didn't even wait for the servant to close the door behind her before she got right to the point. "I've come to tell you two things, Lord Allen. My—"

"Where are your manners, girl?" he cut in tersely. "Sit down."

Julia found herself obeying, sitting in the chair that he pointed to in front of his desk. She did so unthinkingly because of that autocratic tone of his that brooked no argument. He was thinner than she remembered, his hair a duller brown. And having seen Richard recently, she realized father and son bore little resemblance to each other. But she recalled Charles hadn't taken after his father, either. Both sons must pull to their mother's side of the family.

"Now," he added, just to display some of the politeness she'd been lacking, "how is your father?"

Suddenly he was smirking. Because he'd just controlled her without even half trying? She bristled and shot back to her feet. "Recovered."

He sat abruptly forward. "I beg your pardon?"

"My father has recovered. His mind is completely functional again and he grows a little stronger each day."

Apparently, like everyone else, including Gerald's doctor, Milton hadn't expected to ever hear that. His incredulity was revealed for a brief moment before he turned stiff. "How—nice," he said drily.

He didn't care. He was such a despicable man. Like father, like son. In fact, Julia suddenly realized that Milton had probably been delighted by Gerald's disability. If Richard *had* been available to marry her at any time during the last three years, since she had come of age, it would have given the Allens control of everything without having to wait for Gerald's death.

"I also came to tell you that I've seen Richard and nothing has changed between us. We still hate each other and have mutually agreed to never marry."

Milton narrowed his eyes on her. "Do you really think what either of you wants matters? But Richard will have a change of heart."

"He won't."

"Oh, he will. In about seven months. So you have that long to prepare for your wedding."

Julia felt herself approaching a screeching level. How could he say something like that and sound so confident about it, when he hadn't even seen Richard? So she counted to five, ten, should have counted to a much higher number, but the earl was staring at her with his icy blue eyes, adding nervousness to her other frazzled emotions.

She burst out, "What arbitrary number is that? You actually think you can find him in seven months?"

"I know exactly where he is."

"Where?"

"Does it matter? All that matters to you is that he will soon be available to remove the taint of old maid from you. You should be rejoicing."

She was incredulous now. Why did the nobility put so much stock into a young woman's getting married right out of the schoolroom? But he hadn't given her an answer, probably because he didn't know where Richard was, which meant he was just bluffing. He had to be.

She gritted her teeth. "*If* that mattered to me, which it doesn't, it doesn't remove the fact—"

"Are you arguing with me?" he demanded.

"No, of course—"

She stopped abruptly, realizing he was *frightening* her. With his tone of voice? Good God, how had

Richard managed to live under this man's roof all the years of his youth and manage to defy him to the point of earning beatings for it? He'd mentioned at least one of those beatings, even tried to blame her for it. She didn't doubt now that there had been many beatings. She realized if the earl *had* gained guardianship of her, she would probably have run away just as Richard did—no, she wouldn't. That guardianship would have given him complete authority over Gerald's care, too, and there was no way in heaven or hell she'd have left her father to the earl's questionable mercy.

The very thought stiffened her spine and had her amend, "Yes, I am arguing with you. And I understand why you would lie to prolong this intolerable situation—"

"How dare you!" he shouted, his cheeks florid with anger.

She flinched. She was suddenly glad his desk was between them. What had possessed her to utter that gravest of insults to a lord of the realm, even if it was true? If she were a man, he'd be demanding a duel.

"I apologize," she said quickly. "That was a bit harsh, but—"

"You're as disrespectful as Richard is. How alike you two are."

She didn't particularly like being compared to Richard, but at least her apology seemed to have mollified the earl because he'd only sneered at that last remark.

Now might be a good time to leave, before she let her anger rule her tongue again. She had been prepared to offer him money one last time if he couldn't be reasoned with, since the solicitors hadn't yet been summoned to transfer control of the family businesses and finances back to her father, but the man simply didn't deserve a penny for holding on to the contract much, much longer than he should have.

"I came here to end this amicably, but in either case, it's over," she said.

"Over?"

"Yes. I was willing to honor my end of this detestable bargain, but Richard wasn't, and he's quite old enough now to stand by that decision. So I have been stood up at the altar, as it were."

He snorted. "You haven't stood at any altar—yet. But in seven months—"

"I'm sorry, but seven more months will be four years too long. So if you can't produce the groom immediately, I am no longer obligated to wait. I am officially removing myself from the engagement to your son—with my father's blessing, I might add, since Richard long ago removed himself from it. I came here as a courtesy to tell you that, before it becomes public knowledge."

"I see," he said, a distinct iciness entering his tone. "You're going to let your father suffer the brunt of this when he's only just recovered simply because you won't wait a few more months to be married?"

"My father has assured me we'll weather the storm," she said stiffly.

The earl steepled his hands before his face for a moment, then suddenly did an about-face that amazed her. In a tone that actually sounded like concern for her, he told her, "You must realize your father tells you what you need to hear because he loves you. But I would be remiss if I didn't warn you, for your own good, what will really happen if you break your betrothal. It's not just going to reflect badly on you and your family, the social scandal it will cause and the negative effects it will have on the Miller enterprises will cause your father so much aggravation that it will quite likely upset his recovery. I'd hate to see that happen. Do you *really* want to be responsible for making your father sick again? I hadn't realized you were so selfish, girl."

She drew in her breath sharply. He was masking a threat with his so-called concern. She knew he was a horribly greedy man, but piling guilt on her now to manipulate her?

Furiously, her turquoise eyes blazing, she said, "A few more months based on what?! I've already told you I saw Richard last week and he told me to my face that he won't marry me! What could you possibly have said to him to make him change his mind? And if you don't tell me, m'lord, then we have nothing more to discuss."

She was bluffing. He'd made his point well. That damned contract was going to stand for eternity now.

She wasn't about to risk her father's health over this.

Yet he actually answered her this time. "Saying anything to Richard wouldn't have worked. He had to be shown the error of his ways. He was due punishment for the debt he deliberately left for me to settle, and for his thefts before he disappeared. That punishment could have been light, a slap on the hand, if he'd been reasonable, but as usual, he wasn't. Instead he's going to suffer the most extreme punishment."

She hadn't known Richard had committed any crimes, however minor they sounded, but she guessed, "My God, you've put your own son in prison?"

"Prison?" The earl gave her a supercilious look. "Our prisons would seem like a vacation compared to the penal colonies in Australia where he is now being transported. You aren't pleased, hating him as you do?"

The earl smiled mirthlessly as he eyed her closely. Julia fought hard not to show her alarm and to keep an indignant expression on her face.

"I've been assured he will beg to come home within weeks," he continued, shaking his head. "Those convict camps are so harsh. So prepare for your wedding, girl. Richard will be more than willing to meet his obligations here and marry you. Once the conditions of his release are met, I will allow him to come home."

Chapter Twenty-six

Julia was in shock for a good portion of the trip back to London. When she began thinking clearly again, she realized that Lord Allen had no legal right to use a British convict colony in the way he'd described. Men weren't sent there unless they'd been tried first. So the earl had to have pulled strings to bypass a trial, which was something she could do as well. But the only lords she knew who might be capable of that sort of string pulling were Carol's father and James Malory, and Carol had mentioned her father was out of the country this month.

So she didn't even go home first before knocking on the door of the Malory town house. She might have shaken off the shock, but she was still frantic. Time was of the absolute essence if Richard had been apprehended when she'd last seen him, more than a week ago, and the earl had been confident that the convict ship was already at sea. She wanted that ship stopped and Richard removed from it before too much damage was done—to him. But if it had sailed soon after he was placed on it, it could be nearly a week in the lead!

She had hoped to find the Malorys alone so she could put forward her request, but as the butler showed her to the parlor, she could already hear other voices, a few with American accents. She hoped James was at least home and not trying to avoid his wife's relatives.

But then she heard one voice in particular explaining, "I spent the whole week in that part of the country, searching, questioning people. I stopped Richard's brother from departing on a trip he'd planned with his son so he could thoroughly search their house and he did. Rich isn't there. I even checked the nearest jails. And I've run out of ideas, Gabby. He's gone, simply vanished."

Julia recognized the voice as that of Richard's friend Ohr. She reached the doorway just as he finished. James was there, expressionless as usual. Georgina and Gabrielle were sitting on the sofa, both looking concerned, though Gabrielle actually looked upset. Drew stood behind the sofa with his hand on his wife's shoulder. Boyd and Ohr sat on the sofa opposite them.

"We know he wouldn't hie off without giving us word," Gabrielle said to Ohr. "So he's here somewhere, we just have to figure out where. You say he hates his father? That's why he never spoke of him to us?"

"And he hates his fiancée. It's no wonder he never wanted to come back here."

Julia flinched. Apparently Ohr had explained something of her relationship with Richard to the group before she'd walked in on the conversation. But she certainly wasn't expecting to hear him add, "She needs to be questioned. I'll leave that to you."

"You can't really think—?"

Ohr interrupted Gabrielle, "She was in the area that day, and there was evidence of violence, that he was forcibly removed from the inn. And she *has* threatened to kill him."

"Oh, good God, I only said that in the heat of the moment," Julia said in disgust, drawing all eyes to her as she walked into the room. "I wouldn't actually do it."

James was the first to recover from her startling revelation. "*You're* the other half of the engaged couple? Yes, of course, missing fiancé and all that. What bloody irony."

Gabrielle recovered next and with a frown asked Julia, "But why did you claim to have only just met him if you've been engaged to him all your life?"

"He was wearing a mask at the ball and used a false name when he introduced himself. Jean Paul, I think it was," Julia reminded her.

"Oh, of course," Gabrielle said, then abruptly asked, "*Do* you know what's happened to him?"

"Yes."

"Oh, thank goodness!"

"No, there's no reason to be thankful," Julia said gravely. "I've just returned from the country where I spoke with his father. I went to inform the earl that I would no longer honor the marriage contract because I'd seen Richard, and as adults, we've both agreed there will be no marriage. The earl in turn told me that Richard would change his mind in seven months, so I should begin preparing for a wedding. I told him I wouldn't wait even another month. Then he threatened to ruin my family. I thought he was bluffing about the odd seven months' time schedule, so I bluffed as well and told him that without hearing a viable reason why Richard would have a sudden change of heart in that time, I wasn't changing my mind. So he gave me the reason. He mentioned some minor crimes Richard was due to be punished for and—"

"The things he did to get his father to disown him?" Ohr interjected incredulously.

"What prison is he in?" Drew asked next. "We'll get him out."

"That had been my first thought, too," Julia admitted. "But his crimes were minor enough to have been forgiven if Richard had buckled under to his father's will and agreed to marry me. He wouldn't. So the earl has had him shipped to Australia."

"But Australia's only recently been claimed by

England," James pointed out. "There's nothing there yet except . . ."

"Exactly," Julia said.

"Exactly what?" Georgina demanded, looking back and forth between them.

"Convicts, m'dear. When we lost our colonies in America," James said with a sudden grin, because that particular war had led to their first meeting in a roundabout way, "we needed somewhere new to send our worst criminals. They had it easy in America. Indentured servants were all they became. Not so in Australia. The penal colonies there have only been in operation a few years now but have already earned a reputation for their harshness and deprivation. It's a wild, untamed land. The convicts are being worked to death to tame it."

"Well, good God!" Georgina gasped. "Surely Richard's father didn't know that when he had him shipped there."

"He knows," Julia said in a small voice that actually choked up. What contrary emotion was *that*? She had to clear her throat to go on. "The earl has done this to break Richard to his will. He's an unnatural parent. I didn't think anyone could be that cruel to his own child."

"Perhaps Richard isn't his child," James suggested.

Julia just stared at him, but Georgina raised a brow at her husband. "You mean?"

"Yes. There was a Lady Allen making the rounds during my wild London days."

"You didn't!" Georgina gasped.

James chuckled. "No, I most certainly didn't. She was too easy. I might have only just been beginning my jaded career, but I still preferred a challenge. And rumor was she was deliberately cuckolding her husband out of spite and making sure it became a scandal that would reach his ears. Theirs was an arranged marriage and she despised the man."

"So she taunted him with a bastard son?"

James shrugged. "I've no idea what she did. She had her one promiscuous Season in London, then returned to the country. Don't recall her ever showing up again. But that was mere speculation, m'dear. It could likely be as Julia said, that Richard's father is simply an unnatural parent."

"Richard called him a tyrant and mentioned beatings," Julia said quietly, adding, "It didn't stop him from rebelling, though."

James nodded. "That actually sounds more on the mark. Manford wouldn't be the first man to demand absolute obedience from his family and administer harsher and harsher punishments if he didn't get it. Richard escaped his father's wrath for a good number of years and could escape again, so having got his hands on him, Manford might view this as a last resort. The boy is still keeping him from the fortune he expected, after all. And it doesn't sound as if he intends to leave him there."

"No, he doesn't," Julia said tightly. "He expects this brutal experience to utterly break Richard's will. He even implied he wouldn't arrange for his release until that condition is met."

After a moment of silence, Ohr stood up abruptly. "I'll find out when that ship sailed. If it was last week when he disappeared, it may take us weeks to catch up."

Boyd stood up with him. "No, my horse is out front, I'll go. I know these docks better than you, and the sooner we have more information, the better."

Drew said, "One of you stop by *The Triton* and let my first mate know to round up the crew. We can sail with the evening tide."

"You won't be able to get Richard off that ship," Julia pointed out.

"The hell I won't," Drew said with absolute assurance.

She sighed. "Really, you won't. You're an American with an American vessel and crew, and Richard is on a British convict ship. You might be able to get it to stop, but the captain would never willingly relinquish one of his prisoners. You'd have to fire on the ship, and Richard could die in that fight."

"Julia, we can't just let them take him to a penal colony," Gabrielle said earnestly.

"I agree," Julia replied. "I wouldn't be here if I didn't

want to stop them. But the earl pulled lordly strings to get Richard on that ship *without* a trial. It's going to take an equally powerful lord to get him off of it."

Everyone in the room looked immediately at James Malory. His scowl came just as quickly. "No," he said with flat finality.

Georgina stood up and approached her husband. "James" was all she said.

He turned his scowl on her. "Are you out of your mind, George? Think I don't know all this concern is for that blighter who lusts after you? I'll help him to his grave and no further."

Georgina ignored that and reminded him, "You also have the faster ship."

"A crewless ship," he was quick to point out. "It would take days to round—"

"You can have my crew," Drew cut in. "Gabby and I will go with you, of course, since Richard's our friend."

"You're *not* captaining my ship, Yank," James warned his brother-in-law.

"No, of course not."

But Drew was grinning as he came around the sofa to sit next to his wife. Those two at least considered the matter settled. Julia wasn't so sure yet. But then she watched Georgina hug her husband.

"You're a good man," Georgina said.

James sighed. "No, I'm a good *husband*. There's a bloody difference."

Julia finally said, "Thank you, James. I confess I had my hopes set on you. I don't know any other lords well enough to have asked for this sort of assistance."

Georgina hadn't let go of James yet, so he raised a golden brow at Julia over his wife's head. "Just explain to me, if you will, why you came here to get help for a man you profess to hate? Bit contradictory, ain't it?"

She raised a brow back at him. "You think I would prefer that he be brought home broken and willing to marry me when it's not what he wants a'tall?"

"Good point," James said. "And since this engagement is apparently all for the sake of money, I'm going to assume you've already tried to buy your way out of that contract?"

"My father did, more'n once, but the earl always refused. He wants to gain access to my family's entire fortune through the marriage."

"This infamous contract grants him that?"

"No, but he's a lord and my father isn't. He's always assumed that as a relative, he'd more or less have an unlimited supply of funds. And I'll be damned if I'll give up centuries of my family's hard work to one man's greed. I'd as soon kill him than—"

"You want us to kill him for you?"

James said it with such a serious expression and tone, Julia had a feeling he might not be joking! "No, of course not. I didn't really mean that. I have a terrible habit of saying things I don't really mean when

I'm angry, and the earl makes me so furious I could scream."

"Please don't."

She grinned at James's dry tone. "Manford did this terrible thing before he knew of my father's recovery. There's never really been any doubt that I would comply with the contract to honor my father's word—until this week, when my father told me to forget about it. But the earl didn't know this yet, and if he could get Richard under his control, then Milton obviously thought he'd have it all. Now that my father has recovered, that certainly isn't going to happen. But in any case, I would like to sail with you, if you don't mind. Richard and I need to resolve our betrothal and figure out a way to prevent this from ever happening again. And he's not likely to stick around long enough for us to do that when you bring him back here."

"Does that really matter now, when you have your father's blessing to ignore the contract?"

"It does until my father is fully recovered. I'm not going to risk *anything* disturbing that recovery, including the scandal the earl has promised will result from my not fulfilling the contract."

James nodded. "As you wish."

Georgina let go of James and headed for the door. "I'll go pack our bags."

"You'll pack *my* bag, George," James said adamantly.

"You aren't going anywhere near that damned pirate again."

Pirate seemed an odd epithet under the circumstances, Julia thought, even a bit mild coming from James. But no one else there seemed to think so.

Georgina swung around. "You're going to make me miss what sounds like an exciting trip just because of a little jealousy?"

His golden brow shot up once more. "You had doubts?"

"But—"

"You gained one amazing feat today, George. I agreed to rescue the blighter. Don't press your luck."

She nodded reluctantly. He relented enough to add, "You won't miss anything, m'dear. I'm not going to demand his release without documents to back it up. And I know just who to see to obtain those documents. All aboveboard. Quick. We'll be back in a few days."

Chapter Twenty-seven

JULIA HAD BORROWED James Malory's words to assure her father late that afternoon that she wouldn't be gone long. She'd stood in quite a big puddle of guilt while she'd confessed to him what she had set in motion—and related what the Earl of Manford had done to Richard and what the earl had predicted would befall the Millers. The scandal and all repercussions from it weren't going to blow over as her father had thought. The earl would see to that.

"I'm so sorry," she'd ended. "I just got used to doing what needed to be done without discussing it with anyone first, and this needed to be done without delay. So it's all been arranged, Lord Malory has agreed to help. His ship sails with the next tide—and I'm going to be on it."

"You? Why?"

"Because I refuse to reward the Earl of Manford for being evil. There has to be a way out of this contract without his harming our businesses and besmirching our family's good name. Richard's answer was to disappear, but that's not an option for me. So I'm helping Richard out of this horrendous situation his own father has forced on him. Now he will be beholden to help me figure out a way to end this."

"And that's all you're hoping for?"

"Yes—of course."

Why had she blushed when she'd said that? She still didn't know. But he must not have noticed because all he'd said was "You really have grown up, haven't you, dearest?"

She didn't feel grown-up as she stood on the deck of *The Maiden George* three days later. The vast ocean surrounding the ship could make anyone feel small and insignificant. Even the convict ship appeared as only a dot on the horizon.

James and Drew had spotted the other vessel last night. They could have reached it sooner if they hadn't run into a storm while crossing the Channel that first night. James's ship was unusually fast because he'd removed all the cannon for his last trip, when speed had been essential. But the transport ship had left London only two days before they had set sail, not a whole week earlier as they'd initially thought. Apparently, convict ships could be docked in London for weeks, even months, because they wouldn't sail until they had a full load of convicts to deliver.

James had insisted they wait until morning to close the gap between the ships. No one had argued with him because his reasoning was sound. He didn't want British officers who were eager for their beds to be making decisions rashly. That could lead to unnecessary conflict.

Gabrielle joined Julia as *The Maiden George* raced to catch up to the convict ship. Gabrielle said nothing, just offered quiet support. Julia needed that. She was afraid they'd find Richard ill because of this ordeal, maybe even physically hurt again, too hurt to be reasoned with. And she would have only a couple of days with him.

But then she found herself talking to her new friend about her fiancé. Whatever Ohr had told them would have been Richard's version. Not that she wanted to paint herself blameless when she wasn't. Her temper and Richard's snobby, nasty remarks had been a volatile combination. They were equally at fault for never being able to get along.

"I had such a terrible temper back then," Julia admitted, ending the tale. "And he always seemed to know just how to provoke it."

"Do you still?"

Julia chuckled. "I don't really know! I don't recall any tantrums after Richard's last visit. But just thinking about him still makes me angry, so I stopped thinking about him."

"That doesn't sound like the Richard I know," Gabrielle said. "From the time I first met him, he was a happy-go-lucky charmer, always grinning or laughing, always teasing and joking about something with his friends. He appeared not to have a serious bone in his body."

Hearing that, Julia felt a wave of sadness and guilt that turned her stomach. Had she taken the joy of life from him when they were children? She'd seen glimpses of the man Gabrielle knew and cared about. The teasing charmer Julia first met at the ball before she knew who he really was. The gallant man at the hotel who had jumped up and swatted a bee away from her despite his sore body. The laughing man at the hostelry who had tossed her on his bed and kissed her—that definitely hadn't been the old Richard! Of course, he was an adult now, and her old nemesis resurfaced directly after that kiss.

"You're right, we've described two different men," Julia said quietly. "In all those meetings I had with him through the years, I never once, ever, saw him smile. He sneered a lot though."

"Amazing how a few years can change someone, isn't it?" Gabrielle asked.

"Years, possibly, but more likely circumstances. You met and knew the man who had left his troubles far behind. Away from his father and the threat of an unwanted marriage, he found peace, I guess, and became the man he always could have been if he hadn't grown up with a tyrant for a father. And I'm sure he will again be the man *you* know, once he puts all this behind him."

"But you've had it just as hard, haven't you? With this unwanted marriage always hanging over your head?"

"It wasn't so bad when we were children. Once I went home from those visits, or Richard did, my life returned to normal and I was quite happy. It was only when I reached a marriageable age that I began to worry about my future. I do want children after all, a real husband. Love."

"Do you have someone in mind?"

Julia laughed bitterly. "I've been engaged all my life, and to a lord no less. Everyone knows that. The men of my acquaintance treat me as if I'm already married. I was only *just* going to start looking for a husband because enough time had passed and I was having Richard declared dead. Then he showed up and ruined that plan."

Gabrielle flinched. "This is such a sad situation. Richard's never caused me any worry, until his misguided infatuation with a married woman, but that is *nothing,* compared to his being hauled off to a penal colony on the other side of the world! But who could imagine a father like his." Gabrielle sighed. "I wouldn't be surprised if James had the right of it. The earl probably isn't Richard's real father and has treated him so abominably because he was forced to accept and raise his wife's bastard."

"You mean a convoluted punishment for *her* sins taken out on the boy, revenge as it were?"

Gabrielle nodded. "More understandable than a parent being this cruel—unless he's insane."

"No, he's not insane. If he is, he's able to mask it with a normal facade."

"Ohr said Richard truly hates his father, so I don't doubt that he would prefer it if he *was* a bastard."

"That doesn't get him and me out of this situation, though," Julia said. "Throwing that in the earl's face isn't going to make him hand over that horrible contract. By law, Richard bears his name, and so he fulfills the requirement of the contract, bastard or not."

"Time to go below deck, ladies," Drew said as he walked up to his wife and put an arm around her waist. "While it's reasonable that the man's fiancée and friends would come along to see to him released, James doesn't want the distraction of women on deck."

Gabrielle snorted at her husband. "That ship is only five days out of England. They aren't starving for the sight of a woman yet."

"Are *you* going to argue with James about it?"

Gabrielle chuckled at him. "Not a chance. Come along, Julia. We should probably let Richard get cleaned up before we talk to him anyway. I don't doubt it's going to be all he's thinking about, after being locked up for over a week. He's so meticulous about his appearance. He can dress in rags but they have to be clean rags! I always thought that was a little odd, but of course I had no idea he was a lord. More understandable, knowing that. Lordly types do seem to be raised to always put their best appearance forward."

Julia realized how little she knew about the man she'd been engaged to all her life. But she had to agree with Gabrielle's last remark. She couldn't recall ever seeing Richard other than neatly attired and clean. Another edict of the earl's, that his boys weren't allowed to ever get dirty?

They were nearly abreast of the other ship. Julia hadn't even noticed, they'd been so deep in conversation. She was suddenly beset with acute nervousness.

"I'm glad you're so confident of the outcome of our intervention here," she said to the couple.

Drew replied, "Don't worry. Never known a man who could twist arms as well as James Malory can."

Chapter Twenty-eight

JAMES SUMMONED DREW before he crossed over to the transport ship. James had dressed for the occasion. He didn't often make the effort to look so lordly, but today he did. Though his white cravat wasn't excessive, his buff-colored jacket was superbly cut, his boots gleamed, and his waistcoat was of the finest silk.

"You come with me," James said. "If the captain denies his involvement in this plot, someone who knows Richard will have to go down in the hold to point him out."

"I take it you'd rather not?"

"It's not a matter of druthers, Yank. After I establish how bloody high and mighty I am, the captain will find it more plausible if I decline to enter his hold and delegate the onerous task to Richard's manservant. The stink, you know. It's bound to reek already."

Drew choked back a laugh. "So I'm to play the role of servant who can't afford to be so fastidious?"

"Exactly, and not one bloody word from you or you'll give away your nationality."

"Oh, come now." Drew grinned. "Americans make just as good servants as Englishmen do."

"Perhaps, but an English *lord* wouldn't be caught dead with one."

That was an old dig. James was much too fond of referring to Americans as barbarians to ever admit it just wasn't so. And Drew had grown immune to those particular digs over the years. Mostly.

The captain didn't meet them on deck, but they were shown directly to his cabin. Having them brought to him was a rather obvious tactic to establish his superiority. Which evaporated as soon as James introduced himself.

"James Malory, Viscount Ryding. Good of you to see us, Captain. . . ?"

"Cantel," the man answered as he leapt to his feet behind his desk.

"Captain Cantel." James tilted his head slightly in greeting. Drew had to admire James's own tactic. Earlier, Drew had shouted across decks that the matter was urgent, which got the other ship to lower their sails and prepare to be boarded. But James had just put the captain at ease with his cordial greeting. To leave him unprepared for a broadside . . .

The first salvo took the form of the official documents James took out of his breast pocket and dropped on the desk. The captain gave him a curious look as he picked them up and began reading one. He began to frown. James didn't wait for him to finish reading.

"As you can see, it has come to our attention that you are transporting an innocent man. You are to release him to me immediately."

Captain Cantel didn't answer for a moment. He was still reading, then his eyes flared wide. "One of the prisoners is a lord? Mistakes of this magnitude don't happen, Lord Malory. There is no one by this name in my hold."

"Hadn't thought you'd be stupid," James said drily. "But I'll allow that you already fully understand the consequences of your involvement in this plot, so I actually can't blame you for trying to deny it."

Captain Cantel's face flushed with color. "Truly, I have no idea what you're talking about. I can show you my manifest. Every prisoner below is listed and accounted for." Then he barked an order to the crewman who'd escorted them: "Go take a head count."

"Stand where you are," James countered that order in a tone that paralyzed the sailor.

"Now see here—," Cantel began to bluster.

"You don't actually think I'm going to give you the opportunity to hide the evidence, do you?"

"Don't insult me any more than you already have, Lord Malory."

"Or?"

Drew groaned inwardly. James was supposed to be pulling rank, not throwing weight, but Drew had to allow his brother-in-law was much more accustomed to the latter.

James didn't give the man a chance to answer, adding, "You aren't thinking of actually crossing me, are you?" He unexpectedly grabbed the crewman standing next to him by his shirtfront, lifted him by it, and slammed one of his meaty fists into his face. He let the fellow fall slowly to the floor, quite knocked out, before he glanced at the captain again and said with distinct menace, "I wouldn't advise it."

"This is an outrage," the captain blustered, but his statement lacked any heat.

"I quite agree. Lords of the realm aren't dealt with in this manner, no matter their crimes. You do realize that, correct?"

"Of course."

"Very well. Against my better judgment, I'm going to give you the benefit of the doubt that you actually didn't know anything about this. I suppose the earl's son could have been handed over to you with a false name, might even have been unconscious and therefore unable to correct this outrage before it went any further. Although," James added thoughtfully, "he's more'n likely to have been shouting who he really is loud enough to have been heard back in London."

"The guards wouldn't have believed him," Cantel said quickly, obviously preferring James's last version if he had to hand over his prisoner, but he was foolish enough to try one last time not to, adding, "I'll have the guards questioned immediately. You'll see that someone has been misinformed over the whereabouts of Lord Allen."

"And waste even more of my time? I think not. Here are your three options. You can hand Lord Allen over to me now and you might be able to talk your way out of losing your commission when you return home. Highly doubtful, but I'm sure you'll find that option preferable to being arrested at your next port."

"You don't have that authority!"

"Doubt my credentials, do you? Perhaps you haven't heard of my family?" Then James added in an appalled tone, "Good God, am I actually about to drop names?"

Drew almost laughed. But James's attempt to ease tensions, if that's what his last comment was intended for, worked.

"That isn't necessary," the captain said. "Your family is well known, Lord Malory. Shall we adjourn to the hold to see if this missing lord was erroneously placed on my ship?"

Maintaining innocence to the last? James wasn't fooled. Lifting one tawny brow, he said, "Me? In the bowels of a convict ship? Not bloody likely. Allen's manservant here was brought along to identify him. Issue the order directly."

The captain nodded curtly and moved to the door to shout for his first mate before returning to his desk. After a few minutes the man arrived.

The first mate stared pointedly at the unconscious crewman on the floor as he entered the cabin. This prompted the captain's impatient explanation "A disciplinary matter." Then: "These gentlemen have come to retrieve an innocent man we may mistakenly be transporting. If it's true, he's to be released immediately. His manservant here can identify him."

Drew was following the first mate out the door when he heard Captain Cantel ask James, "What was the third option, Lord Malory?"

"That I kill you."

Chapter Twenty-nine

I THOUGHT I WAS done for. You wouldn't believe some of the punishments those guards taunted us with," Richard said.

He'd bathed. Ohr had brought along Richard's bag of clothes so he'd had clean ones to change into. Now all he could think about was food and stuffing himself until he couldn't take another bite.

He hadn't had a good meal since he'd been dragged out of that hostelry near Willow Woods more than a week ago. The ship served nothing but gruel before it departed, but at least fresh bread went with it. As soon as they sailed, the bread stopped coming with the gruel, and one guard had laughed that the slop they were being fed would stop, too, as soon as supplies ran low, because of the lack of ports on the last half of the three-month journey where supplies could be replenished.

Most of the less hardy prisoners weren't expected to survive the trip.

That wasn't even the worst of the guards' taunts of near starvation, backbreaking work, whippings at the whim of the guards, containment in cells so small a man couldn't even lie supine to sleep. The convicts at the colony killed each other just so they would be hanged in order to escape that hell. That's what the prisoners on that ship had been told they had to look forward to *if* they survived the trip.

"Did your father *really* do this to you?" Drew asked.

"Yes, and I'm not even surprised. He used to have servants beat me and lock me in my room."

"Hardly the same thing," Drew pointed out in a somber tone. "But how did they even get you on that ship without proper documents?"

Drew and Ohr were the only ones with Richard in the main cabin. Food had been set out on a table for him.

From the moment Drew had appeared in the convict ship's hold and the chains had been removed from his hands and feet, Richard had been on the brink of laughter. He was still incredulous and overwhelmed with relief. He'd hoped, prayed, to be rescued before the transport ship sailed and had completely given up hope when it did.

"My father is friendly with the local magistrate," Richard explained. "But worse luck, the captain of that ship was the man's brother. The captain wasn't going to take me. They had an argument. But I guess a favor got called in, since I was tossed in the hold with the rest of the prisoners. Don't think the captain was even told who I was. Don't think it would have mattered by then. But how did you find me? Did you beat the hell out of my father to get him to confess?"

Richard asked that of Ohr and would have preferred to hear a yes, but Ohr smiled wryly and said, "No, that didn't even occur to me. After I had your brother search your old home, and he assured me your father was behaving quite normally, I—"

"That man has no emotions," Richard cut in. "So his behavior wouldn't have revealed anything."

"He wouldn't even be gloating that he was finally getting what he wants?"

"Oh, he would," Richard said bitterly. "But he'd keep it to himself. He certainly wouldn't let Charles see it. He knows Charles and I are close. If Charles found out about this, it would sever their relationship for good, pitiful as that relationship is."

"Well, in either case, I erroneously concluded that your father wasn't even involved."

"Wish you hadn't let my brother know I was missing. I don't like to think of him worrying."

Drew laughed. "But it was all right for the rest of us to worry?"

Richard grinned. "I expected you to rescue me and

so you have. But Charles wouldn't have had a clue how to get me out of this."

"I didn't leave him worrying," Ohr assured Richard. "I told him you've taken off on me before and I probably just missed a note you left behind saying so. But he searched that place for me early the next morning, so you must have been taken out of there that same night?"

"Immediately after the interview with my father, yes, straight to jail for the night, then tossed in a coach at dawn for the trip to the London docks."

"Damn, I checked the jails, too, but not until the next day. And after searching the entire area for nearly a week, I ran out of ideas and returned to London."

Richard frowned. "I don't get it. How'd you find me then?"

"How tedious," James said as he walked in. "You could have fed him in his cabin, not mine."

Richard leapt to his feet, his body tensing instinctively in preparation for another pounding at Malory's lethal hands. "*Your* cabin?"

"Relax, Richard," Drew quickly intervened. "We couldn't have done this without his help. The captain of that ship would have laughed at us if we'd demanded your release. A member of the nobility put you on that ship, and it took another lord to get you off of it."

"Actually," James said as he crossed over to sit on the edge of his desk, "as soon as I mentioned the illegality of his transporting an English lord in his hold, Captain Cantel tried to deny he had you. Could smell his guilt, though. So I merely mentioned a few consequences to get his cooperation."

Drew burst out laughing. "You do manage to get your points across quite—unusually."

James shrugged. "A knack."

He'd left the door open. Gabrielle rushed in and, with a shriek of gladness, leapt at Richard and hugged him. Laughing, he swung her around in his arms. Damn, it was good to be back among his friends. He'd begun to think he'd never see them again.

"My God, Richard, don't ever do this to me again!" Gabrielle exclaimed at him.

"You?" He chuckled.

She backed up and slapped his chest lightly. "I'm serious! This was as bad as LeCross putting my father in his dungeon just so he could get his hands on me. But that pirate was an evil man and I wouldn't have thought twice about blasting him out of the water. But this was a British ship. We couldn't fire on them to get you back without starting another war!"

"And I'm glad you didn't! Don't think I would have liked going down with that ship if you'd managed to sink it."

"Well, there was that consideration, too," she huffed.

Then Richard glanced at James and mumbled, "Bloody hell, I suppose I must thank you."

"Don't," James replied. "You and I know where we stand. I wouldn't be here if my wife didn't have a soft heart."

Richard started to beam in delight that Georgina had intervened to help him, but thought better of it. He didn't *really* want another beating at Malory's hands. But he was still confused. Even if Abel Cantel had experienced a pang of conscience about stepping outside the law as he'd done, and Richard couldn't think of anyone else who would have set this rescue in motion, Cantel wouldn't have known who Richard's friends were to tell them about it.

"I'd still like to know how—?" he began, but stopped cold.

Julia had appeared in the open doorway. Looking at her, he felt a strange mixture of anger and desire. She was still the quick-tempered hellcat he remembered, but she had other tools at her disposal now. Her luscious body. Damn, that woman had grown some nice curves, and he resented how much he actually wanted her. But then his eyes met hers and the anger took precedence. It always came back to her, the reason for his father's greed and why he'd nearly died for it this time. He didn't doubt that would have been the final outcome.

"How—unexpected," he said sardonically. "Hoping for a different resolution, Jewels?"

She frowned. "What are you implying?"

"I know we got a bit carried away the last time we saw each other." His eyes swept over her suggestively. "But I guess I should have also remembered that you told me you were going to have me declared dead—or pay someone to kill me. Don't tell me you paid my father to do your dirty work for you?" At her shocked look, he added angrily, "No? Never mind, just stay out of my sight. This wouldn't have happened if not for you and your damned money."

She turned about and left. Absolute silence followed her departure. He glanced around uncomfortably to see his friends staring at him appalled.

James said contemptuously, "What a bloody ass."

But it was the disappointment in Gabby's eyes that made Richard defensive. "What? You have no idea what has passed between her and me. She'd be delighted if my father's form of punishment had ended in my demise."

"Actually, Richard, I *have* heard both sides of that childhood feud," Gabrielle said in disgust. "A feud that got out of hand because you couldn't really fight it out. Had she been a boy, you two would have broken each other's noses when you were children and laughed about it when you were adults."

"She *did* break my nose," Richard said, stabbing a finger at the small bump on the bridge of his nose.

"Pity," James interjected. "I'd hoped I'd done that."

Neither Gabrielle nor Richard acknowledged James's drollery as she continued to berate Richard. "Yes, and because you wouldn't hit a girl, you held her over balconies instead."

He flushed, embarrassed that she knew about that. He wasn't proud of what he'd done. He'd just been sick to death of bleeding every time Julia got near enough to bite him. But Gabrielle wasn't done with making him feel guilty.

"We wouldn't have had a single clue where to find you, Richard, if Julia hadn't come and told us what your father had done. And she did that because she didn't want this to happen to you."

"She spoke to my father?" Richard said incredulously.

"Yes, she's the one who asked James to rescue you. Ohr, Drew, and I just came along in case we could help in some way. Does that sound like a woman who wants you to die?"

Richard sighed. "It sounds like I owe her an apology."

James couldn't resist saying, "D'you think?"

But again he was ignored as Richard said on his way out of the cabin, "Excuse me while I go eat some crow."

Chapter Thirty

JULIA NO SOONER slammed shut the door to her cabin than her eyes filled with tears. Again, anger and hurt were tearing her apart. Unable to control her strong emotions, she felt like a little girl again, helpless, weak, and never able to win when it came to *him*. How could Richard still be so nasty after what she'd done for him?

Wiping tears on her sleeve wasn't effective when the tears kept coming. She picked up a towel from the washstand to dry her face when she heard the doors in the hallway opening and closing. She glanced behind her and stared at the doorknob, then suddenly rushed forward to turn the lock—too late. The door was pushed open.

"You *would* have to be in the last cabin I checked," Richard said as he walked in and closed the door behind him.

He didn't ask for permission to enter her room. That was so like him. And he sounded aggrieved. But all she could think about was hiding the evidence that he'd made her cry. She turned her back on him and swiped the towel over her eyes and cheeks.

"Were you crying?" he asked suspiciously.

"No," she quickly denied. "I was washing my face when I heard all the racket you were making out there and thought to lock my door."

She turned around. He wasn't smirking in doubt, he was actually blushing. He didn't look as if he'd just suffered a horrible ordeal this last week. His long black hair looked clean and was neatly queued back. He was wearing a flowing white shirt tucked into black britches that were tucked into knee-high boots. The boots were scuffed, he'd probably worn them all week, but the clothes were fresh. The bruises on his face had healed, leaving him so damned handsome she found herself staring almost hypnotically at him, and even *that* infuriated her.

"I believe I owe you an apology," he said.

She snapped, "D'you think?"

"Don't go sounding like Malory," he warned.

She drew in her breath sharply. This was the attitude of an apologetic man? "Just get out! You couldn't bear the sight of me? I feel the same way about you. There's the door."

He didn't budge. He looked perplexed when he said,

"Gabby mentioned that you went to see my father and that's how you found out about this. But why did you go there? When? I could have sworn I saw you heading back to London that day you came to the inn."

"I did go home. But I felt I had to make one last attempt to end the contract amicably, so I returned to Willow Woods. It was a futile effort. In the guise of concern, your father clearly laid out what would happen to my family if I didn't prepare for my wedding. I thought he was bluffing about having seen you and was trying to convince me that you'd be a willing groom. He finally told me why you'd be willing and what he had set in motion to assure it."

Richard winced. "I'm sorry you had to talk to that tyrant for any reason. I'm also sorry I lashed out at you. Thank you for organizing my rescue. You do have your moments when you can be a sweetheart." He grinned. "Do you accept my apology?"

She was still too upset to be gracious. She was amazed she had even answered his other question without screaming at him. But this one?

"Are you kidding me?! You'd have to apologize a thousand times to assuage all the hurt you've caused me."

"Must you always exaggerate? I never hurt you, I made you angry. There's a big difference."

"Do you know how many things I missed out on growing up because of you! No boys ever flirted with me because I was already spoken for. I didn't get to have an exciting come-out while all my friends were planning theirs. Why? Because I was already engaged! I should have married three years ago. Now, the *ton* calls me an old maid!"

She'd made each of those things sound like an accusation, which turned him quite stiff. "You would rather I had stuck around so we could have married and ended up killing each other?" he asked her incredulously.

"We wouldn't have done that, you ass."

"You swore you would—"

She cut in, "I say things in anger that I don't mean. Don't you?"

"I'm not talking premeditated murder. I'm talking about the violence of the moment. You know bloody well you never had control of that."

"Doesn't matter. I don't have it in me to kill anyone, even you. So no matter how furious you make me, it would never come to that."

"Like hell. You bit off my ear! Did you forget about that?"

She snorted. "Now who's exaggerating?"

"You tried, Jewels. You *always* went for blood."

She blushed over *that* reminder. "You were too strong. I had no other way to fight you."

"You didn't have to fight me at all!" he said in exasperation.

"You hurt my feelings," she said in a small voice, her

lip beginning to quiver, her eyes turning glassy again. "You always did. I wasn't quick enough back then with a sharp comeback to pay you back in kind."

"Good God, are you crying?"

She swung around instantly. "Get out."

He didn't. She heard him move toward her, not away. He came so close she could actually smell him behind her—then felt his hands on her shoulders. It was too much for her fragile emotions. She turned around to pound her fists against his chest. He wrapped his arms around her to prevent it, but oddly enough she found his touch comforting. He was actually trying to soothe her? It just made her cry all the harder, great racking sobs that wet his shirt and wouldn't stop. It had been so long since she'd had a shoulder to cry on. Actually, she'd cried on her father's shoulder a number of times, missing him so much, but he hadn't been awake to notice, and remembering that brought on even more tears.

"Don't," Richard said softly, trying to wipe her cheek with his fingers.

"Don't," he said again, smoothing a hand over her head now, but all that did was dislodge her hairpins so half her coiffure tumbled down her back. He threaded his fingers through her hair now, dislodging the rest of the hairpins.

"Please, don't," he said, and kissed her brow. Twice. And so tenderly.

His soothing tone was working wonders. She wondered why he'd want to comfort her. Guilt? Or was he finding comfort as well from his own ordeal? He was a man. He probably wouldn't allow himself the luxury of tears, but she found herself hugging him—just in case he needed it.

His soothing touch was also working wonders, though in a different way. One hand in her hair, the other moving up and down her back with just the slightest pressure. He wasn't actually holding her there against him now, but she didn't even consider moving away. She wasn't feeling any angry passion at the moment that could explode into something else. But that something else was happening anyway.

He tried to wipe her cheek again, with his. She tilted her head a little and it worked, and suddenly he was kissing her. This could just be his way of comforting, too, but that's not what it was for her.

Her tears dried up. The escalating warmth running through her veins might have helped. That kiss was so gentle, but it was still churning her insides with exciting flutters. This was—romantic, a careful introduction to the more sensual side of life. It's what should have happened when she was eighteen and married—him. She blanked out that thought. She wasn't going to let their past intrude just now.

The kiss got a little more intimate, his tongue asserting dominance to explore her mouth. Even the taste of him was thrilling her senses. She hugged him more tightly. He cupped her face in the palms of his hands, his fingers spreading to the back of her neck, sending shivers down her spine.

But then he suddenly broke the kiss and looked down at her. His green eyes were hot and questioning. Her eyes remained lambent. Was he giving her a chance to stop what was happening between them? But it was only a brief chance. The next kiss was much more provocative and all the more thrilling for the decision that had just been mutually, if silently, made.

He began unbuttoning her blouse. She pulled his shirt from his pants. They were both moving slowly to keep from breaking that kiss. There was no hurry—yet. Desire was growing stronger, but it was just as exciting to savor it. Her skirt came undone and drifted down her hips. His hand slipped under the back of her drawers to squeeze a plump cheek before he pressed her against his loins.

Oh, God, nothing about that was sensually lazy! She immediately wrapped her arms tightly about his neck with a moan. He lifted her higher and curved one of her legs about his hips, so she did the same with the other. He walked her to the bed like that, with her limbs holding fast to him, and laid her down carefully at the edge. He didn't follow her down. He stood there at the edge and yanked off his shirt and unfastened his pants. She was mesmerized by him. He really had matured into a strapping young man, with thick muscles, limbs tautly corded with them, such long legs, lean hips. And his hair, oh, my, that extremely long, raven black hair that gave him such a wild, primitive look when it flowed loose as it did now.

But the look in his eyes, when she finally caught them again, held her fast. Not the heated passion. That was there, but something else was as well, need, a deep longing, as if this were something he'd waited for forever. Was she imagining it? She could have said that of herself, but him? Yet she was spellbound by the longing in his eyes. It struck just the right chord in her to make her hold out her arms to him.

With a groan he whisked off her drawers and leaned forward to slide his hands up under her chemise. The flimsy strings holding it together easily widened with both his hands stretching it as he learned the feel of her breasts, and they came completely undone by the time he bent farther to capture one of her breasts in his mouth.

She held him fast with her arms, with her legs. The sensations he was stirring seemed to spiral straight down to her core. It frazzled her senses. She couldn't be still. She was pushing at him, squirming, demanding—something. Then she had it, so quickly, that hard, thick pressure at her loins sliding forward, penetrating directly where it was needed. It was such a welcome relief that he knew how to fix what was wrong with her that she barely felt the brief pain before he filled her fully.

How amazing! Such a glorious feeling, to have him so deeply inside her. She was held breathless with anticipation. But he didn't move! At least his loins remained perfectly still, pinning her there to the bed, while his mouth touched and explored hers again. She didn't know why she felt so desperate and needy, but she kissed him back furiously because of it, wildly, tempestuously, about to burst with suppressed passion screaming for release.

He finally broke that kiss with another groan, reared back, and then thrust into her. He didn't have to do another thing. Oh, God, the pleasure that burst forth was beyond anything she could have imagined. It gushed, spread clear to her toes. Each slow thrust dazzled her even more, had her holding fast to him for that glorious ride.

It ended all too quickly. She was only vaguely disappointed that those amazing sensations couldn't have lasted much longer. But he threw back his head, stiffened, actually looked as if he were in pain, then let out the breath he'd been holding in an exultant cry before he dropped his head to her shoulder, panting. After one tender kiss on her neck, she felt his entire body rest against hers.

The tenderness that welled in her was astounding.

Chapter Thirty-one

THE BLOOM HAD worn off, but it had lingered long enough for Julia to know that she didn't want to fight with Richard anymore—at least not today. They were still lying on the bed, lengthwise now. When he'd raised himself off her, he'd immediately picked her up, positioning her on her side with her head on a pillow, then joined her again, curling into her backside. He'd kissed her shoulder and put an arm around her to pretty much keep her there.

At least he hadn't immediately deserted her when she'd still been feeling a unique sort of bond with him. That would have hurt. While they were still fully touching, at least their bodies were, neither of them had moved for the longest time.

She finally began to think he'd fallen asleep, cuddled against her, which might be a good thing. She wasn't sure what to say to him now, after what they'd done.

She was afraid the subject she was there to discuss was going to utterly end this fragile truce. Actually, she didn't even know if this could be considered a truce. She might be feeling exceptionally mellow, but she had no idea how this unexpected occurrence was going to affect him. He'd been angry after kissing her at the inn, blaming her for what shouldn't have happened. This went so far beyond that there was no comparison.

She finally knew what lovemaking was all about, and it had been wonderful. But she didn't deceive herself into thinking she couldn't experience that excitement again with someone she could love. Not only Richard could stir those desires in her. She might be strongly attracted to him, even liked him—sometimes. He could have been that perfect someone for her if only they had met under different circumstances and they didn't have the ugly history of the marriage contract between them. Instead he was her perfect nemesis! Until she got rid of him, she wouldn't find that one man who was out there somewhere, waiting for her to come along.

She ought to get up and dress. The windowless cabin wasn't cold, but it still wasn't warm enough to be lying there naked and uncovered. Yet she wasn't chilled at all, not with Richard sharing the heat of his body. Besides, she couldn't quite bring herself to break contact with him.

She sighed. Why was she even enjoying just lying there with him?

He must have heard the sound she made because he finally spoke to her. His tone was merely conversational, yet the subject was so far from anything she could have imagined, she was floored.

"You scare me, Jewels. I've never experienced this before with a woman. You kiss my shoulder, you could as likely sink your teeth into it. I kiss your mouth, you could try to take my lip off. I take my life in hand, getting close to you. No, don't be insulted." He laughed as her whole body stiffened. "I'm not saying this is a bad thing. It's actually oddly exciting."

The laugh made her hold her tongue. She turned onto her back so she could glance at him. Yes, it was even in his eyes, sparkling laughter, and he was still grinning with it. Gabrielle knew and counted this man as a friend. This wasn't the man Julia knew. She had no way to tell, no reference to draw on, to know if he was joking, so she didn't try for a witty reply, in case he *was* serious.

But, apparently, he was in a speculating mood, or merely a roguish one, because he went on, "It's too bad we were too young for this back then. I guarantee a harsh word would never have passed between us."

"Don't count on it." She grinned, reminding him, "You were a snob."

He laughed again. "A little perhaps, but not toward you. You could have been a queen and I wouldn't have behaved any differently. It was never you that I fought against; it was my father handpicking my bride without even asking me. It was my not having any sort of control over my own life that was the focal point of my rage."

The subject was getting touchy, yet their emotions were remaining neutral for the moment, at least hers were. That they could discuss this without going for each other's throat was amazing.

Then his tone did turn somber when he continued, "When I was sixteen, I'd gotten too big for Father to take a stick to. I took it from him when he tried to hit me with it. He hired his brutes then to enforce his will. Do you know what it's like to be beaten by servants who actually hated the aristocracy and took perverted pleasure in being ordered to teach me a 'lesson'? Then they threw me at father's feet, and all he said was 'Maybe next time you'll do what you're told.' What sort of man is that uncaring about his own son?"

"One who hates you?"

"Hates? Nonsense. All the hate is on my side. I'm quite sure he simply knows no other way to be."

That attitude annoyed her, particularly after the memory he'd just shared, which actually had her feeling sorry for him. "Don't make excuses for him, Richard, just because he's your father."

He raised a brow. "What part did you miss about how much I hate him?"

He was taking offense. The conversation might have

ended abruptly if she hadn't shocked him by asking, "Are you certain he's your real father?"

"Of course he is. How many times I've wished he wasn't, but he is."

"But *how* do you know?"

"Because I wasn't singled out for his harsh discipline. Charles was treated the same; he just buckled under and never fought it like I did. And when Father wasn't dispensing punishments, he was usually cordial to both of us. Not loving, mind you. He was never that. But he never displayed any sort of hate, either, just anger whenever we broke his rules or didn't jump immediately to obedience. And that's how he was raised, you know, so I suppose he thought what worked on him would work on his own sons. Bad parents raising more bad parents," Richard ended in disgust.

"Nonsense, or are you saying you'd raise your own children that way?"

"God, no!"

"Exactly, so that's no excuse for your father's atrocious treatment of his children."

She knew about his mother's promiscuous Season in London, but she wasn't sure she wanted to mention that when it sounded as if Richard didn't even know about it, and he was already much too defensive about the subject. If he and his brother *had* been treated equally, then perhaps James's speculation about Richard's being a bastard had been off the mark.

So she ended with "He's simply evil."

"There we go agreeing again."

Richard didn't sound the least bit amused and sat up on the edge of the bed and put on his pants. With his warmth gone so abruptly, she was acutely aware of her own nakedness, but her clothes were out in the middle of the room where he'd dropped them. As she started to get under the covers, he tossed her blouse and skirt onto the bed, so she made quick work of getting back into them while he was facing in the other direction.

He didn't turn around until he was tucking his shirt back in his pants. "What are you really doing here, Jewels?"

A blatant accusation was in his tone, even in the expression on his face, which made her stiffen defensively and scramble to her feet on the other side of the bed. "I told you. I spoke to your father and he told me to prepare for my wedding—and what he'd done to make it finally happen. This was the only way to stop that."

"I see," he said a touch derisively. "So you weren't helping me, you were helping yourself."

"Exactly!" she was hurt enough to say.

He gnashed his teeth in exasperation. "You could have saved both of us from this nightmare if you had just ignored that contract and married someone else."

"I was going to, with my father's blessing. He thought we could weather the storm that might result from breaking the contract. He didn't know your father would make it a personal vendetta to ensure we never recovered from the scandal. Your father alluded to that when I went to inform him I was getting on with my life. He's a damned nobleman. The trouble he can stir up is—too much."

"Isn't your family already so rich it doesn't matter?"

"You're suggesting my father retire? He's barely middle age!"

"No, but perhaps you're overreacting just a little?"

"When my father has only just begun to recover from a major accident that left his mind damaged for the last five years!? You might have no trouble letting your father be embroiled in a social as well as business scandal if the situation were reversed, but I love mine and I won't let *anything* disturb his recovery."

"I'm sorry, I didn't know your father's condition was so fragile."

She was getting close to tears again and glanced down to try to control her emotions. Her eyes landed on the bed between them, and the rumpled covers, evidence of something really beautiful that had happened between them. That calmed her a little, actually a lot. There had to be a way to convince Richard that they needed to find a way out of this dilemma, not just ignore it anymore.

"He wasn't going to leave you in Australia, you know," she said, raising her eyes to him again. "He just wanted you to suffer enough and *think* you were never getting out of there, so that you'd do anything he told you to do in order to escape that hell."

"That sounds like him. But I doubt he knew exactly what he was condemning me to, that I might not have survived long enough to be 'broken.'"

She reserved doubts about that, but was still trying to make her point. "I was sure, after that ordeal, that you'd hie off and disappear again. That's how you reacted before—you just ran away."

"What choice did I have back then? I was a boy."

"You're not a boy anymore," she said calmly. "And I believe you owe it to me now to find a way for us both to be done with this once and for all."

He stared at her hard for a moment before he asked suspiciously, "Are you suggesting we marry?"

"No! Of course not. But I've run out of ideas. That contract needs to be destroyed, but I have no way of getting my hands on it."

"That would end it? Despite it being well known that we've been engaged all these years?"

"Known, but who knows it was writ in blood, as it were, binding our families, not just us? Any child from either family would have sufficed, you know. It didn't have to be you and me. But my parents had no other children, and I suppose your father already had plans for Charles, so by the time we first met, it was taken for granted that it would be you and I who formed this family tie."

"You're saying Charles could have married you—after he was widowed?"

She blinked. "Yes, I never even considered that. I'm sure your father must have, yet he never brought forth that solution to your absence. Perhaps Charles refused to have a second wife picked out for him?"

Richard frowned. "When I recently saw him, my brother did admit that his son has given him the courage to defy our father, and Father treats him with kid gloves now because of it. Charles and the boy are Father's link to the duke, after all." Richard's eyes swept over her again before he added, "I can't believe Charles wouldn't have agreed to marry you, though, if he was asked to. And you and he were never at war like we were."

She blushed slightly. "Perhaps you can ask him about it someday. But that doesn't help *me* out of this situation. Our tie is well known. Besides, it's also well known that you've been gone all these years, and I expect you to be gone again. With no groom *and* no contract, your father would have nothing to hold me to, which would invalidate his threats."

Richard sighed. "All right, give me a little time to think of something. And we *will* be done after this, right?"

"Certainly, why wouldn't we—?" She stopped, blushing furiously, because *he* was staring pointedly at the bed now.

Chapter Thirty-two

WHEN RICHARD TOLD her they would steal the contract from the earl, Julia's first thought was yes! A perfect solution! But then he told her how they would do it, and she thought he was out of his mind. She still thought that. His plan was far too risky!

So she refused, of course, and was quite adamant about it. She didn't rescue him so he could jump right back into the fire. He didn't get angry that she balked—annoyed definitely, but not angry. She didn't expect him to present the plan to his friends, though, that night at dinner in the captain's cabin, to gain their support.

After Richard laid his plan on the table, as it were, Gabrielle was the first to react. "What a splendid idea and so daring! It almost makes me wish I was going along."

Drew stared at his wife. "Not a chance." Then he

glanced at Julia, his expression quite concerned. "Did you actually agree to this?"

"No, I think it's too dangerous, now that we know what the Earl of Manford is capable of," Julia replied.

"Smart girl," Drew said.

Drew's taking her side made Julia admit, "I *do* think stealing the contract is a good idea, though. I just don't think Richard and I should risk contact with the earl again to accomplish it."

"Then how does it get stolen?" Gabrielle asked.

"I could hire a professional for the job."

"An actual thief?" Richard scoffed, then added, "You think they advertise their credentials?"

She stared at him incredulously. She'd just given him an out, releasing him from any further involvement. Why wasn't he jumping on her revision of his original plan to avoid their participation in the theft?

James seemed to concur with her when he mentioned, "Thieves are easy enough to find if you know where to look. That's how my son Jeremy met his wife, Danny. He needed to hire a thief and caught her in the trap that he set for one."

Julia was surprised to hear that rumor confirmed. "I'd heard people joking that she had an odd background, but I didn't think it was true."

"Indeed it is, but through no fault of her own. The poor girl was separated from her family when a nasty lesser member of it tried to kill her and her parents for the coveted title. She was barely knee-high and too young to even know who she was when a band of young thieves found her and took her in. Jeremy helped to reunite her with her mother, who survived that tragedy. Course he was head over heels by then," James added with a chuckle. "So it wouldn't have mattered if she was an aristocrat or not."

"Which was your case, wasn't it?" Drew couldn't resist pointing out with a smirk.

"Put a lid on it, Yank," James said in a droll tone. "We both know your sister is the exception to any rule. And besides, George can't help it that she has barbarians for brothers."

Julia watched Richard closely as his one true love was mentioned. He didn't appear to even notice! Though with the lady's husband in the room maybe it was simply self-preservation that had him mask his feelings.

But Richard apparently still preferred his plan over Julia's, possibly because it *was* so daring, as Gabby had pointed out, and that appealed to him. Or maybe he felt so beholden to her for arranging his rescue that any option that didn't include some risk to himself wouldn't actually remove his debt to her. He'd definitely want to settle that debt. It had to be sticking in his craw that he owed her anything.

For whatever reason, he seemed to want another

opinion to tip the scale, so he turned to Ohr and asked, "What do you think of my plan?"

Ohr didn't even have to think about it, simply said, "Fate will decide the matter."

More than one of them rolled his or her eyes at Ohr's response, but Richard disagreed. "People decide fate; fate doesn't make decisions for them."

"No?" Ohr asked, and even grinned. "A matter of interpretation then."

Julia sighed. One neutral opinion, one siding with Richard, one siding with her. She hoped to settle the matter by confirming James's support, which she wasn't quite sure of yet, and asked him, "So you do think a hired thief is the better plan?"

"Didn't say that, m'dear. In fact, I should point out that if your thief gets caught, that contract will end up getting so well hidden, it will never see the light of day again. So I'm afraid I have to agree with the blighter. Amazing, ain't it? You'd think a man who covets another's wife wouldn't have the backbone to—"

Richard definitely didn't miss *that* mention of Georgina and snarled, "You've made your bloody point, Malory!"

"Much as it pained me, I was complimenting you, you ass," James said drily.

"I'd rather be insulted, thank you very much," Richard rejoined stiffly.

James shrugged, but then with another glance at

Julia, said, "The risk will be his, not yours, as it should be considering what he owes you."

Julia groaned to herself. She simply couldn't bring herself to disagree with James Malory, and that decided the matter.

Chapter Thirty-three

JULIA SHOULD HAVE stuck to her original resolve! Richard's plan couldn't be enacted without her full participation, and while she might have been talked around to an agreement that evening aboard *The Maiden George,* the more she thought about it, the more she didn't think she'd be up to the task. Yet there she was in her family coach, Richard sitting beside her on the plush seat, and they would be arriving at Willow Woods within the hour.

"Are you ready to discuss this?" Richard asked with some amused exasperation. "You've put it off and put it off, but you really can't put it off any longer."

It annoyed her that he seemed to be treating this like a lark. Was he really this adventurous? He should be as nervous as she was!

It *was* brave of him to do this, after what his father

had just tried to do to him—and could well do again. Her father had pointed that out when she had taken Richard home with her to tell Gerald about their plan.

Richard had been respectful during that meeting. She had told him on the ship about Gerald's accident, but she hadn't mentioned the ramifications of it. Until that meeting with her father, Richard hadn't known that she had pretty much been overseeing the family businesses for the last five years. He'd given her quite a few odd looks that night, as if he couldn't believe it. But convincing Gerald of the necessity of their plan had taken all evening because he kept insisting the better solution was for him to pay Milton more money than he could ever refuse. But money wasn't always the answer, and Richard had balked at that idea.

"Then he wins? And I've exiled myself from England for nine years for nothing? Please don't do that. He doesn't deserved it."

Reward the wicked? She'd agreed with Richard on that point wholeheartedly. Milton should be brought to account, not paid off.

James had actually offered to instigate proceedings against him. He'd already promised to see that the Cantel brothers got their just deserts as soon as the contract was destroyed. He was going to wait until Richard's plan succeeded to avoid tipping off the earl about how angry they were over what he'd tried to do to Richard. Neither Cantel brother was ever going to hold a position of authority again after James was done with them. But a lord of the realm couldn't be dealt with as easily, and Richard had refused Malory's help in that, pointing out that the scandal would also affect Richard's brother and nephew, who were both innocent in all this.

Julia had ended up telling her father, "The scandal, even if it dies down eventually, is still going to prevent me from getting on with my life as we previously discussed." She wasn't about to tell him she was trying to protect him from it until he was fully recovered since he would consider any sort of protecting to be *his* duty, not hers. "But this plan will put this whole thing behind us. It will break all ties without a scandal, so I *can* get on with my life."

Gerald had finally agreed with the stipulation that he send an escort of eight armed guards with them. Witnesses and muscle if needed. Richard had concurred, though he planned to leave that small army in the hamlet nearby under Ohr's direction. They would keep an eye on the house day and night, but showing up with that army would just point out to the earl that they were worried about something. And that wouldn't support the lie.

Julia glanced at Richard now. He'd dressed well for the occasion and looked like a typical young lord today. He even had a cravat tied neatly at his neck. He hadn't cut his hair, but at least it was tightly queued.

They were alone in the coach on this last leg of the journey. They'd needed two coaches for all her baggage, and Richard had insisted her maid ride in the second one with Ohr, so they could talk privately. The weather was warm, the sky cloudless—a nice day for a charade.

"What is there to discuss?" she asked Richard. "You confront him, I agree with you, we settle in for the search. Quite simple."

"Then stop gritting your teeth as if they're about to be pulled. You're going to have to do some lying yourself. Are you up to it?"

"You ask that because I wouldn't lie to my father? I love him. There's a big difference in that."

"Shielding someone you love is sometimes preferable."

"And if your father hies off to London to confront my father about it?"

He sighed. "Point taken."

"Besides, I'm simply going to follow your lead and improvise as needed."

"Then be warned. My father told me once that bedding you would change your attitude. Don't blush too much when I tell him he was right."

"Why must you even mention that?!" She was already blushing.

"He's not stupid. He's not going to believe that out of the blue, for no good reason, we've suddenly changed our minds and want to get married."

She was hoping they'd get lucky and find the contract sometime today. The less time she had to spend under the earl's roof, the better. But there was no way to avoid the initial confrontation that would get them under that roof to stay for however long it took to find the contract and destroy it. The pretense of being a happy couple was going to give them full access to the house, the only viable excuse to be there.

She still found it odd that Richard would even come up with this particular idea. Nor could she forget her father's bittersweet comment about it: "I'd always hoped to see the day when my daughter and the earl's son would be planning their wedding. How ironic to see it happen, but have it only be a charade."

Julia gave a start when Richard suddenly touched her check. He tsked and said, "You can't flinch when I caress you. You're supposed to be in love."

She stiffly disagreed. "That doesn't include carte blanche in public. Such demonstrations are quite frowned upon, you know."

"By whom?" He laughed. "Old dames who come from the last century when most marriages *were* still arranged? Besides, our situation is unique in that it's purely a performance, and performances need those extra little touches to be convincing. We may even need to do this more'n a few times—just for effect."

This was his kissing her, and he did it so suddenly she had no chance to protest. He swept her close, his hand cupping her cheek, and his lips moved over hers with gentle pressure that quickly wasn't gentle at all, got quite out of hand on his part. She was a bit stiff. They shouldn't be doing this again! There was really no need! But her will wasn't powerful enough to ignore something this tempting. Just when she started to melt completely, he pushed her back to where she'd been sitting, a foot away from him.

"I think you get the idea."

Was his voice a little breathless? She had to take a deep breath herself before she leaned her head back against the seat, closed her eyes, and said as calmly as she could, "You will resist giving *that* good a performance, if you please."

"Do you need more practice?"

Her eyes snapped back to his. "I got the idea! Now give me some peace for what's left of this ride so I can compose myself."

"Don't let me down, Jewels. I'm only doing this for you, you know. I'd as soon never clap eyes on the tyrant again in this lifetime."

Chapter Thirty-four

As Julia stepped out of the coach, she was reminded of her very first visit to Willow Woods. Her trepidation was the same as it had been on that day so long ago. She was terrified, really, yet she had to hide it. She wasn't a little girl who hoped so much that her fiancé would like her. She was a grown woman who had to pretend that he did.

They weren't announced. Richard didn't even knock on the front door. He just walked in as if he had never left—as if it were still his home. No servants were in the hall to stop them. Willow Woods had never had a great many servants despite the manor's impressive size. Julia's mother had once remarked, rather cattily, that the Millers must have twice as many, and for a home that wasn't nearly as big. Gerald, frowning at her attitude, reminded her that they didn't *need* all the servants she frivolously employed.

Julia was glad that she remembered her mother's remark today. It was, in essence, the main reason the earl refused to relinquish the contract. His lack of wealth forced him to live so frugally compared to other lords of his stature. It was also the main reason why he might believe them today . . . because he'd want to.

They went straight to the earl's study and entered, Richard's arm tightly about her waist. For effect? Or because he thought she might bolt? But she felt more confident and in control now. She could do this.

Milton was sitting at his desk. He didn't glance up immediately, probably because he thought it was a servant who had come to bother him about something. When he did look up, he just stared at them. He didn't move, didn't blink. Apparently, he was shocked to the point of being speechless.

Which allowed Richard to announce, "We're getting married, Father. I won't say you win"—he paused to glance down at Julia with a loving smile—"when I'm the one winning here."

The earl displayed no sense of triumph, but some color was mounting his cheeks, and his icy blue eyes narrowed on his son. Julia began to wonder if he'd even heard what Richard had said, or if he couldn't get past Richard's no longer being on a ship to hell—where he'd put him.

In fact, that was all he seemed interested in, finally saying, "How is it possible you're here?"

"That was my bride's doing."

"Your—bride?"

Milton's eyes landed on Julia as if seeing her there for the first time. He was still frowning as he said to her, "You lied to me?"

"About what? That your son and I were in agreement not to marry? No, that was quite true at the time. When I met him in London recently and we began to get acquainted, we didn't recognize each other. When we did, it was quite a rude awakening that brought back all the old animosity, so all we parted with were some very angry words. I was convinced he hadn't changed a'tall."

"I thought the same about her," Richard added with a grin.

"But when you told me where you were sending him, you remember asking me if I was pleased?" Her eyes narrowed on Milton now. "I wasn't, not in the least! And before I even returned home, I knew I had to get him out of that horrid situation. I couldn't stand the thought of him suffering. That's when I knew that what I'd felt as a child was gone."

"She's still a little spitfire," Richard interjected, giving her a tender look. "But when she stands in your corner, it's rather endearing."

Julia nearly lost her train of thought over that remark because Richard sounded so proud of her, but she managed to continue, "I went straight to the docks and found the convict ship before it sailed. I found Richard's friend there. He was searching for him as well—"

"Someone else knows about this?" Milton interrupted sharply.

Richard lifted a brow. "Did you really think I would approach the lion's den alone? A friend was traveling with me, he just wasn't in the room when your lackeys pulled me out of it. He knew exactly where to look for me, though. He just had no opportunity to free me from the guards who escorted me to London. And a week was wasted because he thought I was being detained at the docks in a building it would take a small army to break into. He didn't see me taken out the back way and dragged directly onto the ship."

They had agreed to give a completely different account of the rescue for three good reasons. Mainly, Richard didn't want his father thinking only he and Julia knew about his stepping outside the law to have his son imprisoned. Someone else, and a friend in particular, being aware of it would make the earl think twice about trying it again. But mentioning James Malory's involvement could have the opposite effect, causing Milton to panic that another lord knew of his transgression, so this simplified version allowed them to leave James's help out of it. And lastly, the quicker rescue gave them nearly a week to "fall in love" rather than the few days aboard *The Maiden George*.

Julia felt confident enough to finish the tale. "His

friend had only just found out where Richard had actually been taken and was intent on getting him off that ship just as I was, though he was going to do it aggressively. I gave him enough money to do it the easy way instead. Guards are *so* easy to bribe. They couldn't hand Richard over fast enough, for what they were promised."

Milton guarded his emotions as he assimilated how his plan had been thwarted. "And now?" he asked tightly.

Richard actually laughed. "I guess you didn't hear me, Father. Julia and I are getting married, *not* because of that silly contract, but because we want to. An amazing thing, love. It actually encourages you to forgive people who don't deserve forgiveness."

Richard's tone had turned distinctly cold. Julia began to panic. Was he talking about her? Or his father? But of course that was meant for his father. She realized it wouldn't be at all natural for Richard to pretend to *not* be bitter over his father's transgressions. His performance would be all the more believable, too, with the addition of those little touches of rancor.

To distract from the sudden tension between father and son, she said to Milton, "I'm sure you won't mind if I redecorate one of the larger rooms downstairs. Perhaps the music room?"

The earl's gaze swung back to her with a frown. "Whatever for?"

"She actually wants to be married here, of all places," Richard answered. "She fell in love with Willow Woods as a child, despite the fact that I lived here," he added with a chuckle.

Before the earl could refuse, Julia went on, "I'll be turning the room into a lovely chapel. The workers and all the material will be arriving in the next few days. You do have a pastor on the estate? If not, I can arrange for a bishop from London to—"

"Yes, I have a pastor," Milton cut in.

"Excellent, one less thing for me to worry about. I've hired triple crews to make sure the room is finished in time. I might even add an enclosed garden off of the room, if time permits. And please don't worry, I'll have the room restored to its current state right after the wedding."

"Then why not just hold the service outside?" Milton said. "I already have numerous gardens."

"But what if it rains!" she said, aghast. "No, it must be indoors. Nothing is going to stop me from having the wedding I've always dreamed of."

Milton glanced at both of them. Richard's arm tightened about her waist. If that didn't warn her what was coming, the suspicious glint that entered Milton's eyes did.

"I find it preposterous that you could fall in love in the span of a week—even if you didn't hate each other for so many years. Why are you really—?"

"Some of that week was spent in bed," Richard cut in bluntly, adding in an ironic tone, "Didn't you once tell me that would change her attitude? You forgot to mention it would change mine as well."

"Richard!" Julia gasped, as embarrassed as she'd known she would be, and angry, too, but she directed that anger at the Earl of Manford. "We don't need to explain ourselves to you. The *only* reason we are here is for the wedding, but come to think of it, it was more my mother's dream to have the wedding here, than mine. She instilled that dream in me because I saw grandeur in this place through a child's eyes, but quite frankly, your home as it stands simply won't do."

"How dare—," Milton began to sputter.

"Peeling wallpaper," Julia continued, "cracked floorboards, the main chandelier in the hall missing a third of its crystals, frames on paintings rotting away they are so old. It will involve much more than creating a chapel to have Willow Woods ready to receive members of the *ton* in less than a month. Not that I couldn't manage it. Everything needed to refurbish the entire house can probably be found in Miller warehouses. But I'm not so sure I want to now. In fact, Richard, let's just leave. This was a bad idea."

"A moment, love," he said while pinning his father with a curious look. "You didn't actually think this was a reunion, did you? She had to convince me to come here, and you can be certain, it wasn't easy. I would have been quite happy never to step foot here again, and after the wedding, I don't intend to return. She's right, this was a bad idea, but it's an idea already in progress. The banns were posted before we left London, and her father probably has sent out most of the invitations already."

"The location can be changed," she assured Richard.

"That isn't necessary," Milton said gruffly and a bit red-faced now. "You're welcome to have the wedding here."

"When you just questioned the validity of our love for each other?" Richard said to his father. "Do you even realize how hard-hearted and narrow-minded you seem in not understanding how easy it was for me to fall in love with her? But just for the record, Father, we met in London at the beginning of the Season and didn't recognize each other a'tall. I was completely smitten and did my best to seduce her. She nearly succumbed, drawn to me as well."

"Richard, *stop* giving him intimate details!" she protested again.

He didn't quite ignore her, just leaned down to kiss her cheek and say, "Hush," before continuing his improvised tale. "It was a shock when we finally figured out who we actually were, and as she said, we parted in anger because of it. But then, ironically, *you* brought us together again and were responsible for the powerful emotions that consumed us—relief, gratitude, and anger that was not directed at each other for a change, but at you. And, well, one thing led to another, and the recent attraction we'd just experienced took over again."

"My God," she said in wonder. "He *is* responsible, isn't he? We never would have seen each other again if I didn't feel compelled to rescue you."

Richard chuckled at her. She must have looked suitably awed because he was able to say, "You don't need to feel beholden to my father, really you don't, love. But if you still want to be married here, I suppose I can tolerate a few weeks under this roof while you make all the preparations for this grand wedding of ours."

Chapter Thirty-five

THE YOUNG MAID who had shown Julia to a bedroom had wanted to clean the room immediately. She'd had no notice of guests coming to visit, she'd whined, so she hadn't prepared a room ahead of time. Julia shooed the girl off, telling her to come back and clean it later that afternoon while she wasn't in it. She just wanted some privacy immediately so she could tremble in peace.

But collapsing on the bed as soon as the door closed stirred up so much dust, she sat up and coughed and sneezed for nearly a minute. That took care of the trembling, and she almost laughed when the clear outline of her footprints across the dusty hardwood floor caught her eye.

She hadn't been exaggerating about the condition of Willow Woods. The bedroom she had been shown to probably hadn't been used, or even cleaned, in years. With so few servants, the maids—if there was even more than one for the entire upstairs—obviously cleaned only the regularly occupied rooms of the large manor house.

She'd been given a room with blue drapes, walls, and bedcover. At least the decor used to be blue. The wallpaper was so faded it was more a dull gray now. The dark wood floorboards needed to be polished. The room contained a narrow desk, but no vanity, hence no mirror. She needed to make a list soon of all the items she would need from the warehouses in London.

She was filling her mind with these trifles so she wouldn't think about the interview with the earl, which had shredded her nerves so badly. She might have thought she was up to that confrontation, but she'd known how easy it would have been to slip up and say the wrong thing. She wasn't certain that Milton had been completely convinced by their charade, despite his giving his permission for the wedding, which was why she'd started trembling as soon as she left his study.

For a man who had wanted this wedding to happen for most of *her* life, he didn't seem the least bit delighted that it was finally taking place. At least not yet. He obviously had some reservations—or needed more proof that she and Richard were sincere. Such as an actual wedding.

She started to laugh hysterically at that thought, but cut it off abruptly when the door opened again and Richard stepped inside.

She shot off the bed, stirring up another cloud of dust that she tried to wave away as she said testily, "You need to figure out how to knock."

He closed the door softly behind him. "We're soon to be married, no knocking."

She raised a brow. "That doesn't give you privileges." Then dropping her voice to a whisper, she added, "Even if we *were* getting married."

He just grinned at her before he glanced at the deplorable condition of the room and said with a wince, "I was really hoping your room would be in better shape than mine, but obviously not. Willow Woods really has fallen into a miserable state."

"Just one more thing to prove how desperate your father should be for us to marry."

"He's always been greedy, but *desperate* might be more accurate now. The gambling debts I left him with would have pinched his pockets even more. Apparently, he had to borrow from Charles's father-in-law to pay them off."

"You like to gamble?"

"Not really. Those were deliberate losses to get him to disown me back then. It didn't work, so I left instead."

She really knew so little about Richard anymore. But the snob was gone. Had snobbery ever really been there? Or had his rage over the situation caused that nastiness she remembered? And today, he'd been remarkable.

Recalling his performance, she said, "You were amazing downstairs. How did you do that? You mask your emotions so well! You even had me believing you!"

He blushed slightly. "Sorry for embarrassing you, but my father has a suspicious nature. If anything deviates from the norm he wants to know why. And what we're attempting here is about as far from normal as it gets."

"Do *you* think he believed us?"

"It's hard to say at this point. I don't really know him anymore. Nine years ago when I left, he wouldn't have done something as horrendous as what he just did to me. But he *had* slowly been heading in that direction, his punishments growing steadily more harsh. If he didn't believe us, he still can't afford to not go along. The boon we're offering is too great for him to risk losing it. If he does believe us, well, it would be my guess that he's simply forgotten how to be gracious anymore."

"I don't recall him *ever* being gracious."

That wasn't really true. When she'd been young, the earl had seemed like any other grown-up she'd met. His belligerence had shown up only when the situation had begun to turn sour and her father had tried to end the relationship between their families.

She suddenly realized she hadn't been whispering any more than Richard was, and she ran to the door, opened it, looked both ways down the hall, then closed the door with a sigh. "We're really going to have to be more careful around here. We can't afford to be overhead."

"Why don't we go outside and enjoy some of this fine weather?" he suggested. "And give the servants a chance to clean these rooms."

Julia thought that was a splendid idea, especially since they could talk freely outdoors with no one nearby. She grabbed her bonnet and opened the door, but paused to dust off the back of her skirt a little. She *had* left the outline of her body on top of the bedcover, it was so dirty.

"Wait!" Richard exclaimed, staying her hand. "Let me do that for you."

She glanced back to see the roguish glint in his eye and his reaching for her skirt. She swung around to face him. "No, I don't think so."

He was grinning widely now. "Ah, come on, love, what better opportunity than a little dust!"

"Really, you're *not* putting your hands on my arse." She tried to sound stern, but his teasing humor was contagious.

"Be a sport," he cajoled, and reached for her again.

She laughed and quickly backed her way out the door with a firm "No."

He ignored her denial and leapt forward. She shrieked and ran down the corridor. Giggling now, she half turned to make sure he wasn't getting too close . . . and bumped into his father.

Her blush was hot! "Beg pardon," she got out, and hurried down the stairs in embarrassment.

"You sure know how to put a damper on things, old man," she heard Richard complain before he bounded down the stairs after her.

Chapter Thirty-six

Wɪᴛʜ ᴛʜᴀᴛ ʙɪᴛ of silliness upstairs, the last of Julia's nervousness vanished. She was amazed at herself for being drawn into those childish antics with Richard, though she reasoned she'd needed an outlet of some sort, and laughter was a potent cure for dour emotions. Temporarily at least. But even her embarrassment over Richard's father witnessing some of it went away quickly once the afternoon sun touched her cheeks. She even removed her bonnet so she could feel more of the sun's warmth, hooking the tied ribbon over her wrist.

She told her maid, who was standing beside the coaches, that she could direct the luggage inside now and unpack. There had been no point in doing so sooner when their welcome had been in question.

"That was brilliant," Richard said as he closed the front door and joined her at the bottom of the entrance steps.

She gave him a curious look. "Did you do that on purpose so you could chase me around the house?"

"What do you think?"

She didn't know what to think, but since he seemed so triumphant over it, she simply said, "Give me warning next time."

He shook his head with a grin. "Spontaneity plays out better."

In that he was likely accurate *if* it produced the desired effect, but that silliness could have gone either way. Considering their past and her nervous state, she could just as easily have railed at him for not being serious, and Milton would have walked in on a fight.

"Did you suspect he'd be up there to witness our antics?" she asked.

"I suspect he'll be watching us like a hawk. But he also has to be full of questions, so, yes, I had a feeling he'd track me down within the hour."

Richard put an arm around her waist to lead her. The long drive stretched before them lined with trees in full bloom, the sun peaking through the treetops. But not taking this picturesque path, he led them around the house instead. The large terrace back there ran along a good portion of the house, with doors leading to it from the parlor, the formal dining room, even the breakfast room. The place didn't bring up fond memories for Julia, and the lake was back there, too—even worse memories.

She tried not to think of them and blurted out instead, "Did you start the search yet? I don't want to stay here a moment longer than we have to."

He rolled his eyes at her, making her blush with the realization of how illogical her question was. "Our baggage hasn't even been brought in yet," he pointed out. "But allow me to spend a few days with my brother and nephew, who I haven't even met yet. When we do leave here, I'll be returning to the Caribbean."

"Where?"

"The Caribbean. It's where I've made my home."

"Not France?" Then she immediately hit her forehead. "No, of course not France. How silly of me. That was just your fake identity."

His brow formed a slight frown. "I probably shouldn't have mentioned that, so keep it to yourself. I do *not* want Father to know where to find me when this is over."

"You don't think he's going to ask where you've been all these years?"

"Certainly he will, but I wouldn't feel obliged to answer him even if I was delightfully in love as we're pretending to be."

Delightfully? What an odd way to put it. It almost sounded as if he wanted to be in love. Actually, he *was* in love with someone else, or had that just been a silly infatuation with a beautiful, unavailable woman? Actually, the adventure-loving, charming Richard that

Gabrielle had described was the kind of man who probably fell in love easily with a lot of women. She didn't like that thought any better.

"What about you?" Richard asked. "What are you going to do when this is over?"

She raised a brow at him. "You heard me discuss it with my father. I'm going to get on with my life—finally."

"Which means?"

"Marriage. Children. I'm going to find a man who's perfect for me, a man like Harry Roberts."

Richard abruptly stopped walking and frowned. "You've already picked out your husband?"

She chuckled at him. "Harry's my best friend's husband. I was just making the comparison because he's quite perfect. He adores his wife, Carol. He doesn't treat her like a glorified housekeeper, as so many man treat their wives. It never comes down to 'do it my way or else' in their marriage. He always takes Carol's opinions seriously. They compromise, sort of like partners in a business relationship—actually, that describes it very well. Believe it or not, he treats her like an equal partner, and she loves him all the more because of it. And that's what I want, a man I can *share* my life with, not one who tries to dictate how I live it. And of course he can't object that I'm going to continue to help manage the family businesses."

"That's a tall order," Richard said, but he was

grinning again as he continued their walk. "Considering how wealthy your family is, you aren't worried about fortune hunters telling you exactly what you want to hear, then reverting to form right after the wedding?"

She stiffened. "You think my family's wealth is the only thing a man will find attractive about me?"

"No indeed, but it's still something you'll need to consider."

She'd never get married if she had to take that into account, too. How many men out there were like Richard, who didn't give a damn about her money? She was surprised he didn't point *that* out, too.

How quickly a mood could turn sour. She was about to turn around and head back to the house, preferably alone, when he said, "Watch your step, Jewels. This slope has a few uneven spots."

She gritted out, "Would you stop calling me that tacky name you gave me when we were children?"

He didn't take note of her harsh tone, didn't even glance down at her. He was staring reflectively at the lake as he said, "A ship I sailed on was named *The Crusty Jewel*. You can't imagine how much I laughed every time that name made me think of you. No, Jewels it is and Jewels it will always be. Admit it, it's a pretty name—at least when it's not modified by the word *crusty*."

She'd admit nothing of the sort. But she did realize she'd just got testy for no good reason.

For the sake of their joint effort, she changed the subject. "The lake is man-made, isn't it? The slope might be gradual on this side of it, but it's rather steep on the other sides, making it appear unnatural."

"Yes, the first Earl of Manford started digging the lake in the early 1700s."

"Ah, a time that favored long hair like yours. Do you wish you'd been born back then? Your hair *is* as long as mine, you know."

He chuckled at her. "No, it isn't."

"It is."

"Let yours down and show me."

She took out a few pins, shook her head, and her coiffure fell, her hair tumbling down her back. She then turned around to show him, but glanced back at him over her shoulder. "What do you think?"

"Damn" was all he said before he whipped her around and kissed her.

His kiss had no gentle persuasion, was instantaneously passionate, and she was easily swept away by it. So unexpected, and all the more potent for the suddenness of it. God, he tasted so good, he dazzled her senses to new realms of temptation. She couldn't get near him without feeling spurts of unusual giddiness. Just the sight of him did that to her. But being pressed to his hard body magnified that tenfold, a burst of sensual pleasure that spread from her core, heightening all her senses.

Abruptly he stopped kissing her. Apparently Richard had enough presence of mind not to tumble them right there on the lawn. She didn't. She wouldn't have protested at all, couldn't really think yet, could only pant and regret that those wonderful feelings were cooling down.

He was no longer pressing her tightly against him, not that that changed their position much when she was still holding on to him. But his hands came to her shoulders, his forehead touched hers, his warm breath steamed against her face.

"Don't move for a moment," he said in a whisper.

A laugh almost bubbled out of her. She didn't think she could move if she tried.

"Did you do that deliberately?" he added.

She didn't know what he was talking about, but his tone had just turned accusing, which made her stiffen. "I don't know what you mean."

He sighed. "No, I suppose you don't."

One of his hands moved down her arm so slowly it was a caress that actually made her shiver and think they weren't quite done with kissing yet. But he was only after her bonnet, which he removed from her wrist—and set on her head rather roughly.

"You've got beautiful hair, Jewels. Keep it contained," he said a little too sharply.

She gasped and tried to pull away from him, but his hands were back on her shoulders and he wasn't letting go. "Don't get huffy on me, we're not done with this demonstration. The tyrant is watching us from the house. So be still and put your hand on my cheek."

She did, though she replied tartly, "Or he's not watching a'tall."

"I brought us to the back lawn because it can be viewed from more rooms, including his bedroom, than can the front of the house. He's watching. I can almost feel the malevolence coming from that house."

"You're probably feeling what's coming from me!"

He glanced down at her, then started to laugh. That could so easily have set off her temper to explosive levels. But she realized he wasn't mocking her, he was genuinely amused, and it wasn't hard to figure out why. Here he was making every effort to help her rid their lives of the marriage contract, and she was being difficult, argumentative, and defensive. When they'd been doing so well at getting along!

"Maybe we should talk about the lake again," she offered sheepishly.

"Good God, yes! Let's do that."

He was chuckling as he took her arm and led her down the gentle slope to the water's edge. It wasn't big enough to be considered a lake, it was really a large pond, but she knew that it was deep, even near the edges, which was probably why the Allens called it a lake.

"The aristocracy was quite frivolous back then in their clothes, their wigs, in their spending," he told her.

"They say the first Earl of Manford employed an entire village to dig this hole. When he ran out of funds, it was left unfinished for years, a great gaping hole in the backyard. Unfortunately, rain never collected there, it just seeped into the ground. Snow sometimes filled it in the winter, but once it melted, it never succeeded in leaving more'n a mud puddle come spring that would dry up by summer."

"So who finished it?"

"The next earl married well, but his wife wasn't a generous person. Whenever she replaced her wardrobe, which was a yearly event, of course, she wouldn't donate her old clothes to the poor, she simply had them thrown away. And she decided her first year at Willow Woods that the huge, ugly hole in the backyard would serve very well as a place where she could discard things, including her clothes. Of course, the earl's gardeners couldn't allow a rubbish heap on the property. The solution was to cover the pile of clothes with dirt. But servants, being naturally efficient since the sooner they got a job done the more time they would have to themselves, spread out that enormous pile of clothes so only a few shovelfuls of dirt here and there were needed to cover them sufficiently. Come springtime that year, the muddy puddle formed as usual, but this time, it stayed there and got deeper whenever it rained."

Julia laughed. "So without figuring out how to finish that lake properly, they did it by accident?"

"Exactly. A generation later fish were brought in to spawn and the little dock was built."

They were standing on that dock now. Julia impulsively confided, "I was very jealous of your fishing prowess. My mother didn't think it was an appropriate activity for me, so of course that made me want to try it even more. My father finally gave in and took me fishing without her knowing. It was our little secret. But seeing those poor worms stuck on hooks that day quite cured me of my infatuation with fishing."

He chuckled. "Did you ever learn to swim?"

She glanced at him sharply. How unkind of him to mention that, and yet, no, he didn't seem to be gloating over his adolescent attempt to drown her. He astonished her when he added, "You scared the hell out of me that day. You were only supposed to get wet, not sink."

Her eyes flared wide. *You were only supposed to get wet, not sink?* How many other things had she been wrong about back then? Should she give him her interpretation of his actions that day?

She turned to him, but he'd moved behind her, rather close. She had to crane her neck to look up at him, only to find that teasing glint in his eyes, and then she was suddenly in the water.

She came up sputtering, her skirt bubbling around her waist, her loose hair covering her eyes so she couldn't see. He'd pushed her in the lake? Again?! She shoved her hair back, but before she could glare at him, a large wave splashed over her face as Richard landed next to her.

"Looks like you can swim well enough now," she heard him say. "So much for another valiant rescue."

He was treading water, laughing. She splashed at him. "You call that valiant?"

"You ruined it by not being in peril," he complained, but he was grinning widely at her. "Do I have to show you how it's done?"

She shrieked when he dove under the water, and sure enough, he pulled her down with him. But just as quickly he released her and she came easily to the surface again to find him still grinning at her.

"Nice legs you've got, Jewels." He stuck his head in the water to ogle them.

Her skirt no longer bubbled up around her now, but she still couldn't get it to stay down and cover her legs. Her emotions were bubbling up, though. She really couldn't help laughing at his antics.

Richard's head came back up. He was actually tall enough to stand in that one spot with his head out of the water. She tried it, but couldn't quite reach the bottom, so she was completely submerged again.

"Are you in peril yet?" he asked when she bobbed back to the surface.

"No."

"Let me try harder."

"Don't!" was all she got out before she went down once again.

She realized she was *not* going to win this game, but that didn't bother her in the least. It didn't stop her from trying, though, and while she was still under the water, she twisted around and used Richard's chest as a springboard to push him back and swim away from him. And so they spent the rest of the afternoon, playing like children, frolicking in the cool, clear water, laughing with each other.

As they should have done when they were children. . . .

Chapter Thirty-seven

THE AFTERNOON HAD been so enjoyable, even though it was just a demonstration for Richard's father to show how well they got along now. At the time, Julia had been having too much fun to even think of that. But pretending from afar was much easier than pretending while they were in the same room with the earl, so she had been dreading going down to dinner that night.

She dressed a bit formally in a cream-colored evening gown, high-necked and adorned at the cuffs and neck with tiny white pearls. After all, she was dining with an earl, and she distinctly recalled that he had always dressed elegantly for the dinners he'd shared with her parents.

Richard walked over to a chair at one end of the long table, likely as far as he could get from the earl's usual seat. He moved one of the side chairs even closer to his and sat her next to him.

He couldn't have been more casually attired that evening, in his white, open-necked, flowing, long-sleeved shirt and black trousers. But his father didn't show up to remark on it. When the footmen began serving them, she and Richard realized he might not be joining them at all. One servant confirmed that.

"Indisposed, m'lord," said the man who was filling Richard's glass with wine, nodding toward the empty seat at the head of the long table.

Julia relaxed immediately. Richard didn't, probably because the footmen didn't actually leave the room, two of them remaining on duty just inside the doorway. This was a normal practice in most households that employed a great many servants. But in a household so short on servants? So she kept in mind that she and Richard were likely being spied upon. If that was so, they really needed to appear more relaxed with each other and not eat dinner in silence.

"Your brother isn't going to join us either?" Julia asked as the first course, fresh fish with herbed cream, was set before them.

"He's not here," Richard replied with obvious disappointment. "Mathew's other grandfather had some business to see to in Manchester. He invited them to join him there for a few days. He's the Duke of Chelter, you know."

"Yes, I know. My family was invited to Charles's wedding. You don't remember?"

"I guess *you* don't remember that I wasn't there."

"Actually, that did slip my mind. Why didn't you attend your own brother's wedding?"

"Because I refused to watch him make such a serious mistake. He couldn't stand his wife, you know, even before the wedding."

That sounded so similar to their own situation that it sobered both of them. But she couldn't just end the conversation like that. "All I remember about her was she had a very high-pitched voice."

"Call a spade a spade, m'dear. Lady Candice screeched like a stuck pig."

Julia nearly choked on her fish. She really couldn't stop the giggle that followed. "As a child, I thought her voice was quite unique, but let's not be unkind. There was probably something wrong with her vocal cords at birth."

He stared at her for a long moment before he said, "Bloody hell, never thought of that. But she was a chronic complainer, too, and you don't inherit *that* at birth."

"Quite right." Julia grinned at him. "*But,* she wasn't very pretty—"

"Don't forget the spade," he interrupted with a grin of his own.

She nodded her concurrence. "Very well, rather ugly, with an odd voice, couldn't find a husband on her own—I'd say she had reasons to complain."

"You're taking her side because you're a woman?" he asked curiously.

"No, just viewing her from a different perspective."

"Well, consider this perspective," he said as he gave her a bite of his fish. "The poor and the sick have reasons to complain. She was a duke's daughter and was spoiled . . . rotten."

She wondered why he'd paused until she realized he was staring at her with an expression that looked like fascination. He'd been feeding her from his own plate every so often, loverlike. A good touch, she'd thought, and she went along with it. She even pretended that his food tasted much better than hers, putting on a dreamy expression each time he gave her a bite. But now much more heat was in his eyes.

He even confirmed the direction his thoughts were taking when he said, "I'm about to toss those two out of the room and have *you* for dinner."

She felt a sudden rush of warmth and her stomach seemed to flip right over with delicious fluttering. And he wasn't even serious! She knew that, yet she had to fight an urge to climb into his lap and throw her arms around his neck. But he'd said it loud enough for the two male servants to hear him, so she didn't blush as deeply as she would have if she weren't sure this was just another "demonstration" of his.

How was she supposed to respond? What would a

lover say to such a provocative statement? She had a feeling it might be "Behave—until later."

"With a promise like that, I'll force myself to," Richard said with a seductive smile.

Oh, good Lord, she'd said that aloud? But his grin, a real one, assured her he was pleased with her contribution to the "demonstration."

That more than anything else enabled her to return to their neutral subject of conversation, albeit with a deep, composing breath first. "So nothing made Candice likable?"

He didn't answer immediately, took a deep breath of his own, even glanced up at the ceiling for a moment before his eyes came back to her and he said, "When Charles gets here, ask him if he ever got around to liking her."

Julia shook her head. "I always liked Charles, but that question is a bit too personal—even for my future brother-in-law. I'll trust your word on it."

He raised a brow at her. "Liked my brother, did you?"

She chuckled. "No need to get jealous. What was there not to like about him? He was always kind to me." *And you weren't,* but she kept that thought to herself.

He didn't. "And I wasn't."

"Shh," she tried to stop him.

"Don't shush me, the whole world knows we hated each other."

"Don't exaggerate."

"Very well, all of England."

He was still exaggerating, as only their respective families and servants had known. But she wasn't sure why he'd brought up a subject they shouldn't be discussing—when the walls had ears.

She was beginning to feel uncomfortable when he lightened the subject by adding, "We don't need to tiptoe around it, love. It's our past. It's certainly not how we feel now."

No, it wasn't. There was nothing to hate about this Richard. Like the man she'd been drawn to in London at Georgina's birthday ball, he could be quite charming, even gallant. He also had a wonderful sense of humor. And he was honorable. He didn't have to be here doing this for her, *just* for her. But he owed her, so he was paying his debt.

A stunning thought came to her—she liked this man. A lot. How oddly disconcerting.

Chapter Thirty-eight

Soon after dinner Julia retired to her freshly cleaned room. She wanted to be up early to direct the workers when they arrived. She and Richard had decided to bring large work crews to the manor for several reasons. It would add credence to their wanting to marry. It would also create so much commotion that the earl might be distracted by it—and not think so much about them. But, mainly, it gave them an excuse to enter all the rooms downstairs as they had to determine what needed to be done to them before the wedding guests arrived.

She was sitting cross-legged in the middle of the bed combing her hair. She usually performed this nightly ritual at a vanity, but none was in the room. She'd actually added a mirror to the list of items she had included in the note she'd sent to her father, apprising him of their reception. He'd insisted on being informed immediately. He might still show up to give Milton a piece of his mind, if he gained enough strength to travel before they accomplished their task. But she was still hoping she and Richard would be out of there in days, not weeks.

She should have been exhausted after all that frolicking in the lake today, but oddly she was wide-awake. Too many thoughts were clamoring for attention, but she was trying her best to ignore them by counting the strokes of the comb through her hair. She was almost to one hundred strokes when the door opened.

She froze. She wasn't dressed to receive anyone, much less Richard, yet there he stood, frozen as well at the sight of her. She was wearing her favorite summer nightgown, sleeveless, V-necked, made of white silk spun so thin it was the softest thing she owned. And the most transparent.

He came out of his daze first. A slow smile began to form on his lips, but then he groaned and did an about-face.

He didn't leave, though, merely closed the door and said a bit tersely, "Get decent."

She immediately dove off the bed to the wardrobe where her robe hung and quickly donned it. Made of the same thin silk, it wasn't that much of an improvement, but at least her arms were covered now and an extra layer of silk crossed her chest. But for good measure, as soon as she pulled the belt tight, she flipped a lock of hair over each shoulder to also lay over her breasts.

"Are you decent yet?"

She glanced up and tsked. "If you would get in the habit of knocking, you wouldn't get embarrassed seeing what you shouldn't."

"I'm bloody well not embarrassed. I'm bloody well fighting tooth and nail to stay on *this* side of the room."

Her mouth formed the *Oh* though no sound came out. He sounded so aggrieved! Impassioned by what he'd seen? That he was having difficulty over the mere hint of nipples under silk almost made her smile.

"Yes, it's safe to turn around—and tell me what you're doing in here."

He faced her. His eyes still covered her slowly from head to foot before he said, "We're spending the night together."

Oh, God! An image immediately filled her mind of the two of them entwined on her bed on *The Maiden George* and she nearly melted on the spot so much heat washed over her. But he couldn't mean they'd be doing that again! That couldn't be what he'd come there to tell her. He'd just had a very male reaction to her scanty attire.

Really, the man needed to choose his words more carefully. A bit miffed at how easily he'd excited her, she said, "I beg your pardon?"

"Don't get huffy. I won't touch you. You've my

word on it. It's just for effect. I want the maid to find us together in the morning and report it to my father."

He was serious! How could she survive an entire night with him *not* touching her? She couldn't. This was *not* a good idea.

She quickly reminded him, "We were quite demonstrative today. Do we really need to do more?"

He merely said, "I didn't like his not making an appearance tonight at dinner. When I don't see him, I don't trust him."

"And when you do see him?"

"I don't trust him period, but at least it's easier to gauge what he's thinking if I can *see* his mood."

"He probably just still doesn't know what to make of our desire to get married. It's the very last thing he was ever expecting to happen, us falling in love. And besides, it's my maid who'll open that door in the morning, not your father's upstairs maid, so nothing's going to be reported to him."

"Do you trust your maid?"

"No, she's new, but she likes the job because I overpay her, so she isn't going to jeopardize it."

"Do you overpay all your servants just because you're rich?"

She wondered why he sounded so annoyed. Did he resent her wealth? Or was he still upset over finding her half-dressed?

She tried not to react to his sour mood with one of

her own and simply said, "As it happens, it's my opinion the average wage isn't enough to feed pigs, much less people. And my family has always paid our employees what we feel they are worth, not what the standard dictates. You get much better results when a worker is happy and well fed, you know. Or would you know?"

He chuckled at last. "Good point. No, I wouldn't. I've never in my life paid for a servant of any sort."

"Never? All the years you were gone?"

"Didn't I mention I lived at sea mostly? Or in someone else's house?"

"A lord without a valet. I'm—amazed."

"Don't be. It's not hard to polish your own boots or wash your own clothes. Now, cooking? No, never tried that, if you must know."

He grinned, then added, "As for my new plan, it's still a good one. Father's only heard that we've slept together from me. And that's really the clincher in this charade. So I want him to hear it from someone else. And if your maid can't be trusted to take the tale to him, come along, we'll use my room."

He didn't wait for her agreement, just grabbed her hand and led her down the corridor to one of the two corner rooms at the end of it. She still didn't like this new plan of his at all, despite the logic of it.

But she felt some shyness mixed with avid curiosity. She really wanted to see the room he'd grown up in. But when she entered the room and glanced around it, she saw nothing that indicated a child had ever lived here. Faded jade wallpaper, old yellow drapes open to the night, an empty fireplace with nothing on the mantel, not a single painting on the walls. As it was a corner room, one set of windows looked out on the side yard, the other faced the front lawn. None were open, so the room smelled a bit musty despite having been cleaned. There was a small desk where Richard might have done schoolwork. A bookcase, empty of books.

"This wasn't your room when you were a child?" she asked as he closed the door behind them.

"It was."

Not a single thing in the room suggested it had ever been used except as a guest room, so she asked, "You took everything with you when you left?"

"No, it was probably all thrown away when it became obvious I wasn't coming back. I just took what I could carry, a pocketful of childish mementos, and some clothes. I was running for my life—well, it definitely felt like it. I'd just had my hair butchered, every single lock of it cut off to the scalp with a knife because I wouldn't cut it when I was told to."

She gave him a sharp look. "That isn't funny."

"No, it wasn't."

Her eyes widened in horror at his somber tone. "You aren't joking?" Then she guessed, "Is *that* why you wear it so long? Because your father wouldn't let you?"

"A matter of choices that I never had, and a reminder I always carry with me of what I escaped."

He didn't really leave England because of her, she realized. She was just another of his father's choices that had been forced on him. But he wasn't a boy anymore, and his father could no longer make the choices for him—except by illegal means. Harsh measures of that sort were unnecessary, as long as Milton *believed* their charade.

"Now laugh," he told her.

She snorted at such a ludicrous suggestion. "I don't think so."

"Don't feel sorry for the boy, Jewels," he said with some exasperation. "He doesn't exist anymore. I'm well pleased with my life now, at least I will be again as soon as I get the hell out of England." Then he nodded toward the wall to his right. "That's his room. I want you to laugh loudly, so he knows you're in here."

She couldn't help but blush. Talking about setting up this new part of their charade, however innocent it actually was, wasn't the same as actually doing it.

But seeing her blush, he rolled his eyes at her and said, "Don't be silly. The whole point of this is letting him think we're having fun in here. Now laugh."

She sighed. "I can't just laugh for no reason, especially after what you just told me."

"Then let me help you."

She was positive that no bit of humor, however silly, would get rid of the sadness she was feeling because of what she'd learned about his horrid childhood. But she hadn't anticipated Richard's tickling her. He did just that, pulling her to the bed, pushing her down on it, and tickling her all over. She succumbed immediately. She did some shrieking, too. She'd had no idea she was so ticklish. But she was also laughing and was quite out of breath by the time he stopped.

He leaned beside her, his elbow bent so he could rest his head in his hand. He looked quite satisfied with her performance, was giving her a pleased smile. He had such a sensual mouth. When he looked like this, his green eyes flashing, his lips curled just so, she felt wildly attracted to him.

She stared at his mouth, hoping he'd kiss her. He didn't. Without looking at her chest, he gallantly pulled her robe back over her breasts. That was a potent reminder that he'd said he wouldn't touch her. So she pushed all carnal thoughts away and tried to relax. But as she'd guessed, it wasn't easy with him this close to her.

She tried to distract herself by running a finger down the bridge of his nose over the slight bump. "So this *is* the break I made?"

"Yes, scarred me for life, you did."

"Nonsense, it adds character to your face. You were too pretty without it."

"Are you insulting me already?"

He didn't sound serious, but she still said, "You call my telling you that you're handsome an insult?"

His tone got huffy. "You couldn't have used that word instead?"

She giggled, teasing him, "Well, when you were a boy, you *were* pretty. Really you were."

He did some teasing of his own. "You were waiting for me tonight, dressed so scantily, weren't you?"

She gasped. "Of course not."

"Because if you were, I would have come up much sooner. You're sure? We don't *have* to sleep here like strangers, you know."

Was he teasing, or was that a hopeful look in his eyes now? But she couldn't bring herself to encourage him, even if she had just been thinking about his kissing her. Making love with him once had been an impulsive act, and she'd been quite carried away by passion. But to consciously decide to—she just couldn't do it.

"I'm sure," she said.

But he continued to stare at her, and she was suddenly holding her breath. "I'm not so sure *you're* sure." He leaned in closer, then ended with a husky challenge whispered against her lips: "Prove it."

Her eyes flared just before his mouth captured hers in the kiss she'd been longing for. His arm drew her flush with his body. She heard a groan—whose? She clung to him tightly, tasted him deeply. Prove it? In a moment she would, just another moment. . . . No, she wouldn't. How could she not want this when it felt so right? But how could she allow it when it really wasn't right? It would be awkward in the morning, might even ruin the charade.

With her last bit of will, she pulled her head back. "Richard, what are you doing?"

He stared at her hard for the longest moment before he mumbled, "Driving myself crazy." Then with an aggravated sigh, he added, "Strangers it is then, and I think we better get some sleep."

He sat up to remove his boots. Her feet were already bare. Then he stood up and removed his shirt as he walked around to the other side of the bed. She held her breath, watching him. But all he did was pull the covers down on that side and nod for her to get under them on her side. Small details, such as being found under the covers in the morning. But that allowed him to keep his pants on, and she wasn't about to remove her robe, which could be assumed to be part of her nightgown as long as she was half-covered.

He hit his pillow a few times before he put his head on it, turned on his side away from her, and said simply, "G'night, Jewels."

"Night," she mumbled.

So easy for him! He'd probably be asleep in minutes. It was fairly warm in the room, so he'd only drawn the sheet up to his hips, which gave her a view of the entire breadth of his back. She couldn't take her eyes off him. Could she change her mind before he fell asleep? Why did she have to be sensible!? It wasn't as if they hadn't made love before. She wanted to feel his hands on her body again.

He got out of bed abruptly, as if he could read her thoughts. She blushed, but didn't try to pretend she was already asleep. However, he didn't glance down to see that she was still wide-awake, merely marched to one of the windows to open it. Some cool air filtered in, enough to make her snuggle deeper under the covers.

He stood in front of the window for a few moments. She turned on her side away from him before he returned to the bed. He snuffed out the dim lamp on his side before he got back in bed. No wonder she'd been unable to take her eyes off him! At least now the room was truly dark.

She moved about, trying to find a position that would lure her to sleep. Her knee accidentally touched his arse. She groaned and knew she ought to apologize. She hoped he was asleep and hadn't even noticed.

He was quick to dash that hope. "Dammit, Jewels, I'm holding on by a thin thread here." But then he apologized, "I'm sorry. We'll laugh about this tomorrow—or at some point in the next century!"

His brief attempt at humor didn't help. Thirty minutes later, she knew the darkness wasn't helping to lull her asleep either. He was still only a foot from her, and she couldn't get him out of her mind. So she was still wide-awake when the coach rumbled up the drive to the front of the house.

She sat up and would have gone to the window to see who was arriving at that hour of the night, but Richard beat her to it. "Bloody hell, what a wasted performance," he said with a drawn-out sigh. "Father isn't in his room. He hasn't even been in the house."

"Where would he have gone?"

"To find a London newspaper to see if banns really were posted, would be my guess. Damned old man can't just take us at our word."

"I should return to my room."

"Stay where you are."

"I'm really too tired now to go through all that laughter again."

"So am I." He turned away from the window with a slight grin. "But I still want the maid to find us here in the morning and report it to him."

She groaned. She wasn't going to get a bit of sleep tonight, she was sure.

Chapter Thirty-nine

Richard was awake long before the knock came at the door. What a hellish night. He'd hardly slept at all. Sharing a bed with Julia to strengthen the charade had seemed like such a good idea when it occurred to him. But he hadn't taken into account what it would be like, having her luscious body next to him all night and being unable to touch it. He'd foolishly assumed he could keep his carnal urges at bay by concentrating on their unhappy past and the reason why they'd come to Willow Woods. More fool him.

He'd even reviewed in his mind every one of their prior vicious meetings. It didn't help. She simply wasn't that little monster anymore. She'd changed so much she was like a completely different person.

They could actually hold normal conversations without either of them getting angry. She laughed with him. She succumbed to his teasing. What a surprise and delight that had been! And what could he say about her rescue of him? Had it been self-serving as he'd first thought? Or was she simply possessed of enough compassion that she'd had to help him even though she hated him? Did she still hate him? He couldn't even tell anymore.

Frankly, the changes in Julia amazed him—and enticed him. It had taken guts for her to come here to enact this charade after what his father had done. That was self-serving though. The contract meant nothing to him when he lived in a different part of the world now and would marry whomever he pleased when he was damned ready to. But she needed to destroy the contract so she could get on with her life and marry someone else.

He shook that thought off when whoever was at the door knocked again, and he called out, "Come in."

Julia stirred beside him, but she didn't awaken. Was she really that sound a sleeper? Or had she spent as hellish a night as he did? What an interesting thought, but he found it unrealistic. She might have succumbed to passion on Malory's ship, but she'd been highly emotional at the time, and he'd been a cad to take advantage of that.

But, damn, she looked stunning now, like a sleeping angel with that ash blond hair spread out around her pillow. Aside from his first sight of her when she'd been a howling five-year-old with splotchy cheeks, she'd been a beautiful child. He should have known she'd grow up to be a prime piece.

The opening door drew his eyes away from Julia. A young maid came in with a pitcher of fresh water. She halted immediately upon seeing him still abed, a hot blush climbing her cheeks.

Obviously embarrassed, she started to back out of the room. In case she hadn't noticed Julia, he said, "Leave the water," so she'd come farther into the room and see his sleeping companion. But really, how could anyone miss that bright splash of white-gold hair?

Annoyingly, the maid nodded, but kept her eyes glued to the floor as she hurried to the washstand, then hurried back to the door without once glancing in his direction again. He sighed. There was no help for it but to spell it out for the maid; otherwise, that hellish night he'd just endured would have been for naught.

"There's no need for embarrassment. We're getting married in a matter of weeks!" he said before the door closed.

She had to have heard him, although she gave no indication. But he reminded himself they weren't going to need weeks. He was fairly confident he could find the contract after a few days of searching. His father might have set up numerous locked hiding places in the house, but they were located in only two rooms, his father's study and his bedroom. The only thing that worried him was that if *he* were his father, he wouldn't keep the contract locked away. Given the circumstances of their showing up so unexpectedly, he'd keep it on his person night and day. What a horrid thought.

Extremely annoyed now, he got out of bed and dressed. He walked to the bed to wake Julia, but stopped abruptly. He didn't dare touch her when he could attribute some of his annoyance to still wanting her! That desire was riding him hard. He could have just nudged the side of the bed and said her name loudly to awaken her, but he wasn't sure he could handle seeing her all warm and sleep-tousled, sitting up in bed in that revealing nightgown. He went downstairs for breakfast instead.

Unfortunately, his father was still at the table in the smaller breakfast room. After all these years, his gut shouldn't twist up in Milton's presence, but it still did. All those beatings in his youth had left a brutal mark. A hell of a thing, to associate a parent with pain—and nothing else.

"You're late to this meal," Milton said in disapproval as Richard took a seat across from him.

Richard stared at him. "Do I look like a child who needs to be told when to eat?"

"You look like the recalcitrant rebel you've always been." Milton stared at the tail of hair Richard had allowed to fall over his shoulder. "Are you going to cut that for the wedding?"

"No, I'm not."

"You're going to embarrass this house—?"

"No one will give a damn what I look like, Father, and it's not your decision, is it? Are we clear?"

Milton didn't answer, possibly because of the servant who'd just arrived with a plate for Richard and set it down before him. Food predetermined. No choices to make. He grit his teeth, but then as quickly he relaxed his jaw. He was nitpicking. The food was tolerable and plentiful. At least his father didn't skimp when it came to feeding himself and his family.

But Milton did seem to rub in that lack of choice as he admonished, "We eat at precisely eight in the morn, precisely at one in the afternoon, and precisely at seven in the evening. It allows the cook, who doesn't have very many helpers, to plan her day accordingly."

"Can't imagine old Greta complaining about anything. She's a wonderful cook and one of the few servants I remember fondly. And why haven't I seen—?"

"I had to let Greta go. In fact, all of the old servants were fired long ago, replaced with young ones who don't expect as much wage."

From the expression on Milton's face, Richard could see his father blamed him for that, because of the debt Richard had saddled him with. But Richard wasn't going to discuss *that* again, if he could help it, when his father hadn't resorted to the simple solution he'd wanted him to use—disowning him.

" 'Fraid I'm not very fond of *precisely*," Richard said,

then conceded, "If there's no food around when I feel like eating, I'll make do."

"And where is your bride this morning?"

"Still asleep," Richard said, and immediately had that alluring image of Julia again in his mind.

"She's accustomed to the late hours of the London crowd, I suppose?" Milton asked disdainfully.

Milton had never liked London. The upper crust who either lived there or frequented the city to enjoy the Seasons were mostly rich. He wasn't. But his question provided a perfect opportunity to allude to how they'd supposedly spent the night.

"Not a'tall," Richard answered his father. "I'm afraid it's my fault for keeping her up late. But might I suggest you avoid using those nasty, offensive tones with her? She's already having reservations about holding the wedding here, after the reception you gave us."

Milton said something under his breath. Richard chose to ignore it and tried for a neutral topic. "The butler mentioned Charles should be back today. Is that correct?"

"Indeed. Your brother is very predictable, and dependable. He said he'd be back today and so he shall."

Richard didn't miss the implied insult in that statement. He could be quite dependable, though he'd rather not be predictable. But Milton admired those qualities, so Richard had strived to develop them as a child—until it became obvious that nothing was going to endear him to his own father. Richard gave up talking to the man and concentrated on finishing the meal. But Milton wasn't fond of silence.

"You forgot to mention that army you brought with you. Cantel informed me about it."

Richard raised a brow. "So that's where you went last night? Afraid your lackey didn't follow through on your orders and went to confront him about it?"

"The magistrate isn't my lackey," Milton mumbled. "And he'd already reported last week—," he started to explain, but narrowed his eyes instead to ask pointedly, "Why did you try to hide such a large escort from me?"

Richard laughed. "You're amazing, you know that? Does anything *ever* sit right with you? The simple fact is, we didn't want to worry you unnecessarily by showing up with all those guards, which is why we left them down the road. And they're not mine, they're Gerald Miller's. Shall I bring them to the house? They might as well be put to use and help with the remodeling."

"Leave them where they are," Milton said testily.

Richard laughed to himself. Had his father really thought he'd caught them in a lie? Obviously.

But for good measure Richard added, "Do you really think Julia's father would let her come near this place unprotected, after what you did to me? They are her escort. I don't need one. You and I know where we stand. If I didn't *want* to marry her, you can be damned sure I wouldn't be here."

Chapter Forty

SHE'D OVERSLEPT! A glance showed Julia that Richard hadn't. He'd left her alone in his room. But why the deuce hadn't he awakened her before he left? He knew the work crews were arriving today and would need her direction.

She rushed to her room, didn't bother to summon her maid, just found a dress she could don without help, then hurried down the corridor again. But she stopped at the top of the stairs and took a deep breath, even took a moment to braid her hair. The hall below was empty. The crews hadn't yet arrived. She was being silly trying to create a crisis just so she wouldn't have to think of last night. But those thoughts assaulted her now with a vengeance.

Never again was she going to subject herself to that sort of frustration, not for any reason. Richard had been true to his word and hadn't touched her again after that kiss! The one time she could have wished he wouldn't be so honorable, and he was. Of course, she'd insisted that they avoid any physical contact in bed, but she'd had no idea how difficult and uncomfortable it would be. But if he really believed that sleeping in the same bed again was absolutely necessary, then they would bloody well do it properly and not pretend. No indeed, and she'd be perfectly clear that she was willing to make that sacrifice for the sake of the charade.

She groaned to herself and continued down the stairs. She wasn't going to say any such thing to him. He might not only take offense at her choice of words in referring to making love to him as a sacrifice—but, really, how else could she put it when she certainly couldn't say that she *wanted* to make love to him?—but he might also not like her taking control of the charade when it was his plan, not hers.

She found Richard in the breakfast room. Unfortunately, the earl was there as well.

Richard stood up as she appeared in the doorway. "Bad timing, love, I've just finished."

He was going to leave her there alone with his father? She put on a smile for him. "I'd prefer a walk before I eat anyway. It's such a beautiful morning."

"Breakfast won't be served much longer," Milton said.

Was that a censuring look he just gave her? Still no improvement in his attitude then? Or maybe he hadn't been informed yet about their sleeping arrangements. She tried to recall how she'd felt after she'd *really* made love. Utterly tranquil, tender, benevolent—happy.

She turned a serene smile on the earl. "Won't it? I didn't notice the time. I still enjoy walking before I eat. I usually ride, but I didn't bring my horse—or do you have mounts in your stable?"

"Aside from Charles's mount and Mathew's pony, just coach horses. I don't ride myself."

"Do you think Charles would mind if I borrow his horse?"

"I do," Milton said.

"I don't," Richard added, giving his father a reproving look.

Milton ignored his son and told her, "There are no saddles for females."

The man really was determined not to be accommodating. It was becoming laughable, but she refrained and simply said, "No matter. A walk will do."

Richard took her arm and got her out of there before anything more unpleasant occurred. She sensed his tension. He was bristling, actually.

"That was difficult?" she guessed as he led her outside.

He started down the long drive, away from the house. No demonstrations for his father planned for this walk apparently.

"He can't even be civil to you! He was never this

obnoxious or unpleasant before. Of course he always got furious when one of us broke his rules, but after administering the punishments, he went back to ignoring Charles and me, or just treating us normally."

"What do you mean by 'normally'? The way a normal parent treats his children?"

"No, not that. If he cared about either of us, he never showed it. His attitude was more like he'd treat a guest in his house, cordial, but without any sentiment. I wonder if the gambling debts I saddled him with pinched his pockets a little too much and have turned him this bitter. This place was never run-down like this before I left home. He was never, ever extravagant back then. We never had the best of anything; in fact, he did harp on expenses from time to time, but we didn't live like paupers either. It must bite hard, that he's had to let the place get so run-down."

Richard turned them around to head back to the house. She hated to see him so upset and felt a strong urge to hug him.

Instead she quickly said, "Perhaps your father is being so unpleasant because he just doesn't believe us."

"Or he's guessed why we're here," Richard said with a groan.

That thought worried her as well. "Do you really need to extend this in order to visit with Charles? Can't you arrange a visit with him after we've accomplished our goal?"

"Indeed, I actually tried to get into my father's study last night while he wasn't downstairs, before I came to your room. It was locked. And one of the footmen suddenly appeared, as if he'd been hiding in the shadows, and told me my father wasn't in there. The damned fellow *could* have told me he wasn't even home, but he didn't."

"You think the contract is in there?"

"That would be the most likely place. If a servant continues to be stationed outside the study, I'll have to attempt access from the outside through a window. He had a locked floorboard under his desk as I recall."

She chuckled. "He locked the floor?"

He grinned with her. "Actually, yes. He had a box that fit under the floorboard, and a keyed lock was set into the board, so it can't be lifted without the key. But he was fanatic about not leaving money around for servants to steal, so that's not the only place to look. One of the drawers on his desk also has a key lock. For that matter, all three of the top drawers on his bedroom bureau have locks, as does the little chest he keeps his watches in. And come to think of it, there's even a locked door inside his clothes room."

"It's not for a bath?"

"No, there's a separate room for his bath on the other side of the wardrobe. Charles and I always wondered what he kept in there, but we never found out.

We were punished once for being in his bedroom, so we never went there again."

She groaned. "How on earth are you going to obtain that many keys?"

"Wasn't planning to. I brought a set of tools that can serve as keys."

She had no clue as to what he meant. "Oh?"

"Jeremy Malory, James's son, offered them to me before we left London. They belonged to his wife, Danny. Jeremy said his father suggested the loan." Richard snorted with a shake of his head. "There's something absolutely wrong with James Malory helping me."

"Why? He's a nice man."

"The devil he is. Did you know he used to be a pirate?"

"I'd heard joking references to it, but I didn't believe it."

"It's true."

"How do you know?"

"Gabby's father saved his life long ago and told me the whole story."

"Go on with you." She laughed. "I'm still not believing it."

"I suppose you wouldn't believe I used to be a pirate, too?"

She laughed harder, couldn't help it. But since her amusement wasn't amusing *him*, she choked it off and tried to present a serious expression. And failed.

He ended up rolling his eyes at her and adding, "Would you believe I was a treasure hunter?"

That was too intriguing to scoff at. She gave him a curious look. "Really?"

He no longer looked annoyed with her and nodded. "My old captain is enamored of treasure hunting, always has been, and has finally made it his only occupation."

"Have you ever found any treasure?"

"Enough for me to continue to find the chase extremely exciting. Ask Gabby. My captain is her father." They'd reached the house, but instead of opening the door, he glanced down at her and asked, "Do you really like to ride?"

"It's one of my passions."

"One?"

She blushed. Definitely a poor choice of words around him. But she was saved from answering when he turned abruptly at the sound of a coach approaching the house.

"Charles?" she wondered.

"I hope so."

And in fact his brother bounded out of the coach before it quite stopped and engulfed Richard in a bear hug. "What are you *doing* here?" Charles exclaimed. "I thought—"

Richard quickly cut him off. "I'll explain this visit later."

"And Julia?" Charles gave her a smile. "Does this mean——?"

"Yes," Richard said, eliciting a delighted laugh from his brother.

Julia managed not to frown. Richard wasn't going to confide in his brother about their charade? But then she guessed that he simply didn't want to take the chance of being caught there on the porch discussing it. It would take quite a bit of explaining.

The door to the coach hadn't stopped swinging, but as soon as the coach came to a full stop, a small hand pressed it still and a young boy stepped down. A handsome boy who very much resembled his father, but looked quite reserved now, and confused.

Charles said to his son, "Come meet your uncle, Mathew."

Richard knelt down and held out his arms to the boy. But Mathew was shyly hesitant, glancing at his father for guidance.

Charles smiled. "He's my brother, Mathew. The only one I've got."

The boy finally grinned in understanding and rushed forward. It was such a touching moment, Julia almost cried as she saw the tender look on Richard's face as he held his nephew for the first time.

Then Milton opened the front door and, with a delighted smile, held out *his* arms to the boy.

Mathew laughed and ran to his grandfather for a hug.

"Did you miss me?" Mathew exclaimed.

"You know I did," Milton said, and took the boy inside the house.

Richard stood up slowly. "My God, pinch me, I didn't just see that."

Charles chuckled beside him. "I warned you he's on his best behavior around my son. To Mathew, he's everything a grandfather should be."

Richard glanced at his brother sharply. "You mean the father we never had?"

"Yes."

Chapter Forty-one

RICHARD WAS SOAKING wet as he sat beside his brother on the dock. Though he'd removed his shirt, water still dripped from his cutoff pants and down his chest and back from his wet hair. It wouldn't take long to dry, the day was so warm.

He often used to share this peaceful setting with his brother when they were growing up. Stately, old trees dotted the area, and wildflowers grew in abundance beyond the manicured lawn. It had been easy to forget where they were if they didn't look back at the house.

Richard had found out during luncheon that Mathew had never learned to swim, and he'd volunteered Julia and himself to teach him. The boy had politely declined the lesson, but wanted to come along to watch them swim, so they ended up going down to the lake anyway.

Charles had joined them. As Julia and Mathew

walked ahead of them hand in hand, Charles explained to Richard, "He's afraid of the water, so don't be surprised if you can't coax him in, even where it's shallow. One of the gardener's boys was drowning a few years back. He could swim well enough, but had cramped up or something, and Mathew, who had been playing on the back lawn, heard the boy's screams and thought he could save him, when he couldn't swim either! Father actually rescued them. He'd been on his way to speak with Mathew and was the only one near enough at the time to help. Mathew has declined all my attempts to teach him to swim since then. I blame myself, for not teaching him sooner."

Richard was determined to teach the boy after hearing that, but Charles was right. Even though Richard had showed Mathew how much fun could be had in the water, and Julia had been a good sport to participate in that, he couldn't lure Mathew in to try it. But in the end, Julia succeeded! She'd merely had to promise to hold him all the while, until he got the knack of it.

Watching how patient and gentle Julia was with the boy, Charles remarked, "She seems to have a way with children, doesn't she?"

Richard had been thinking the same thing. But then Mathew had taken to her right away, while he was still quite reserved with Richard, not seeming to know what to make of an uncle he'd never before met. God,

Richard thought, he'd missed so much in the nine years he'd been away.

"Give Mathew time," Charles continued when he noticed Richard's pensive look. "I've told him so many stories about you, all good, and I made sure Father never said a bad word about you in front of him. It might be your hair, since he's never seen a man wear it so long. But it's more likely your height that makes him a bit uncomfortable. He's very self-conscious right now that he's a bit short for his age. But with Julia, well, he doesn't get much exposure to young women who aren't servants. And I wouldn't be a bit surprised if he's smitten!"

Charles didn't need to make excuses for the boy. Richard knew you had to be around to gain trust and love, and he hadn't been here, nor would he be in the future. And yet, *this* was the family he'd always wanted for himself, he realized with a profound sense of sadness. Woman and child frolicking, brothers sitting on the side watching, fun, laughter, a sense of togetherness, and it probably wouldn't happen again. He and Julia would soon be leaving.

He hadn't had a chance yet to explain to Charles what they were doing there. Milton had called them into the parlor when they entered the house, then they'd all gone into the dining room for luncheon. Milton had continued to amaze Richard because not once while the boy was present did Milton's manner turn caustic or nasty.

Richard and Charles were far enough away from the activity in the water to speak privately, so he wasn't surprised when Charles said, "Rich, what's going on between you and Julia, and why are you really here at Willow Woods? Your behavior contradicts everything you told me at the inn."

Now that the subject was at hand, Richard almost decided to give Charles the same account they'd given to Milton. It wasn't that he didn't trust his brother, but the charade had to be kept secret and Charles wasn't good at keeping secrets. But this was his brother, and Charles might even be able to assist them in finding the contract more quickly. At least he could shed some light on their father's daily routine, which would aid Richard in his search.

Richard shook his head and gave his brother a brief account of the truth, ending with "He's not exactly displaying any happiness over our upcoming wedding, and you'd think he'd be ecstatic, finally to be getting what he wants."

"Then he simply doesn't believe you, which doesn't surprise me. *Skeptical* might as well be his middle name. But then he's always been suspicious about anything out of the ordinary, and this is about as unexpected as it gets. You don't remember that?"

"I'd gathered as much, though it means we just have

to 'perform' more convincingly—or get the damn job done. Do *you* know where he keeps that contract?"

"I'm sorry, I haven't a clue. All these years, he wouldn't talk about you, and whenever I tried, he'd just get furious. I even brought up the contract after you first showed up and told me what Julia was going to do."

Richard was given pause. "You told him you saw me?"

"No, of course not. But her plan didn't sit well with me a'tall. I'm too superstitious, you know. Her declaring you dead would be like jinxing you so you really would die. I had to at least try to stop that by convincing him to release her from the contract. Of course, he fobbed off my reasoning."

And with Milton's suspicious nature, he guessed that Richard might be in the neighborhood to have prompted that plea? But Richard was *not* going to mention the trip to Australia that Milton had arranged, in case Charles was indirectly responsible for Milton's finding Richard.

Richard still needed to know his father's current habits and mentioned, "Father was out rather late last night. Is that typical for him not to be at home for most of the evening?"

"He spends time with a widow nearby."

Richard raised a brow. "A mistress? Him?"

Charles shook his head. "Don't think he's keeping

her, not that he could afford to. She lives comfortably on a small pittance and, apparently, enjoys his company."

The idea that any woman could enjoy Milton's company was ludicrous. "Must be something wrong with her, then."

Charles chuckled. "Not really. She's his age or thereabouts, and untitled gentry."

"So she's hoping for his title?"

"Possibly, or it could simply be she's lonely. She frequently invites him to dinner, so a few times a week, Mathew and I eat alone. And every week or so he'll come home late, so while you can't really say she's his mistress, they do probably share a bed occasionally."

"You think he would marry her?"

"No," Charles said, then added bluntly, "If she were rich, maybe, but she's not."

"Not enough money for him, how pathetic. You realize he's always been obsessed with money?"

"Rather hard to miss, that. But do you know why? Yours wasn't the first debt he was forced to pay. Our maternal grandparents were heavily in debt, and when they died soon after our parents married, every one of their creditors came knocking at Father's door. Mother's family actually thought Father was rich, so they wouldn't let him out of that arranged marriage any more than he would let us out of ours. And actually, this estate has enough tenants that it would do very well if so much old debt hadn't piled up. Mother ran up extreme debts, too. And Candice didn't come with a dowry. Her father figured that marrying a duke's daughter was dowry enough, and it was. That connection was all my marriage was about. *You* were supposed to fill the coffers again and pay off all the old debts."

Richard winced. "And instead I added to them. Do you feel pinched with your home in such a deplorable state—due to lack of funds?"

"I have funds," Charles said surprisingly. "The allowance that Candice continued to receive from her father after we married was doubled when Mathew was born and now comes to me, to make sure he never lacks for anything. The duke would spoil Mathew horribly if I let him, but I won't let him."

"Then you could have refurbished this place?"

"Yes. Easily. But then father would know I have money and consider it his. That's not going to happen."

Richard laughed. "Good for you. But Jewels is going to fix up the place—if we're here that long." Considering the subject, he was reminded of his conversation with Julia when they'd wondered why Milton hadn't put Charles forward to fulfill the contract. Richard brought it up now. "Did Father ever ask *you* to marry Julia? After you became a widower?"

Charles chuckled. "Actually, he did about three years ago, when Julia was about to turn eighteen and you still hadn't returned to marry her. He even tried to pull out the big guns, pointing out that Mathew, at the tender age of five, needed a mother."

"You disagreed with that point?"

"Mathew had a nurse as well as a governess that I employed, two very motherly women who got so attached to him that they won't leave now that he's older! So he's never lacked for women doting on him. But Father brought it up a few more times, carefully. Remember, he treats me with kid gloves now, so he never insisted I marry her."

"You obviously refused." Richard stared at Julia as he said it, and the beautiful smile on her lips as she spoke to Mathew. Richard couldn't tear his eyes away from her, even as he added, "I take it you didn't know what a beauty she'd turned into?"

"Oh, I did."

That made Richard turn his attention back to his brother. "And you *still* told him no?"

Charles grinned. "He rarely asks anything of me these days, and never orders, so I don't get to tell him no often, now that I have the guts to. I rather enjoyed it." Then in a more sober tone Charles added, "Besides, I know why you didn't want her. How many times you railed that you wouldn't reward him for the hell he'd put us both through. I wasn't about to give him the very thing you left home to deny him."

"Thank you," Richard said with a half grin. "It would have been quite a shock to come home to find her in the family. But enough about that. Tell me, why do you even still live here?"

Charles chuckled. "Well, one reason is because I *do* have a mistress nearby."

"Leave with her."

"I can't. She has a husband, an old chap who pretty much became an invalid not long after they married. She's a good, kindhearted woman. She won't abandon him."

"You love her?"

Charles's warm smile was answer enough, but he said, "She's grown on me—yes, I'm more than a little attached to her. It was just sex to begin with, but it's been six years now that I've been seeing her. She's not gentry, but I don't care. I intend to marry her once her husband passes on. I love her enough to wait."

Now *that's* the sort of love Richard had always been looking for: enduring, defying obstacles, reciprocated. He found himself staring at Julia again.

"But you saw the other reason I'm still here when we returned," Charles continued. "Mathew loves his grandfather. I'm not going to deny him this opportunity to know what a family is like."

"You're never going to tell him what Milton is really like, are you?" Richard guessed.

"Probably not."

Chapter Forty-two

JULIA HADN'T INTENDED to put on her bedclothes until she was ready to get under the covers, but by the time she entered her room that night, she didn't think she'd last for her nightly rituals, even though she had a mirror now that had been brought in from Manchester that afternoon.

She couldn't remember ever being this tired, but then two vigorous days in the lake and so little sleep last night had definitely caught up to her. And the dinner she'd just had with the Allens, minus the earl, had been so relaxed she'd almost fallen asleep there at the table!

Milton's absence at dinner twice in a row would have concerned her if Richard hadn't leaned next to her at the table and whispered, "He visits a lady friend."

Those were the only private words they'd exchanged since the morning, prior to his brother's return. The work crews had arrived and she'd taken them to the music room and explained the improvements she wanted made, then she and Richard had spent the rest of the day with Charles and Mathew. After the swimming lesson at the lake they'd played a few hours of croquet on one of the side lawns that was level. Without discussing it, all of the adults had wanted to make sure Mathew won those games. Julia found that rather funny, particularly the groans of the two men as they deliberately missed their shots.

She didn't begrudge Richard his day with the two members of his family that he loved. But she hoped that would be enough for him and that he'd focus on locating the contract. It was nerve-racking to be in that house with the earl, who was so unpredictable. Look at his behavior with his grandson today! He'd behaved like a completely different man from the one who had sent his son on a trip to hell. Without a qualm. Without remorse.

She groaned when the knock came at the door only minutes after she'd closed it. She didn't doubt it was Richard and was glad now that she hadn't changed out of her clothes yet. While she was afraid he was going to suggest another night of "fun" in his bedroom, even though his father wasn't home yet, the thought did manage to wake her up a little.

But when she opened the door, Richard grabbed her hand and started leading her down the corridor as he said, "Come on, I need you to keep an eye out for me. With Father out of the house again, now's our chance."

Finally! She was wide-awake now! But halfway down the stairs he stopped. They could see the footman stationed at the beginning of the narrower hallway on the left that went on beyond the stairs and led to the earl's study. Richard was going to have to go outside and enter through the window if he was going to get into that room tonight.

She thought of mentioning a reason for them to go outside, loud enough for the footman to hear her, but she held her tongue when Richard's hold on her hand tightened. She could almost feel the rage suddenly coming from him, the kind that his father could easily inspire, but when she leaned to the left to see what had caused it, she saw it wasn't Milton he was staring at.

A giant of a man was lumbering down the side hall from the back of the house. He was middle-aged, rather ugly, and almost grotesquely muscular. As he passed the footman, he made a playful punch toward the man's belly. The poor fellow blanched, causing the giant to laugh as he continued toward the stairs and started to mount them.

Seeing Richard, the giant snickered, "Better cut yer hair for the weddin', eh."

Richard let go of her hand, took hold of the banister for leverage, and vaulted both feet into the man's chest. The crash in the hall as the giant hit the floor might have broken some of the old floorboards. Dazed, the man didn't get up, but Julia was horrified at what was going to happen when he did. He had to be twice Richard's weight, and like the rest of him, his hands were abnormally large.

Richard certainly didn't seem to take any of that into account or was simply still too enraged to care. He quickly followed the man down the stairs.

"Get up, Olaf. Get up and give me satisfaction! Or have you no guts without my father's permission?"

Olaf didn't move, just lay there groaning with his arms trying to protect his belly, no doubt anticipating a kick from Richard.

But all Richard did was lean over Olaf, and she'd never heard such an ominous tone from him as he said, "Get out of this house and don't ever come back. It won't matter that an earl gave you orders to attack me at the inn and drag me back here. It only matters that you violently laid hands on a lord. They used to hang men for that, you know. Come to think of it, I think they still do."

The other footman just stood there trembling, yet pretending not to notice the commotion around him. Julia gathered her wits and rushed down to Richard's side. It was a perfect opportunity for her to say, "Why don't we take a walk outside—so you can cool off."

Richard nodded and took her hand again. Once outside, with the front door closed behind them, he paused to take a few deep breaths, then glanced down at her with an apologetic cringe.

"I'm sorry you had to witness that."

"It was—unexpected."

"But long overdue."

She didn't have to ask. That giant had to be one of the brutes that his father had set on him long ago. A giant like that against a defenseless boy—she was actually surprised Richard had been lenient and hadn't beaten the man senseless.

He led her around to the side of the house. The yard was well lit. Several of the rooms on that side of the house still had lamps burning in them, even the study. Julia thought that was odd, until Richard glanced through the window, then abruptly ducked down and dragged her away again.

"Son of a bitch," he whispered. "He's left one of the servants inside the study as well. The chap's sleeping in a chair, but opening that window will probably wake him. That's got to be the place then."

"If it's always guarded, we're not getting in there, are we?" she asked in disappointment.

"We will. During the day, when the servants will be too busy with their other duties to stand guard."

"You know that's too risky."

"Not if Father starts to relax his guard. He hasn't yet. He's still too suspicious. I doubt that maid has said anything to him yet about finding us in bed together this morning. But one more night in bed when he can actually hear us cavorting should convince him. We can time it right tonight, just as he gets home."

"The moment my head touches a pillow, I'm going to fall asleep. I'm too tired tonight."

"Tomorrow then, or the next night, when we're sure he's in his room."

Two more days at Willow Woods? She abruptly changed her mind. "All right, tonight."

Chapter Forty-three

JULIA MUST HAVE yawned three times on the way back upstairs. She didn't really know how she was going to manage this, fighting sleep, fighting her attraction to Richard—weren't the two incompatible? She sighed in frustration and tried to think of another way to convince the earl they were sharing a bed, without actually doing so, but as tired as she was, she couldn't think clearly, or she wouldn't be walking down the corridor to Richard's room again.

At his door he paused and nodded behind him toward the earl's door. "While I'd wager that the contract is in the study, the joke would be on us if Father has set guards there just to make us *think* it's there."

She had to disagree. "While that could have occurred to him, I highly doubt he'd bother."

"When I could knock out a guard, take what we're

after, and be gone? I have a feeling that Olaf was on his way up here to guard my father's room. And he'd be more difficult to knock out than one of the footmen. This is the perfect opportunity to search his room just to be sure. Charles said he only goes out like this a few times a week, so he isn't likely to be out of the house again while we're here."

Unless they were still there next week, Julia thought with dread. "By all means, check it now."

He did, but then said, "Locked."

Before she could express her frustration, he grinned at her and fiddled with the lock for a moment. Then he grabbed the lamp on the hallway table and swung the door open. Julia went straight to the window on the side wall and opened it so she could listen for the coach. She wasn't about to let Milton catch them in his room because they had no warning of his return until he was walking down the hall.

She kept glancing behind her to keep track of Richard's progress as he picked open the locked drawers on Milton's bureau. The tools he was using worked nearly as fast as a key! She would have to thank James Malory when this was over. When Richard and the lamp moved into the wardrobe, she knew he was almost done, with only the secret closet still to be unlocked.

She was starting to close the window when she heard Richard say in surprise, "Son of a bitch."

He'd found it?! She rushed into the clothes room

and over to the open door inside it, then halted in her tracks.

"Oh, my" was all she could think to say and even said it again. "Oh, my."

The long, narrow room was lined with floor-to-ceiling shelves. Cluttering every shelf were vases and urns in all shapes and sizes, some quite odd-looking, but most of them beautiful.

"These aren't ordinary pieces you'd use to decorate your house," she said in awe. "The smaller ones appear to be made of real gemstones, not colored glass. And look at this one." She picked up one that was nearly the size of her hand. "As I thought, this has the weight of pure gold, not painted metal."

"I don't understand it. He lets his debts pile up while he keeps this fortune locked away up here?"

Julia didn't understand it either. "Well, they're probably locked away because they're so valuable. Every one of these can actually be considered a work of art. I would have said they must be family heirlooms—"

"That he never shared with the family?"

"I recognize this one," Julia said, inspecting the gold vase more closely. "I almost bought it myself. It was in one of the more expensive import shops on Bond Street. But I'm not so frivolous to waste thousands of pounds on a vase just because it's supposedly one of a kind and thus considered priceless. That's something my mother would have done. So while some of these could be heirlooms your ancestors acquired over the years, not all of them are."

Richard had been looking inside every vase to make sure nothing was hidden inside them. Finished, he handed her the lamp and pushed her out of the room so he could relock it. In quick order, he got them safely back to his own room.

Tossing the packet of tools into his traveling chest, he mused, "No matter the why or how of it, he's still got a fortune in there, yet he's been obsessed with *your* fortune? It makes no sense."

"Your father isn't an ordinary man by any means. Nothing he does makes sense. Consider his horrid treatment of his own sons? And him holding on to a hope for nine bloody years that you'd come happily home to do your duty? And his 'grandfather' persona, which is everything you could hope for in a grandpapa? But at least when we leave here, I'm not going to feel guilty now about pulling the work crews out before they're done, not with all the wealth he possesses in that collection of vases and urns. I've become rather fond of your nephew already, so I was starting to feel bad about leaving him here in this rotting old place."

Richard chuckled at her. "It's not rotting. The foundation is solid. Can't deny it doesn't need a lot of work, though, but children don't pay attention to that sort of thing. And Charles has his own money, so you needn't worry that Mathew will ever lack for anything."

"That does relieve my mind, thank you."

He came over to her and pushed her toward the bed. Her heart skipped a beat, until he said, "You might as well take a nap, as tired as you are. I'll wake you when Father's coach pulls up. Oh, and Jewels? Might as well get comfy, too. If for some odd reason he doesn't come home tonight, I'll let you sleep the night through."

"I can't reach my buttons," she said with a yawn.

"Was that an invitation?"

"What?"

He chuckled. "Never mind, you're nearly asleep on your feet, aren't you? Let me help you."

She knew she should be paying attention. He was undressing her. She didn't want to miss that or what might happen afterward. But she'd expended her last bit of energy on her nervousness in the earl's room, and she had none left now. She even started to nod off once, Richard was so gentle in removing her dress, her shoes and stockings, and pulling the blanket over her scanty underclothes when he was done.

Then she felt the kiss on her brow and heard him whisper, "Sweet dreams, love."

How'd he know she was going to dream about him?

Chapter Forty-four

HE'S HOME. D'YOU need help waking up?"

Julia didn't remember falling asleep, remembered nothing after her head touched the pillow. But her eyes opened now as she felt Richard's warm breath on her cheek, her neck. His lips were even warmer. He was kissing her awake. She wasn't going to answer him to let him know it had worked. Her belly was already fluttering with excitement. She wasn't experiencing any frustration now, no indeed. But she soon had to revise that thought when she realized he was *only* trying to wake her.

The moment he sensed her awareness he said, "We should bounce the bed. With no carpet on the floor, it will make quite a racket."

Imagining that, she couldn't help laughing. "That implies quite a bit of exertion. I happen to know you have more finesse than that."

"Do you?" he asked, his voice turning husky.

She realized she must have provoked some carnal thoughts in him with that compliment because his mouth moved over hers and he was kissing her deeply now. But they were too quiet, emitting only a soft groan, a labored breath now and then. This wasn't for his father's benefit at all, she realized. This was him wanting her, and that brought forth her own passions with quick abandon.

So easily, she forgot why they were doing this. She wrapped her arms around him, enjoying the feel of his warm skin under her hands. He'd removed his shirt in preparation for the morning demonstration for the maid again, but she didn't care why. She loved the feel of his body, the wide stretch of his chest, muscles rippling under her fingertips. In the past, she'd always hated his strength, even held it against him, but she laughed at herself for those childish notions when she was so thrilled now by his big, muscular body.

He leaned over her, his tongue delving for another deep kiss as he slipped a hand beneath the loose top of her chemise, pulling it down low enough to expose both of her breasts. He cupped one in his large hand, then the other. When he tore his mouth away from hers to capture one of those breasts in it with such scalding heat, she arched forward, her head thrown back.

His arms slipped under her back, holding her in

that position for a few tantalizing minutes before his mouth moved up to her neck, then her ear, causing gooseflesh to spread over her shoulders. Little nibbles followed, spreading the exciting sensations further. Shiver after shiver joined in, while his mouth traveled down her arm, his tongue licking at her pulse points, then he actually took one of her fingers into his mouth and sucked on it. It was so oddly erotic, her breath caught.

With a last kiss to the center of her palm, he leaned over her again, pressing his chest against her breasts, kissing her deeply as he slipped his hand under her drawers to raise her temperature even higher. It worked, too well!

Too many clothes were still in the way! She knew he could change that quickly enough, so she tried to control her impatience, but it was almost impossible. God, she wanted him so much, deep inside her, taking her to those magical heights of pleasure again.

But he came to his senses! God, not again! Yet he dropped his forehead to her chest and groaned, "This better work this time, because there's no way in hell I can do this again and *not* make love to you."

She started to tell him that she felt the same way, that he didn't need to restrain himself, when the door burst open. They'd been so involved with each other they hadn't heard the earl coming down the corridor. He walked into Richard's bedroom with three men crowding in behind him, two of them holding lamps high so the entire room was lit. Startled, Julia had leaned up, and now she froze in shock, all color draining from her face.

Richard shot out of bed instantly, tossed the covers up over her half-naked body, then stood there furiously, facing his father. Richard looked as angry as he'd been downstairs when he'd confronted a man big enough to tear him apart. This was the reckless, unpredictable side of Richard, and she was actually more afraid of what he might do than of what his father was up to.

Milton didn't leave them wondering for long. Much too congenially he said, "I didn't really expect this to play out this way, but just in case it did, I brought our parish pastor along."

Knowing exactly what that meant, Julia began to panic, but Richard didn't acknowledge the danger they were in. "What for?" he demanded.

Milton smiled, exuding triumph. "You've compromised her. You aren't going to try to deny it, are you? After you've already admitted it and when I'm standing here seeing the proof of it along with these good witnesses, who will, of course, also bear witness to your wedding—tonight."

Richard said nothing, but his fists clenched. Julia found her voice and quickly pointed out, "This isn't legal when the banns—"

"—are irrelevant when I have a special license that doesn't require the posting of banns," Milton cut her off. "I've had it for nine bloody years."

She was beginning to see there was no way out of this. Here she was lying in bed next to the man she'd been betrothed to since childhood, and it wasn't just the earl who had caught her in this compromising position. A pastor was present, too. But she knew Richard was going to refuse to go through with the marriage, and then what? Would they both be shipped off to Australia this time?

"Why are you doing this when we're planning to be married at a proper wedding ceremony?" she asked frantically.

"You can still have your grand wedding, m'dear. This is merely *my* insurance."

"No, this is you forcing the issue and putting a tawdry stain on it," Richard said furiously.

Milton tsked. "It's nothing of the sort. If you love her as you say, you should be delighted to marry her sooner." But then Milton added with a knowing sneer, "Or were you not really intending to marry at all?"

Richard didn't answer. Julia said quickly, "If you had a license and were going to force a wedding, why didn't you just send for me when you had Richard before, instead of putting him on that convict ship?"

Milton flushed angrily at her mentioning that in front of the pastor and the other men, but he said quickly, "Would you have come for a wedding? No, you would have sent someone to verify that Richard was back and agreeable, and finding out that he was still against it, you would have run in the opposite direction, wouldn't you? Can you deny it, when a week later you came to tell me that nothing had changed between the two of you so you weren't getting married? No, *he* needed to be willing before you'd come to the altar, and he wasn't—yet."

She noticed it only made Richard angrier to hear Milton's previous motives spelled out, but she insisted, "That isn't true. I never said I wouldn't marry him if he was here to be married. Whether he was agreeable or not, I would have honored that contract."

Milton waved his hand impatiently, dismissing her words. "I don't believe you. But since you've both had such an amazing change of heart and claim to love each other now, it doesn't matter, does it? Enough talk. Please rise and prepare to take your vows."

The silence was suddenly deafening. Richard didn't even try to conceal his rage, it was in his posture, in every line of his face, pouring from his eyes, and the tension in the room grew apace. He wasn't going to let his father win this long-standing battle. He simply wasn't going to answer, and that was answer enough. Julia held her breath, waiting for Milton's reaction, unable to think of anything else to say that might prevent or delay what was going to happen.

Richard finally spat out, "I knew it was a mistake to come here," and Julia braced herself for the violence that was sure to follow that remark. But then she stared at him incredulously when he added, "Hurry up, Pastor. My bride has been embarrassed enough."

Chapter Forty-five

SHE WAS MARRIED, to *him*. Julia was so close to tears she didn't dare say anything yet, didn't dare even glance at the angry man sitting across from her in the coach on the way back to London.

She was still so embarrassed she didn't think it would ever go away. She'd had to stand there with a blanket wrapped around her for her wedding. They wouldn't even give her an opportunity to dress first. The pastor had immediately begun the ceremony. She'd had to be nudged for her replies, she'd been in such a mortified daze, and nudged again for her signatures. Three times she'd had to authorize that travesty with a pen, for the parish ledger that the witnesses had also signed, for the document Milton wanted for himself, and for the document that was handed to her, her proof that she was married, as if she needed proof after that.

When that door had closed behind all those witnesses, and Milton's laughter could be heard on the other side of it, Richard had looked as if he wanted to kill something, really kill something.

She was still too shocked over what had just happened to feel angry, but she did realize they'd made that much too easy for the earl. She tried not to sound accusatory, but she had to ask Richard, "Did you consider this possibility when you decided on our demonstration?"

"Hell no, I didn't. And now isn't a good time to talk to me, Jewels. Go pack, we're leaving."

He'd said no more. She didn't argue because she wanted to leave Willow Woods as much as he did.

Leaving at night didn't make for a fast exit though. Most of the servants had retired so they had to be awakened to help with the baggage and to bring the two coaches around. But they wouldn't be racing down too many dark roads. She was sure Richard would find them an inn where they could spend the night once they were far enough away from Willow Woods. But he didn't. He stopped only long enough to gather Ohr and a few of the guards, who could spell the drivers of the two vehicles because he intended to reach London before nightfall the next day.

Julia slept the rest of the night, despite the emotional turmoil that had begun to get worse. She was simply too tired not to nod off, even while sitting up. At one point Richard leaned over to push her down on the seat she had to herself so she could be more comfortable. She barely noticed, going right back to sleep.

She finally woke at midday, feeling rested, yet not a bit more prepared to deal with having a husband who was furious that he *was* a husband.

Richard still said nothing as she sat up and wiped the sleep from her eyes. He just handed her a basket of food they must have stopped for. It didn't look as if he'd had any of it himself. It didn't look as if he'd slept, either.

He was staring broodingly out the window. Every so often a muscle ticked in his jaw. His hair was loose and had been since she'd pulled it free of its queue last night in bed. But he was wearing a jacket and a loose cravat. Such an odd contrast that long hair made with his finely tailored clothes. He was half aristocrat, half daring adventurer, but still so handsome, even though he was putting up this cold, angry wall between himself and the world. It made her wonder what he'd really been doing all these years. What had made him so unconventional? He'd given her silly, teasing answers that she couldn't possibly believe when she'd asked before. But now that the knot was tied, as it were, she had a right to know the truth.

"You *are* a pirate, aren't you?"

She regretted the question the moment after she blurted it out. This was no time to discuss his past when they hadn't even discussed what they were going to do about their future. And it didn't yet look as if he'd calmed down at all.

He didn't look at her, but he said, "No—not anymore."

She hadn't expected to hear him confirm it. "You used to be?"

"Yes."

"Why didn't you try to convince me of it?"

"When you found it so hilarious that I could have lived such a life?"

"But a pirate, Richard?" Then she said in her defense, "I didn't find it ludicrous that you could *be* a pirate, I simply didn't believe that pirates still exist. You do know what century this is?"

He glanced at her. A half smile formed on his lips. Had she just cracked that wall of anger?

"I have a feeling you're thinking of bloodthirsty cut-throats. "You're right, they lived in another age. Let me tell you about my captain, Nathan Brooks. He's Gabby's father and a kind, good-hearted man—who used to be a pirate."

She was soon fascinated, listening to him, and watching the way his eyes lit up when he spoke of his adventures aboard *The Crusty Jewel*. He told her how he'd met Ohr, and then Nathan and the rest of his crew, how they were like family to him now. Yes, they had loosely called themselves pirates, but they were treasure hunters, too.

"That was always Nathan's real passion and what we spent at least half our time doing, hunting down old pirate treasure. And that's actually all we do these days. After Nathan spent some time as a hostage himself, he washed his hands of anything to do with pirating. It was an easy decision for him to make, though, with Gabby marrying into the Skylark shipping family, who quite frown on that sort of thing."

"So you really like the Caribbean?"

"Like it? I love it—but not everyone does. It's beautiful, but there isn't a single thing about it that's similar to England. It's a completely different way of life from what you know, harsh at times, the heat extreme. The English who go there soon wilt and return home."

"You didn't."

"I was forced to adapt because I didn't have a home to return to."

He turned back toward the window, the wall firmly back in place now that he was reminded of why he hadn't had a home to go back to. She looked down at her lap, sadness overwhelming her. The ring on her finger caught her eye, her wedding ring. Milton must have quickly bought it off one of the servants to present it at the wedding. It didn't fit and was as ugly as her marriage ceremony had been.

A tightness formed painfully in her chest. She wished she hadn't learned these things about Richard's life away from England. A part of her, an emotional part, *liked* that she was married to him. She was afraid that she'd grown too attached to him over the last month and now she'd fallen in love with him. But from everything he'd just told her and how he loved the new life he'd made for himself in the Caribbean, there was obviously no place for her in it. But even if she could fit in, she couldn't ignore that Richard didn't like their current state at all. He couldn't have made that clearer. So she had to make it right for him and at least offer him a way out. Yet, hesitating to broach the subject, she waited too long.

The coach stopped in front of her home in Berkeley Square, and Richard opened the door for her and handed her down to the curb. He didn't leave the coach himself. Too angry even to come in with her to tell her father that they were married?

There was no help for it. She felt he was going to close the door without even a good-bye.

"I'll start divorce proceedings immediately," she promised him. "You needn't—"

He cut in sharply, "You want a divorce?"

No sigh of relief? No thank-you? Anger still spewing forth? She grit her teeth. "Yes, of course. Neither of us expected or wanted this to happen."

"Whatever you want, Jewels," he said with a poignancy that she didn't quite understand. But she must have mistaken it, because he added brusquely, "I'm leaving."

He started to close the door. "Wait! You'll need to be present for the divorce. It shouldn't take more than a few weeks. Where can I reach you?"

He stared at her for a long moment before he said, "I guess you better pack for a long trip. If you want that divorce, you'll have to come with me. I'm not staying in this country another day. If *The Triton* isn't ready to sail, I'll catch another ship. I'm going home where I can breathe and forget about that ruthless bastard again."

"You're not thinking logically. It will only take a little while longer, then we can be done with this."

He shook his head adamantly. "If I stay here another day, I'm going to go back there and kill that son of a bitch. I need to get far away from that temptation. Immediately. So take it or leave it, Jewels. You've got the rest of the day to think about it."

"Just like that? Wait! Where are you going? I'll need to be able to find you to let you know if I—agree."

"You can send the message to Boyd Anderson's house, since that's where Gabby and Drew are staying, and I'll be meeting up with them."

Richard closed the door and slammed a fist against the ceiling for the driver to move on. She stared at the departing vehicle incredulously. My God, what had just happened? She was doing him the favor of getting him out of this quickly, yet he wouldn't cooperate?

Chapter Forty-six

THE DECISION TO leave England with Richard wasn't as hard to make as it should have been. Julia made it before she even entered her home that day.

Waiting for her maid to get out of the second coach, she told the girl, "Have more trunks brought down from the attic and pack them today. I'm going on a long sea voyage with my husband."

But stepping inside the house, she immediately glanced upstairs where her father was and knew that the hardest part of that decision was still to come. She didn't like having to admit she'd failed at anything, and that farce at Willow Woods was the biggest failure of her life.

Her father was in his room, but not in his bed. Arthur was helping Gerald exercise his legs by walking him back and forth across the room, Gerald's arm over Arthur's shoulder for support. She was glad to see they were diligently working on getting his muscles back into shape.

"Welcome home!" Gerald beamed when he caught sight of her. "I didn't anticipate your being successful so soon. Come, let's sit on this delightful balcony you had built for me and you can tell me all about it."

The doors to the balcony were open wide, letting in the warm, fresh air. Arthur led Gerald in that direction. Julia followed and sat next to him. How many times had she read to him here in the summer months? She'd been sure he never absorbed a word, but that hadn't stopped her from trying, just in case he did.

She sighed at his expectant look. "It didn't work, Papa. The earl called our bluff."

"Called it how?"

"With a special license to marry immediately and a pastor at his heels. We're married."

Gerald frowned as he asked carefully, "That isn't a happy statement, is it?"

"No indeed.

He sighed. "I'm sorry, I shouldn't even have asked that. But you and Richard appeared to be getting along so well when you were here together, I got the notion that you might be liking each other after all these years and that something might still come of it."

Feeling a tightness in her throat, she glanced away before answering. "We do like each other, we're just not the least bit suited for each other. He lives a life of high adventure across the ocean, where he spends most of his time at sea. I'd rather be adding up profits in an account book—here."

"Then if you two didn't want to marry at that point, why did you? I told you I would deal with any scandal. Why didn't you just refuse?"

She wished he hadn't asked that. She could feel a blush mounting her cheeks. While she hadn't actually made love to Richard that night, witnesses would say otherwise.

"I was sort of in my underclothes—in Richard's room."

Gerald cleared his throat. "I see."

She winced. "Actually, there's more to it. It was part of our charade. We wanted the earl to think we were, well, sleeping together, so he'd believe we really did want to marry and relax his guard. He'd been highly skeptical. We thought that might convince him. It never once occurred to us that he'd pounce on it as an excuse to marry us immediately instead. He barged into Richard's room with a pastor and some other witnesses. Just as Milton no doubt hoped, he caught us in a compromising position. So the whole charade backfired on us. And Richard won't even stay in London long enough for a divorce."

"You mean he won't agree to one?"

"Oh, he will, just not *here*. He's leaving the country tomorrow. So if I want the divorce, I have to go all the way to his home in the Caribbean to get one. He's so angry that it came to this, he won't listen to reason."

"I'll talk to him."

"That's just it, he won't discuss it. If there were more time for him to calm down and think logically, he might see reason, but there isn't. And I even understand why he's so furious. All these years he stayed away, but it wasn't to avoid me, it was to keep his father from getting what he wanted. Yet the earl just won the battle with this marriage."

Gerald said in disgust, "Milton Allen isn't going to get anything out of this other than the dowry I committed to."

"I'm glad to hear you say that. I wish he wouldn't get even that, after everything he's done, but I understand the dowry was promised to him in the contract. Yet he could have had more. It makes no sense that he turned down your other offers, does it? And he *still* thinks he's going to get a lot more, which—I hate to say this, Papa, but it makes me fear for your life. And Richard is playing right into his hands by leaving again. If you die, Milton will have control of everything through the marriage."

He chuckled at her. "Don't let your imagination run wild, dearest. The answer is as simple as my not breaking the tie when I should have because your mother always begged me to wait. Then the accident incapacitated me and Milton continued to think the marriage would still make us all one happy family. And families take care of their own, even their black sheep."

She understood what he was getting at. Even her cousin Raymond, who could be considered their black sheep because he disdained any responsibility and led a frivolous life, was still supported by Gerald and would always be. He was family. And now Milton was family, unwanted, but dammit, family nonetheless.

"That implies you'll help the earl out when he comes knocking at the door," she pointed out. "And I don't doubt he plans to, endlessly."

"No, it means nothing of the sort. It just explains why he still *thinks* I will help him. You should have let me talk to Milton. I would have made it clear that I don't forgive or forget. And he's earned my enmity, for what he did to his own son, and for the tears he's caused you."

She chewed at her lip, still worried. "But he doesn't know that yet. And what if he's beyond reasoning with, due to his obsession with your wealth and—"

Gerald gently put his finger to her lips. "Hush. If it will relieve your mind, I'll have a legal document drawn up today that will prevent him from ever inheriting anything of mine and have it delivered to him posthaste."

"I like that idea. I also want everything put back in your name before I leave, so we can do that at the same time."

Gerald nodded, but then sighed. "So you really are going all the way to the Caribbean?"

"It won't be for long. A few weeks and—"

"It's three or four weeks just to get there."

She sighed. "Well, I'm going to find a bright side to it—somehow. I've never traveled before, other than here in England and to France a few times, so I suppose it will be an interesting trip. And once Richard calms down, he's easy to get along with."

"Is he?"

"Yes, very. He's nothing like the man—well, the boy I used to know and hate. Living abroad for so many years away from his father has changed him dramatically—at least when he isn't around his father."

Gerald gave her a curious look. "Are you sure you want a divorce?"

That odd emotion was welling up in her again. All she could think to say was "I'm sure he does."

"That doesn't answer my question."

No, it didn't, so she confided sadly, "I can't deny there were moments when I began to think he actually would be perfect for me. But our way of life just doesn't match anymore, Papa. He'll never come back to England, not as long as his father still lives here. But can you imagine me living in the tropics where it's always so hot I'd be longing for a flake of snow? I can't imagine it, and—and he doesn't love me."

"I see." Gerald sighed. "This isn't how I wanted you to get out of this mess I got you into."

"I know, but at least that damn contract has been satisfied and will never haunt me again."

"But a divorce is a serious matter. The *ton* that you hobnob with will consider it a scandalous solution. There will be repercussions that won't be pleasant, at least in a social sense. You may find yourself not invited to their parties, even snubbed."

"Are you suggesting—?"

"No, dearest, if this is something you feel you must do, then I will support your decision. And I've merely mentioned the worst that could happen, but it may not be so bad as that. Your situation is unique, after all, with a fiancé gone for so many years, and you were even kept waiting for three of them. That may gain you sympathy, or at least understanding for why you couldn't forgive him."

With the *ton*? If they considered something "simply not done," the reasons wouldn't matter. She could well lose all her friends over this.

Her father seemed to read her mind and suggested, "Why don't you contact Carol before you leave and see what she has to say about all this? Arthur told me she hasn't lived next door since she married, but does she live too far away for a quick visit? I didn't think to ask when she stopped by the other day to express her delight over my recovery."

"She and Harry do live at his country estate, but they

also have a London house, and with the summer Season of parties under way, she's probably still in town. That's an excellent idea, Papa. I would like to see her before I leave for my brief vacation in the Caribbean."

He chuckled at her choice of words. "If, as you say, Richard's company doesn't aggravate you like it used to, then you might as well enjoy the trip. The islands in that area are reputed to be quite beautiful, though perhaps a bit warm at this time of the year."

"A bit? Richard made it sound a lot hotter than that. But I don't intend to stay any longer than I have to. I wish you could go with me."

"That isn't possible. Even if I were physically fit, one of us still needs to hold down the fort here. But would you like to take Raymond?"

"Good God, no. Then the trip would be nothing *but* aggravating."

As soon as she left her father's room, she wondered if she would have time for everything she needed to do that afternoon. She sent off a message to Carol first, hoping her friend could come to her so they could talk while she was packing. She didn't want to leave and miss the solicitor, either. And since she hadn't seen Carol since the Malory ball, they had a lot to catch up on.

But she'd barely sent the footman off with her note when Carol burst into her room while she was laying out clothes on the bed for her maid to pack as soon the extra trunks were brought down.

Obviously, Carol had already been on her way to visit, and her first question was "*How* did you end up married?"

Amazed that Carol already knew, Julia asked, "How did you find out?"

"Are you joking? Your servants downstairs are talking about nothing else since your maid spread the news. Your butler mentioned it the moment he let me in."

Julia sighed. She was going to have to give her maid a tongue-lashing. The girl really was too quick to gossip.

But Carol surprised her even more when she added, "But I already knew what you were *supposed* to be doing at Willow Woods."

"How?" But then Julia guessed. "Never mind, Father said you paid him a visit while I was gone. I take it he mentioned it?"

"Yes, I came by to see you, but once again you weren't home—it's almost laughable how many times you and I must have just missed each other that week. So I visited with your father instead, since I hadn't seen him since his recovery. But he only mentioned where you'd gone and why because he assumed I already knew. He knows you and I tell each other everything. I was *so* disappointed that I didn't hear it from you. Your father didn't exactly go into detail when he realized I didn't even know your fiancé was back in town."

"I told you about him that night at the ball—"

"You did not!"

"Yes, I did—well, indirectly," Julia said. "Actually, I didn't *know* it was Richard yet, either. The Frenchman? You remember now?"

"Him? Oh, my. But didn't you say he was in love with someone else? A married woman?"

"Georgina Malory."

Carol gasped. "He has a death wish?"

"No, and I'm sure that was merely an infatuation. He never once appeared melancholy again when she was mentioned. As daring as I now know he is, I don't doubt he was just enamored of the risk of pursuing her."

Carol sighed. "But this means you aren't really married, doesn't it? You just let your maid think you are for some reason?"

"You should probably sit down," Julia said, then brought Carol up-to-date.

And after hearing it all, even the more intimate details that Julia would never tell anyone else, Carol said in amazement, "That's quite a—predicament. No, don't cry!"

Julia couldn't help herself. "The irony is, he's my perfect someone, but I'm not his."

"Good God, you love him? After all these years of hating him, you actually *love* him?"

"I didn't say that."

"You didn't have to."

"But I don't want to live so far away from everything I know, in a place that sounds so foreign."

Carol rolled her eyes. "You won't know that you don't like it until you've actually been there. So what other doubts do you have?"

Julia said in a small voice, "He doesn't love me."

"Are you sure?"

"Well, no, but—"

"Maybe he's having some of the same doubts you are?"

Julia bit her lip. "I'm not sure."

"Then you'll have to find out, and you'll work it out. You've got a whole ocean to cross before you stand before an official to end a marriage maybe neither of you wants to end. Let Richard know how you feel."

Chapter Forty-seven

GABRIELLE AND DREW had been waiting for Richard to return to London before they set sail for the Caribbean, so making the preparations to depart in the morning wasn't an inconvenience, Drew assured his friend. Richard was relieved that Gabrielle wasn't at Boyd's house when he arrived there because he knew she would insist on a full accounting of what had happened at Willow Woods. His emotions still volatile, Richard wasn't ready to discuss it. He merely told Drew that it didn't go well.

What an understatement that was. When he'd stood in his old bedroom at Willow Woods, watching his father smirk, he'd realized his detestable sire was actually forcing on him something he wanted! The woman he'd been tied to most of his life. Yet getting what *he* wanted meant his father won, too. That's what was so bloody unacceptable in his mind.

He didn't stay at Boyd's house any longer than to drop his bag in the room he was shown to, which he would share with Ohr for the night. He needed to find a solicitor who would see him today. If anything should happen to him, or to Julia before she got her divorce, he wanted to make damn sure his father couldn't step in and try to lay claim to any part of the Miller fortune. He wanted a will drawn up that would expressly exclude Milton Allen from anything of his—or his wife's.

His wife. Good God, that sounded so nice. But Julia didn't think so, and she was probably right. What did he have to offer her, after all? He wasn't broke. There was nothing really to spend money on in the Caribbean, so he had a few thousand pounds stashed away, but that was like pocket change compared to what Julia was worth. He owned no property, not even a house of his own. And he was a second son, so no title other than *lord* came with his name, which he didn't even use in the islands. Take Julia away from the world of high society she was so accustomed to? From the business empire she'd been running by herself for the last five years? In good conscience, how could he do that?

He had to let her go, and that meant not fighting her decision. He could see no way around it. But he couldn't bear to do it yet. It had been pure impulse, insisting she come with him, but he was glad now that he'd done it. At least, it would give him a few more weeks with her before they parted for good.

But she might not come.

After he returned to Boyd's house late that afternoon, it felt as if he were holding his breath until her message was delivered, informing him that she'd meet him at the docks in the morning.

Ohr appeared in the open doorway. Richard hadn't closed the door after Julia's message was brought up to him. He was so deep in thought, he only barely realized Ohr was saying something to him.

"What?"

"I said, what happened at Willow Woods?" Ohr repeated.

"Our bluff got called. We're married."

Ohr chuckled. "Wasn't expecting to hear that. Then why are you mooning again?"

"I wasn't."

"You were. After recent events, I was sure you'd be done with that."

Richard didn't want to discuss Julia yet, so he simply said, "It's a complex situation."

"Seems simple to me. Or did it never occur to you that you were enamored of the *danger* of loving her, simply because of who her husband is?"

Richard choked back a laugh over Ohr's mistake, tried to interrupt him, but Ohr held up his hand, determined to have his say. "Malory threatened us the very day you met his wife when we dropped Gabby off at their house. He was extremely intimidating, as he tends to be, and that could have influenced you right then. He presented you with a unique challenge. But you've finally had a taste of his jealousy, so I have to ask, do you really *think* you still love her?"

Richard chuckled as he shook his head. He didn't *have* to explain the mistake. Ohr wouldn't pry. So he just said, "No, whatever that was, it's gone."

"So you're mooning over your own wife?" Ohr pried anyway. "How—odd."

Richard's mouth tightened. Nothing about that was amusing. "I'll work it out."

"Well, if you'd rather talk it out, we have time before the party."

"What party?"

"Gabby and Drew's farewell party this evening. We've been invited."

"Invited when we're already here? Was there any doubt that we would be welcome?"

"Oh, the party isn't here," Ohr said with a grin. "It's at James Malory's house."

Richard never imagined he'd actually be invited to James's house. Malory must not know, he figured. Yet when he and Ohr were shown into the parlor where Andersons and Malorys were gathered, James noticed him and didn't even raise a brow over his presence.

Gabrielle pounced on him though, the moment he walked in. Ohr had warned Richard that he'd mentioned his marriage to Drew, and Drew had joined his wife earlier at the Malory house.

"I'm so delighted!" Gabrielle told Richard.

"Don't be. My father won, Gabby."

"Well, there is that, but you did, too, didn't you? I saw the way you were looking at Julia on *The Maiden George*. You could barely take your eyes off of her. And you married her!"

She was too happy for him. Richard didn't have the heart to tell her about the upcoming divorce, at least not at this party in her honor.

He said simply, "She's sailing with us."

"Well, of course she is, why wouldn't she? Oh, wait, she must have *so* much to pack, to move to another country. Does she need help? Do we need to delay our departure a day or two?"

"No delays, Gabby, please. I was prepared to find another ship if *The Triton* couldn't sail in the morning. I can't bear to spend another day on the same continent with my father."

She peered at him closely. "What else happened?"

"Let's not discuss it tonight. And Julia will manage just fine; she's probably got more servants to help her than we can count. Go enjoy your party."

He pushed her toward her husband while he quickly headed across the room to escape any more questions. James's son, Jeremy, caught his eye and Richard went over to him.

He'd never seen Jeremy's wife before. She'd probably been at Georgina's ball, but he wouldn't have noticed as besotted as he'd been with Georgina. He couldn't help noticing her now as she turned to face him. He even caught his breath. Danny Malory had an ethereal sort of beauty that was mesmerizing and made even more angelic by her pure white hair, which was so unusual on a young woman. Though cut extremely short, a highly unfashionable style for a lady, on her it was stunning.

Jeremy poked him in the ribs to get Richard's eyes off his wife. Richard chuckled as he realized he had indeed been staring.

"Sorry," he told the couple with an abashed grin. "I suppose it happens a lot?"

Jeremy nodded. "She's lucky I'm not the jealous type."

"No, I'm just lucky," Danny said, and gave her husband a loving smile.

Richard was envious—of their happiness. Actually, all of the couples in the room seemed to be blessed with happy marriages.

Jeremy, noticing Richard's glance about the room, said, "You don't know everyone here, do you?"

" 'Fraid not. Your father would never let me in the house before."

"Really? That's interesting. Before he knew you were a lord?"

"No, I just got on his bad side," Richard said evasively.

"Ah. Well, all must be forgiven if you're here now," Jeremy assumed. "So let me introduce you to my side of the family. They aren't all here, of course, just those who were in town and could come to the party on such short notice. And I'm sure you probably know Drew's side of the family already."

Richard had never actually met Drew's older brother Warren, but since he'd married a Malory, too, Jeremy introduced Warren's wife, Amy. "A gamine imp" was how Jeremy described this cousin of his, and he warned Richard never to bet with her. She never lost, apparently.

Another of Jeremy's cousins was present, Regina Eden, who had hosted Georgina's ball, and her husband, Nicolas. "If you hear my father disparaging Nick, think nothing of it," Jeremy said with a chuckle. "My father and his brothers all had a hand in raising Reggie after her parents died, so they're a little overprotective of her and make sure Nick knows it, least my father and Uncle Tony do."

Also present was Jeremy's uncle Tony, an exceptionally handsome man whom Jeremy resembled more than his own father! Jeremy laughed when Richard mentioned that.

"Drives m'father batty, so don't remark on it where he can hear. It's this black hair, really. Only a few of us Malorys have it. Everyone else in the family leans toward blond."

One of Jeremy's older uncles was there, too, Edward Malory, and his wife, Charlotte, who lived over in Grosvenor Square. Another of Drew's older brothers, Thomas, was in attendance, too. The eldest Anderson had been in town, but had already sailed.

Of Edward, Jeremy said, "A shame Uncle Eddie won't have a chance to meet your wife before you hie off with her. He's the financial genius of the family. Julia doesn't appear to do too bad in finance herself, so they would have had so much in common to discuss."

At the mention of Julia, Richard's mood took a downward swing. But he remembered the lockpicking tools in his pocket and handed them to Jeremy now. "Thank you for lending me these."

Jeremy handed the tools to his wife, who grinned and said, "You're welcome. I don't have any use for them these days. I just keep them as a memento of the friends I made in my youth."

"They worked like a charm," Richard assured her.

"Glad to hear it."

"You've monopolized him enough, puppy," James told his son as he approached them, then said to Richard, "Come along, I've a bone to pick with you."

Richard groaned, but followed James to the unlit fireplace, which was a good distance away from the other guests.

Resting one arm on the mantel, James didn't actually look at Richard. His eyes were on his wife as he said, "What's this I hear that you actually came to your senses and did good? Trying to bowl me over before you leave town?"

"Very funny," Richard replied, unamused.

"Just don't even think of moving in down the block from me, old boy. Ever."

"You've my word on it: that will never happen."

James finally glanced at Richard, one golden brow raised. "Not even to visit? I suppose I can make exceptions for visits."

Richard couldn't help laughing now. "You're all heart, Malory."

"It's a gift," James said without expression.

Since James seemed to be in a good mood, probably because Richard was leaving the country again, Richard asked carefully, "Would you mind if I apologize to Georgina while I'm here, for any distress I might have caused her with my infatuation?"

"Yes, I mind."

"It will only take a moment."

James's tone turned abruptly ominous. "I said I mind."

Richard sighed. "Then would you convey my apologies to her? Tell her she's one of the loveliest women I've ever known—"

"You're pressing your luck."

"—but I'm fully aware of the difference now between a minor infatuation and love," Richard finished quickly.

James gave him a steady look before he said, "If you think I'm going to tell my wife she came in second place, you're out of your gourd. I'll convey the apology and not another bloody word."

"Fair enough." Richard grinned.

"But I'm reminded that George will likely miss Julia. Living so close, they were quite chummy."

"Julia will be back," Richard said simply.

"She? Not you?" At Richard's hesitant nod, James added, "Splendid. Couldn't have asked for a better arrangement. Wouldn't let George out of my sight that long, but as long as Julia travels on Skylark ships, you can at least be assured of her safety."

Richard should have let it go at that. He didn't owe Malory any explanations. But he ended up saying, "You misunderstand. She's only going to the Caribbean to get a divorce."

James stared at him for a moment, a brief moment, before his stonelike fist landed in Richard's gut. "Wrong answer. Try again."

All Richard tried to do was get some air back in his lungs and keep the wince off his face. When he was finally able to straighten up and breathe at the same time, his eyes narrowed on James. "It's not my idea. I love her. But she won't be happy where I'm going, away from everything she knows and loves. I can't do that to her."

"Then you move back here. Or you figure out another way. But you don't let true happiness slip out of your grasp without one helluva fight."

"That's what he did," Anthony Malory said as he joined them and caught the last of James's advice. "James had to get around the fact that his wife's brothers wanted to kill him and take her back home with them. Deuced hard to maintain a marriage from different sides of the ocean. But he forced them to see reason. He's good at that."

"Put a lid on it, Tony," James said.

Anthony grinned. "I was being helpful."

"You were being obnoxious," James disagreed.

Richard slipped away as the two Malory brothers began to bicker in what *might* have been a friendly way, though it was hard to tell. With his thoughts so far removed from the revelry all around him, Richard left the party early. But before he summoned the carriage to take him back to Boyd's house, he stared down the street toward Julia's home and slowly began to walk in that direction. He didn't hesitate to knock on her door. But when the butler answered, it wasn't Julia he asked to speak to. It was Gerald Miller he wanted to talk to before he sailed in the morning.

Chapter Forty-eight

OH, GOOD LORD, it's raining," Raymond said as he stepped down from the coach and reached for Julia's hand to help her down. "You're going to be soaked before you get on board."

"Nonsense," she replied, glancing curiously around the docks. "This is barely a drizzle."

Even at such an early hour, the area was bustling with activity. *The Triton* wasn't the only ship sailing with the tide. Fresh supplies were still being carried aboard Drew's ship, with several more wagons waiting to unload even more. A line of sailors soon showed up to take her trunks aboard.

She looked at her cousin, who was frowning up at the gray sky. It was too bad the nice weather they'd been having hadn't lasted for her departure. But the clouds didn't look too dark yet, and the brisk wind meant the overcast sky might clear soon.

"Don't forget to check on my father—often," she told Raymond as her last truck was carried up the ramp. She should follow it, or she *would* soon be soaked.

"Yes, yes, but at a decent hour!" Raymond said, and gave her a hug. She heard him mumble as he got back into the coach, "I still can't believe you got me out of bed before dawn *again!*"

Her cousin's grumbling was so familiar she barely noticed it. But she was still a little perplexed over her father's good mood this morning before she left the house. He'd had a much more positive view of her voyage than he'd had the day before. Just putting on a good face for her benefit?

Julia boarded the ship. It was just as well it was raining. She didn't want to watch *The Triton* sailing away from England anyway. She might cry. Again. But in her cabin, she sat on the bed staring at her trunks, which took up all of the available floor space, trying *not* to think about why she was here. Four trunks. She'd brought too many clothes, obviously. But she'd never traveled so far from home before.

The small cabin, being fitted with a normal-size bed, had only room for a tiny table to eat at, the smallest, circular bathing tub she'd ever seen, a washstand, and a normal-sized wardrobe. She was going to have to un-pack so those trunks could be removed to give her more space. She wondered if she ought to take a nap first. She might have caught up on her sleep the day before in the coach on the long drive back to London, but she hadn't got much rest last night with this trip on her mind—and what was going to happen at the end of it.

After she'd sent off her message yesterday to Richard, he'd sent back a note with directions to the dock where *The Triton* was berthed and advising her to be there before dawn. He could have said he'd pick her up, but he didn't. That would have given her one more chance to break his resolve to leave England so quickly, before it was too late. And she didn't find him on the ship, either, before the anchor was raised, though she'd been assured he was around somewhere.

She was at least glad that Gabrielle and Drew had agreed to sail this quickly, but she wondered if Richard had even told them about their marriage. She'd been given her own cabin, so maybe he was keeping that to himself—no, he would have had to explain her presence.

Carol had said, *You've got a whole ocean to cross before you stand before an official to end a marriage maybe neither of you wants to end. Let Richard know how you feel.* She'd made it sound so easy. But Julia didn't think her friend had ever had to deal with someone like Richard. He had demons eating at him. Those demons had made a monster of her when they were young. They had controlled most of his life. They could burst out at any time spewing rage and bitterness. But when those demons were quiet, when he wasn't thinking about his

father, he was another man completely—the one she'd
fallen in love with.

Still staring at the trunks that were in the way, she
gave up on the notion of napping when there was so
much on her mind and started unpacking. It didn't take
long to realize there wouldn't be room in the wardrobe
for even half of what she'd brought, so she just took out
her favorite dresses. The rest would have to be stored
with the trunks.

She paused when she heard a knock at the door and
immediately held her breath. She hoped it was Richard
if he was ready to talk to her, but hoped it wasn't him
if he was still beset by those demons—she was afraid
she was going to get angry if she had to deal with them
again.

But it was Gabrielle who poked her head inside, gave
her a bright smile, and entered, asking, "Where's your
maid?"

"Her husband wouldn't let her leave England. She's
young and they haven't been married very long. And
there was no time to find another."

Gabrielle rolled her eyes. "I know what you mean.
It was time for us to go home, but Richard insisted we
had to leave *today* or he'd find another ship. So rude of
him and he wouldn't even discuss it. But don't worry
about a maid. Mine is here and she can help you, too."

"Thank you. I don't need much help, mostly just
with my hair. I'm terrible at putting it up just right."

Gabrielle chuckled. "You might as well forget about fancy coiffures on the ship, unless you intend to spend the entire voyage below deck. *The Triton* makes good speed, which means it's usually very windy on deck. I find it much easier to manage my hair if I just braid it."

Julia barely heard any of that, was still surprised that Richard wouldn't even talk to his closest friends. She finally said in his defense, "Richard is angry."

"It was apparent something was wrong, but that's no excuse for him to be so abrupt with his friends," Gabrielle huffed.

"He told me the same thing, to be ready to leave today or—good-bye."

"But you're his wife!"

"So he did tell you that?"

"That's *all* he told us," Gabrielle said, looking at Julia expectantly.

Julia didn't really want to talk about the catastrophe at Willow Woods yet again. Tears kept sneaking up on her every time she did, and she'd had quite enough of those.

But Gabrielle didn't take the hint from her silence and said, "You know, when I said you could be his salvation, I wasn't thinking of—"

"It's all right. It didn't work anyway."

"It didn't?" Gabrielle said with a blank look. "But he married you!"

Julia sighed. There was no help for it. She sat on

the bed and patted the spot next to her so Gabrielle would join her. Then as briefly as she could, she told her new friend the same story she'd told her father, she just didn't mention all the fun she'd had at Willow Woods when the earl wasn't around. She was beginning to think she'd dreamed all of the fun she'd had with Richard and with Charles and Mathew.

Staring at the floor thoughtfully, Gabrielle said, "You won't consider staying married to him?"

Hold him to a marriage that had been forced on them? Carol seemed to think that if Julia told Richard she loved him, that would change everything. It wouldn't. How could it, when he didn't feel the same way about her?

So she avoided all the reasons why that wouldn't work and simply said, "My place is in England."

"But with most of Drew's family usually there, we'll visit often. You'd be welcome to join us anytime. And Richard will make such a good husband!"

Julia was taken aback by Gabrielle's certainty. "Will he? I know he can be charming, fun, caring—you should have seen him with his nephew. That was so touching, so I imagine he'd even make a good father. He's shown me how nice he can be, but he and I live in two completely different worlds. After the exciting adventures he's had since he left home, he wouldn't be happy to live in England now, any more than I would be happy away from the world I've grown up in. Besides, if we stay together, his father wins."

Gabrielle rolled her eyes. "His father has already won, but it was only a minor victory. You and Richard haven't really lost—yet. So don't let that tyrant be an issue anymore, or he really will win."

Chapter Forty-nine

W<small>HEN</small> J<small>ULIA</small> <small>WENT</small> up on deck once the British isles were no longer within sight, she immediately looked for Richard, but she didn't see him anywhere. Gabrielle had given her even more to think about. *Don't let that tyrant be an issue anymore.* He wasn't an issue, not for her. But would Richard ever see it that way?

She didn't think to look up to find him. But then she heard the laughter above her and glanced up to see Richard and Ohr. Hanging from a mast? And laughing? That was quite unexpected. His anger had dissipated that quickly, just because he was getting away from the homeland? Or maybe it was Ohr who had laughed.

Richard was helping his friend to hoist more sails to take advantage of the strong wind. Gabby had been right in advising her to style her hair simply for the duration of the voyage. Even queued, Richard's long hair was flying about his shoulders, and the coiffure she'd come on board with that morning had fallen apart within minutes of her standing in that wind.

She couldn't take her eyes off Richard. He was barefoot, probably for a better hold on the mast, but at that height it was still dangerous when the slightest slip could send him tumbling to the deck. Yet he looked fearless up there, as if it were something he'd done so many times he could do it blindfolded!

Her neck was beginning to crick as she watched him. Her hair was becoming quite a nuisance, blocking her view. Was he never going to notice her? Then he did. Their eyes locked. Such intensity in his, everything she felt in hers, but the wind blew her hair into her face again! When she shoved it back this time, she saw that Richard was climbing down to the deck.

She glanced down and waited, well aware that he might head in another direction, still unwilling to talk to her. But then his legs were within her view and he took something out of his pocket. His hands came to her shoulders. She gasped. But all he did was spin her around, gather her hair in his hands, and quickly tie it off.

"Thank you," she said.

She was surprised, aware that he had to feel very familiar with her to do that. She turned expectantly to face him, but his expression was completely inscrutable, giving her no clue about how to proceed.

She began carefully, "I thought I heard you laughing

with your friend. Are you feeling better now that you've succeeded in making a quick escape?"

"Not—yet."

A tightness rose in her throat with that reply. There was no help for it. She couldn't stand seeing him like this, with those demons still riding him so hard. And she could remove them.

She began again, "There's something you should know, Richard. Your father didn't really win. He'll never get more than my dowry."

"He still won," Richard said bitterly. "His damn contract has been fulfilled. And he obviously believes that will lead to greater things."

"But he's mistaken. Milton doesn't know my father. He never forgets a wrong."

"I know that now," Richard said with a slight smile. "Gerald assured me of that last night when I went to see him."

She tried to mask her surprise. "You came by last night?" And he didn't ask to see her? And why didn't her father mention that?!

"Yes, I couldn't leave without promising him that he wouldn't need to worry about you while you were gone."

"That was very thoughtful of you," she said, emotion welling up in her. "And it worked. He was in much better spirits this morning."

"Well, it's nothing to cry over!" he teased.

She swiped at her eyes. "You're too nice. Why couldn't you be like this when we were children?"

"You know why, but you're right. At some point, I should have told you why I was against the marriage back then. There was no reason we had to become enemies simply because I was outraged at being used to fill my father's coffers—and given no choice in the matter." Then his hand touched her cheek. "We don't need to discuss this again, Jewels. I'm never going to feel better about that whole episode, so let's put it behind us for now. I want you to enjoy this voyage as much as possible."

She couldn't believe he was saying that, and so tenderly. But he suddenly glanced behind her, back toward England, then abruptly grabbed her hand.

"Let me get you safely back in your cabin before that storm reaches us," he said, pulling her along behind him.

"What storm?"

"The one that followed us from the Channel. Drew had hoped to outrun it, which is why we were putting on more sails, but it's nearly here."

He entered the cabin with her and glanced around it. "The large furnishings are nailed down, but douse the lamp. That isn't safe. And to avoid injury in a fall, I'd suggest you simply stay in bed until you get the all-clear signal."

She thought he was being overly dramatic in his

warnings, until the ship pitched under her feet. But she didn't miss that he'd made sure she was safe before he rushed back to the upper deck to help secure the ship. His concern for her, coupled with that amazing conversation they'd just had in which he didn't seem to be angry anymore—did that mean he cared about her? She smiled to herself and barely noticed the pitching of the ship.

Chapter Fifty

TONIGHT THERE WAS to be a celebration dinner because the ship hadn't sustained as much damage as they'd feared. When Gabrielle came by to escort Julia to the captain's cabin she mentioned one of the small masts had cracked, but they wouldn't know until morning if they would need to return to England for the repairs, or if the ship's carpenter could fix it. She also mentioned other storms that she'd been in, none of which had been as bouncy as this one, although they'd all posed a degree of danger.

Julia actually hoped they wouldn't have to return to England now. She was afraid that would bring back Richard's demons, and she much preferred his improved mood and wanted more time to fully explore what it meant. She wasn't going to speculate anymore, but she was going to tell Richard how she felt before they made port. She had to at least do that. If there was *any* way for them to resolve the differences between their lifestyles so they could actually remain married, she owed it to herself and to him to find out.

Her spirits lifted, she was even laughing with her new friend as they entered Drew's cabin. Richard was there—and smiling at her! She couldn't resist smiling back. She'd never been able to resist his smiles. She still couldn't get over this change in him. Then she realized she hadn't exactly been in a good mood since they'd married because of all her doubts. Had he been reacting to that all along? And he'd just seen *her* laughing. . . .

He stood up to seat her. She didn't hesitate in joining him, even though other chairs at the table were empty that were not next to his.

Both seated, he leaned a little closer to ask, "Weathered the storm all right?"

"Yes."

"No bruises?"

"None."

"Maybe I should do a thorough examination, just to be sure."

He said that with a roguish grin! Good God, he was teasing her? She loved it when he was like this, with laughter in his eyes. And it continued as her companions all began to fascinate her with descriptions of the Caribbean. Balmy breezes year-round; warm, crystal-clear waters to swim in; magnificent sunsets; exotic fruits she'd probably never tasted before. They made it sound so wonderful, she realized she probably *would* like living there—if she didn't have solid ties to England.

They all seemed to be trying to convince her to give their islands a chance, and Richard didn't intervene. He was himself once again, that laughing, teasing young man who was so much fun to be around. As long as she didn't mention what was going to happen at the end of the trip, would his mood stay this way for the duration? That would mean he was just going to ignore their divorce plans for now? Or was he just glad that they would end their marriage amicably?

But she couldn't ignore that in their earlier conversations he'd given her quite a different impression of his new home. Pinning a curious look on him, she asked, "Why didn't you tell me all this, instead of making me think I'd wilt in such extreme heat?"

"Because I didn't think you'd be there long enough to adjust to the tropical climate. Tell her, Gabby."

"It might seem a little too hot at first," Gabrielle admitted. "But once you get used to it, the tropical breezes will be enough to cool you off, and a house can easily be designed to take advantage of them. And consider never having to bundle up again against the cold: no more hot bricks at the foot of the bed, no more dreary browns of winter where so much of the landscape withers. Just imagine seeing trees that never go bare, flowers that bloom year-round. There are only a few days out of the year when I might complain because the trade winds go still and it gets overly muggy, but that's a small price to pay for such beauty and lush vegetation no matter what month is it."

Drew, having traded in the Caribbean for years, mentioned the commercial aspects of what could be found there, products that were unique to the tropics—fruit, rum, sugarcane, tobacco—and that's when Julia's eyes really lit up with excitement. With her father recovered and running the family businesses again in England, she saw endless opportunities for them in the Caribbean. She could actually expand Miller industries.

She didn't realize she was thinking aloud until Richard remarked, "You're going to make the Millers farmers now?"

He was joking, but she replied, "We've always been farmers. Our businesses are based on the land. We breed the sheep, the cows, grow the wheat, process the raw materials in our own factories and mills, employ the craftsmen to turn it all into the products that get transported to our own shops, or are sold in bulk to other markets. Most everything we do, make, sell, comes from the land."

"I never realized your family dabbled in so many things," he said in surprise.

"Oh, my, yes. If it looks profitable, why not? And it sounds like there's so much potential in these islands, things we've never considered because England doesn't have the right climate to produce them."

"There are already a lot of suppliers of these products," Drew was compelled to point out.

"So?" Julia laughed. "There's always room for competition, or untapped markets, and besides, Millers do things on a grand scale."

Her excitement became contagious, at least for Drew, who was suddenly seeing new customers for his family's fleet of trade ships. They discussed that over dessert. But she finally realized that Richard had stopped contributing to the conversation, and when she glanced at him to discover why, she saw him looking at her in amazement. Did she sound too businesslike for his aristocratic tastes?

Color rose in her cheeks, but halted when he said impulsively, "Marry me."

She blinked. "We're already married."

"Marry me again. For real."

"You *want* to marry me?"

"Did it look like I was going to let you go?"

She gasped. "*This* is why you wouldn't get a divorce in England?"

She didn't realize they had an avid audience listening to every word. She was too overcome with emotion to get beyond his *wanting* to marry her to even remember they weren't alone. But he realized it and grabbed her hand and led her away, leaving his friends complaining that they were going to be denied such fascinating entertainment.

Once he'd closed the door to her cabin, he put his hands lightly on her hips and hesitantly asked, "Are you angry?"

"I should be."

He grinned slowly. "You're not."

"Of course I'm not. I thought it was rather obvious that I didn't want a divorce either."

"It was nothing of the sort. You were utterly forlorn to be leaving England."

"No, I wasn't. I was utterly forlorn—actually, *heart-broken* is the correct word—because you didn't want me."

"My God, Jewels, I couldn't want anyone more than I want you. I love you! I suspected it was happening when you showed up with the big guns to rescue me. And there wasn't much doubt left when I held you in my arms aboard *The Maiden George* and I'd never felt so complete. But I knew it was permanent, that I wanted you by my side for the rest of my life, when I watched you let my nephew choke you just so he would feel safe in the lake."

He kissed her softly, with no passion, just pure long-ing to have his love returned. But they each had too much desire for the other not to get swept up in pas-sion. Rather quickly on her part. She'd just heard what she'd wanted to hear from the day they'd first met. So many years these feelings had been there and had been denied, but no longer.

They undressed each other. She wouldn't wait for him to take off her shoes, so they laughed as they fell upon her bed. She had a feeling that laughter was going to fill the rest of her life with this man. What a wonderful thought, and such an unexpected bonus of loving him.

But just now, with his hands all over her, she did more gasping than laughing. He could ignite her so easily. He'd always been able to do that—in one form or another—to push her passion over the edge, beyond her control. But this passion was welcome! This passion was thrilling, and knowing the pleasure it would lead to made it all the more exciting.

He was leaving no part of her untouched. Following his lead, she lavished the same attention on him. She even pushed him back and climbed on top of him.

Sitting in this position was an exciting new experience for her. With his arousal pressed against her, but not inside her, teasing her, tempting her, so much of him was at her fingertips now! She moved her hands over his wide chest, circled his strong neck, and threaded her fingers up through his soft hair. She leaned forward to kiss him hard, but only for a moment—she could tease, too.

She was in more control than she'd thought! He was letting her play with him, explore his hard, beautiful body. But everything she did was tempered with her love. She was sure she was getting more pleasure from touching him than he was—or maybe not. The sounds he was making were rather telling.

That hardness pressing at her apex was still teasing her. When she finally straightened and looked down, she was arrested in complete amazement to see that his arousal had grown. She put her hand over it, heard him groan. She wasn't sure if she was hurting him or pleasing him, but she was too fascinated to stop! But when she glanced at him and saw such intensity in his green eyes, such heat, such straining tension in the muscles of his neck, his shoulders, she knew she wasn't hurting him a'tall.

She had no idea he was fighting not to flip her over immediately. But she guessed, and with a sensual smile, she raised her hips just enough to guide him where she wanted him. The pleasure of him filling her! Her head dropped back, her hair spilling over his thighs like a silky caress. But she'd already pushed him beyond his limits. He gripped her hips and thrust so hard she had to hold on, and that quickly he exploded in her. His groan of satisfaction filled the room.

"Damn," he said when he caught his breath. "You excite me so much I feel like a youth again, unable to control myself. I'm sorry."

"For . . . what?" she gasped out with a trembling shudder, then another, as she moved against him to prolong her orgasm.

He laughed when he realized he had nothing to

apologize for, but explained, "I thought I'd left you behind, unsatisfied."

She grinned at him. "Don't worry. I won't ever allow that to happen."

He chuckled. "I think you've been in control of your family empire too long. You're going to be bossy in bed, aren't you?"

"I just might, but I'll make sure you enjoy every minute of it."

He settled them comfortably on the bed so he could hold her close. There was no thought to leaving it, but then it was late enough in the evening they didn't have to. Julia wondered how she was going to survive being this happy. She had such urges to laugh, to shout for joy, to jump up and down in giddy delight. She'd made him feel like a youth? She guessed the feeling was mutual.

She sat up abruptly when she realized something important. "I didn't leave you wondering, did I? About how much I love you?"

"You did." He grinned. "It was a good guess, though."

She blushed a little. "Don't be surprised when I tell you I've always wanted you for my husband. When I first clapped eyes on you, you can't imagine how thrilled I was. My parents really did find me the perfect match. I think I hated you so much because you didn't feel the same way about me."

He sat up and hugged her. "I'm so sorry I let what I felt for my father influence me to push you away."

"Shhh. No more apologies. You've made me more happy than I can describe."

"Which I'm still finding incredible. If I've been a boor since we married, it's because I was so sure you wouldn't like living in the Caribbean with me—until I saw your reaction to the conversation tonight."

"I have no doubt a'tall I'm going to love it then."

"But it wasn't just that."

"What else?"

"I don't have anything to offer you but my love. I don't even have a home to take you to. I live on a ship, or at my captain's house, or at Gabby's house. I've never needed a house of my own."

She leaned back and chuckled at him. "You think I can't buy us a house?"

"I didn't say I couldn't afford one. I'll do the house buying, Jewels."

That absolutely male-prerogative tone made her ask cautiously, "You aren't going to be silly about me being rich, are you? I know Anthony Malory is like that. He refuses to let his wife spend a copper of her own money."

Richard's eyes flashed with laughter. "Does he? Well, I'm not that arbitrary. *You* will have the choice of spending your money on whatever you like. But I'm still buying our first house."

She started laughing herself. "You call that a choice?"

"I call that *me* knowing more about island living than you do—yet. But I didn't say you couldn't buy a house, too. We'll have two—or more. Hell, however many you want, but at least one in England, and one in the islands."

She was thrilled beyond measure. "You mean it? We can live in both places?"

"Whatever your heart desires, Jewels."

Chapter Fifty-one

THEY STOOD OUTSIDE Julia's home in Berkeley Square. Richard took her hand in his, brought it to his lips, and kissed it. They were back so soon! But they wouldn't be staying long, only a few days to get *The Triton* back into shape. A few days was enough to share their happy news—and put paid to an old account. Richard just didn't know yet about the "paid in full" stamp she wanted on that part of their lives.

"My father is going to be so happy," she said as they mounted the steps, then added carefully, "Is there any chance that you might ever reconcile with yours?"

"Are you joking?"

His expression confirmed that was never going to happen. "I had to ask," she said, "because I would like closure with him. I want him to know, without any doubt, that he'll never be a part of our lives."

"He won't be."

"We know that, but I want him to know it, so he will never attempt any more plotting or planning where we're concerned. Can we put an end to it, once and for all, so neither of us has reason to concern ourselves with him again?"

"You actually want to go to Willow Woods again?"

"Yes, one last time."

"Let me mull that over, Jewels. I really wasn't planning on ever seeing him again."

She nodded and took him into the house. She wasn't going to argue the matter. It had to be his choice. He was never, ever going to be denied choices again, if she could help it.

They actually found her father downstairs in his study. "You can walk!" Julia exclaimed.

Gerald said at nearly the same time, "What are you doing back so soon?"

They chuckled at each other. Gerald explained first. "Arthur found a stretcher to use to get me downstairs easily. I've missed this old chair. And it just felt wrong, taking care of business from a bed."

"So you're back to work?"

"Only as much as Arthur will allow," Gerald grumbled.

Arthur tsked from his seat by the door. "Most of the day still has to be devoted to exercise. Doctor's suggestion. But we're doing it down here now. He's bloody well tired of that bedroom."

"Don't blame him a'tall." Julia grinned. "As for our timing, we'd barely got to sea when a storm overtook us. We're only back for repairs, though we do have good news."

She was beaming, so Gerald guessed, "Of the permanent sort?"

She chuckled at her father. "I know what Richard told you the night before we sailed. He confessed. But why didn't you tell me, Papa?"

"That he loves you? I almost did. But he was so sure he needed time on that voyage to convince you of it. And you've worked so hard these last years, Julia. You never should have had to shoulder all this responsibility as young as you are. I thought the trip would do you good, give you time to relax and enjoy yourself as you should be doing at your age. And . . . well, I hoped it would end up being a real wedding trip for you."

She held up her hand to show him the beautiful silver wedding ring Richard had bought for her the day before they'd sailed out of London. This morning before they'd docked, he'd taken the ugly ring Milton had supplied for their wedding and tossed it into the Thames River before he'd slipped the new band on her finger, telling her, "You'll only have to remove this once, the day we have a wedding worth remembering. Either on a beautiful beach in the islands, or in an old cathedral here in England—you decide."

"When we come back next time," she'd told him as

she hugged him to her heart. "I want my father to be strong enough to walk me down the aisle."

Gerald raised a brow at Richard now. "Didn't take long at all, did it?"

"No, sir."

Gerald laughed. "I never thought I was going to get to say this—welcome to the family, son."

They spent the rest of the day with her father. She infected him with her own excitement, about expanding the Miller holdings to include raw materials and products from the tropics.

"One of these days you're going to have to open your own banks, just so you'll have a place to store all your wealth," Richard joked.

"That's not a bad idea!" Julia agreed. "And a good project for you, actually."

Richard rolled his eyes. "From pirate to banker? Somehow that just doesn't sound right."

The ride through the countryside the next day was solemn. Richard had agreed to go to Willow Woods because he wanted to let his brother know of their changed circumstances. That night in an inn along the way, while Richard was holding her so tenderly in bed, Julia broached the last subject she hoped to see resolved. She was still so sure that Milton Allen wasn't Richard's real father. The way the earl had treated him smacked of a man abusing a bastard that had been foisted on him. Richard had scoffed at the notion before, but if she was right, that knowledge was bound to make him happy. Wouldn't it?

Richard just hugged her tightly when she mentioned it and said, "I know you think that would resolve issues for me, but honestly, Jewels, it doesn't matter to me one way or the other. As far as I'm concerned, he's no relation of mine and hasn't been for most of my life. But if it will make you happy, I'll ask him."

Now she had doubts. If Richard really didn't care, maybe she should leave the matter alone. But she didn't get around to saying that. He had other ideas about how they would spend the rest of that night. Nice distracting ideas indeed.

Chapter Fifty-two

AT WILLOW WOODS they were met at the door by an exuberant Mathew, who had apparently decided during their absence that he liked having an uncle around after all. Richard was delighted that the boy was no longer shy in his presence. Julia was already thinking about inviting Charles to visit them in the Caribbean. Mathew would love it, she was sure.

Ruffling the boy's hair, Richard asked where the earl could be found, then sent him off to let his father know they were there. Milton was in the small library reading. He didn't stand up when they entered. He didn't look surprised to see them, either. In fact, he looked as if he was still gloating, exactly as he'd been the last time they'd seen him. Which didn't make much sense.

The house looked the same, too. Julia's workers, who had been told to leave when she did, had at least cleaned up, but nothing had actually been refurbished yet. Of course, they'd been gone for only a week. But the dowry had been delivered, along with Gerald's promise that no more money would be forthcoming. You'd think the earl would be furious over that.

"You left in such a hurry," Milton said, setting his book aside. "Forget something?"

Richard obviously didn't care for Milton's smirk and got right to the point. "Didn't Julia's father tell you that you wouldn't get anything more from the Millers?"

Milton scoffed. "Gerald will change his mind after you give him a few grandchildren."

What an amazing delusion. Richard's tone was incredulous as he pointed out, "We could be getting a divorce. Did that never occur to you?"

"You won't," the earl said confidently. "Divorce causes the worst sort of scandal in our—"

"You *really* didn't think divorce was a possibility?"

"Of course not."

"When I don't give a damn about scandal?"

"That scandal would have touched your brother and your nephew. You give a damn about them, don't you?"

Richard suddenly laughed. "They're protected."

Milton didn't like Richard's humor, even asked suspiciously, "What's different about you?"

"I'm in love," Richard replied.

"You said that before."

Richard nodded. "Before I hadn't realized the depth

of my feelings for Julia. Now I have. Before we were putting on a charade for you—"

"I knew it!"

"Now we're not," Richard finished. "So, no, there won't be a divorce."

"I thought you'd see it my—," Milton began to gloat again.

Richard interrupted this time. "But that's no benefit to you. Like Gerald, I've made it legal. Nothing of mine will ever come to you in my lifetime, or beyond. I have, in fact, disowned you, which effectively removes you from my new family."

Milton's eyes flared. "You can't do that."

"It's already done."

Milton shot out of his chair, furious. "How dare you ruin years of planning?"

"What planning?" Richard asked curiously. Julia had slipped her hand into his for support, but she realized he was quite calm in the face of his father's fury. "I'm an adult. What's hers is mine, not yours."

"We were to be one family, and families take care of their own. I expected to never want for anything again."

"The Millers offered you a fortune to release Julia from that marriage contract," Richard reminded him. "Why didn't you take it when you had the chance?"

"It wasn't enough."

"It would have been more'n enough if you sold that collection you have upstairs in your closet."

Milton nearly screeched, "Are you mad? I've been collecting those vases since I was a young man. It's the only real passion I have!"

Julia suddenly guessed, "My God, you've already spent the dowry on more vases, haven't you?"

"Of course I did. Do you know how long I've had to wait to buy the pieces I wanted? What little was left of our family wealth ran out long before my wife died, thanks to her parents. I was fine before then, able to buy the occasional vase I coveted. But then the prices started getting too steep and that infuriated me. You have no idea what it's like to love something so much and be unable to obtain it. It's important to have things of beauty in your life that you can value and love. But I couldn't afford them anymore! Year after year my suppliers would show up with a vase they *knew* I would want, and I had to turn them away, again and again."

"Do you realize how pathetic that sounds?" Richard said. "And what a fool it makes of you, that you'd place more value on hard, cold objects than you do on the people in your life?"

"Don't you judge me, boy," Milton snarled. "It was your mother's fault! Her debts, her parents' debts. And on top of that, she saddled me with *you*! But you were going to tip the scales and correct the injustice. You were going to make this family prosperous again. And now look what you've done, you ungrateful whelp."

"Are you even my real sire?"

"I raised you, didn't I?" Milton asked defensively.

"That doesn't answer the question. But you call life with you being raised? If I'm not yours, I would rather you had given me away, even to the poorest dirt farmer. *Any* other life would have been preferable to the one I had here with you."

"It's what I should have done! Of course you're not mine. She couldn't wait to throw that in my face as soon as she got back from London, or tell me what a whore she'd been to assure it. She laughed when she confessed there were so many men, she had no idea who your father was. You can't imagine how much I hated her."

"And me," Richard said.

"Yes! *And* you."

"I'm afraid that's not all of it," Charles said from the doorway behind them.

"Charles, get out of here," Milton ordered. "This is no concern of yours."

"Actually, it is," Charles said as he came farther into the room. "And it's high time I spoke up. Mother told me everything, you know. I was her only confidant. It was to be our secret. I was barely old enough to understand, and her rage more often than not frightened me. She hated you so much. I tried to hate you, too, but I couldn't. Richard *is* only my half brother, but I'm the bastard she produced from cuckolding you. Richard is your real son."

Milton fell back into his chair, his complexion gone white. "You're lying."

"No, I'm finally telling the truth. She craved revenge and hers was twofold. She wanted you to love your bastard and hate your son. My father is the man she loved, the one she wanted to marry. She'd known him all her life. But his family wasn't rich enough to suit them, so her parents gave her to you instead."

"You're lying!" Milton said again.

Charles shook his head sadly. "She loved my father till the day she died. They trysted daily in the woods near here until an emergency called him home. Then he died—suspiciously. She blamed you. She really thought you'd found out about them and arranged his death. So she devised the ultimate revenge. She wanted you to think your real son was her bastard. She was already pregnant with Richard when she went to London. But she knew she was having her lover's child soon after your marriage. Did you never wonder why she came to your bed, begging for a child, even though she hated you?"

Milton was too shocked to reply as he stared at Richard with new eyes. Julia was speechless, too. This wasn't a real family, being so filled with hate, lies, and revenge. That her husband had risen beyond this legacy to become the tender, caring man he was, was a marvel. Ironically, Richard seemed unaffected by what he'd just learned.

"Well, that was certainly short-lived relief," he remarked drily.

"I'm sorry, Richard," Charles said, shamefaced. "I was supposed to tell him at an appropriate time, and you. There were so many appropriate times, but—I never had the guts to do it."

"It's all right." Richard said, and he even smiled at his brother. "As I told my wife, whether he is or isn't my sire changes nothing. I would have *liked* to think he wasn't. I can't deny that. But all these years I've never doubted he was, which accounted for such a rotten feeling inside me, that I couldn't love him. That seems to be gone now and I have you to thank for that. It's a relief knowing he had his reasons, however selfish and wrongheaded, for treating me as he did."

Milton found his voice. "Richard—?"

"Don't," Richard said, cutting off what sounded like a conciliatory tone coming from his father. "You know it's too late. You let hate govern your life, and because of it, you made it govern mine, too. That's the only legacy I have from you. But I'm cutting myself off from the source for good."

"But this changes everything."

"My God, how delusional you are. All bridges have been burned here. You can't change what you've wrought, old man. There's no going back. As far as I'm concerned, you don't even exist anymore."

The room fell silent. No one there other than Milton

might have thought Richard's statement was harsh. Milton had sundered his own family, deliberately, obsessively. There was no room for pity for someone like him.

"Let's get out of here," Charles suggested. "Mathew and I are leaving, too. I was misguided in thinking he needed to know both of his grandfathers, when he only really has one."

"Don't take him from me. Please."

The pleading tone from Milton was so incongruous it didn't even sound real, but it stopped Charles long enough for him to say, "A burden has been lifted from my shoulders today. You're not going to put it back there. Mathew is no relation of yours. *I'm* no relation of yours."

"That doesn't change the fact that I love Mathew."

They were incredulous, and while the brothers weren't going to ask the obvious question, Julia wasn't so reticent. "Why couldn't you love your own sons?"

Milton glared at her for her impertinence. "Because they were *her* sons and I despised her. But she died so many years ago, and nothing about Mathew has ever reminded me of her."

"I could almost pity you, but I don't," Julia said. "You, sir, are a disease, and you've infected the people in this room long enough, myself included. You've placed value on objects instead of people. You've hurt innocent children because you didn't like their mother.

You had a family and you didn't cherish it, didn't even try. You don't deserve another. My husband has put 'paid' to this account. The receipt stands before you. Now you live with what you've wrought, having no one left who gives a damn about you."

"Mathew loves me!"

"Mathew doesn't *know* you! It doesn't matter what face you show him. The taint is still there and thank God he's going to be removed from it."

Chapter Fifty-three

J ULIA WAS ONLY slightly embarrassed when they left Willow Woods—for the last time. She hadn't meant to display her no-nonsense business instincts in that meeting with the earl. She hadn't meant to display her disgust either. But she'd been unable to stop herself. Now she was a bit concerned about Richard's reaction not only to what he'd learned today, but to her indecorous behavior.

But she didn't get a chance to discuss it with him until that night when they were finally alone at the inn they'd stopped at to break up the journey back to London. Charles and Mathew had ended up sharing the coach with them.

Charles hadn't wanted to spend another moment in that house any more than they did, not even long enough to pack. He would send for their belongings later. Right now, he wanted to spend as much time with his brother as he could, before *The Triton* sailed again. Then he intended to stay with Mathew's real grandfather briefly, until he found them a house of their own in Manchester.

Julia worried that that would be too close to Willow Woods and mentioned it to Richard on the way into the inn when Charles and Mathew went ahead of them. She was actually delighted to hear about Charles's lady friend and that he couldn't bear to move too far from her. But she got Charles to promise that they would visit the islands after she and Richard were settled there. Mathew was already excited by the idea, so she didn't expect them to wait too long.

The four of them shared a relaxing dinner that evening, the tension gone, the burdens gone. Mathew didn't yet know that he and his father were no longer going to live at Willow Woods. Charles had told Julia in an aside that he would eventually tell his son a story about two brothers and a not-so-nice father and let him decide for himself if he wanted such a person in his life. Again, choices were very, very important to these two men who'd never been allowed to make any of their own while growing up.

She retired first, leaving the brothers a little time on their own. But Richard wasn't long in joining her in their room. She'd been sitting cross-legged in the center of the bed, combing her hair, but she immediately got up to meet him in the middle of the room and put her arms around him.

"I'm so glad this day is behind us," she told him.

"So am I. But I've been dying to ask you since we left there—you're not feeling sorry for him, are you?"

"Me?" she asked, somewhat in surprise. "I was going to ask that question of you."

He chuckled. "Well, my answer is a resounding no. What about yours?"

"The same."

"Glad to hear it. Because he really did kill whatever love I had for him when I was a child. That I'm apparently his only son now is simply an amusing irony. As I said before, I couldn't care less."

She grinned. "You know that means his title will eventually come to you."

Richard snorted. "I don't want it. I don't want anything of his. I'd rather it went to Charles as I always assumed it would, then to Matthew after him. I'm sure Milton will consider that, too, and tell no one of this. Besides, you're the only thing I want, Jewels. *But . . .*"

She leaned back and swatted his chest lightly. "You *can't* put a *but* after that statement!"

"*However?*" he teased.

"No *however* either."

"Then maybe you should just let me finish. I can't deny you got my hopes up that I was a bastard, and now I'm a little disappointed that I'm still related to

Milton Allen by blood. But I'll get over it." Then he grinned roguishly. "Will you help me get over it?"

That was practically the same question he'd asked her when he came back into her life the night of the Malory ball. She laughed and leaned into him suggestively and said, "That's—very likely."

He laughed with her. "God, I love you. And that's yet another irony, isn't it?"

"I beg your pardon? You're *really* stepping on thin ice now."

He pulled her closer despite her huffy warning. "I thought my forced marriage would be just like my father's." He gave her a loving smile before he kissed her, then kissed her again. "The irony is, how wrong I was."

She'd been touching him too long. Any more discussion could wait until later. She wrapped an arm around his waist, drew his lips down to hers with the other, threaded her hand through his hair—and finally realized what was missing! With a gasp, she turned him around to verify that his long queue was nowhere to be found.

"Good God, what'd you do?" she cried, aghast. "I *liked* your hair!"

"I thought it was time to finally cut it, since I don't have anything to rebel against anymore, so Charles, Mathew, and I hunted down a barber after dinner. But I'll grow it back for you."

"No, not for me. It's your choice."

He laughed at her effort not to sound disappointed. "You're my choice, Jewels, and whatever makes you happy makes me happy."

She wondered if he realized he'd just ceded all his future choices to her. But not really, because perfect matches—and he was certainly hers—had many benefits. Happy compromises, for one. With her loving him so much, whatever made him happy would always make her happy, too. It could be no other way.

Read on for an excerpt from
Johanna Lindsey's next novel

When Passion Rules

Coming soon!

A<small>LANA WAS SHOWN</small> to a big anteroom in the palace that was furnished with only a few uncomfortable-looking chairs. No one was sitting in those chairs and she didn't sit, either. She was still too nervous to relax, almost sick to her stomach with it.

She tried repeating to herself what her guardian had said to her when they parted outside the palace gates. "I am very proud of you, Princess. Garner your confidence. Your blood is royal." She sighed. It didn't really help, because she would be meeting her father, the King of Lubinia, *today*.

Alana knew that the king would be shocked and overjoyed when he learned that she was still alive and he had a legitimate heir after all. She hoped she would be able to keep her distance from him emotionally, so she could return to London without any regrets as soon as the rebellion here was quelled. But what if she and her father were both overcome with familial feelings and instantly took to each other? That would be wonderful—as long as he didn't expect her to stay in this backward mountain kingdom.

As she looked around the room, she was dismayed to see more than twenty people waiting to see the king! She was tired of delays. She was tired of keeping her identity a secret. She wanted to be rid of this apprehension that was making her queasy.

Nervously, she walked about the room. She passed a group of big, brutish-looking men laughing at a ribald story one of them was telling. She got away from them and nearly tripped over a goat herder sitting cross-legged on the floor eating a haunch of something with his hands. And he had a goat with him! Probably a gift for the king, but really, inside the palace?!

As Alana moved farther into the room, looking for a safe place to stand and wait, she noticed that the other women in the room appeared submissive to the men they accompanied and were dressed so differently from her. She was in the height of English fashion, her long elegant cloak and cap fur-trimmed for winter. In stark contrast, one of the Lubinian women was wrapped in a togalike garment, another was wearing a long shaggy vest that appeared to be made of thick untreated fur. One middle-aged woman was garbed in a more European style, but so gaudily, with half her breasts showing, that it was rather obvious she had loose morals and was happily letting the men there know it.

Every so often an official-looking fellow opened the

double doors at the far end of the room, which she assumed led to the king's receiving room, and escorted a petitioner or a group of petitioners through them. But more people continued to arrive, keeping the anteroom crowded.

Alana finally approached one of the two guards standing by the doors to the inner chamber and asked, "When can I expect to meet the king? I've already been here an hour."

He didn't answer her. He didn't even look at her! She asked the other guard the same question, asked it in every language she knew, but he, too, treated her as if she were invisible! Was it because she was an unescorted woman, or was there some custom she wasn't aware of?

Fuming over being treated like that—she was their princess!—she moved to sit in one of the chairs. A brutish man she'd noticed earlier actually approached her after a while. She glanced up expectantly. He didn't say anything. Instead, he boldly fingered the fur on her cloak. Outraged, she came to her feet, but he didn't move away. He just laughed as she glared at him. The guards standing nearby did nothing. Fortunately, an old woman shooed him off.

"Stay away from the men," was all she said to Alana.

Blushing because she hadn't approached that lout, she went back to pacing the room, convinced now that Lubinian men had a barbarian streak in them.

More than an hour later, Alana suddenly forgot about how tired, hungry, and exasperated she felt when a new palace guard entered the anteroom. She was amazed to see the other guards actually speaking to him when they hadn't even spoken to each other, let alone to her. This new guard wore an identical uniform, a tight double-breasted black jacket with gold buttons, cut short to the waist in front. The back of the jacket was longer, split for ease of movement, she supposed, the two tails reaching nearly to their knees. In contrast, the tall stand-up collars and the cuffs on the jacket sleeves were white and embroidered with gold braid. The tightly-fitted trousers were also white.

The gold-fringed epaulets on the uniform made the new guard's shoulders look extraordinarily wide. He was also taller than the other guards, possibly six feet. And there was something else that made him stand out. He was very handsome. As if that mattered, but it did cause her to stare at him much longer than she should have. She was still staring when one of the guards pointed her out to him.

She tensed slightly when he glanced her way and then immediately walked toward her. He had better not tell her it was time to leave, not after she'd spent half the afternoon there without having gained an audience with the king.

The thought produced a strong burst of annoyance, so she tried to look away and compose herself. But she couldn't quite manage to take her eyes off him. He was *that* handsome.

He had dark gold hair, worn no longer than his nape, yet it draped off of his forehead in soft waves, half covering his ears. She verified that he had deep blue eyes when he stopped before her and gave her a brisk military bow. She had to look up even before he straightened. He was taller than the six feet she'd estimated, and young, probably in his mid-twenties. His face was thoroughly masculine with thick brows, a square jaw, and a strong lean nose that was perfectly straight. Seen this close, he no longer looked like a common soldier. No, indeed, there was nothing common about him . . .

"Is there a problem?" she asked when he didn't speak immediately.

She'd almost used English, but caught herself in time and addressed him in Lubinian.

"No," he replied, and a grin slowly formed as his eyes moved boldly over her face—and then lower! "Though my men wonder what such a pretty lady is doing in here."

Was he—flirting with her? Something that wasn't the least bit unpleasant stirred inside her with that thought. She felt so flustered she had to take her eyes off him for a moment to gather her scattered wits.

"Your men?" she asked.

His military bearing became more pronounced. "I am Count Becker, their captain."

Alana felt a surge of relief. *This* was a man she could deal with more easily, a formal official, whose mouth was set in a hard, straight line. But why did a man this young wield so much authority? Just because he was a member of the nobility? Or maybe he was older than she'd guessed. The deep timbre of his voice supported that thought. The tone seemed almost familiar to her, though she'd heard so many Lubinian voices today, that had to be why.

"I, too, wonder why you are here," he added in that same formal tone.

"I was led to this room by one of the guards at the palace entrance. Are these other people not waiting for an audience with the king, as well?"

He nodded. "Indeed. But there is another room where the nobility wait. It is much more comfortable. Your rich apparel indicates you should have been taken there. So what did you tell the guard that made him show you to the commoners hall instead?"

Blast it! Had she really wasted so much time because she was being too cautious? Yet what other choice did she have? Her guardian had warned her not to tell anyone except a highly placed official why she wanted to see the king. Alana wished this captain had shown up sooner.

"I told your guard nothing more than that I wish to speak to the king," she admitted, abashed. "I'm not going to discuss my business here with just anyone."

"Ah, very well. If you don't state the nature of your business, you don't get very far," he said simply.

"But I was told that King Frederick had an open policy of receiving his people."

"You aren't one of his people."

"I am more than that."

"Oh?"

As captain of palace security and a nobleman, as well, he seemed the ideal person to help her. She wanted to trust him. She just hoped she wasn't being influenced by her strong attraction to him. But he *was* an official, and that made her decision.

She leaned slightly closer to him so he would hear her low-voiced entreaty. "Is there somewhere we can go so we may speak in private?"

His demeanor changed abruptly again. His golden brows rose as if she'd surprised him, and his blue eyes gazed at her warmly. When his hard mouth softened into a grin, she felt that fluttering in her stomach again, but more strongly this time. Good God, he was handsome. And as attracted to her as she was to him? Or was he just relaxing, letting down his guard? She wished she hadn't been so sheltered in London and knew more about such matters.

"Come with me," he said.

He grasped her hand immediately, surprising her. She didn't like that at all. It wasn't how an Englishman would behave upon first meeting a lady. But this wasn't England, she reminded herself. Lubinians might think nothing of a man treating a woman this way. It might even be customary here for men to behave like barbarians and drag women about. She groaned at that thought. Yet it *did* feel like he was dragging her, though she allowed that it simply felt that way because his much longer stride was forcing her to quicken her step to keep up with him.

He led her out of the anteroom and deeper into the palace until they came to a side entrance that opened onto a wide courtyard. But it wasn't a private courtyard where they could talk; it was the ward that lay between the palace and the old fortress walls that surrounded it. Soldiers and even a few opulently dressed courtiers passed through the area.

There was still daylight, though the sun had already dipped below the mountain ranges to the west. Alana tried to slow her step but couldn't. Where exactly was the captain taking her?

When he stopped in front of the door to a building that resembled a fancy townhouse but was adjoined to the ancient fortress walls, Alana took the opportunity to pull her hand away from his, though she actually had to yank a little. He glanced at her and started to chuckle, but it was abruptly cut off when an angry woman swept through the doorway and attacked the captain, pounding her fists on his chest.

Alana adeptly moved out of the way. The captain didn't even try. The woman, who was young, blonde, and finely dressed, pounded on him rather hard, but he gave no indication that he even felt her blows!

"How dare you have me thrown out!" she shouted.

He took her wrists, one in each hand, and thrust her away from him into the ward. Not very gentlemanly, Alana thought, but the woman *had* been attacking him and his annoyance was now obvious.

Yet his voice was absolutely calm when he asked the young woman curiously, "How is it you're still here, Nadia?"

"I hid from your men," she stated rather triumphantly.

"Who will now be disciplined because of it," he said and waved at two passing guards.

Nadia glanced behind her to see the guards' swift approach, then somewhat in a panic, she yelled at Count Becker, "We haven't finished our discussion!"

"Only a fool doesn't know when to quit, so how much of a fool does that make you, eh?" That brought a gasp from the blonde woman, but it didn't keep him from adding, "Now, would you finally open your eyes to see that the past will no longer protect you from my contempt?" To the men who had reached him, he said, "Take Countess Braune to the gates. She is no longer to be allowed entry to the palace."

"You can't do that, Christoph!"

"I just did."

Distinctly uneasy now—that had been quite a beautiful woman he'd just dismissed so cavalierly— Alana said, "Is she a former lady friend of yours?"

He took a moment to shake off his annoyance before he glanced at her. Once again, it was a long look that took in more than just her face. But then he smiled at her and her breath caught in her throat, it so dazzled her.

"Not as you mean," he answered.

Then he grasped Alana's arm and ushered her inside the building, closing the door behind him. He was gentle with her now, not rough as he'd been with that harridan, not even as firm as he'd been when dragging her there.

She took a moment to glance around and get her bearings. They were in a large room that seemed to serve as a parlor and a dining room, but she didn't think it comprised the entire first floor of the building. And then she couldn't think at all.

She didn't realize the captain was still holding her arm until he turned her toward him. His other hand slipped behind her neck and drew her forward, right up against him. And then he bent his head and pressed his lips to hers.

No training she'd ever had had prepared her to be overwhelmed by her first kiss.

With the soft touch of his lips on hers, Alana's senses were overwhelmed. She felt her heart racing, and the pleasant fluttering in her stomach she'd felt earlier was now a powerful, exciting swirl. Both his hands were suddenly warm against her cheeks, caressing her, which meant she was leaning against him of her own accord! This was madness!

She tried to lean back to take her mouth away from his and for a brief moment she felt something close to frustration when he let her. Opening her eyes, she saw his smile. That was all she saw, because she couldn't take her eyes off of his mouth, which had just stirred up so many startling, pleasurable feelings in her.

In wonder, she touched her own lips. "Why did you do that?" she asked in a breathless whisper.

She looked up at his blue eyes before he answered. That was a mistake. He was too appealing like this, with the seductive warmth in his gaze and a charming grin on his face. Did he find something humorous in her question?

He raised a brow slightly before he said, "You aren't here looking for a protector? I'm going to be very disappointed if you say no."

He didn't sound disappointed. He sounded confident of himself and amused, as if he were teasing her. Of course, she was here looking for a protector. Her father was going to be her protector. Was she missing something in what he'd just said? Did he mean something else? How could she think with him this close to her?!

"Yes, but—" she began.

He was kissing her again, and this time much more passionately. Now she was thrilled to a new level, every wonderful sensation he'd provoked earlier was back and so magnified, she had to grip his shoulders to keep from falling. He slipped his arm around her back, holding her tightly to him. His mouth slanted across hers, his tongue pushing past her innocence, thrusting deeply, deliciously into her mouth. His other hand was sliding up the side of her leg.

Her gasp was lost in his mouth. Oh God, what was she doing?!

"Stop!" She pushed away from him, gasping for breath, grasping to keep her balance now that she was no longer holding on to him. She was shocked by what she'd just allowed him to do, what she'd allowed herself to do!

He was watching her with something akin to suspicion in his eyes. "I don't mind a little teasing, as long as we both understand where it ends."

She had no clue what he seemed to be accusing her of, but she'd regained enough of her wits to say stiffly, "I'm not sure what kind of mistake you've made, but it *is* a mistake."

He leaned back against the door, slamming it hard. "You can't be serious."

He glanced down at her again for an answer. She didn't need to say anything more. Her accusing look seemed to convince him that she was serious. But instead of apologizing, he swore under his breath and moved toward her. She was instantly unnerved. He was much too big and tall to stand that close to her with such an angry visage.

"What sort of ploy is this?" he demanded. "You melt on me like sweet butter, then cry foul?"

She sucked in her breath. That didn't even deserve a response. She pushed around him to get to the door instead. He grabbed her by the waist, stopping her, and even drew her back against his chest.

Her whole body tingled as he embraced her so intimately. "You want to talk terms first?" he asked impatiently. "Fine, I will give you whatever you want. There, we have talked terms. Now melt on me again."

The husky tone he'd ended with made her close her eyes tightly. She was *not* going to be drawn back into his web again. She wiggled out of his hold, hoping to break through to the captain of the guard she'd first met, the polite if mildly flirtatious man she'd been willing to trust. He let go of her as she turned to face him instead of reaching for the door again.

"I asked to speak to you in private because no one else can hear what I am going to confide in you," she said and even sighed. "How could you think I meant anything other than talk?"

A number of emotions crossed his countenance:

frustration, self-disgust, and finally, regret. He turned away, saying, "Your whisper suggested something else."

"What?"

"Many foreign women of quality, mostly widows, come to this court to find a protector," the captain explained, facing her again. "We are not unique in that. We are just one of many courts they visit across Europe, until they find a gentleman of power or wealth to their liking. A few even aspire to be a king's mistress and so they request an audience to make themselves available, yet are too embarrassed to mention it to the guards—"

"I understand!" she quickly cut in. "You thought I was one of those women trying to see the king. You couldn't be more mistaken. I'm his daughter."

"Whose?"

"The king's." A moment of silence followed.

"Are you?"

He said that without inflection, making her realize her wish had come true. She was now dealing with the real captain of the guard who would actually attend to duty, not that tempting seducer, thank God. Yet why wasn't he more surprised by her revelation?

"I can explain," she said. "As it was explained to me. If you aren't surprised, I certainly was. I've only known about this for the last month. I—"

Alana stopped. Was she rambling? She was still in the grip of too many emotions she wasn't familiar with.

She moved to one of the sofas in the room, but not to sit down. She just wanted to put more distance between herself and the captain.

"Why was I really kept waiting today?" she asked. "I saw at least one man who arrived after me summoned into the inner chamber."

"Bureaucracy," he said simply. "If you don't state your business, you are placed at the end of the line."

"So I should have told a mere guard who I am? When my life has been in jeopardy since I was an infant? I was warned not to do that."

He shrugged. "It is of no matter. You would have gone no further in either case. We would merely have had this conversation sooner, since you would have been brought to my attention, not the king's."

She sighed. Such a waste of time. Had she really thought it would be easy to gain an audience with the king? She had hoped, foolishly, it now seemed.

"Sit down," he said. "Make yourself comfortable. I suspect you will be here for quite a while."

"Not unless my father is scheduled to leave the palace today and I have to wait for his return," she disagreed.

"The king isn't leaving."

"Then can you at least take me to him, so I don't have to repeat myself?" she asked. "The story I have to tell is not exactly a brief one."

"When you aren't the first princess to show up with this claim? I think not."